ALL FOR LOVE

ALL FOR LOVE

A Novel

DAN JACOBSON

METROPOLITAN BOOKS
Henry Holt and Company
New York

F
Jac

m

METROPOLITAN BOOKS
Henry Holt and Company, LLC
Publishers since 1866
175 Fifth Avenue
New York, New York 10010

Originally published in the United Kingdom in 2005
by Hamish Hamilton, London.

Library of Congress Cataloging-in-Publication Data
Jacobson, Dan.
    All for love : a novel / Dan Jacobson.—1st American ed.
        p. cm.
ISBN-13: 978-0-8050-8103-9
ISBN-10: 0-8050-8103-8
    1. Louise, Princess of Belgium, 1858–1924—Fiction. 2. Mattachich, Geza
von, 1858–1923—Fiction. 3. Princesses—Belgium—Fiction. I. Title.

PR9369.3.J3A79 2006
823'.914—dc22

                                                                    2006043363

Henry Holt books are available for special promotions and
premiums. For details contact: Director, Special Markets.

First U.S. Edition 2006
Designed by Lorie Pagnozzi

Printed in the United States of America
10 9 8 7 6 5 4 3 2 1

Errors, like straws, upon the surface flow;
He who would search for pearls must dive below.

—JOHN DRYDEN,
PROLOGUE TO *All for Love* (1678)

ALL FOR LOVE

I

CHAPTER ONE

SHE WAS A PRINCESS, LOUISE BY NAME, the daughter of a king who was one of the richest and most hated men in Europe.

Her lover, Géza Mattachich, a second lieutenant in the Thirteenth Regiment of Uhlans, was the stepson of a backwoods Croatian count, who had lived for many years in a ménage à trois with Géza's mother and father.

And then there was Maria Stöger, the keeper of a canteen inside the prison in which Mattachich was confined for several years.

Both the princess and the young uhlan (who improperly assumed his stepfather's title) wrote books about their lives.[*] In these they describe their chaste, honorable, self-sacrificing love for each other and the exorbitant price they were made to pay for it. Not everything they write is to be trusted. In neither book, for example, is Maria Stöger's part in the story acknowledged, nor is any reference made to Mattachich's illegitimate son, whom she managed to conceive and produce during his imprisonment.[†]

Also involved in the story were Prince Philipp of Saxe-Coburg, Princess Louise's husband, known to her and to some of his friends as

---

[*] See *Autour des trônes que j'ai vu tomber* by Princesse Louise de Belgique (Paris, 1921), translated into English by Maude M. C. Ffoulkes as *My Own Affairs* (London, 1924): the page numbers given here refer to the original French edition of the book, from which all translations have been directly made. See also *Aus den letzten Jahren: Memoiren* by Géza Keglevich-Mattachich (Leipzig, 1904).

[†] The relationship between Mattachich and Maria Stöger is documented, along with much else, in Gerd Holler's biography *Louise von Sachsen-Coburg: Ihr Kampf um Liebe und Glück* (Vienna and Munich, 1992). In his memoirs Mattachich refers to Maria only twice: once by name, once anonymously. Louise does not refer to her at all in her autobiography.

Fatso (*der Dicke*); the prince's lawyer, Dr. Adolf Bachrach, described by a socialist deputy in the Austrian parliament as "a little Jew with feudal pretensions" (*ein kleiner Jude mit feudalen Allüren*); and the king-emperor of Austria-Hungary, Franz Josef, last but one of the Habsburg monarchs, of whom Louise wrote that "he could have been taken for a headwaiter, had it not been for his uniforms and retinue."* Professor Richard von Krafft-Ebing, the heavily bearded author of *Psychopathia Sexualis,* a book which before his death and after it gave guilty pleasure to schoolboys in many parts of the world, contributed to the proceedings too.

So did a half-trained black stallion whose plunging and kicking led to the first encounter between Géza Mattachich and Princess Louise. This was on a late spring morning in 1895, in the Prater Gardens in Vienna. She looked on from her coach while he struggled to control the beast. A glance passed between them. Years afterward Mattachich wrote, "I felt as if I had experienced an electric shock. Something had happened to me, but I did not know what it was."† How could he possibly have known "what it was"? That exchange of glances changed his life. Ahead of them both lay assignations, adultery, flight, the squandering of a fortune (not his; not hers either, as things worked out), a duel, imprisonment, bankruptcy, morphine, madness (or alleged madness). Mattachich chose to write as if the consequences of their meeting had been fated from that first moment. Yet he had to work hard, though blindly too, in order to bring those consequences about.

Later the princess took up the running—and the writing. Later still it was the turn of the humbly born Stöger, who made sure that she too played a significant role in some of what followed but who left no book behind her.

Each of them—the princess, the hussar, and the canteen worker—was thrilled by the apparent remoteness of the others' circumstances from his or her own. The improbability of their association was one of the closest bonds between them.

---

* Louise, *Autour,* p. 105. She also wrote of Franz Josef that he "had two bad habits: when perplexed he would tug and stroke his muttonchop whiskers, and at formal dinners he studied his own reflection in the blade of his knife" (p. 107).

† Mattachich, *Memoiren,* p. 17.

❖

People are what they do. They are what they say. They are what they want. They are what they remember and what they have forgotten; the motives they reveal and the motives they try to hide. They are their bodies, their voices, the movements of their eyes and hands. Beneath these and other such manifestations of selfhood, it is impossible to go. The "reasons" why people are as they are will always remain hidden, not only from outsiders but from themselves too.

Can you give wings to the peacock and feathers to the ostrich? Does the hawk fly by your wisdom?*

Exactly.

Imagine, then, that first exchange of glances between the princess and the hussar. A fine May morning in the Prater: sun, trees, shadows, grass; carefully nurtured gardens and extended avenues in every direction; human voices rising and falling; a brass band shaking the air in the distance; carriage wheels grinding on gravel roadways and hoofbeats falling dully on churned-up sand; the sharp smell of horse dung mingling with the deeper, darker aroma of horse sweat—a smell heady to horse lovers and rancid to others. Imagine, in the midst of this leisured throng, a pair of brown eyes meeting a pair of blue eyes and the passage of an "electric shock" between them . . .

No. Go back twenty years. Imagine a very different garden on the outskirts of another city, Brussels this time, and at a different season. From a distance this one looks less like a garden than a palace or small city of glass. There are buildings like basilicas and cathedrals, their domed or pitched roofs scattered among others no bigger than suburban villas and small cottages. Their walls are of glass and so are their roofs; all are sustained by squared-off or concentric iron frames. Between the buildings are driveways and pathways, open squares, flights of stone steps, rows of upreared stone lions grasping heraldic shields to their breasts. Fountains send spray

* Job: 39: 13, 26.

hissing into the air and the water falls back into star-shaped or shell-shaped urns and stone basins, from which terra-cotta demi-monsters peer out.

Within the buildings a heavy, steamy, breathing growth. Palms of all heights and dimensions. Trees festooned with creepers or swathed in what looks like decaying fur. Multileaved ferns much taller than a man and many feet in circumference. Blooms of every color flaunting their dark cavities and shameless pistils. Leaves of all shapes, some drooping of their own weight, others as light as feathers. A hundred shades of green mixed with improbable hues of silver, custard, purple, scarlet. Textures ranging from silken to something like crocodile skin; from gossamer to cartilage and muscle. Above all this and seemingly intertwined with it hang cast-iron gantries and spiral staircases that look as if they too have taken root and sprouted, emulating the growth around them. Black hot-water pipes of cannonlike bore, ticking irregularly, run around the walls at floor level.

Each house is a miniature jungle, an imitation Congo: the re-creation by the dreadful Leopold II of the Belgians of that huge tract of Africa he is already scheming to own outright. Any hour now scores of gardeners, painters, and builders will be arriving to continue their toil on this make-believe kingdom of glass and jungle. But for the moment all is a blur. It is early morning. Winter too. The coming dawn is a dilution of night's shadow, nothing more. Alone in one of the buildings sits Leopold's daughter, the Princess Louise. She is young, not yet a woman, though her figure is full. She wears a silver wrap tied with a cord around her waist. Her hair is covered by a white lace shawl, and on her feet are slippers lined with white fur. She is Leopold's oldest child, but he has never cared for her. She is not a boy; she will never replace the king-to-be, the only son whom he cherished and lost (pneumonia) a decade before. For this loss he finds it impossible to forgive her. (Her two younger sisters are abominated for the same reason.) She is merely a female whom he has at last succeeded in bargaining away in marriage to a wealthy, undistinguished kinsman.

Imagine now that a shudder of silver shows the child-woman to have moved. She has opened her wrap. She looks down at the nightdress beneath it. The dark stain on it is not large, but it is enough to keep her occupied.

She stares at it, holding it away from her body for a few minutes. Her head does not move. Her face is expressionless. As she was to write years later:

> *I am surely not the first woman who has lived in the clouds during her engagement, only to be suddenly thrown to earth on her marriage night. . . . I am not the first victim of an excessive* pudeur, *based perhaps on the hope that a husband's delicacy, together with the guidance of nature, would make up for her ignorance of what awaits her in the marriage bed.*
>
> *However that might be, at the end of the reception at the palace of Laeken, and while all Brussels was dancing in the specially illuminated streets and buildings, I fell from heaven onto a bed of thorns, a heap of boulders. Psyche, who was more guilty than I, was better treated.*
>
> *The day had hardly broken when I took the chance of a moment's solitude in the bedroom to put on my slippers, and with a cloak pulled over my nightgown I ran to the orangery, looking to hide my shame there. I found refuge among the camellias, and to their pallor, sweetness, and purity I spoke of my despair and the suffering I had been through. Their comforting sweetness and silence, like the chill light of the winter dawn, gave back to me something of the innocence in which I had lived and which I had now forever lost.**

❖

That was her version of her wedding night, anyway. By the time Louise wrote her account she had had decades in which to perfect it; she had rehearsed it for the benefit of a variety of listeners. Among them were Mattachich, lovers who had preceded him, her ladies-in-waiting, and many of the doctors and psychiatrists who examined her both inside and outside the various institutions in which she had been confined. Not to

* Louise, *Autour,* p. 77

speak of guards and maids. And herself too, of course, for she had a habit—an indulgence that was also a compulsion—of speaking to herself, passionately and at length.

Naturally her husband, the prince, Fatso, told a different tale. He never wrote down his version of events, but he talked about that nuptial night almost as indiscreetly as his spouse. He was a gregarious man; he had a naturally trusting disposition; he felt ill-used. He had rank, money, and a cosseting mama; he lived with her, his brother, and various other members of his family in the Saxe-Coburg palace in Vienna: a huge, bleak, high-ceilinged place, abounding in oversized rooms, faded wallpapers, dusty cornices, musty drapes tied by cords thick enough to keep a yacht moored, oil paintings encased in tormented, gilded, ton-weight frames where more dust accumulated. Paintings of long-dead Saxe-Coburgs they were, chiefly, and of stags with ravening dogs at their necks, to whom kindly death would never come.* Yes, he had all these advantages, and servants in livery, a stable of horses, several carriages, many preposterous uniforms, and sets of day clothes and evening dress. Also an extensive collection of pornographic statuettes in china and bronze, acquired on his travels to the Far East.

Yet nobody took him seriously. Not even his servants. How could they, when he barely seemed to take himself seriously? Oh, he suffered all right; he felt pain; he was conscious of his insufficiencies; embarrassed, even humiliated by his inelegant figure, his high-pitched voice, and myopic eyes. And the grander the cloaks he was obliged to wear, the more hung about they were with orders, stars, sashes, and tassels, the larger the hats of fur or astrakhan, brass, leather, or velvet he donned for important occasions, so the more doubtful he felt about the figure he cut. Especially

---

* The Saxe-Coburgs were rulers of the relatively obscure duchy of Saxe-Coburg-Gotha, which was then a part of the German empire. However, the family's two major palaces were in Vienna and Budapest respectively—i.e., within the empire of Austria-Hungary and therefore under the rule of the imperial Habsburg dynasty. For that reason, among others, once Louise had married and moved to Vienna she was subject to the jurisdiction of the Lord Marshal of the Habsburg court, an official whose decisions with regard to her status could not be set aside by any other judicial authority within the empire.

in comparison with his best friend, his favorite drinking, whoring, and hunting companion, Franz Josef's only son, the doomed Crown Prince Rudolf. The imperial beard he had cultivated, Philipp knew, had not given his circular face the triangular severity he wished it to have; his rimless oval pince-nez and their dangling black ribbon he regarded as another humiliation but was too shortsighted to do without; his gait was a waddle. In short, he was one of those people who suffer and yet are absurd too—and know it—and who for that reason seem to turn their grievances into absurdity and their absurdity into yet another grievance.

Is it done deliberately? How is it done? Why is it done? It is a mystery. Imagine him, then, fixing you or some other interlocutor with his steady injured stare, his pince-nez trembling slightly, while he again tells the story of that wedding night, when his and Louise's marital misfortunes began. Imagine him insisting with his solemn face close to yours, in a high, almost treble voice at odds with his girth, that everything up to a certain point had really gone off all right, according to plan. They'd been declared husband and wife at a solemn mass in the palace and driven in an open carriage across Brussels, with thousands of people looking on. Then they had gone on to the palace at Laeken, on the city's outskirts, where there had been any amount of feasting and drinking to get through.

He and Louise hardly exchanged a word through it all, but so what? They'd never had much to say to each other even when they'd been courting. Or what passed for courtship between them. Each knew the other to be a suitable match, and so did their respective sets of parents. Given that they were cousins about six times over, Saxe-Coburgs both, it could hardly be otherwise. His branch of the family was not poor; hers, as a result of Leopold's depredations of the Congo and its peoples, was on its way to becoming rich beyond calculation. (Yet Leopold never ceased calculating, plotting, driving harder those beneath him, demanding more from every possible source of income.) So who could have raised objections on either side? Not even the long-faced lawyers who had drawn up the papers could manage that.

Still, he knew there would be . . . problems. He wasn't a fool. He wasn't a bully. Or a beginner. He'd had his first real taste of women at the age of thirteen, fourteen, something like that; before then—well, he couldn't even remember at what age he'd started fooling about with nannies, chambermaids, kitchen girls, anyone of that sort he could get his hands on. Squeeze, chase, smack, pinch, press, grab, rub, push into cupboards: that sort of thing. With the serious business starting just a few years later. And since then—well! (An eyebrow goes up briefly, and something like a smile moves within his beard.) Whereas she, his bride, knew nothing about men. Would he have married her if she had? During their previous days together all that had passed between them were a few kisses and the holding of hands: that sort of thing. Chaste schoolgirl stuff. With her mother constantly hanging about, for her own reasons. So much so that he could remember wondering if the mother thought she had to keep an eye on him, to stop him having a go at the girl before the wedding night. Also perhaps that she was hoping he would have a go at *her,* his *chère belle-mère* to be? Among that miserable set anything was possible.*

Anyway, he'd done his best not to frighten or disgust her. He really did try. He didn't want to hurt her; why should he? Poets can babble as much as they like, but everyone who's ever done it knows that getting in there for the first time is always an awkward business. Ungainly. And not only the first time either. There's always some . . . maneuvering involved. Not so? But then (his half-hidden lips again stir within his beard) where would any of us be without it?

He was entitled! That was the main point. He knew it, she knew it, so what the hell was going on? All right, you have to make allowances, but was it so unreasonable for a newly married husband to expect *some* willingness from his bride? Curiosity at least. Or a sense of duty, a wish to become a real woman, to leave her childhood behind? To start off on the right footing?

---

* Louise later suggested that Philipp had actually come to Belgium in pursuit of her mother, who had got rid of him by diverting his attentions to her daughter (*Leopold the Unloved* by Ludwig Bauer [London, 1934], p. 181).

Hah! Not a chance of it. Not with this one. Never. It took years before he'd understood that he, Philipp, fourteen years older than she was, was the real innocent in that fiasco. Her whole performance—and it was a performance!—had nothing to do with girlish *pudeur* or stage fright. It was all obstinacy, selfishness, perversity. . . .

When it came to other men, afterward, she seemed to manage well enough.

Her father's daughter—that's what she was, in every respect. That was why she and her darling papa hated each other so much. They knew what they were dealing with, on both sides: Louise with her brown eyes and fair hair and round cheeks, and him, the old goat, the girl chaser, with his ax of a nose sticking out in front of him, a nose you could chop logs with, take out a man's eyes with, use to tap rubber with from those trees of his in the Congo. With his great beard hanging down from his chin like a feed bag on a horse. And skinny legs, each one like a carpenter's measuring rod, you know the kind, with brass joints, opening up, always stretching out farther than you'd ever expect them to go.

That was him. A grotesque. And without conscience. Everyone knows now what his people did to those miserable blacks in the Congo! Chop their hands off, rape, thieve, swindle, kill, anything as long as it made his moneybags grow.

And his daughter, also a grotesque, though a handsome one, if you like them fleshy and somehow . . . *off*. Yes, that's the word. Tainted, like food—not so that you could smell it, but not right either. Also without conscience, just like the old man. Crazy for money, just like him again. But who would have known it to look at her, at the age of sixteen or seventeen? The only difference between the father and the daughter was that he was a great miser, except when he spent money on himself and the teenage tarts he was always chasing, and she was a spendthrift, especially when the money she spent was her husband's. That was always a double pleasure for her.

"First, it made her feel rich. Second, it made me poor."

His lips quivered, a deep vertical frown appeared, he took off his

pince-nez, revealing his mild brown shortsighted eyes and curiously truncated eyebrows. His eyes brimmed with moisture. A man was only
human, after all.

❖

Now take another twenty-year leap, forward this time. Imagine that
the girl—who was then already tall, round-armed, large-bodied, big-
bosomed, with plenty of hair, forehead, and chin—has acquired more of
all these: a bigger bust, thicker hair (with that of other, anonymous
women tied into it), a larger chin, a wider neck. Her complexion has lost
its gleam and elasticity; the skin itself looks as if it has been flattened
against the tissue accumulated beneath it. She has developed a knowing
eye, a loud laugh, and a taste for spending money on luxuries of all kinds
that is extravagant even by the elaborate, bejeweled standards of her
period and her caste. She has had two children by *der Dicke,* a boy and a
girl, the girl now almost as old as her mother was on her infamous marriage night, and the son, her firstborn, who has just begun his army service in an artillery regiment attached to the king-emperor's household.

Within a dozen years this son of hers will die in a way so frightful that
in her autobiography she will write that "it cannot be mentioned."* As
she sets out for a drive in her carriage along the avenues of the Prater this
fine spring morning, toward her first encounter with Mattachich and his

---

* "My son Leopold [named after his grandfather in Belgium] reached adulthood just when I had
rejected a way of life that had become odious to me. He believed that in refusing to live any longer
under the roof of the Coburgs I had taken from him the hundreds of millions he would one day
inherit from his grandfather [Leopold]. . . . So I have felt the unnatural hatred of a son for his
mother. I have wept as only those who have been cut to the heart by their own flesh ever can. But
God knows that though I have suffered from their greed for money, that root of all evil, I have
always forgiven them" (Louise, *Autour,* p. 99).

The manner of the young Leopold's death, which Louise says "cannot be mentioned," was
frightful indeed: a prostitute whom he had offended flung a vial of acid into his face (see Holler,
Ihr Kampf, p. 346). She also says, however, that "at the time of his death he had long since ceased
to be alive in my heart. . . . The one who was truly stricken was the father, Philipp, who had
turned this tainted son into an image of himself! I believe he has survived for no other reason than
to repent" (*Autour,* p. 148).

rebellious stallion, she has no inkling that her son's life will end in this manner. Nor does she know that she will scarcely mourn him when he is gone. But she does know, has known for years, that something is wrong, missing, blank, unfilled, worse than unsatisfactory in her life and her relationships with everyone around her, her children included. What feels like a stone of disappointment and resentment seems to be lodged inside her, just above her diaphragm; at moments of anxiety or anger she presses on that place with both beringed fists, as if to push deeper into herself this indigestible thing she is condemned to carry about. It feels as hard as any of the diamonds and sapphires that hang from her neck or earlobes but much larger than any of them. She even has a picture of it in her mind. On the outside it is incised with an obscure pattern of whorls, like a peach stone or a fingerprint or the illustrations she has seen of the human brain.

But as for getting rid of it, how is that to be done? She cannot ask her dresser to unclasp it at night, as she does with her other jewels. If only she could! She has consulted various doctors and healers about it (fearing a cancer), as she has about all the other unforgiving complaints she suffers from: irregular and painful periods; patches of inflamed psoriasis-like skin that appear on the backs of her knees and between her fingers; troubles with her digestion—cramps in the stomach, constipation, the opposite of constipation. She has pressed the spot to show the doctors and quacks where this stonelike thing is lodged, and they have palpated her stomach, drawn her blood, put their ears to this spot and to others, peered down her throat, invited her to breathe in and out, stuck their fingers into her most private places, asked questions about her intimate relations with her husband, scribbled prescriptions on pieces of paper, or sent her to other quacks like themselves who have told her to take the waters, sleep on an east-west axis, eat bran, wear rubber belts around her stomach and magnets around her wrists.

One of these doctors, or so-called doctors, a self-confident charlatanic *Volksdeutscher* from Bukovina with long clammy-looking hair, loose joints, thin fingers, a sallow skin, and a man's head attached to a boy's slight figure, had insisted—for strictly medical reasons, of course—that what she needed was "internal massage" of a kind he had been trained to administer while on a protracted visit to India. During his sessions with her he did in fact come closer to temporarily dissolving that stone inside her than had any of the other men who had also "massaged" her in much the same fashion. (From the way in which she writes about them, it can be assumed that her husband's brother, Prince Ferdinand—also a fatty, as well as a necromancer and a wearer of crazy uniforms, who was later to become king of Bulgaria—was among her lovers, and that so was her sister's husband-to-be, the Imperial Archduke Rudolf.)* However, when her Bukovinian healer made the mistake of demanding ever-larger sums of money from her for his treatments, and finally threatened to expose her if she did not pay the preposterous fees he took to demanding for his services, she had him physically thrown out of the Saxe-Coburg mansion and nothing more was ever heard from him again.

Which didn't stop her, for weeks after he had gone, from walking up and down her private chamber, fists clenched into her midriff, enacting and revising everything that had passed between them and imagining what she would say to him if they were ever to meet again. She gestured, whispered, scowled, threw her head back angrily; she even composed lengthy narratives dealing with their relationship, as if dictating them to an interviewer or to a bosom friend she did not have.

The habit of going through secret, creative performances of this sort had grown stronger as the years passed. The pleasure they gave her was

---

* "From the moment I entered the court, the archduke Rudolf and I were friends. I dare say we were alike in many respects. . . . I soon felt there was something more than trust in his attitude toward me. It was often the case in my early years in Vienna that I was not as wary as I should have been. . . . God knows therefore that it was meritorious for me to have said to him, in the free and easy way we used with one another, 'My younger sister looks like me. Marry her!'" (Louise, *Autour*, pp. 130–131).

And on Ferdinand: "We gave the old palace whatever life it had; with him I could forget my boredom and bitterness. . . . But it was because of me that the Coburg brothers fell out with each other, though their situation demanded an outward show of amity. I mention this because it helps to explain the hostility that was one day to be directed against me. And all from the same unhappy source that lies behind so many dramas: male jealousy and frustrated appetite" (*Autour*, p. 148).

always painful; it was like surrendering to the spasms of scratching at inflamed patches of her skin, as she sometimes did, or tugging at hanks of her hair. Occasionally the vividness of these imaginary dialogues and monologues frightened her; she would devise schemes to stop them in their tracks: by counting up to one hundred slowly, with a mind empty of all but the accumulating numbers, say, or reconstructing in the fullest possible detail a favorite path through the woods that she used to follow as a child, when holidaying on her grandmother's estate. But she would lose count of her numbers, or abandon the path, and find herself first drifting and then rushing once more into these compulsive, exhausting, strangely rewarding bouts of sotto-voce reverie.

Still, the habit came in useful when she finally settled down to compose her memoirs.

❖

"The stallion had to give way to my will," Mattachich writes proudly about the first encounter between himself and Louise on the Prater on that unforgettable spring morning, "and thus it came about that I rode past the Princess several times that day."[*]

You bet he did. You can imagine the ardor of his glances and how briskly his gloved hand flew to the gleaming black peak of his cap, each time he passed by. And how he surreptitiously drove his spurs into the flanks of the stallion, to make it start and rear and throw its head about so she would have yet another opportunity to admire his horsemanship.

Did she know what he was up to? Of course. Was she impressed by it? Amused, rather, that this dapper little fellow, this Lieutenant Nobody in uhlan cap and shiny boots should have had the nerve to put on such a performance before her. And to stare nakedly at her while he went about it. She had no doubt that he knew who she was: on the lacquered door of her coach, which was even blacker and shinier than the peak of his cap, there

---

[*] Mattachich, *Memoiren*, p. 17.

was a coat of arms he would have recognized; and in any case he would certainly have seen her seated in carriages much more ornate than the open boat-shaped affair in which she was then sitting, or on reviewing stands with behatted females like herself, alongside their cockaded and uniformed menfolk. Moreover, the knowledge of his own impudence shone in his wide brown eyes and the gleam of his white teeth under his mustache, not to speak of the tilt of his head as he went about his tricks. Possibly she had seen him before on parades and state occasions; but how could she tell? He would then have been one among hundreds of others like himself, whose duty was to be nothing more than single decorative elements in the spectacle unfolding before her. Their whole point then was to disappear as individuals, to be divorced from their separate lives for the sake of the whole of which they were a part. So who cared if this one's eyes moved as she caught his gaze, or that one had a swarthier skin than those around him, or another had a face comically like that of his own horse?

Yet this particular nobody, this assemblage of cap and leggings, bright buttons, and horseflesh who she decided was at least ten years younger than herself, dared to cut a figure in front of her! Now he cantered ahead so that he could turn around and come trotting sedately back; now he ambled along just in front or just behind her carriage, where the wide bridle path ran parallel to the carriage drive, before dashing forward to go ahead and return once more. Had he been less handsome than he was she would have been less amused. Less tolerant too. But he was a good-looking fellow—and he knew it and knew also that she had noticed it. Clearly he'd had plenty of practice in drawing and dealing with admiring glances from women of various ages and classes. His tunic and breeches fitted him closely and so, somehow, did his features. Smooth high-colored cheeks, neat brows, and dark eyes innocently open like a child's, yet appraising too, like a man's; sharp shapely nose; firm cropped chestnut hair that fitted his skull almost like a cap, under the smaller round cap he was wearing, with its black peak and black strap passing under his chin; soft lustrous mustache that nestled promisingly on his upper lip. Yet an irrepressible and unyielding part of herself noticed also that his ears, sticking out on both sides of his cap, were too large and had a squashed, rumpled, somehow inferior look.

❖

For Mattachich it was enough, on that first morning, that she had not turned her head ostentatiously away from him or fallen into conversation with the lady companion seated alongside her or told her top-hatted roly-poly of a coachman to bring this outing to an end—and with it, his antics. Nor, he realized, as succeeding days went by, had she used her connections or her husband's to let the commander of his regiment know how offensively a junior officer was behaving before a woman recognized to be of royal rank, though not precisely regarded as a member of the Habsburg family. Astonished at his own nerve, looking at his own impudence as if it were a performance by a stranger, he had a single thought in his mind. If she dared, then he dared! She would never out-dare him! Every direct exchange of glances between them he regarded as a success in itself and an incitement to bring about the next.

For weeks on end I rode daily in the Prater [he wrote later] *and often encountered the princess. It belonged to my life, so to speak, that I should see her. With anxiety to know whether we would meet I would ride out in the morning; when I had succeeded in doing so I rode home happily, my heart filled with the thought,* If only I shall see her again tomorrow.

This went on for months. I made great progress with the training of my stallion, and I had the feeling that Her Highness the Princess looked on us as old acquaintances. Though there was no other connection between us, it nevertheless seemed self-evident that these meetings should take place. It sometimes happened that I went to the opera without knowing what was driving me to do so, and there I would see her. I waited on street corners filled with the conviction that

she was bound to ride by—and I was not disappointed. And when I
heard the song "I know a heart to which I pray, and in that heart I
find my solace," I understood just what it meant.*

Ah, for the mystic bond that draws true lovers together, the telepathic understanding that guides them toward each other, the sense of a common destiny that confounds the laws of chance or uses its laws to bring about the ends they both half-consciously yearn for. . . . Only it wasn't quite like that. He had carefully reconnoitered the Coburg palace: a pompous unbeautiful building like a cross between a department store and a major government office, with a row of pillars on each of its two tall floors, balustrading and allegorical figures along its roofline, and a great concave shield in the middle. The size and appearance of the palace impressed him, but it depressed him too. How would he ever be able to penetrate it? Make any kind of mark on it? Yet every time his eyes and the princess's silently acknowledged each other's presence, whether in the Prater or elsewhere in Vienna, he knew a breach in that fortress had already been made. All he had to do now was take advantage of it. Though as yet he had no idea how it might be done, he comforted himself with the thought that the moment before he had looked up from his struggle with the stallion and seen the princess looking at him, he had had no idea that she was there. And look how things had changed for him since.

He needed a go-between, and set about getting one with a ruthlessness that contrasted strangely with the vacancy in his mind as to what he would do if he succeeded. Across the road from the palace was a small park where handfuls of Saxe-Coburg servants spent some of their leisure time; and it was there, not on random street corners in the fashionable quarters of the city, that Mattachich actually did most of his purely speculative hanging about. There was a kind of kiosk or café at the far end of the park, with little metal tables scattered about, some in the open, some under cover, and he went there as often as he could. Imagine him dressed

---

* Mattachich, *Memoiren*, p. 17.

in civilian clothes (which he wore with a military neatness), smoking, studying a newspaper, taking his time over a cup of coffee—and finally, on his fourth or fifth visit, getting into conversation with one of the maids, Fiorenza by name, who worked in the private chambers of Prince Philipp and his wife. She was small, plump, gullible, dark-haired (soft hair it was, with a wave, and worn shorter than was fashionable); she explained to him that her father was an Italian from Venetia, which accounted for her name as well as what she spoke of as her "romantic temperament" (with a delayed, sideways glance up at him). She also told him that she had a young man, back in her village near Graz, and intended to go back and marry him in due course. The tip of her small pale arched nose moved up and down in sympathy with her lips when she spoke, a peculiarity that Mattachich had never come across before and that amused and roused him. Yet he knew it to be the sort of thing a man might soon grow tired of—might soon find positively objectionable.

Two years later Mattachich was to be described by the Lord Marshal of the imperial court, in the course of his inquiries into the whole affair, as a man who had been "corrupt in his sexual inclinations since his schooldays" (*schon als Mittelschuler in sexueller Richtung verdorben*).* Should you consider it a mitigation of those "inclinations"—or a manifestation of them—that from adolescence onward he had always been much moved by his own conquests? (He certainly thought the better of himself for the emotion he felt each time.) The more modest the girl, the more timid she was, the more haunted by the teachings of her priest or the fear of unwanted consequences, the more affected he was by her eventual surrender to him. To the point of tears sometimes. As he saw it, the poor creatures *wanted* to be led astray; they wanted to be put into danger, to have their hearts broken. Why else would they permit him to do with them what he did? That was what made their malleability so touching. The same was true of their helplessness later, their unavailing incredulity when they realized that it (whatever it had been) was now over.

* Quoted in Holler, *Ihr Kampf*, p. 19.

❖

It does not take long for Mattachich to decide that the time for conversation and coffee at the kiosk with Fiorenza, and for sentimental strolls around the Stadtpark, interrupted by pauses for passionate kisses behind trees, has come to an end. The restaurant he chooses to celebrate its ending displays plenty of red velvet upholstery, white napery, blue and gold drapery, waiters eyeing Mattachich like a confederate and Fiorenza like a whore. Upstairs a *chambre séparée* awaits them, with its table set for two and a couch against the wall opposite. The couch has cruelly curved legs, like a bandy dwarf's, and it too is swathed in red velvet. Fiorenza is in a cream-coloured, inoffensive dress, which shows off her pale neck and immature arms. For the first time in her company he is wearing one of his walking-out uniforms—not the full parade dress but a dark blue outfit with braid and gold buttons on the tunic and claret-colored stripes down the sides of his trousers. Once they are seated, Fiorenza's little straw hat comes off. Plenty of wine and conversation accompany the meal. She talks about the princess (one of her favorite topics): She is so lazy, she is so rich, she is too fat, she looks beautiful in her new gown, she has a foul temper sometimes, she can be so sweet at others. To these confidences Mattachich listens without much interest, certain that at his distance from Louise he already knows more about her than Fiorenza, from her servant's propinquity, ever will. The talk on his side is mostly about his gambling, his horses, and his previous conquests. He knows from previous experience that the last of these topics will make her feel both jealous and emulous. After brandy and coffee, the buttons at the back of her dress are undone; later, a long soft band of cloth, tied tightly around her rib cage and knotted at the side in order to push her breasts forward, is unwound. It lies in loops on the floor, like a flattened snake. She has told him that she is a virgin, but when the moment finally arrives that problem is dealt with effectively.

Afterward, more words and kisses and a few tears on both sides. Before they leave the restaurant he tells her he has a favor to ask. He wants her to provide him with information about the princess's movements. He's doing it, he reveals, on behalf of a friend who is of such high rank he cannot reveal his name. But there's nothing political about this man's interest in the princess, he assures Fiorenza. Nobody wants to assassinate her employer. Joke.

"The man is lovesick, that's all, just from seeing her. It happens all the time. Look what's happened to us."

The idea of taking part in two intrigues at once excites Fiorenza. She promises to help him and to keep it secret from everyone in the palace. As a reward for her gullibility, Mattachich gently kisses her once, twice, three times on her eyelids. His heart softens to feel their delicate fluttering under his lips and the resilience of the unseen and unseeing eyeballs beneath. Who would dare say to him that he does not love her at that moment? It has been raining outside; the streets are now drying gently, unevenly, in the warm summer air. From a distance they hear the slither and grind of one of the electric streetcars that have recently been introduced to Vienna. They walk arm in arm for a few blocks before he puts her in a cab. He continues on foot, slowly making his way through the restless, slumbering mass of the city. All its darkness and light, silence and noise, roadways and buildings, its great outer and inner rings, seem to arrange themselves around him as he walks, so that he always feels he is at their center, in whatever direction he turns. This grandiose, axial notion of himself had come to him during his very first visit to Vienna; though he knew it to be a delusion he loved it then and loves it still.

❖

Hence the knack he had developed, with Fiorenza's clandestine help, of waiting for Louise on appropriate street corners at the appropriate times, or of going to the opera on the same evenings as herself. Street corners were cheaper, which was not a small consideration, but visits to the opera or to the theater were more effective. Sometimes he saw her two or three times a week, either in the Prater or in town; once she disappeared for several weeks, and when he saw her again he knew at once from her expression that he was not the only one who had been afraid that her absence (in the country, as he learned later) might have brought these silent encounters of theirs to an end.

What lover does not know that look of searching in the beloved's eyes, and the relief registered there when it is answered?

Imagine the two of them, so close physically even then and so distant in circumstances. She was a Belgian princess, nine years older than himself, a member by blood and marriage of a family that was busy peopling the thrones of Europe, a woman of great wealth and of inconceivable wealth yet to come (once her father and her mad childless aunt, Charlotte, relict of the Emperor Maximilian of Mexico, had been buried with the pomp their rank would demand). She was also, through both her sister's and her husband's connections, a frequent visitor at the Hofburg, the royal and imperial palace of the Habsburg dynasty, and the occupant of an honored place at all major occasions of state. He was an unknown, undistinguished, unmoneyed twenty-eight-year-old subaltern of dubious origin: a gambler, an idler, a spendthrift; a man repeatedly in trouble with his superiors for absenting himself from his duties and for being careless with other people's money and wives. What connection could there be between the two of them? What could he hope to get from her? Or she from him? It was grotesque for him to dream of her as his friend or patroness, let alone as his beloved, his mistress, an older woman who would lie naked in his arms, listening to his tales of army life.

Yet such waking and sleeping dreams seldom left his mind. He looked for her name in newspapers and magazines; he went to libraries and tried to trace her family connections through encyclopedias and the *Almanach de Gotha*. The life she had led since her childhood was unimaginable to him; but as he went about his "researches," picturing her as a cherished, cosseted child, cheered and admired by all who saw her (he was to be amazed to learn from her how harsh and empty of comfort and affection her childhood had actually been), his thoughts constantly went back, as if in rebound, to his memories of the bleak secretive house of his childhood in Tomasevich, among the stone- and tree-laden hills of northeastern Croatia. The three adults there, his mother and the two men, his drunken father and her lover, Count Keglevich, sharing their obscure connubiality; the uncouth glances and gestures of the servants in his direction and the sniggering talk he heard from them about his "two fathers"; the sense he had of something that was both shameless and shameful in their circumstances and his; the conviction that there was nothing at home for him to be proud of—all this had been a part of his consciousness from an early age. And outside the home? So much useless space given over to random bristling trees, each one an unneighborly distance from the next, with boulder-broken slopes leading up or down to more of the same; a view around the house that was viewless, in effect, in revealing nothing but more and more of what had already been seen. He could remember how, like a little madman, he had put a coin under a loose, flat, gray stone lying near the wooden gate to the backyard of the house, where the cattle went by, and how, when he came back from boarding school at the end of his first term three months later, he had found the same coin still lying under the same stone—and what a bizarre and degraded sense of vindication he had felt at the sight of it! You see what the place was like? You see how nothing changed? You see how nothing would ever change—neither him nor the place nor the people? And if they died, others would merely take over and the whole thing go on in the same way as before.

Subsequently the inspection of the coin under its stone became a ritual he had to perform each time he left the house and returned to it. That's what his home was. That's what it made of him. That was what drove him, now that he was far from it, to swagger and take risks of all kinds, sometimes privately, where no one would know of them; more often in public. Show them! Show them! He was not a gifted man, and he knew it; even his horsemanship, of which he was proud, had been described by his superiors in the army as merely "good," not "very good" or "outstanding," the grade he had hoped to receive. Yet he was ambitious and always had been. He burned to show them, the vacant-eyed yawners and belchers and scratchers at home, his bored fellow officers in the Thirteenth

Regiment, officers in grander regiments than his own, the native Germans and Austrians who recognized Croatia in his speech and instinctively patronized him for that reason, the shifting, anonymous, multiracial crowds in Vienna, drawn there from all quarters of the ramshackle empire he had sworn to defend: Croatians like himself, Hungarians, Serbians, Galicians, Italians, Poles, Czechs, Slovenes, Ruthenians, Jews, Gypsies—even Turks and Albanians. Show them!

No, if he didn't raise the stakes now, he would be finished; he would never do anything worthwhile. And what reason would he then be able to give himself for not even having *tried* to follow up the wordless acquaintance with the princess that an incomprehensible chance had thrown in his way? What defeat, what humiliation could he suffer that would be worse than the humiliation of never having tried? He alone would remain as judge of himself, and his finding would be that he was a nothing—forever. A coward. A jackass. The son of an idle drunken cuckold who had lived for years off the largesse of his wife's lover. Yes, that's what his father was, and his son now found himself staring at the possibility that he would turn out no better. A man who would spend the rest of his life knowing he was exactly what he deserved to be, a failure who had been too timid to make a grab at the most implausible prize anyone of his rank had ever dreamed of winning.

So he wrote a letter to the princess, to be transmitted to her by the faithful Fiorenza. In order to conceal the fact that the fictitious admirer of the princess for whom he claimed to be acting had much the same handwriting as himself, he wrote the princess's name on the envelope in block capitals (IHRE KÖNIGLICHE HOHEIT PRINZESSIN LOUISE VON SACHSE-COBURG UND GOTHA) and used a different pen and ink of a different color from those he had used when writing to Fiorenza herself. She suspected nothing. Full of excitement and self-importance, she carried the sealed note to her royal mistress.

"What happened?" he asked, when they next met. (Imagine being Fiorenza, claiming to be in love with him, and not seeing the fierceness of his eyes, not attending to the thickness of his voice.)

"She took the letter."

"And then?"

"She asked who'd given it to me."

"And then?"

"I gave the princess your name. You told me I could. I said the letter wasn't from you, it was from someone else."

"And then?"

"She read it right away."

"And then?" (Almost screaming by now.)

"She said 'I understand' and put the letter away."

CHAPTER TWO

BARRACKS AND OFFICERS' QUARTERS, PARADE grounds and armories, stables and bathhouses; bugle calls and echoing commands (in German only); platoons of men on foot or horseback passing by; superiors to defer to; inferiors to give orders to; fellow subalterns to drink, argue, and gamble with; animals and equipment to inspect; elaborate route marches and maneuvers, some lasting for weeks and taking him across entire provinces, countries indeed, he would otherwise never have seen— these were the settings and routines that had given Mattachich's life a continuity he would not have been able to find elsewhere. For him, as with everyone else in a peacetime army, boredom and irritation were always a problem. Something like thirty years had passed since the empire had been at war, so his chosen career had an air of permanently unfulfilled expectation, of enforced futility, about it. Yet he took much pride in his uniform and the place it gave him in one of the handful of institutions through which the empire knew itself as an empire. A Croat in a Croatian regiment, he was aware that his unit would never be stationed in his own country; and that the same was true for all the other soldiers drawn from the empire's "subject" or "nonhistoric" peoples. For reasons that were plain to him, and which he accepted with a perfect cynicism, he knew too that only Germans and Hungarians were exempt from this iron rule.

So what? Should he feel injured on that score, as some of his fellow Croatians and the other non-Germanic types did? Sometimes, perhaps, but usually not. *In deinem Lager ist Österreich* the army boasted (for want of a clearer definition, no doubt, of how Austria was to be defined),* and that sentiment had always found its echo in Mattachich's Croatian heart. In his view Croatia was better off subordinate to the Habsburgs any day than to an independent Hungary, which would otherwise have been its fate. As for himself, a man in flight from what he used to be and famishing for what he could not define, both the idea of the empire, and the reality too—railway lines and postage stamps, bureaucrats and coinage, parades and public ceremonies—had a glamour he could not resist. The empire was ramshackle, yet it remained one; it was crisscrossed with a thousand prohibitions and discriminations, yet it offered to its disparate races opportunities they would never have had without it.

Croats like himself included. Why should he look only to provincial Agram† as his capital when (with luck) a great capital like Vienna, the second city of Europe, as he liked to think of it, might be his too? Only in Vienna could he have spent a free morning displaying his horse and his horsemanship before all the grand people parading along the avenues of the Prater. And see whose attention he had been able to draw to himself there.

❖

Yet look at him now, hurrying anxiously across the regiment's lines in Lobau, on the outskirts of the city. He has just been summoned by messenger to report forthwith to the regimental office and is convinced that he is in trouble. Over the last months he has been taking more liberties than usual in order to free himself to pursue his obsession with the responsive yet still unattainable princess. He has bribed fellow officers to take his watches, fiddled times and signatures on the duty roster, reported sick and crept out of bed when he thought it safe to do so, absented himself from camp without even bothering to fabricate any kind of cover.

Which of these offenses has been uncovered? What is his punishment

---

* "Your camp is Austria." Or perhaps, "Where your camp is, there Austria is also."
† This is how Mattachich invariably refers to Zagreb in his *Memoiren.*

to be? All he can hope for at the moment is that the orderlies in the front office will tell him what he needs to know before he goes in to see the commander. But that hope is thwarted the instant he arrives. An anonymous arm points silently toward a door. He knocks and enters. Colonel Funke, his hands clasped before him, sits at his large bare desk. He is thin, bald, tall, dry-mannered. His features are immobile; his eyes are so light in color they appear to be almost transparent, even empty. The unnerving result is to produce an effect not of vacancy but of secrecy, reserve, penetration. He is famous in the regiment for his intimidating stares. Unusually for any grown man at that time, and especially so for a soldier, his face is clean-shaven. Across his forehead is a red line made by the cap he has set aside on his desk. It is near his right elbow, and its gilt badge and black peak are turned toward Mattachich, as if it too is eager to take part in the forthcoming interrogation. There are shelves behind Funke's head, carrying stacks of buff-colored folders, like flat pillows piled on top of one another. Aside from Funke's intimidatory cap, the only item on the desk is a single sheet of paper with a stamped heading and some scrawled writing on it.

Funke does not acknowledge Mattachich's salute and does not invite him to sit down. Silence. Mattachich waits. He has always known this man does not think well of him. Funke clasps and unclasps his hands. Then Mattachich sees something strange in his commander's empty gaze; something he has not seen there before and would never expect to see. It is unease. He looks almost shifty. He is not a man to show discomfort when issuing rebukes and punishments. So what is on his mind?

The moment he opens his mouth, unable to put off speaking any longer, the source of his discomfort is made plain. He hates being the bearer of good news for Mattachich.

"I am instructed to inform you," he declares in a dead voice, "that you have been promoted from second lieutenant to lieutenant."

Mattachich begins to gasp out some words of thanks but is cut short by a gesture. "This is not because of any recommendation of mine, you understand. It seems you have friends elsewhere in Vienna. You can go now."

"Sir."

The newly promoted Oberleutnant closes the door behind him. The men in the front office lift their heads to stare at him curiously. He ignores them. Some yards from the set of wooden office buildings is a clump of birches in which he takes shelter—not from the rain, for there is none, but from the astonishment within him. Louise! It is her doing. It has to be. Five times his name has been put forward for this modest promotion; always the list of successful candidates has been returned with his name among those struck out. And now, with no notice, no warning, outside the season for the announcement of promotions, this! Who else could it be? What other source of patronage does he have? Full of gratitude and excitement, he walks back and forth among the skinny birch trees. The ground is littered with their fallings: curled strips of bark, small serrated leaves, and stringlike twigs, some longer than the span of a man's arms, like those still hanging down from meager branches as if out of sheer weakness, unable to sustain their own negligible weight. He takes a few brisk paces, turns, takes another few paces, turns once more, and does it again and again, like a man who has to cover a specific distance in a limited period and a confined space. Or a prisoner with nowhere to go. His heels grind the fallen stuff into the damp dark soil. His thoughts move from Louise to the humbling of the colonel—yes! that's what it was, the bastard swallowing his own bile!—and from there to vague dreams of kissing gloved hands, embraces, greater liberties and honors than these, whispered words, undying love, journeys, God knows what. He sees himself as a general, a duke, a governor of a province, an ambassador in Paris.

No, no. Such fantasies are rubbish compared with what he has in his grasp, this precious moment here, on his own, the familiar sounds of the camp's half-industrious, half-indolent routine going on around him. Eventually his pace slackens; he goes slowly back to his room and settles down to write a letter to his benefactor. It will duly be carried to her by another benefactor, the gullible and (he has now begun to believe) dispensable Fiorenza. In the letter he thanks the princess for what she had done for him (*I have no doubt, your royal highness, that this is your doing*) and speaks of himself as her eternally grateful and faithful servant. *I still wait to hear your voice,* he pleads. *Even a glimpse of your handwriting has been withheld from me. But no matter. You have my fealty unto death.*

He likes that last phrase especially. It moves him as he writes it. Surely she will respond directly to him now.

❖

She did not do so—not directly. Nevertheless, the sign he longed for was not long in coming. It was brought to him by a tearful Fiorenza. She had lost her job. The princess was going to spend much of the winter in Abbazia* on the Adriatic coast, where her sister Stephanie, the widowed crown princess, had rented a villa. Louise would be following her in a few weeks' time—not to the villa but to a suite in the Quarnero, Abbazia's biggest and newest hotel. She was taking only a small entourage with her. So she had told Fiorenza that she would not need her there, and in fact had decided to let her go. Her advice was that she should return to Graz and marry her young man. It was time she did so.

"I asked her what I'd done wrong," Fiorenza sobbed, "why she was sending me away, but all she said was no, I'd done very well, I'd already done everything for her that I possibly could. Now she can manage without me. What does that mean? Why does she say it?"

"I have no idea," Mattachich said untruthfully, concealing his delight at what he had just heard. Taking tactical advantage of the moment, as a soldier should, he then told her (also untruthfully) that his regiment had just received orders to entrain shortly for Slovakia. He hadn't wanted to break the news to her, he claimed, but there was no point in keeping it from her now. No, he did not know when they would return to Vienna. Never, perhaps. He had to go where he was sent. Of course he would remember her. Of course he would write to her. Of course they would meet again. She was his darling.

* Now Opatija.

Kiss, kiss. His performance, though, was a perfunctory one, and he did not care if she sensed it. What did she think he was—a fool? A man who couldn't read the signs? The princess had secured a promotion for him, she was leaving Vienna, and at the same time was getting rid of their go-between. This conjunction of events could not be an accident. Fiorenza was no longer needed. She had just carried to him her last and most thrilling message.

Some weeks later he read in the Court News section of the newspaper (of which he'd become a keen follower) that the princess had left for Abbazia, where her sister, the widowed Crown Princess Stephanie, had already taken up residence. Within two days he was on the train en route to the same destination. (His stepfather, he told the regimental adjutant, had suddenly been taken ill, and his mother was begging him to return home.)

There in Abbazia, away from Vienna, away from the court and the hundreds of dependent aristocrats who clustered around it like wasps on an overripe fruit, they would be free. He and his Louise.

❖

With a little harbor at its center, where sailing craft and a few steam yachts were moored, the newly established Adriatic resort of Abbazia straggled in optimistic fashion around its bay. Little headlands jutted into the pale blue sea; farther out, islands of rock seemed to recline at their ease, like swimmers looking back at the row of florid hotels along the shoreline. Day and night, modest Adriatic waves collapsed without ado on the sands; they gurgled beneath the wooden bathing huts provided by the hotels for their clientele and washed over the bottom steps of the ladders that led directly from the huts into the shallow water. On the landward side rose steep, dark, solid-looking slopes of wild laurel, into which yet more hotels had begun to make their inroads. Magnolias and palm trees, still groggy from their transplantation, adorned the main promenade. So did cafés and restaurants, a toylike bandstand, an undersized casino, shops with some of the smartest Viennese and Milanese names on their awnings, and a much-patronized institution for hydrotherapy and colonic irrigation. At all hours of the day, early morning and early afternoon aside, visitors sauntered back and forth, the men doffing their hats and eyeing the women; the women eyeing other women's clothes and, more discreetly, the other women's men as well.

After making a languid survey of this brand-new "pearl of the Adriatic Riviera" and of its patrons, Crown Prince Franz Ferdinand had dismissed it as a "Jew aquarium." He had also complained of the number of "Slavs and irredentists" who frequented the place.* Yet aristocratic and fashionable patrons continued to come to the resort. They gambled in the casino, immersed themselves gingerly in the sea, went on journeys by steamboat along the coast, took carriages into the mountains, and gave "small soirées" (Mattachich's term)—at one of which he and Louise met and spoke to each other for the first time.

Neither had ever before been so close to the other, or seen the other bareheaded, or heard the other's voice. Never before had they simply stood face-to-face and directly confronted the presence of the other. Their own voices sounded strange in their ears, as if they were taking parts in a drama written by someone else. This was at the villa Stephanie had rented. Mattachich had found out about the soirée from one of Stephanie's servants and chosen simply to gate-crash the party, confident that if he were challenged Louise would vouch for him. The reception itself was much like any other, though the guests were more relaxed than they would have been at a similar occasion back home. Tall doors stood open; vases of flowers filled fireplaces from which the grates had been removed; tailcoated waiters bustled about with trays in their hands; two men in

---

* Quoted in Holler, *Ihr Kampf*, pp. 44–45. Less than twenty years later, this same Franz Ferdinand, who had become heir apparent after the suicide of his cousin Rudolf, was to be assassinated by Gavril Princip—who, as it happened, was both a Slav and an irredentist (a member of a nationalist group dedicated to "redeeming" territories governed by a neighboring power). The assassination precipitated the outbreak of the First World War and the end of the Habsburg monarchy.

black jackets scraped away at their violins with swaying shoulders and screwed-up eyes, while a less impassioned member of the trio fingered the keys of a piano; voices rose and echoed back from the ceiling, where molded plaster wreaths encircled crossed flambeaux, also of plaster, that forever strained and failed to touch each other; discreet traffic to and from an unseen room betrayed the final touches being given to an informal sit-down supper still to come. Shaven, shining, smelling of cologne, Mattachich bowed deeply. Louise stretched a gloved hand toward him; he raised it to within an inch of his lips, his head dipping over it, before he relinquished it to her. "Your Highness," he said, "Lieutenant Géza Mattachich, Thirteenth Uhlans, at your service."

His voice was low, his gaze intense. She looked at him in silence, also intensely, but with a hint of the amusement he had seen in her eyes during their first encounter in the Prater—and many times since.

"You have waited a long time for this," she said.

"It seems no time at all—now."

"I wondered if you would come to Abbazia."

"Once I'd got your message, there could be no doubt of it."

"My message? Oh, yes."

Their eyes remained locked. Moist, quivering light on both sides: that was all either could see. Yet the moment was fateful for them both. Each sensed in it the possibility of a transformation from what they had previously been: a promise, a phantom, a threat that could not be denied. What had already happened between them, however tenuous it had been—their first exchange of glances, the silent encounters that had followed, his pursuit of her in public places, his unanswered letters and her repeated solitary readings of them—was over now. Something else had begun. The game they had been playing no longer belonged to them; rather, they belonged to it. It possessed them. He may indeed have been, as he was to be described in an official volume after his death, *un escroc . . . aussi dénué d'argent que de scrupules* and she (according to the same authority) *capricieuse et difficile,* but neither was mistaken about how momentous this occasion was for them both.[*] For several long moments after their first exchange they were silent, hanging away from each other, though there was no inclination on either side to retreat. The stillness between them was an acknowledgment that a new life was on offer. If they so chose.

Her eyes flickered and lost their intensity. Those moments were over. Yet she gazed at him still. "Have you brought your stallion with you?" she asked.

Smiling, shaking his head, he felt an unexpected pity for her, this princess, this woman older than himself—and who looked it too, for all the care that had been taken with her dress, her jewels, her powdered face and solidly loaflike head of shining hair—and who had not the faintest notion of how a man like himself lived. The idea of a debt-ridden lieutenant with his third-class return rail ticket to Vienna in his pocket, who did not know how long his funds would enable him to eke out his stay in Abbazia—the idea of his bringing with him his only mount!

"A fine animal," she went on heedlessly. "What is his name?"

"Rebel," he answered, instantly giving the horse a brand-new name.

"Like his master?"

"Your highness, you know what you've done for me—and to me. All I ask is the chance to do whatever I can for you. Anywhere. Always."

"Yes, we've got a lot to learn from each other."

They parted, he wishing that he were taller, she that she were younger, both content for the moment, relieved at least that his silent doglike courtship—which to her had always had been edged with absurdity and for him stained through and through with incredulity—was at last over.

❖

Two nights later, he and the princess lay together in the bedroom of her suite on the first floor of the Quarnero Hotel. He had arrived there in

---

[*] *Biographie Nationale de la Belgique,* vol. XVIII, supplement 10. The description of Mattachich translates as "an adventurer as devoid of money as he was of scruples"; that of Louise needs no translation.

high romantic fashion by climbing one of the pillars that held up the terrace outside her room. It was 2 A.M. when he appeared at the tall French windows. She had pointed out the windows of the room with her parasol while strolling with him along the promenade: he dressed in a buff linen suit, complete with tie and stiff white collar; she in a many-layered light dress, her face shaded by a close-fitting round straw hat with a preposterously wide brim that made her face beneath it look like the planet Saturn with all its tilted rings. *Tap-tap-tap* on her window, he now went; and again, *tap-tap-tap,* a little more anxiously than before, for though he had taken her pointing parasol as an invitation, he had not warned her that he would be coming. His aim was to give her no choice, to surprise her with his boldness and ardor. But he did not want to frighten her; still less to wake up the whole hotel.

Once more: *tap-tap-tap.* This time she heard him. Waking, she knew at once what the sound meant. She was not afraid. She did not even put a wrap over her long nightdress. She went to the windows and saw a vague male figure through the glass. A turn of her hand and the single vertical brass bolt securing both the upper and lower latches of the windows moved obediently sideways. He eased himself into the room. A by-now familiar smell of cologne, cigar smoke, and soap filled her nostrils, mixed with a new male acridity of anxiety and desire. She drew him to her and for the first time used the word for him that she never abandoned when they were alone together, through all the years that followed: "*Geliebter.*" And he—for the first time and always thereafter, when they were alone and long after they had ceased to be lovers, when they had merely become one another's fate, nothing else—he called her simply "*Prinzessin.*"

Done. Done in a welter of disbelief, pride, strangled breath, tangled bedclothes, the strangeness of the other's body (textures, smells, tastes), and the making plain of what each sought. This was the hidden territory to which the last few days of horseback riding, dancing, and talking had led them; now, finally and irreversibly, they entered it.

Ingress at last.

❖

To Stephanie's spoken and unspoken questions about this man who had first insinuated himself into her house and now clicked his heels whenever they met, bowing and smiling at her as if they were old acquaintances, Louise gave evasive, offhand, sometimes even nonsensical answers. Oh, he's a wonderful horseman. *Is that why you go riding with him every day?* Oh, people on the General Staff speak so highly of him. *Which people? Who?* Oh, he was so brave and kind; he had saved her life. *What?* Oh, there'd been a horse that was just about to bolt in the Prater and he'd stopped it from coming near her. *When? How?* Oh, he comes from an ancient and truly aristocratic Croatian family. *A Croatian what?*

The more incoherently Louise spoke, the more convinced Stephanie became that Mattachich's sudden appearance in Abbazia had been carefully planned between them. Now she understood why Louise, while foisting her lumpish daughter, Dora, on her, had declined to share the villa Stephanie had rented just south of town and had chosen instead to take a suite in the Quarnero Hotel, where the *nouveaux riches* goggled at her every time she appeared in its public rooms. Obviously she and this follower had deliberately chosen to use her holiday plans as cover for their arrangements. And when the story got back to the Hofburg in Vienna, as it certainly would, who would be besmirched by it? Not only Louise, that was for sure. Stephanie may have been a younger sister, but she was senior in rank; she was the one whose residence remained the great palace itself, her widowed state notwithstanding. Naturally they would assume there that she had been complicit in the whole dirty business from the start.

With her large body, sloping shoulders, and heavy breasts, Stephanie resembled her older sister; only the shape of her small, pale, oval face was wholly her own. Both women had inherited their father's prominent nose (though in more shapely versions); both were crowned with thick heads of implausibly golden hair worn in the same double-layered round-loaf fashion; both moved in a forceful, awkward manner, as if their legs and upper bodies were at odds with each other. Their voices were alike too, deep and inexpressive in every one of the several languages they spoke: French, German, English, Spanish, and—poorly, in Louise's case—Hungarian. (Not Flemish, however, or any of the empire's Slavic tongues.) They kissed when they met and kissed again when they parted, even if it was only for an hour or two; often they sat together conversing quietly; throughout their time in Abbazia there was nothing approaching a scene between them despite Stephanie's conviction that she had been used, even swindled.

With Mattachich, Stephanie was less restrained—which is to say she was even more restrained. Silent, in other words. She ignored him or did her best to do so; she directed no remarks to him, responded to his salutations with the smallest of nods, made it plain that she did not need his help to mount her horse or get into her coach. But if Louise herself, in the excitement and distraction of having this new young cavalier in her presence, remained in the dark about how wounded and exploited Stephanie felt, Mattachich was wholly out of his depth with her. Habits born in the chill distances and silences, the savagely enforced proprieties and secret improprieties of Leopold's household, and confirmed by a marriage that (like Louise's) had begun disastrously and continued unhappily until it was brought to an end by the sensational double suicide at Mayerling of Stephanie's husband, the archduke Rudolf, and his last mistress—all this was quite beyond Mattachich's comprehension.* Nor could he have guessed that from the moment of her arrival in Vienna many years before, Stephanie had suspected that her new husband had previously been Louise's lover. Her pride had kept her silent at the time and had done so since, but her relations with Louise were never the same again.

---

* Stephanie's description of her wedding night is almost as horrified as her sister's: "We had nothing to say to each other, we were total strangers. In vain I waited for a tender or kind word from him which might have distracted me from my thoughts. . . . What torments! What horror! I had not the ghost of a notion of what lay before me, but had been led to the altar an unsuspecting child. My illusions, my youthful dreams, were destroyed. I felt that the disillusionment I experienced would kill me. I was freezing, shuddering with cold; fearful and feverish tremors ran through me." (*Ich Sollte Kaiserin Werden* [Leipzig, 1935], pp. 82–83, by Princess Stephanie of Belgium, translated into English as *I Was to Be Empress* [London, 1937].) Not surprisingly, she gives no indication in her book that she had been infected with venereal disease by her husband—which is why, after producing a daughter, she was unable to bear him another child.

Mattachich had no notion of any of this. He did his best to ingratiate himself with Louise's slow-witted, six-foot daughter, Dora, and believed he made some progress there, unresponsive though she was. Like a simpleton he also believed he was making a good impression on Stephanie. He even began to suspect that she too fancied him a little. At the very least he believed she and he had an understanding. Louise and Stephanie were sisters, after all; why shouldn't a man who appealed to one not interest the other?

It was a misapprehension that was, much later, to have disastrous consequences for him and his princess.*

❖

From their quasi-honeymoon on the Adriatic, Louise and Mattachich returned to the still-wintry streets of Vienna, where leaves and buds lagged far behind their Mediterranean counterparts and a Siberian wind pinched every ear and finger exposed to it. For the lovers it was as if they had gone back in time to a city that was as they had left it, climatically and in every other way, while they themselves had passed through an irreversible change in relation to each other and the world at large. Before Abbazia they could not have guessed what they would do when they at last managed to meet and speak face-to-face; now they knew—and much else besides. That mystery had been resolved; other unguessable possibilities were still to reveal themselves, one by one.

So: back to Vienna, 1896. The end of the century approaching. The high point of a period that would lead historians of a later generation to make exaggerated reference to the city as "the birthplace of the modern world." Which presents a temptation here that has to be resisted. There is no need for you to imagine that this slight, bearded, firm-gazed, intensely respectable Jew, who looks on with interest as Louise and her

---

* Louise makes many references to Stephanie in her autobiography (not all of them hostile), whereas Stephanie refers much more sparingly to Louise. She does not mention Mattachich at all.

retinue pull up in front of the Coburg palace in Seilerstrasse, is Dr. Sigmund Freud (author so far only of *Studies in Hysteria*). Or that the abstracted, faintly smiling twenty-five-year-old on the far side of the park is Arnold Schönberg, listening inwardly to a piece of music that will eventually become his tone poem *Verklärte Nacht*. Or that, several city blocks from him, Egon Klimt is striking a price with a consumptive prostitute whom he is eager to paint in the flat desperate colors he is making his own. Or that the little boy with a wide forehead, sharp nose, and intense eyes, walking with his plainly intimidated governess toward the Franziskaner Kirche, is Ludwig von Wittgenstein, who himself has no idea that within a few decades he will transform the direction of philosophical inquiry in the English-speaking world. Equally there is no point in imagining that any of these people—or any other Viennese poet, thinker, or artist who will eventually achieve a stature comparable to theirs—is going to be casually snubbed by Louise or Philipp or Stephanie (at a formal reception, say, or a theatrical performance), who will never know just how important that unknown person will appear to be when they themselves have been all but completely forgotten.

No doubt Louise and Philipp attended a Schnitzler premiere or two; and Stephanie might (later) see Gustav Mahler mount the rostrum in the *Stadtsoper,* after he had painstakingly converted from Judaism to Christianity in order to make himself eligible for the conductor's job. But none of this mattered to them. They were preoccupied with what had always been truly significant to them: their health, their relations with each other; the exact degree of precedence given them on royal occasions; their clothes, public appearances, shopping, affairs, gossip, hunting, gambling; occasional political crises; the scanning of the newspapers for mention of their names. In one of the memorable phrases that Louise produces from time to time in her autobiography, she summarizes life in and around Franz Josef's Hofburg as a "combination of Spanish etiquette and German discipline": a society in which it was unthinkable that families of royal and ducal blood should marry out of their kind; where male members of the imperial court and the high aristocracy (the First Society), let alone underlings like cabinet ministers and senior civil servants, usually wore military uniform in public; and where status and styles of address were as carefully calibrated as the stars, ribbons, sashes, and epaulets that embellished the men's jackets and tunics. Among the womenfolk the signs of relative standing were even more elaborate, and changed more from season to season, but they were always plain to the eye that had been trained to recognize them.

Yet it was into this world that Louise attempted to insert her lover, the murky stepson of a Croatian baron whom no one in Vienna had ever heard of. (Of his real father, if he had ever had such a thing, even less was known.) If she had discreetly taken a lover from an "acceptable" family whose presence in her life Philipp could have tacitly acknowledged and ignored, people would have talked of it and let her get on with it. So many years had passed since Philipp and Louise had had anything but formal relations with each other that he felt no jealousy, no prurience even, in thinking about her with another man or men—merely a patronizing, faintly incredulous wonder as to what they might find in her and why anyone in his right mind would choose to have anything to do with her.

But a low-grade upstart like Mattachich! That was another matter. *A Mattachich!* That was how Philipp could not help thinking and speaking of the man, as if he were a breed of dog or horse.* However, even a connection with a person of that sort, Philipp believed—or later came to believe—might have been tolerated if only Louise had had the sense to keep him out of Vienna. If only—and here, during the months and even

---

* When everything about Louise and her lover was known, plain, undeniable, all over the newspapers, Philipp made a formal statement before the State Attorney's office in Vienna. In it he declared that nothing but a profound mental disturbance (*Geistesstörung*) could have allowed his wife "so to forget herself as to go wandering about little Croatian villages in the company of a Mattachich . . . and other persons of that ilk." Nothing else, he went on, could explain how a high-born lady, the daughter of a king and the wife of a prince of Coburg, "could so thoroughly have lost any sense of her rightful position and of the royal values in which she had been raised" (quoted in Holler, *Ihr Kampf,* p. 117). The "royal values" invoked with such unction by Philipp had permitted King Leopold to treat his wife and daughters with brutal disdain and to specialize in the serial debauching of teenage girls. Of the policies those same "royal values" encouraged Leopold to introduce into his African possessions, more below.

years that followed, he would fall into a kind of daydream—if only she had bought a secluded hunting lodge, say, with a bit of ground attached, and left the fellow there to mind the horses and pigs, shoot what was available for shooting whenever he felt like it, lord it over a handful of peasants, and of course have Louise visit him from time to time . . . well, in that case things might have been . . . arranged. More or less. Given what he liked to speak of as his easygoing nature (and which you might choose to think of as his fondness for his own sense of failure, his not-so-secret readiness to see himself as a butt of misfortune), he could have put up with it. Easily. No problem. Once the man was out of sight and people had got over the novelty of the whole thing, it wouldn't have mattered a damn to anybody. And no doubt the wretched couple themselves would have got tired of each other soon enough.

❖

Some hope! Not long after getting back to Vienna, Louise made a series of announcements to her husband. First, she had just appointed Mattachich to be the master of her private stable, her *Stallmeister.* Previously Philipp's man had overseen her mounts and grooms as well as his master's, but this would no longer do. Second, her friend on the General Staff had arranged for this new *Stallmeister* to be granted special leave for a year from his regiment. Third, accommodation had to be found for him.

"Not in the palace," Philipp said sharply. "I won't have it."

"Why not? What have you got against him? You've never met the man."

"I don't intend to meet him."

"Why not?"

"I know enough about him."

"Who have you been talking to?" Then, because Philipp stood silent before her: "Dora? Stephanie? The servants?"

He turned away. "This conversation is over."

"Is it? Is it? Is it?"

Philipp knew that trick of hers: repeating a brief question over and over again, her voice growing louder every time she uttered it. He knew all her tricks. In response he did what he always did. He left the room, closing the doors behind him. Within minutes he wrote a message to Stephanie, begging for a few minutes of her time. The following morning he and she sat side by side on a couch in the Chinese morning room of her apartment in the Hofburg. Delicate porcelain coffee cups, which they had just emptied, stood on the tiles (also Chinese) of the tabletop in front of them. Sunlight came in through tall windows and glittered off black-and-gold lacquered cabinets and dragon-entwined mirrors. Some of the dragons had gilt scales, some green; all had open mouths, revealing curled scarlet tongues and sharp white teeth within. When either Philipp or Stephanie moved, so did many fragmented images of themselves, reflected sharply in mirrors or subaqueously in the leaded glass and lacquer of the cabinets, like eavesdroppers unaware that they too could be seen and overheard.

Having exchanged the usual civilities, Philipp got down to business. He told Stephanie about his conversation with Louise and asked for her advice. After all, she knew Louise better than anyone else. Even before her return to Vienna, he'd heard about this fellow turning up in Abbazia, but had hoped that the end of the holiday would be the end of the matter. You know, that this . . . ruffian . . . would simply vanish. But it hadn't happened.

Leaning farther forward and lowering his voice, he looked confidentially across his shoulder at Stephanie. His neck was short and his shoulder plump, so it was an effort for him to do it. She'd been there when the creature had first appeared. Did she know how long the affair between them had been going on?

"No, no idea," Stephanie answered. "I know nothing about it. You mustn't think it's got anything to do with me. I'd never seen him before. Never heard of him. Not from Louise or anyone else."

Her voice and expression convinced Philipp that she was telling the truth. He leaned back alongside her on the couch. "I understand," he said reassuringly. "I wasn't accusing you. But I had to ask." Then he tried another tack. Perhaps, he suggested, Louise was going through "a phase," as women did when they reached a certain age—behaving erratically, doing unprecedented things, going out of their way to find unsuitable friends. They were famous for it, no? What did she think. "If we take no notice, perhaps she'll just get over it? If it wasn't this it could be something else—like hot flashes. Or who knows what?"

His courage had failed him well before he had finished. Stephanie gave his last suggestion short shrift. "It's got nothing to do with hot flashes."

"So what is it?"

In silence each turned over various possibilities. Infatuation. Lust. Vindictiveness. Despair. Boredom. Stupidity. *Nostalgie de la boue.* Fear of age.

But neither offered the other any of these unattractive terms. "I tried to talk to her," Stephanie said eventually, "but she wouldn't let me. She gave me no chance. You've seen what she's like. She thinks she's found something in this Mich-Mach-Mich fellow, God knows what. . . . You could bribe him to go away, perhaps. It might work."

In much the same tone of voice she added, a moment later, "Or have him killed."

Beneath her gleaming solid-seeming head of hair, with not a strand of it out of place, she looked straight at him; he did the same, at her, from behind his frail glasses. He sat in silence, knowing abjectly that he could not tell if she meant what she had just said. Was she mocking him? Challenging him? Asking him to do it?

Impossible to tell, with these strange outsize sisters.

So he made his excuses and left. On his return to the Coburg palace his triumphant wife informed him that she had arranged to rent a pair of rooms for her *Stallmeister* not too far from the palace. She did not say where the rooms were exactly, however. Mattachich's first duty would be to look for accommodation for her horses, which she no longer wished to keep in the palace stables. However, her coaches and chaises would remain where they were.

To these announcements Philipp made no response. Over the next weeks, and then months, as gossip about the princess and her "groom" spread more widely among people who knew her and people who did not, Philipp remained silent. Inactive. A kind of lethargy had come over him. He behaved as if he thought it beneath his dignity to speak or act in connection with the affair; or at least wanted people to think this was how he felt. Yet he knew it was not beneath his dignity to place himself behind shutters and curtains of various upstairs windows at the back of the palace, from where he could look down on the cobbled stable yard and spy on the *Stallmeister* supervising the preparation of Louise's vehicles and mounts before he sent them around to the front of the building, where they would wait for her to descend the stone steps. Or rather, Philipp *did* know this activity to be beneath his dignity, and that was why he couldn't stop doing it; it was a means of mortifying himself. The trimness of Mattachich's figure depressed him; so did his youth and the cocky way he carried himself, with the small of his back pulled in and his lewd backside stuck out behind. Not to speak of his tight-belted brown tunic and its high black collar and cuffs, his boots of the finest cut and softest leather (and guess who had paid for them), his gestures, the movements of his mouth under his mustache as he ordered the grooms about. Everything. All he was. Loathsome.

At social gatherings Philipp was conscious of people conversing with one another and drawing apart as he approached, their amused, curious eyes sliding away from him. He was surprised to find how little he cared; for the moment anyway. He felt much the same when he was at home, in his own palace, with its retinue of servants for each member of the family who lived in it: himself, wife, widowed mother, his brother and wife, his reprobate son away in the army, silent daughter. With its gilt-and-dust-encrusted state rooms and long, gloomy corridors, the palace was less like a private residence than a neglected small town.* At this or that corner of

---

* "Everything was old, tasteless, somber. No flowers, no comfort, nothing intimate, nothing with a welcoming air. As to a bathroom [in her own quarters] there was not a sign of one. There were only two baths in the palace, far away from each other and with fittings that were completely out of date. Of the 'hygienic' arrangements of the rest, it is better not to speak!" (Louise, *Autour*, pp. 83–84).

it the servants exchanged whispers and smirks. Those of them who had seen Mattachich in action during his days as Fiorenza's suitor were particularly scornful of what was going on and also gleeful about it: they had a lien on the scandal, they felt, that was denied to the others.

One of them even took the liberty of handing Mattachich a letter to him that Fiorenza had sent with a covering note. Like a sensible fellow, Mattachich tore it up without reading it.

❖

Around this time, Mattachich wrote to his stepfather telling him it would be helpful to his career if he were now formally to be "adopted" as the count's son. The older man responded after a pause: yes, he would do it; he would put the process in hand. With that assurance given him, Mattachich took to instructing everyone in positions inferior to his own, in the palace and elsewhere, to address him as *Herr Graf*.* He also added the count's surname to his own and took to signing his letters *Mattachich-Keglevich*. He felt that these changes befitted his changed circumstances, especially as he told himself that he was doing it less for himself than for the princess. If, as he said, it was "only fitting that an officer should be bound in service to a king's daughter," it was fitting too that such an officer be the bearer of a title. At the same time he was gratified that this particular king's daughter, his employer and lover, was indulging in fantasies that ran parallel to his own, though in a directly opposite direction. Now that she had taken this outsider into her bed and her life, Louise had begun to make a parade of her democratic instincts, her informal tastes, her contempt for rank and court etiquette.†

---

* Holler (*Ihr Kampf*, p. 54) points out that Mattachich needed a special dispensation from the emperor in order to adopt the title. This was never granted.

† "My strongest sentiments are those of distaste for all that is insincere, overdone, needlessly elaborate. I seek what is simple in thought and action: that was why my family condemned me from my earliest years as a revolutionary. . . . How happy I would have been had I not been born a princess!" (Louise, *Autour*, pp. 16, 18).

So they abetted each other in the complementary myths they culti-vated about themselves. Masquerading under a self-endowed baronial title, Mattachich expressed his wonder that someone as "majestic" as Louise, "a figure from a fairy tale translated into reality," should have no interest in "rank and royal life"*—while she, "strongly democratic by instinct" though she claimed to be, looked around for a position that would be more fitting to his role in her life than that of *Stallmeister*. It did not take her long to find one. Philipp, she decided, should sack Baron Gablenz, his adjutant, and replace him with Mattachich. The impudence of the suggestion was irresistible to her. So was the humiliation it would inflict on Fatso, regardless of whether he acceded to her request or turned it down.

The post itself was a sinecure, a fiction. Since Philipp held the hon-orific title of a general in the imperial army, by virtue of his princely rank, he was entitled to have a military man permanently on his staff. Gablenz had served him in this capacity for several years. A pleasant, corpulent, open-faced bachelor of about Mattachich's age, Gablenz was always respect-ful toward his master, listened to his tales, organized his diary, played cards and billiards with him (frequently doing his best to lose), and accompanied Philipp on hunting parties, drinking bouts, and other expe-ditions of a more intimate kind. Now, all of a sudden, here was Louise demanding that he be chucked out of the palace to make room for this rubbishy Croatian cavalryman from whom, like an infatuated seventeen-year-old, she would not be parted. How could he possibly do it?

Louise had barely spoken to Philipp since her failure to bring Mattachich into the Coburg palace; now she pursued him with slanders against the innocent Gablenz. He was dirty, he was lazy, he was impudent, he stole, he was a glutton, he had made sexual advances to her, he encouraged Philipp to go whoring and drinking. When these attacks failed to pro-duce results, she turned to insulting not Gablenz but Philipp himself. Not even his careful closing of the painted sets of inner and outer doors

---

* Mattachich, *Memoiren* (p. 23).

with which each of the major apartments of the palace was equipped could keep from the ears of the servants, the wretched Dora, or his mother the abuse she directed at him. He was a fat pig, a whoremonger, a bully, a coward, not a man, a *"Scheisskerl."* Though the couple usually spoke French to each other, she repeated that last word over and over again in a peculiarly triumphant tone, apparently believing it to be one of her own invention. In return, keeping his voice much lower than hers, Philipp told her that she was carrying on like a madwoman, an infatuated creature, a menopausal mouth, a plague, a prostitute. While this was going on, Gablenz crept about like a felon awaiting sentence: dry-lipped, yellow-complexioned, unable to look his employer in the eye. Eventually he fell ill and lay in his bedroom with a pillow over his head, wondering which would be the worse course for him to follow: to resign or not to resign. He thought of suicide too, but the prince talked him out of it.

Mattachich's name never crossed Philipp's lips. Nor, though Louise yelled at him to do it often enough, would he send for Mattachich, so that the two of them could talk matters over "man to man"—another phrase she seemed to have adopted as her own. She and Mattachich would go off two or three times a week on their outings, she usually inside one of her carriages and he riding alongside it; or, more disturbingly, both mounted and accompanied by just a single groom, they would set out for an unseasonal ride in the dripping Vienna woods. These departures too were shamefacedly monitored by Philipp. About the bribability of the groom accompanying them he had no illusions. Doubtless the man would ride away on his own whenever they told him to and would stay away for as long as they needed. The hostility of the weather to these outings, and presumably therefore also to the couple's couplings, did at first give Phillip some satisfaction. But the spring foliage continued to unfurl, the skies above the city softened and retreated, and the sun shone more strongly day by day; soon the horse chestnut trees would again be transforming themselves into great green candelabras, lit up once more with a starry lavishness by their white and red candles, just as they had been when the lovers first set eyes on each other.

By the time the chestnut candles had been quenched, and were transforming themselves into clusters of spiky, green, grenadelike objects, Louise had abandoned her attempt to drive Gablenz out of the palace; she and Philipp now communicated by way of written notes only, carried back and forth by the servants. Nevertheless, when it was necessary for them to do so, the couple occasionally went out together and sat silently side by side in their carriage or in a box at the theater, or at special parades and state ceremonies. She and Philipp's mother never exchanged a word, either spoken or written. Dora fled the palace with her governess and a servant or two whenever she could: in effect, whenever she was invited to visit one or another of her innumerable relatives in Austria, Hungary, or the various German statelets. Philipp accompanied her occasionally; more often, he visited one of the Coburg estates on his own, where he came as close as he ever did to what you or anyone else might think of as working: that is, letting his estate managers lead him by the nose through the rent rolls, accounts, bills of sale (timber, crops, cattle), and so forth.

Louise stuck it out in Vienna, even in August, which she had never done before. She could not bear to leave her lover, and she could not take him with her—not without the kind of cover that Stephanie had provided for them in Abbazia. And no one volunteered to perform this service.

So much of 1897 went by. Soon the summer, late in coming, began to stiffen, to curl upon itself, to rust away, burn away, fall away into drifts of dry leaves that gathered wherever wind or the brooms of gardeners and street sweepers took them. Then the rains of autumn turned them into a sodden mulch. As if he had been positively waiting for this change of weather, and though nothing was said or done between him and his wife that hadn't already been done or said by them many times, Philipp suddenly acted. He was like a man flinging his bedclothes from him in disgust at his own torpor. He went to see the Minister of the Interior, who was an old acquaintance, and told him he wanted the secret police to watch the couple and to bring him a report on what they got up to when they went out together. He needed evidence, he said, law-court evidence.

A few days later the minister's deputy turned up at the palace. The discussion with him turned out to be not at all embarrassing, as Philipp had feared it might be. In fact, it came as a relief. The deputy told him that the ministry's spies had been keeping an eye on the couple ever since their return from Abbazia. A whole dossier about them was already in existence.

"It's our job," the man said. "Everything about this person is suspect. We are not even one hundred percent sure who his father is. Is he a drunkard named Mattachich or this Keglevich? And you know how it is with Croatians: scratch any of them and you'll find a nationalist underneath. So who knows who he's working for? Where his loyalties lie? What he's really after? To have an outsider in such close relations with an exalted personage like her highness . . . and others of even higher rank . . . we couldn't possibly ignore it."

Between sentences or half sentences, Philipp's overweight guest paused for breath. Or perhaps just for effect. A disheveled, gray-streaked, Nietzschean cascade of mustache hid his upper lip and left only a fragment of lower lip exposed; for the rest he was clean-shaven. His fat cheeks quivered every time a *b* or *p* emerged explosively from them. "We're not asleep," he insisted, his eyes half closed, as if to demonstrate how dozy he could look in order to deceive a suspect. "We're always on the watch. The empire is surrounded by enemies abroad, which is bad, and infested by them at home, which is worse still."

An aide had been left outside, in an antechamber. He was now summoned into the room and ordered to extract a single sheet of paper from the leather portfolio he carried. This he laid before his master, who groped for his glasses in a pocket of his black waistcoat, failed to find them, and so read the document holding it at arm's length from himself, as if it had a bad smell.

On six occasions the princess and Mattachich had left their horses with their groom in the woods and climbed into a waiting closed fiacre, which returned an hour later. On many other occasions they rode away from the groom on their horses for shorter periods. On one further occasion (which by chance had also been observed by the Archduke Ludwig Viktor, the emperor's youngest brother, who had reported the matter directly to his majesty) they had been seen entering a *chambre séparée* in the Hotel Sacher.*

Neither the minister nor the emperor, Philipp was told, had acted on this and other items of information supplied to him—apparently out of consideration for the prince's feelings. Now, Philipp assured the deputy, neither of them need hesitate any longer.

* Ludwig Viktor was also among those who were suspected of having been one of Louise's lovers in earlier years. "For many years he made a display of his affection for me. Everyone in Vienna knew of it, the emperor included—the emperor especially, in fact, because of his love of gossip. He lived in hope of hearing that his brother had had his way with me" (Louise, *Autour,* p. 109; see also Holler, *Ihr Kampf,* p. 34).

CHAPTER THREE

SIX WEEKS LATER, LOUISE AND MATTACHICH HAD in effect been sacked, expelled, driven out of Vienna. You can imagine their outrage. With hindsight, though, there is something ironic about their indignation at the treatment they received. If Mattachich had been dealt with more harshly—if he had been ordered to go back at once to his regiment and then dispatched to some remote Ruthenian or Polish backwater and left there to kick his heels indefinitely—he and Louise might have been spared much subsequent suffering. Other officers who had made a nuisance of themselves were banished to the provinces often enough, so why was that not done to him? And if the authorities intended to put an end to the attachment between him and Louise, why, once he had been expelled from Vienna, did they make it virtually impossible for her to remain in the city, where she would have been safer than before from his approaches?

It is a mystery. In all likelihood the officials in the Hofburg simply didn't know what to do with them. Both of them, anyway, would later speak of their expulsion from the city as evidence of the cruelty of the imperial court. "From that moment," Mattachich writes, "[the princess] was a deserted, unprotected woman and I was an officer of the imperial army forbidden to reside in the city."[*] Her view of what they had to go through was, if anything, even more melodramatic than his: "I have no

---

[*] Mattachich, *Memoiren*, p. 23.

idea where I would have gone and what might have happened to me if God had not sent to me the one man with the courage to tell me, 'Madame, you are the daughter of a king. . . . A Christian woman takes revenge on the iniquity of her enemies by rising above it.'"*

For them, even in hindsight, there was no mystery and no irony about the whole business. They were victims. They were punished by a false, oppressive society for their virtues, not for their vices.

❖

One fine day (Mattachich's phrase) an officer turned up at his door with a large stiff envelope in his hand. On the back of the envelope was the royal seal: a flattened scarlet lump of wax, like a severely squashed tomato.

Unshaven, dressed in pajamas and a full-length silk dressing gown of alternating stripes of pale and dark green (a gift from his beloved), Mattachich had been caught at a disadvantage. He had been about to begin his breakfast, but the seal on the envelope and the looming presence of its bearer left him with no choice. He had to crack it open and take out the note inside. As he did so he remembered the scribbled-on sheet of paper brought to him by a humble regimental orderly that had summoned him to Colonel Funke's office. He had come a long way since then. This communication had been brought by a uniformed official of higher rank than himself and came directly from the royal secretariat, the *Kabinettkanzlei,* in the Hofburg.

"Yes," the man said, the moment Mattachich looked up from it. "I'm to take you there right away."

Holding the thick embossed note in his hand, Mattachich wondered vaguely how these people had known where to find him. Louise had assured him many months before that she had given his exact address to nobody, her husband included. Well, that was the business of those who

---

* Louise, *Autour,* p. 82.

had tracked him down; his was to get shaved and changed. His modest breakfast of coffee and a roll, brought in moments before by his landlady, had to be foregone. After some thought he put on his standard service uniform, complete with tall steep-visored cap. The visitor, who had not troubled to give Mattachich his name, waited in the little hall of the apartment; then they stepped silently into the street, where a two-wheeler with a man up front was waiting for them.

The brief drive to the Hofburg had a strange recapitulatory quality for Mattachich. Back in camp, on his way to answering Funke's summons, he had felt the humiliated anxiety of a schoolboy—and after a few minutes had emerged triumphant. Now, summoned by an incomparably higher authority, and with little expectation that he would receive good news when he stood before it, he felt perfectly calm, even self-satisfied. Whatever the *Kabinettkanzlei* wanted of him, whatever judgment it was about to pass on him, the fact was that it had been compelled to recognize his existence, to send for him by name, to demand his presence. In the Hofburg, no less! And why not? He was now the lover of a king's daughter, a man who would soon (to his own satisfaction anyway) be the bearer of a title; someone who could look any Hohenlohe in the eye, any Kottwitz or Möllendorf.

A nobody from Croatia no longer. Never again a nobody.

❖

So he enjoys the ride to the Hofburg. He is not going to allow his companion's silent hauteur, or the fact that the man is taller, younger, and of higher rank than himself, spoil his pleasure in the summons. The same applies to their march across the palace grounds, or a part of them, after they get out of the vehicle. He looks eagerly about him as they go, but later it was what he heard, rather than saw, that he remembered most clearly. The crunch of gravel underfoot; the clatter of heels on the flag-stones of a courtyard shut off on one side by an ancient wall; the multiple echoes produced by a tunnel-like arch piercing that wall; the sound of a military band in the distance, now loud, now occluded; the slither and click of their boots over cobbles polished to a silver shine by centuries of use; and finally, their march down a long wide passage floored in black-and-white tiles that produced a harsh ringing note of their own at every step.

Still not a word said between the two of them. Halfway down the passageway a white-gloved flunky emerges from a cubicle, as if he has nothing to do all day but wait for them there. He ushers them into a high-ceilinged yet surprisingly populous and cosy-looking office. A log fire burns in an open grate. Cupboards rise to the ceiling, some with their doors open and boxes within. At various large desks, young men much like Mattachich's escort are seated. At an even larger desk sits an older, heavier man with thinning, neatly combed hair. The top button of his tunic is undone, and his shoulders are adorned with a generous supply of crowns and oak leaves.

He is plainly the master of this particular corner of the palace, so it must be by his wish that he works in this domestic companionable manner. He has a genial air—spectacles, silver eyebrows, kindly frown lines on his brow. His voice is unnervingly calm and soft and his words seem to emerge from his mouth with no visible effort; not even a drawing-in or expulsion of breath. All he has to do, it seems, is to open and close his lips and the words become audible, as if of themselves. Unnerving too is the speed and lack of emotion with which he deals with the matter at hand. It is literally in his hand: a single sheet of paper with its blank side toward Mattachich. No greeting, no hesitation, barely a glance at the man standing in front of him.

"It is the wish of the highest authorities that you leave Vienna immediately. I do not propose to specify the grounds for this decision. No doubt you are aware of them."

Everyone in the room seems to attend as intently to the silence that follows as they had to the three brief sentences produced a moment before. Somehow, from somewhere, with an effort that contrasts painfully with the nonchalance of the man in front of him, Mattachich manages to bring out a few words of his own.

"Excellency, I beg you. I have—I need—there are matters—"

"How long do you want?"

"Two weeks, sir?"

(Why two weeks? Don't ask Mattachich. It is merely what comes out of his mouth.)

The adjutant general does not nod or say yes. He says merely, "Don't fail me."

❖

Later the same day, another formal interview took place in a room in a different part of the Hofburg. There, seated at a table, the aged Franz Josef, emperor of Austria and king of Hungary, awaited the arrival of Stephanie and her sister.

Contrary to what Louise was to write about him long after his death, he did not look at all like a headwaiter. Nor did he pull at his whiskers. Nor, as she claimed, did he look like a heartless fool.* Imagine him instead to look like the person he was: an old, tired, hardworking man, bound to protocol and ritual, expecting to be regarded with a respect that approaches veneration, but on the whole well-meaning, who had come to the throne at the age of twenty, and in the almost fifty years that had since passed (with another seventeen years still to go) had suffered many disappointments and griefs. Among these were the suicide of his only son Rudolf, which meant that no son or grandson of his would succeed him as ruler of the Habsburg lands; defeats in war for which he blamed not only his enemies and his underlings but himself too; his unrequited, incurable infatuation with his wife, the beautiful half-mad Elizabeth of Bohemia (which not even his long-standing arrangement with the actress Katti Schratt had greatly affected); his foreboding, which amounted to a

---

* "Take from him his title and position, his rituals and decorations, his fawning courtiers and formal speeches, the ritual of state occasions and receptions, and what will you find? A fool without a heart. A mechanical man in a uniform" (Louise, *Autour,* p. 107).

conviction, that the seven hundred years of Habsburg rule over central Europe, received by him in sacred trust from his ancestors and from the mysterious God he prayed to, would probably come to an end with his own demise.

So there he sat, with yet another duty to perform that he would gladly have spared himself, had his conscience permitted it. The room was unfamiliar to him, but as there were literally several thousand rooms in the sprawling Hofburg it did not surprise him that he could not recall ever having been in this particular one before. Nor did it surprise him, at the same time, that nothing in it struck him as novel or unexpected— chandeliers and sconces, china-crammed cabinets, delicate rococo moldings (wreaths, swags, leaves, and quantities of gilt), a ticking clock in a boulle-work frame, wallpapers in silver and dark red, a large portrait of two children in the court dress of a century or two before, whose names he knew no more than he did those of the dogs at their feet but whose blood without doubt ran in his own veins. In the complex, pale, intensely polished grain of the walnut table he was sitting at he could discern a vague reflection of his face and his plain military tunic, with just two small decorations on its breast, one of them like a brace of dark red cherries. As if to check something he would have restrained himself from inspecting if others had been in the room, he pushed his chair back a little and looked beneath the tabletop at the legs that sustained it. Yes, they were as he had seen them on coming into the room: tubby, fluted affairs, almost like garden urns. Then, as any other idle old man might have done, he felt the thickness of the tabletop with both hands, trying to guess if it really needed such massive supports. No, he decided, it did not. So he studied his hands instead. To his eye their palms had a more friendly and youthful look than their buckled and liver-spotted backs, where veins ran in seemingly haphazard directions, like blue rivers on a map.

The room for this occasion had been chosen by Stephanie. She called it her salon and seldom used it. Together with his *chef de protocol,* Franz Josef had decided it would be inappropriate for him to meet Stephanie and her errant sister in his own living quarters (since that would imply that Louise was of her own right a member of the imperial family—which she was to be pointedly reminded she was not), or in one of the rooms he used for the transaction of state business (since that would imply that the business he had to transact with Louise was of a constitutional nature— which, once again, it was not). These misgivings were duly passed on by his man to Stephanie, who, as expected, promptly begged the emperor to be gracious enough to use a room in her apartment for the occasion. The *chef de protocol* then inspected the location she had proposed, found it suitable, agreed with her both on a time for the meeting and on the desirability of the emperor being in possession of the room before she and her sister entered it.

Much of Franz Josef's life was taken up with considering matters of this sort. They mattered greatly to him. He gave them the same degree of attention he devoted to state papers received from his ministers and governors and to dispatches from his ambassadors abroad. Now, his thick mustache and luxuriant white muttonchop whiskers beautifully shampooed and brushed into backward-curving rolls, his shaven chin and cheekbones by contrast nakedly exposed, the skin of his scalp without luster but remarkably blotch-free for a man of his age, he awaited the arrival of two women he had never liked or trusted and toward whom he had always behaved with a courtesy that was second nature to him.

❖

The clock in the room chimed discreetly, prompting clocks in other rooms and in a courtyard outside to respond successively in lightweight, welterweight, and heavyweight fashion. Instantly the doors opened and a silver-buttoned black-stockinged footman appeared in the vacancy he had just created. He bowed to the emperor, stood aside, and waited for the sisters to come through, Stephanie first. A moment later the footman had disappeared behind the doors he was closing. Standing side by side, shoulders touching, the women curtseyed as deeply as their stiff dresses and half bustles permitted. Only then did they step forward. They remained standing in front of the sovereign just as Mattachich a few hours before had stood before the sovereign's representative in an office at the other end of the palace.

The business to be conducted in both cases was much the same. But the emperor took longer over it.

He cleared his throat, fixed his eyes on Louise, and began. "It has been brought to our attention, madame. . . ." His voice was high, an old man's voice, but it was assured too; his eyes were small and blinking yet he kept them fixed on hers; his face was expressionless. He pulled toward him a leather folder that had been lying on the table and opened it. Once it was there, however, he did not refer to it. The charges followed. She had been seen entering a *chambre séparée* with a man who was not her husband. On several occasions she was observed getting into a closed fiacre with the same man. She was seen repeatedly riding alone with him in the Vienna woods. In each case it was apparent that she and her companion had done their best to elude observation, which they had frequently succeeded in doing. What Franz Josef also knew, but about which he said nothing, was that Stephanie had told him how Mattachich had shown up in Abbazia and the manner in which the couple had compromised themselves there.

The recital done, and with no change in the tone of his voice, he invited Louise to respond to what he had just said.

"I was so outraged," Louise wrote years later, "that I simply had to express to his face what I felt about him."*

Self-righteousness was one of her gifts. So was her capacity for feeling badly done by. So out it all came. Amazement at being spied on. Anger at the guilt of others. Denial of wrongdoing. Scorn for all slanderers and plotters. Insistence on her *Stallmeister*'s probity. Affirmations of loyalty to the house of Habsburg. Warnings of her father's wrath when he heard of

---

* Louise, *Autour,* p. 112. See also Mattachich, *Memoiren,* p. 22.

the accusations made against his daughter. Dark hints about how his anger would be expressed. Tears at the thought of her mother's shame. More tears as she pleaded for the emperor's protection against conspirators. More tears, hotter than before, accompanying the confession that her husband could no longer be relied on to protect her reputation against the tongues of liars and scandalmongers. Her need, therefore, for the emperor to shelter her from the unmerited hostility to which she had been exposed.

All of it, Louise writes, without giving any details, "may be imagined." Franz Josef listened patiently to her outburst, his eyes blinking from time to time under his thick white eyebrows. Eventually he had had enough. He held up a hand. Louise fell silent. He waited to make sure that she had herself under control. Then he spoke.

"We know everything. It must be plain to you that we have been closely informed about what has been going on." He sought his next word carefully. "Errors . . . have been committed." He paused, as if considering whether to go through the accusations against her once more. He decided against it.

"We know everything," he said again, with the air—and the stare—of a man who knew that she had shot her bolt and would not dare to interrupt what he was about to say. "We advise you to leave Vienna, to go abroad for the next few months, and to stay away until this scandal has died down. Then we will review your position. It is not possible for you to attend any of the state functions arranged for this season. The invitations to the palace you have already received are now withdrawn. You will not try to communicate with us until we have indicated to your husband that you may do so."

Before she could make any response, and using the first person singular for the first time, as if he were speaking in the bosom of the family, he said once more, "I know everything."

Those were the last words she was ever to hear from him. He reached for a silver handbell standing on the table and rang it briskly. Like the

wings of a pigeon opening, the high-shouldered doors parted, the footman appeared, bowed, and vanished. The king pulled himself upright,
grasping with both hands at the table he had tested earlier. The women
curtseyed, Louise less deeply than before: a gesture, or absence of it, that
he noticed. As they rose he looked for and caught Stephanie's eye. She had
not said a word throughout, and for that she was given a tiny nod of
approbation. Louise he ignored. He and she were never to see one another
again. Each was left with a wholehearted detestation for the other.

❖

So what now?

Imagine the lovers aware of themselves as figures in a real-life drama
of their own invention, speaking for effect (not least to each other),
reordering their view of the past, manipulating their hopes for the future,
changing the roles they play as their circumstances change. Now go on to
do something that may prove to be more difficult. Imagine that to them
there is nothing "period" or outlandish about the world they live in: the
look of its cities, the clothes they wear, the expectations they have about
how other people are likely to behave, the carriages they ride in, the candles and gas lamps that light their rooms and streets. They are uncon-
scious of the contrivances they lack: antibiotics, combine harvesters,
heart-lung machines, laser-guided missiles, radio, television, supermar-
kets. Nor do they miss the innumerable noises that those who come after
them will regard as commonplace: cars changing gear, airplanes over-
head, pneumatic drills, the nutlike rattle of computer keyboards, zippers
opening and closing with their distinctive little *mew*. Since they know
nothing of these things, their absence does not make the lovers feel
underprivileged. On the contrary, they are proud of what they do have
and what their parents and grandparents lacked: a European-wide net-
work of railways and electric telegraphy, electric streetcars in some of
their cities, automobiles (of a kind), airplanes (also of a kind), the earliest

cinematographic pictures, machine-manufactured goods of all varieties. Machine guns too.

❖

What Louise and Mattachich felt was relief, first of all. Excitement. Almost a feeling of omnipotence. Here they were, about to be expelled from the city that had dominated the life of the one and the dreams of the other since adulthood. So what further harm could come to them? Disgrace was no longer to be feared; nor expulsion They were free to do as they wished, answerable only to themselves, subject to none of the social constraints that had bound them for so long. Their world had just done the worst it could to them? Very well. Did it matter? If Louise now chose to leave the Coburg palace on her own for the first time since she had entered the house as a bride in her teens, who could stop her? She had left the palace on foot before—to go for a stroll or to accompany the children (when they were still children) to the park. But this was different. No lady-in-waiting, no footman to carry whatever she thought she might need, no groom and pony trap to accompany her should she become tired, no nannies, no husband to return to, thank God: just Louise, herself, on her own, doing something she had long thought of and had always been afraid to attempt.

Then let her leave behind her the gaping servants and the ugly overblown building with its balustrades and its sky-high statues in a row, looking down on her in a manner more stupidly aghast than ever. It was like being a naughty child again but without the fear. What did she have to lose? Nothing. What did she have to gain? Entry to her lover's apartment, which she had paid for but not seen since he had moved in.

There they fell on each other as if he had just returned from a battlefield and she from exile or imprisonment. No one could bully or threaten them now and no one could stop them from doing with each other whatever they liked, here, in the confinement of Mattachich's apartment, with its rented brass and iron bedstead which in all its years of service had never been compelled to perform so loudly, to creak and jingle so vulgarly, as it did that late afternoon for the princess and her self-styled count.

It was shameless, degraded, and wonderful. All of it. And it went on for a long time. Repeatedly. Excruciatingly. Then they lay together and watched the meager whitish sunlight of an early February evening invade a corner of the room, high up, where two walls met the coarse molding of the ceiling and two squares of light also met, one on each wall like the pages of an open book, before both rapidly disappeared, leaving no stain behind. Now only shadows remained, some darker than others, undoing the objects they enveloped. Sounds from outside—wheels and people's feet, cries, bells, talk, laughter—grew louder before suddenly sinking, each sound again becoming distinct from every other once the shops had closed and people went home to drink and eat and raindrops began to *tick-tick-tick* irregularly against the single window of the bedroom, as if something out there had not dared to make itself known before and was still timid about doing so now.

Night. Disheveled, suddenly estranged, they looked at each other by the light of the gas lamp Mattachich had lit. "I must get back," Louise said abruptly and did not move. She could not. Elsewhere in the house someone ran up the stairs, opened a door, spoke, was answered, came downstairs slowly, sneezed. Silence again. She had spent time before in rooms as humble as this, when forced to take shelter while traveling or in some of the rougher hunting lodges she had visited. But this room was different. It was in the middle of Vienna, not in some unknown rain-sodden tract of countryside. It was only a few blocks from the palace that had been her home for twenty years. It had a naked man in it. It smelled of what they had just indulged in. It was like a whore's room, she thought, though she had never seen a whore's room and this one was not at all like the gravure illustrations of such rooms she had studied in her husband's collection of pornographic books. Most of those were Japanese anyway, which he had brought back from his travels, so how could she tell?

"Yoshivara . . ." she said to herself. The strange syllables took possession of her tongue and she found herself muttering them over and over again, turning her head this way and that on the skimpy pillow.*
Alarmed by this seeming gibberish, Mattachich propped himself on one elbow and tried to cup her temples in his hands and hold her head still. He wanted her to look at him but she resisted, laughing at first, until her laughter developed a life of its own, as the word had done. He poured some water into a glass and stood over the bed, trying to get her to drink it. When she had calmed down enough to explain to him what the syllables meant and how the name had come to mind, he smiled, though he did not enjoy having his bedroom compared to a whore's (which he knew it did not resemble at all; it was bare, bleak, masculine).

He got back in bed and they continued to lie side by side. As if in a vision that was also a sensation, both at once, she saw and felt herself as a part of the house, nothing more, as immobile as the stones of which it was built. Every stone was rammed against others on all sides; the house itself was rammed between the houses adjacent to it; the basement somewhere below was rammed into the earth. But the earth at last was rammed against nothing; it was a hanging object, turning in space, or so she had been told, and herself somewhere within it. Where was she and what was she doing there? What would become of her? She couldn't live in a place like this with a man like this one, who owned nothing except what she herself had given him. What would he do if she had no more to give? And she? Would her father take her in? Would she ever see her children again?

"I must get back," she said, in the same tone as before, but this time she did manage to get up from the bed. She dressed, and they rode back to the palace in a cab. The faint rain had stopped, leaving no puddles, yet everything still glistened, as if with a black dew. Mattachich accompanied her to the entrance and left her there. She asked one of the footmen where her husband was and went straight to the room the man indicated.

---

* "In the Saxe-Coburg palace in Budapest I saw some very 'curious' pieces: souvenirs of Yoshivara that no young woman could see without shame, even after having lost her innocence at the hands of their owner and her teacher. What a school!" (Louise, *Autour*, p. 58).

Philipp was smoking a cigar in what he called his study. Gablenz was there, also smoking.

She stood at the door. Her clothing was disheveled, her face blotched, the plumped-out skin under her eyes stained with iodine-like hues: brown, violet, yellow. She gestured at Gablenz to leave and Philipp gestured to him to stay. Gablenz stayed.

"I'm leaving Vienna," she said.

"You have no choice. You've been told to go."

"I want Dora to come with me."

"I'm not discussing arrangements with you. Or anything else. Bachrach will call on you tomorrow. You can speak to him."

"I must speak to your Jew?"

"Yes, Bachrach."

Earlier in that long day, she and Franz Josef had exchanged the last words they were to address to each other. Though neither knew it, Louise and Philipp were also never to exchange words again. She stayed on in the palace, making arrangements for her own and her daughter's departure. Sometimes she heard Philipp's voice from a distance; sometimes he heard hers. But the messages that passed between them were carried by servants or by Dr. Adolf Bachrach, Doctor of Jurisprudence, *Geheimer Justizrat, Regierungsrat, Hof- und Gerichts-Advokat.**

Of Bachrach, more later. For the moment he can be left doing what he has always done best: going about his duty as his master's indispensable middleman and counselor, a man who knows where his loyalties lie but who tries at all times to be as fair to others as circumstances permit. Or at least to appear as if that is what he is doing.

❖

Mattachich did not wait out the fourteen days of grace he had asked for when told of his banishment from Vienna. There was no point, he felt,

---

* Privy Councillor, State Attorney, Supreme Court and High Court Advocate.

in doing so. After Louise had visited him in his apartment, the messages he sent her produced only brief, distant replies, as if she could not forgive him for something he had said or done to her. His requests for a meeting she ignored. She did not attempt to visit him again. Remembering how strange her mood had been when he had last parted from her, he did not dare go to the palace to seek her out. In any case he had no wish to see Philipp accidentally or be turned out of the grounds because the servants had been told to keep him away. A fracas was the last thing he wanted.

So, after collecting from camp various things he had left there, and having made sure that officially the army still had him down as being on an extended leave of absence, he left Vienna for Lobor, Croatia. From the telegraph office in the nearest market town he sent Louise a telegram telling her where he was but giving no indication of what he intended to do next. This military tactic—as he thought of it—worked. The first telegram he received from her was reproachful. How could he have left Vienna without telling her? What had she done to deserve such treatment? He did not respond. Her next message was beseeching. Thereafter messages went back and forth between them fairly frequently, though each one he sent or received involved a morning's journey—by horse, pony trap, or bicycle—to and from the town. They were both cautious in the language they used in these messages, since they suspected the authorities were monitoring them. Coming or going, however, it pleased Mattachich to think how impressed the local telegraphist must be by what he was transmitting to Louise, and to imagine the man talking about it to others. How many people in that dead-and-alive place sent telegrams to a royal highness and received affectionate telegrams from her in return?

And if it was part of the telegraphist's duties to pass copies of these telegrams to the police in Agram, or direct them to some office in Vienna, why should he care? What could they learn about him that they didn't already know? What could they do to him that they hadn't already done?

❖

Mattachich had been a child when his stepfather, Oskar Keglevich, had been driven out of the family home, Schloss Lobor, by his own father. In old Keglevich's view it was bad enough that his son, Oskar, had taken up with a married woman, Anna Mattachich; to make it worse, she was the illegitimate daughter of a Roman Catholic priest and thus doubly, irredeemably, even sacrilegiously tainted in his eyes.* Oskar responded to his banishment from the Schloss by moving into the house in Tomasevich that his mistress shared with her husband and her son—and remaining there. Fifteen years later, old Keglevich died and the Schloss fell into Oskar's hands. He returned to it almost immediately, and Anna followed not long after.

Her husband, Mattachich's father, remained behind in Tomasevich, where he set about quietly drinking himself to death. Or so everyone thought. But he knew better. He went on drinking and did not die. Géza, the son, was in his last year as a high school student at the time of his mother's move and he chose her new abode over the old one. He never went back to see his father. The only thing about the house in Tomasevich he missed occasionally was the talismanic coin he had buried and exhumed so many times in the past. But it was not enough to draw him back. Nothing would draw him back. Eventually Anna's husband agreed to divorce her (after being paid to do so) and Oskar Keglevich was at last free to marry her and thus make an honest *gräfin* of her.

It was in this way that she became the official chatelaine of the Schloss Lobor.† Its stuccoed front and sides, painted in a faded lemon color, looked over plowed fields and roughly mown meadows; beyond were

---

* See Holler, *Ihr Kampf,* p. 18.

† "Here we have one of the grandest country houses . . . built and rebuilt from the seventeenth to the end of the eighteenth century. It was built by the Kegleviches and became their main seat. Oskar Keglevich (1839–1910) was the last member of his family in Croatia. In 1905 he sold the house to the merchant Moric Setlenger. Until 1935 it was not used and then it was bought by Janko Pejas. During the Second World War the house unfortunately acquired a negative image, as it was used as an assembly point for Jews who were later transported to concentration camps. Today it is used by the Institute of Social Health supported by the State" (http//:www.lobor. netfirms; passage translated from the Croatian by Dr. Ivan Danicîc).

steep hills strewn irregularly with firs and birches. Not far off, in the nearest cleft in the hills, lay the ancient settlement of Lobor, complete with a church steeple, an inn, two or three stores, a mill, a bridge, a doctor, and other such amenities. Looking out of the upper windows of the Schloss one could see some of its buildings thrust forward from the cleft, like the pale projecting paw of an animal.

Mattachich had only occasionally visited the place since he had left school. On his first evening back he told Keglevich and his mother that Princess Louise and her daughter, Dora, were about to go traveling in France and Germany and that he had accepted the princess's invitation to accompany them as her *Kammerherr,* or chamberlain. His friend, a fellow Croatian and fellow uhlan by the name of Artur Ozegovich, would be taking over his job as the princess's *Stallmeister.* No, he did not know how long he would be away or how far his employer's travels would take her. He had come to Lobor simply to see his mother and Oskar before he set out on these travels. Also to find out if there he was anything he could do to speed up this adoption business—for which he would always be more grateful to the count than he could express.

He was calm, measured, detached, minimally truthful. He had always protected himself from them both, and from his father, in this manner.

Over the following days nothing changed. Louise's messages told him she was "arguing about money"; she wasn't going to let herself be "hurried" by Philipp's lawyer, who was trying to "swindle" her out of what she was entitled to; she would let Mattachich know immediately once things were "sorted out." Sure once again of her dependence on him, he telegraphed back that he was content to wait until she sent for him. He knew few people in the neighborhood, but it was easy enough to get on with the tenants of the estate and the people he drank with in the inn, who treated him with a gratifying deference. The count's name may not have cut much ice in Vienna, but it meant a great deal here. He went into Agram twice and stayed overnight on both occasions; there too the name Keglevich was recognized. The city was livelier and more populous than he had remembered it; since his last visit it had acquired some ambitious new public buildings and gardens. He found it pleasant to be a Croatian in the Croatian capital once again, and constantly to hear around him the language he had learned first and would always know better than any other.

The short days were cold but sunny, with occasional sudden cloudings-over and brief falls of snow. In Lobor the snow clung to the fir trees' thick swatches of needles but left the birches bare. They stood like inverted besoms, their handles stuck in the ground and their heads raised toward the hard blue sky. At night he went to his bedroom and stared at the sweet-smelling log fire that was always burning there, or stood at the window looking into the darkness. Stars came out in handfuls, in fiery swarms. The hills cut oblique shapes out of the display; and so did passing clouds, discernible only by the disappearance of the stars. Then they emerged again, shining more brightly than before. The house creaked in the cold; footfalls resounded along its wooden-floored corridors; muffled voices came from the servants' quarters at the back. After the upheavals he had been through, the silence inside the house and the vacancy outside it came as a relief. Nobody here knew what had been happening to him, and he liked them better for it. He liked himself better for it too. He marveled at how much there was in the world at large that was not himself, and wondered why from childhood onward he had always felt this so-much-elseness as a threat instead of finding in it a strange reassurance, even happiness. If trees, mountains, stars, night, winter, an owl vehemently hooting in the darkness outside—if they had not existed, then he would not have existed either. He too took up space and had weight as they did; he was made of the same materials as they were. The difference was that he knew how transient he was and they did not. But what would they be without his awareness of them? How diminished they would be, even if they did not know it! Why had he repeatedly buried and dug up that coin in the ground in Tomasevich if not to humiliate himself, to exacerbate his feelings of exclusion and powerlessness? Why should he want to do something like that?

During one of these half-vacant, half-intense spells of idleness, the prospect of staying on in Lobor suddenly presented itself to him—as a temptation. In the same moment (or so it seemed) he knew why the idea had entered his head. He could *afford* to be tempted now. Look what he had done over the last months. He had pursued and conquered a princess— a princess!—and that was precisely the reason he was now free to turn away from her if he wished. When the test had come he had not flinched. He was in no danger of falling prey to the shame that might otherwise have gnawed away at his life: the shame of having been too craven and too humble to reach for what the world considered to be forever beyond him. That fear was done with, behind him. How many of the subalterns in the regiment, some of them born to grander families and raised more advantageously than himself, would have recognized the challenge that had suddenly risen before him in the Prater—would have been capable of recognizing it as a challenge—and dared to seize hold of it? How many of them would have dared to find themselves in the position he was now in, sitting by the fireplace, staring out of the window, drafting his next message to Louise?

What a question!

❖

The next morning he got up with the intention of telling his mother the truth about his life during the last several months in Vienna. And in Abbazia too. It seemed logical, somehow. Over a solitary breakfast he learned from one of the servants that the count had left for Agram that morning and that the countess was in the "office." He finished his meal rapidly and went to see her, fearing a change in his own mind if he did not do it immediately.

The "office" was the room from which Anna Mattachich managed not only the household but the entire estate. (Lordly, underemployed Oskar had little taste for such matters.) The room was one of the oldest in the house, a survivor from an earlier building: a sunken affair with leaded windows running high up along its external wall and five great naked beams across the ceiling. From the middle beam hung a circular cast-iron candelabra with a chain and pulley, anchored to a bolt in the floor, to lower and raise it. As big and heavy as a cartwheel, it had many thick upright candles fixed onto it. They were not alight now but on the lumpy, yellowed ceiling above there was a ring of discrete stains that showed exactly where the smoke from each candle holder had risen over the last hundred years and more. The only advantage this room had for his mother's purposes, as far Mattachich could see, was the open door to one side that enabled her to listen to everything going on in and near the kitchen.

She was alone, seated at the large scarred table, with various papers lying on it. He kissed her hand and her averted cheek. He asked if she could spare some time for him. She pushed her papers aside and put on top of them a paperweight in the shape of a bronze hand with an erect pointing finger. As always, he felt uncomfortable under her gaze. She had curiously flat blue eyes with little or no curve to their white and iris; they looked out at close quarters to what was in front of her, while allowing no access for others to look into her mind. Her black satin dress was buttoned severely to the neck and down to the wrists; her thick graying hair was compressed as closely to her skull as brisk brushing and fierce pinning could make it; even the bun sitting high up at the back of her head was as tight as a fist. Yet for all that was stiff, stuffed, almost bolsterlike about her appearance, her neatly proportioned features were clear, her brow was calm, and her pale cool skin always had a seemingly new-washed freshness.

He began, or tried to begin, by confessing that he had something to say that he'd been holding back from her and Oskar. It was about—

She let him go no farther. "Yes," she said. "We know all about you and your princess."

"You know!"

"Of course. Where do you think we're living? In Africa?"

"Why didn't you say anything to me?"

"Why didn't you say anything to us?"

That silenced him. Then: "I didn't want to worry you."

Her pale lips widened but remained secretively closed, as if her amusement—if it was amusement—came from something remembered, not from what he had just said. "That was very considerate of you."

Again they sat in silence. She glanced toward the papers she had put aside. The moment seemed to be slipping from him. So he began again. He tried to describe Louise as he saw her and as he wished his mother to see her: her boldness and insecurity, her unhappiness with her husband, her loneliness and naïveté, the extraordinarily formal, ceremonious, hemmed-in life she had led and how little, he thought, it had affected her and how little she had got out of it. As for himself, he went on, struggling still, how exciting it was for him to be with her. How amazing. Unbelievable. A lieutenant in the Uhlans! How she made him feel that everything he did with her was important.

But it was hard too, he confessed. He felt . . . empty sometimes. As if she was too much for him, and he not enough for her.

His mother listened without questioning or prompting him, her gaze resting evenly on him, one hand at the collar of her dress, the other flat on the table, palm down.

After a silence he said abruptly, "I've been thinking since I've been here. Maybe I shouldn't go back. To her, I mean. It would be a struggle for me and for her too if I broke away, but . . . I'm here and you're here and Oskar, and I see how you live, and I think, I can live like that. It's not so bad. It's nothing to be ashamed of."

He hadn't known the last phrase to be lurking in his mind, lying in wait for his unguarded tongue. Instantly he wanted it unspoken. But it was out now. His mother responded with a swallowing movement in her pale throat, nothing else. Her eyes remained fixed on his. He waited. When she spoke at last, it was as quietly as before.

"That's what you've always felt about me, isn't it? Don't say anything: I know. Now listen to me. I have never, never been ashamed of myself. Not for a moment. Even when I was wretched, and I've been wretched often, it wasn't because I was ashamed of who I am or what I've done in my life. It made me suffer to know that you were ashamed of me, but that didn't mean I had to share what you felt. Never. You have your life; I have mine. If this great lady gives you what you want, some of what you want, take it. Don't throw your chance away. Make the most of it. Do what you can. There's nothing here for you. Believe me," she said. "I know." She pointed scornfully at the chair on which her husband usually sat when he was in the room with her. "So does he."

The desolation of childhood welled up in Mattachich; it occupied its old place inside him, as if nothing else had ever been there. He thought angrily, she still looks down on me. Also, she was right; there was nothing for him there.

Before he left the room—they had sat silently together for some time, as much at peace with each other as they ever would be—she said to him, "You must speak to Oskar. You must tell him what you've said to me."

"But he knows it all, surely, if you—?"

"Of course. But he must hear it from you. He said you'd never leave us without boasting about what you've been up to in Vienna."

❖

That night he found himself tumbling over and over again into dreams that flowed remorselessly into and out of one another and yet remained the same, always telling the same incoherent story. He was alone in various unfamiliar sets of buildings (an army camp it could be, or a railway station, or a school, or a government office, or all of them at once), thronged with people who were strangers to him, though occasionally someone he did not know emerged from the crowd to stare intimately at him from just a few inches away, as if he or she knew him well, and to say words addressed to him that he could not hear in the hubbub. Always he had some duty to carry out (meet someone, find something, pass on a message) but could never recall why he had been chosen for the task and what was to come after it—nor, often enough, what the mission itself had been. All he was left with was a sense of its importance and urgency and a conviction of his ignominious failure to carry it out.

Then he woke and knew just where he was, with dawn showing itself slate-blue against the window and a faint wormlike glow among the cinders in the fireplace.

Another morning. Surely he had been waiting here for too long. He sent a telegram by messenger to Louise, saying he had had enough of Croatia and couldn't bear to be away from her any longer. The next day he cycled to the telegraph office, hoping to find a reply from her. But there was no message. Instead, outside the office he bumped into his stepfather, who had just got off the coach from Agram and was waiting to be picked up by someone from the Schloss. So they left a message for the man and went into a small, brown, sticky private room in an inn nearby, with high-backed settles and scarred tables and an ineffable reek of vanished meals, spilt drinks, pipes and cigars smoked to extinction.

Once they were seated, Oskar told Mattachich that while in Agram he had been to his lawyer's office and signed the last of the adoption papers.

"So you are now my son," he announced solemnly.

The two shook hands. For a moment neither knew what to say. Keglevich withdrew his hand and said, "We must drink to it." A bottle of grape spirit was brought to their table. Two small glasses of the transparent liquid were filled and clinked together. First, a toast to Keglevich. They drank it off at a gulp. Then a toast to the *gräfin,* put away in the same manner. Finally a toast to Mattachich-Keglevich, as the younger man, he told his newfound father, had been styling himself for some time past.

Another silence followed. At heart each had always regarded the other's existence as unnecessary, an embarrassment, even an affront; something they would have preferred to do without if the choice had only been offered to them. They were tied to each other through the woman between them: nothing else. Taking a deep breath, Mattachich launched himself into his "confession" and Keglevich listened greedily, asking questions from time to time about Louise and his relations with her that his wife had been too proud to ask. All in a tone of indifferent, blasé know-ingness about such matters, of course. Tall, slender, gray-bearded, high-colored, halfheartedly a dandy, always ready to talk about the two years of his late adolescence he had spent in Paris, Keglevich looked younger than he was. His movements were lithe; his suits hung loosely on his frame; around his neck he invariably wore a bright silk cravat in a single color (yellow today); across his flat stomach there hung a gold chain in a hammock-shaped curve, from which several seals and a small watch were suspended. His voice was loud and his laugh a series of discrete, humor-less, coughlike sounds that expressed not mirth but the intention to express mirth. Occasionally his lips could be seen working and the muscles around his right eye flickering before the words he wanted came out, not because he was deliberating deeply but because some blocked thing within him was showing itself stronger than his will.

"You still haven't told me what made you come here . . . and tell us a pack of lies . . . about what you've been doing. As if we wouldn't know, and wouldn't feel insulted at being treated like fools. . . . *Stallmeister?* *Bettmeister!*—that's the job for an ambitious young man with a rich old lady friend."

Mattachich stood up, a little unsteadily. The three drinks he had put down so rapidly had had an effect on him. "I will not permit you to speak about her highness the Princess Louise in that way."

"Excellent! Excellent!" Keglevich exclaimed. He laughed, producing from the roof of his mouth three hollow sounds of no meaning. "That's right, defend your lady's honor. Always. I expect nothing else from a son of mine."

Mattachich was still on his feet. "I'm not going back to your house after this. You can send my things here, to the inn."

"Excellent. Excellent!" Keglevich repeated, in the same manner as before.

After this exchange of angry words and scornful looks, they went on drinking together for another couple of hours. It was easier for Mattachich to talk to this man, whom he disliked, than to his mother, whom he feared. Also, they got on better in her absence than they ever did in her presence.

However, he was true to his word in one respect. He did not return to the Schloss. The driver from Lobor took Keglevich and the bicycle there and reappeared the following day at the inn with the luggage Mattachich had left behind. He remained where he was while waiting for instructions from Louise.

❖

Three days later he left Agram for Paris. In Vienna he changed trains but did not leave the station. The bustle, the throngs of people, the noise that rose to the station's high glassed-over roof, reminded him of the dreams he had had in Lobor. But he was not bewildered by what was around him. He knew why he was there and where he was going.

He was to stay in Lobor just once again, about eighteen months later, accompanied by Louise. During the decades that followed he occasionally thought of those wintry weeks he had spent in the Schloss as a lost opportunity; a chance he had passed up of leading another life altogether. In these moods he blamed his mother for not pleading with him to stay. Who could say what might have happened if she had? At other times the whole episode seemed to him absurd: a piece of playacting that he had briefly persuaded himself to take seriously. Dreams! Freedom! A quiet, provincial life! For him? What nonsense it was.

CHAPTER FOUR

IN THEIR MEMOIRS, LOUISE AND MATTACHICH have little to say about the weeks and months that followed their reunion in Paris.* In their bid to retain their readers' sympathy they avoid direct statement, except when blaming others for virtually everything that went wrong. In neither book do they ever admit that they were lovers in any ordinary, physical, adulterous sense; they write of each other only in lofty spiritual terms and dwell on how self-sacrificial their relationship was on both sides. Thus Mattachich on Louise:

> *Magnanimity and strength of purpose are the fundamental traits of this poor woman, who through all the infamy that has been heaped on her has retained an extraordinarily childlike soul. . . . With a truly majestic form, a classical profile, every feature delineated in noble fashion {she was} a figure from a fairy tale translated into reality. . . . Nobody knew who she belonged to, nobody cared what she wanted, no lawyer could tell her what her position was, everywhere she felt her husband's hunger for revenge. . . . I could tell such things—were it not that I shrink from describing the campaign that was waged against this unfortunate woman.*†

---

* More than fifteen years passed between the publication of Mattachich's book (1904) and Louise's (1921). Hers appeared not long before his death.

† Mattachich, *Memoiren,* pp. 8, 24.

And Louise on Mattachich:

> *People see only what they want to see. It is beyond their miserable comprehension to understand superior beings with lofty souls and aspirations, and they describe as infamy what is in reality sacrifice. . . . His enemies have credited him with their own base motives. They did not want to see, and they denied that he was, by his greatness of soul, far above all miserable calculations of self-interest. In vain he threw into the abyss all that he had, all that he was likely to possess. What sublime abnegation, stifled by hate beneath its hideous inventions.*[*]

Mixed with displays of mutual admiration and high-mindedness of this kind are countless references to conspiracy, persecution, treachery, corruption, and so forth. Of details—events, places, facts—there is a striking absence, at least in dealing with this period of their lives. At no point do they come close to confessing how erratically they behaved after they were reunited; still less do they acknowledge that what followed their reunion was in fact a species of *folie à deux*—a state of mind during which they incited each other to behave more bizarrely than either, alone, would ever have done. Ironically, the closest they get to confessing their irrationality is in their vehement insistence that Louise was never mad, as various specially empaneled doctors later declared her to be.

Nor do they offer any explanation of their fifteen-month zigzag journeyings across half of Europe. From Paris, which was as unwelcomingly cold and wet as only Paris in some moods knows how to be, they went to Cannes; it was during the stay there that Mattachich was for the first time described in official documents as Louise's chamberlain (*Kammerherr*). From Cannes they traveled to Carlsbad, where Louise was given a civic reception and Sergei Rachmaninoff, the composer and piano virtuoso, played at a soirée in her rented villa. From Carlsbad, with minor diversions on the side, they went to Merano in the southern Tyrol; from Merano

* Louise, *Autour,* pp. 186, 218.

back to the French Riviera (to Nice this time, where they were joined by Louise's daughter, Dora); from Nice briefly back to Paris; from Paris to London (in the hope of getting financial help from the widowed Queen Victoria, Louise's distant cousin and great-aunt by marriage); from London back to Paris; from Paris (their options now running out fast) to Breznica, in Croatia, which was the home town of their follower Ozegovitch, still occupying Mattachich's former post of *Stallmeister*. And after Breznica, with their situation getting more desperate by the day, on to Lobor, where Mattachich hoped they might find some kind of sanctuary.

Nothing doing there. By then, scandalous stories about them and their activities had appeared in newspapers in several countries, so Oskar Keglevitch greeted his adopted son and the fugitive princess by clearing off as soon as he heard they were headed in his direction. Behind him he left his wife, who had recently entered into a liaison with the manager of the Lobor estate, Claudius Fiedler by name: a post to which he had been appointed by the countess soon after her son's last visit.*

❖

You may be tempted to imagine these crisscross journeys as an unreal, absurdly speeded-up jig of the kind that movie and television directors in search of comic effects are so fond of. But it would be more accurate to think of them in the form of a cumbersome camel train forever making its way across the desert. The princess set out on the first stage of her wanderings accompanied by roughly one hundred trunks of clothes, her own horses (with a coach and a lighter carriage to match), her dogs, a lady companion, a *Stallmeister* (Ozegovich), a *Reisemarschall* (travel manager, unnamed in the records), a *Kellermeister* (wine steward, ditto), and clusters of chambermaids, dressers, chefs, kitchen hands, footmen, grooms, baggage handlers, and the like. To transport this number of people and animals, and that weight of baggage and equipment (the servants' baggage

---

* This compressed itinerary of their travels is drawn from Holler, *Ihr Kampf,* pp. 60–107.

included), Louise hired a special train, an *Extrazug,* for each of her major journeys. Naturally, since Mattachich had brought nothing with him, she bore the whole cost of their journeys and the longer or shorter periods between them: rent, wages, food, alcohol, accommodation, stabling, the livery that members of her entourage were obliged to wear.

How did she manage it? The answer is, she didn't. She couldn't. Before leaving Vienna she had negotiated an agreement with Dr. Bachrach, *Geheimer Justizrat, Regierungsrat,* et cetera, that she would receive from Philipp an annual stipend of 36,000 gulden. In addition it was agreed that her father would continue sending her his regular yearly allowance of 30,000 francs. Translating these sums into their present-day equivalents is an impossibility, given what has happened to currencies since then, not to speak of changes in "patterns of consumption." But by any standards other than those Louise set for herself and her lover, she was generously provided for. They could have eaten, drunk, and idled their time away in resorts and watering places all over Europe, if they had so chosen, like the crowds of other *rentier* types who abounded in such places.*

However, it was never for the sake of a spa water–sipping, tennis-playing, casino-visiting subrespectability of an aristocratic high-spending kind that Louise had bolted. She was a royal princess, the oldest daughter of a man believed (rightly) to be among the richest of all Europe's monarchs, and she had married into a princely family from which she herself was descended. Now that her circumstances had changed, she was determined to cut a figure in the world, to demonstrate how she should be viewed and in what regard she held herself. Finding herself an outcast from Vienna and Brussels, she was also determined to get her revenge on the lot of them—on her black-hearted father for the misery he had inflicted on her during her childhood and for his failure to denounce her

---

* For the figures and some of these details, see Holler, *Ihr Kampf,* pp. 54, 58. Initially the party that set out from Vienna also included Louise's daughter, Dora, who was accompanied by a governess and a few servants of her own. Dora later decamped from Nice with her fiancé, Ernst Günther of Schleswig-Holstein, who foresaw disaster and hurried her away from Nice to the relative safety of his home and dukedom. (On Dora's departure, see Louise, *Autour,* pp. 147–150; also Holler, pp. 89–90.)

husband's treatment of her; on the husband whom she had hated from their wedding night and every night thereafter (or so she now claimed); finally on Franz Josef and the entire Habsburg court.

So much for her enemies. As for her lover, she wanted in equally determined fashion to bind him as closely to herself as she possibly could.

How was it to be done? Instinct and appetite guided her to the demented banality of the answer she found. Shopping! That was how. Shopping! That was how she chose to punish her ancient enemies and dazzle everyone she encountered in her new life. Who could stop her? Certainly not the transported Mattachich (transported in every sense), who was astonished to discover the style in which she had set herself up in Paris—and who within a few weeks had adopted it as his own. From then on, neither could blame the other for what was happening to them; nor could an outsider have said which of the two worked more recklessly toward their common undoing.

❖

Living and traveling as they did would have crushed them anyway, sooner or later. But they were in a hurry. Wherever their caravan halted they went on spending sprees that dwarfed even their day-to-day outlays. For him, new suits, fine wines and brandies, cigars, diamond tiepins, guns, days at the races, and nights at the gaming table. For her, and on a far more extravagant scale, jewelry, dresses, furs, lace, lingerie, cosmetics, perfumes, porcelain—whatever happened to catch her eye. For them both, the schoolboy thrill of unconstrained grabbing, grabbing, grabbing. And the irresistible extra thrill of being admired and fawned on for doing so. To their rented villas and hotel suites, Europe's most expensive jewelers and fashion houses hastened to send their representatives: chunky frock-coated top-hatted men with beards on their chins, pince-nez on their noses, and leather valises chained to their wrists; more elegantly dressed men and women accompanied by porters carrying wicker baskets filled with the latest notions from this or that establishment; creatures more artistic still (of both sexes again) in smocks and floppy bows at their necks with portfolios of designs that could be "made up" overnight, or by next week or whenever her royal highness wished. Not far behind came those who offered "personal" services of various kinds, mostly to her: doctors (licensed and otherwise), hairdressers, manicurists, pedicurists, masseurs and masseuses, eye exercisers, bowel-movement regulators, wrinkle removers, unwanted-hair pluckers, blood-circulation rejuvenators, fortune-tellers.

They lifted silks and brocades to her waist and bosom, bracelets to her wrists, rings to her fingers and earlobes, necklaces to her throat, boots and shoes to her feet; they crawled around her (literally); they patted, stroked, squeezed, pulled, snipped, combed, pinned, stood back to gaze, and came respectfully forward to touch her again and to tilt their heads in earnest contemplation of what they had achieved; they stared at her meaningfully across boxes opened for her eyes only (or so they said) where, trapped in crustaceanlike settings of gold and silver or left temptingly naked on tiny velvet and satin shelves, yellow-green Brazilian and white South African diamonds sparkled shamelessly, gleaming pearls lay back in graded rows, flecked lunar opals and ice-deep sapphires winked their eyes discreetly at her, as if they alone understood her innermost nature. The salesmen and women marveled at how beautiful and clever she was and what wonderful taste she had; they simpered and whispered sums of money into her ear like people disclosing intimate secrets; they departed when she showed the faintest sign of fatigue and sent messengers the next morning to inquire when they might call again or to inform her of newly arrived wares which they were now "in a position" to offer her before any other client had a glimpse of them.

And all this under the gaze of her young lover. He gorged himself on the spectacle. Only when he had appointments of his own, or when the intimate "treatments" she submitted to made his presence inappropriate, did he absent himself. For the rest he was always there, ready to play the connoisseur, to offer his opinions on styles, qualities, and colors: Yes, yes, it suits you, charming, wonderful, perfect, it's just right, this one, that one, why not both? When they went (by her choice) to the merchants' own establishments, instead of having them come to her, much the same performance took place. These outings had the advantage of their knowing that they would be stared at enviously by complete strangers, whether out in the streets or inside the shopkeepers' densely carpeted and gilded showrooms—a pleasure that was not as new to her as it was to Mattachich, for she had enjoyed it from time to time as the wife of Philipp of Saxe-Coburg (whom she referred to only as Fatso when speaking to Mattachich). But never had she enjoyed expeditions like these as she did now. Never before had she been free to indulge herself so intensely and incessantly, with such an encouraging companion by her side and with no need to refer to any inclinations other than her own—not her husband's or those of her husband's benighted family, or Stephanie's, or the dictates of the imperial court. When she thought of what she had put up with for so many years, what she had believed herself to be enjoying—ceremonial occasions of all kinds, ambassadorial receptions, balls, parades, memorial services, formal levees, and the rest of it—it seemed to her that she had been sleepwalking throughout. Never before had only her own and her lover's predilections counted, and he had as little interest in restraining her as she had in restraining him.

Never before. Never before. The words tolled in her ears; she said them to herself and to Mattachich and to the imaginary interlocutors she still had the habit of addressing when she was alone. Look what they had done to her, she told him when he was available and to the walls of her room when he was not, look at the life the people around her had forced her to lead from infancy onward: telling her this, telling her that, forbidding her this, forcing her to do that, feeding her with lies, enforcing their wishes over her own, shunting her from childhood into marriage to a man she barely knew, giving her no time and no opportunity to look about her, to do things for herself, to learn what sorts of people lived in the world and where she might find her place among them. Her childhood overborne by her elongated, ungainly, beak-nosed father; his presence then replaced by the roly-poly figure of Fatso, ungainly in a style even more contemptible than her father's yet no less hateful; waking in a foreign city to find herself bound to him and his family and, at a remove, to the vast imperial court and its countless hangers-on—what sort of life had she lived? That she had despised Fatso from the beginning, had occasionally betrayed him and more frequently quarreled with him and spoken ill of him to others, made no effective difference to her servitude to him. How could it? Whatever she did—infidelity, tantrums, blackening his name— she remained his wife; being his wife was the only role available to her. Fatso would always be the center and fulcrum of her life.

Never again! Never again! It was as if a bell were swinging back and forth in her head, not funereally, far from it, always in celebration. Going back it called out, *Never before! Never before!* and, going forward, *Never again! Never again!* At the age of forty, or very nearly so, she had found her freedom at last. She could do what she liked. She had no master. Mattachich was not her master; he was her lover and abettor and dependent, whom she feared for one reason only—that he might leave her. She dreaded that some police or military machination had already been set to work in Brussels or Vienna to take him from her; she was tormented too by the fear that some whim—or, more likely, some woman—would lure him away. This fear was accompanied by a bizarre mathematical fantasy she could not put out of her mind. It was that the difference in age between them was actually growing greater, somehow extending itself with every week or month that passed, as if time moved at a different speed for each of them, so the effects of it would become more and more evident to him. Clothed or unclothed, his physique and movements had that distinctive trimness that many long-serving soldiers acquire, and which they retain until it is finally wrecked by old age. He also kept himself in shape by regular exercise on horseback and with fencing masters hired by the hour. For her everything was different. When she scrutinized herself in the bath or in a mirror, she saw all too much to worry about: droopings, swellings, dimplings, stretch marks, cavities, slackness, usedness. She stuck her extended forefingers angrily into her flesh over and over again and watched and felt what happened to it under their attack. Look at it! Look at it!

All the more reason, then, to make the most of him. To let him enjoy whatever he wanted of her. For them both to glut themselves on whatever they could ransack from the world at large. Forty! How much longer did she have to enjoy her freedom? How soon would she be old and ugly in the eyes of her lover? How soon would she be dead?

"Don't talk like that," Mattachich scolded her, when she was unable to keep her anxieties and shame to herself. "To me you're more beautiful than ever. When I go out with you I see people turning their heads to look at you." And, "Remember, *I'm* the one who followed you about in Vienna, *I'm* the one who stood on street corners for you; it was the madness of the love in *my* head that made everything possible between us." To assure her how desirable she was, he even invented passions of jealousy he had never felt. "That Frenchman, I hate him, the one with the teeth like this"—miming the man's protruding teeth by pulling up his upper lip and wrinkling his nose above it—"the one on the Promenade des Anglais this morning who wouldn't leave you alone." And there were others he claimed to have seen doing the same: that cheeky headwaiter here; that German there; that countryman of hers, that stinking Belgian in San Remo; that politician from Munich who slavered all over her hand? ("Thank God you were wearing gloves or you'd be dead of rabies by now.") He also said, "When you die, I'll die." And on another occasion, and in a different tone of voice, "No, I'll die before you. I've always known I'm not going to have a long life. That's why I followed you all over Vienna. Time is precious; we mustn't waste it."

"I know, I know," she answered, catching his hand and bringing it to her bosom. So they kissed, in public, on a hotel terrace overlooking the Mediterranean, indifferent to all those who might be gazing at them from the hundred windows of the building above.

Well, not quite indifferent. When they drew apart he glanced up hopefully in that direction.

❖

The debts they were accumulating were by and large a source not of anxiety for them, but glee. At first, anyhow. Why should they worry? In addition to paying out her monthly allowance, Philipp had already silently met bills that soon totaled some 600,000 gulden and that had been charged by Louise directly to his name.* Most of the merchants who flocked around them were ready to extend them virtually unlimited credit; all they feared was that rivals might snatch these invaluable customers away. However, for those who insisted on heavy down payments in cash for their purchases, as well as for meeting the exorbitant, unstoppable, day-to-day expenses of sustaining her household, Louise also had recourse—at Mattachich's suggestion—to various Viennese moneylenders whom he had got to know in his days as a dashing subaltern. These black-jacketed, black-hatted, gray-bearded men, with names like Reicher and Spitzer, who spoke German with a strong Galician-Yiddish accent, were obviously prepared to advance sums to the Princess Louise that were incomparably larger than any they had handed over to the cash-strapped pre-Louise Mattachich.

True, a stink of sexual scandal hung over the lovers' heads; but so what? It was barely conceivable to any of Louise's creditors that King Leopold of Belgium and the House of Coburg would refuse to clear up the litter of bills she was scattering behind her. The Coburg holdings in Germany, Austria, and Hungary were immense; Leopold (a Coburg by birth) was both King of the Belgians and "King-Sovereign" (a title invented himself) of the "Congo Free State" (another self-invented designation)—a tract of Africa bigger than the whole of central and western Europe put together. Over this territory he ruled not as representative of the Belgian state, in the manner of other imperial monarchs, but in his own name, as

---

* This is twenty times the size of the annual sum he had "officially" agreed to pay her (see Holler, *Ihr Kampf,* p. 89).

titleholder to it all. It was his personal fiefdom, literally his private possession. Its ivory had already given him one colossal fortune; its rubber was now giving him a second. Even in a period of gold madness, diamond madness, railway madness, America madness, Leopold stood alone.

Which raises an unavoidable issue. Imagine that when the lovers began their spending spree (in mid-1897) they were as ignorant as most people in Europe then were of the methods used by Leopold's agents to extract from the Congo every tusk of ivory and every bucket of wild rubber they could lay their hands on. Imagine also that Louise and Mattachich knew nothing of the tortures, mutilations, hostage-takings, and wholesale murders that kept the indigenes of the "Free State" at work and that far surpassed in both scale and atrocity the crimes committed by any of the other marauding colonial powers in Africa. Once you have made this kindly assumption about the couple, however, you are entitled, even obliged, to ask a hypothetical question. Would they have cared if they had known?

To this the answer is plain. The evidence they offer speaks—silently—for itself. In his *Memoiren*, Mattachich has many nasty things to say about Louise's family in general and about her father in particular. By 1904, when his book came out, the story of what had been done to the peoples of the Congo was no longer a secret; it was becoming the subject of outraged official reports and newspaper headlines all over Europe and the United States. Mattachich makes no mention, however, of the scandal that had broken over Leopold's head. All he complains about is the man's stinginess toward his oldest daughter.

The same is true of Louise herself. Or worse. In her autobiography (published twelve years after Leopold's death) she works off many grudges against her father, while at the same time presenting herself to the reader as a loving, virtuous, dutiful daughter. In fact, she makes a parade of her loyalty to his memory precisely because she wants to emphasize how badly he behaved to his daughters both as children and as adults. But when she comes to speak of his acquisition of African territories and what his minions did inside them, her language about him changes; she has only praise for his "genius" in developing "the gigantic enterprise" of the Congo Free State and "the value of his work [there] which History knows." Naturally, she goes on to point to the contrast between the "Great Man and Great King" (her capitals) and his "private failings" that "harmed himself and his family alone." This in 1921! She then devotes several pages to condemning the Belgian government for not doing the honorable thing by overturning the king's will—from which Leopold had explicitly excluded her—and handing over to her a fair proportion of his plunder.*

All this appears alongside some wonderfully high-toned justifications of her readiness to squander her father's and her husband's money without bothering to get their permission beforehand. Thus: "Confident, not without reason, that my sisters and I would inherit great riches, I believed that we should put into circulation the means at our disposal, thus making our wealth of use to others." And again: "It is true that at certain times I have spent money too freely. I have said it already and will say it again: *This was my way of taking revenge on the meddling, stifling, small-minded avarice that surrounded me.*" And this: "*I have pitied above all my persecutors' bewilderment at my contempt for the money god they venerate!*"†

❖

Now an interlude. An absurd one, if you like. Also a matter of life and death.

Not that anyone died as a result of it. For this relatively benign outcome, Mattachich immediately claimed the credit. The busybodies who had engineered the affair accepted his claim at face value—and then condemned him for making it. It is difficult to say which aspect of his claim they purported to find the more shocking: that he had deliberately held

---

* "If Belgium is to be regarded as a sovereign being, susceptible to the claims of honor and reason, attentive to the judgment of history and mankind as a whole, sole master of the Congo and its millions, would it be entitled to renege on its duties to the daughters of the one who had bestowed these gifts on her? Surely not!" (Louise, *Autour,* p. 270).

† Louise, *Autour,* pp. 13, 214, emphasis added.

himself back from killing or seriously injuring another man or that he had boasted afterward about his restraint in having done so. In their view, both these "irregularities" reflected badly on him. That they themselves might emerge meanly or absurdly from the episode never entered their self-important protocol-ridden heads.

One morning, Mattachich writes, he was "not a little surprised" to be accosted in the foyer of a hotel in Nice by two high-ranking officers of the imperial army. One, *Feldzeugmeister* Baron Géza Fejérváry, was the commanding officer, artillery, in the War Office in Vienna; the other carried a name and rank almost as improbable: *Feldmarschalleutnant* Hugo Count Wurmbrand-Stuppach. Stiff-visaged, dolefully kitted out in dark civilian suits, white cutaway collars, striped neckties, and tiny badges of merit in their lapels, their expression and dress were so much alike that Mattachich half-consciously expected them to take turns in delivering their message, like a performing duo of some kind. But only Fejérváry, who was evidently the higher in rank (though the lower in stature), did the talking. Staring directly into Mattachich's eyes with a distaste he made no attempt to hide, and without putting his hand forward in greeting, he introduced himself and his companion. They had come to Nice, he announced, on behalf of his highness Prince Philipp of Saxe-Coburg, to "demand satisfaction" from Mattachich "with weapon in hand." This challenge was being made for reasons the prince was not prepared to enter into, but which would be known to his opponent.

He paused. Mattachich made no comment. So, with a slight knitting of his brows, Fejérváry continued. He and Count Wurmbrand-Stuppach would therefore expect to receive Mattachich's two seconds at such and such a place in Vienna, at such and such an hour, where the terms and conditions of the duel would be settled between them. It was the prince's wish that the encounter itself should take place in Vienna as soon as possible after that meeting. Preferably the next day.

Yet another summons from on high! Over the last few months Mattachich had got out of the way of being instructed to do this or that, to present himself here or there. Telling others what to do had become his style. But he had no choice in the matter. He nodded and brought his heels together. The two men merely responded with a nod and turned their backs on him.

❖

So an additional journey must be included in the account just given of the travels undertaken by Mattachich and Louise. This one was a solo affair however: namely, the dash he made from Nice to Vienna, in order to exchange pistol shots and saber blows (if the pistol shots did not finish the business off) with the quivering Philipp.

No contest. That was Mattachich's first thought, once the two men had departed and he sat himself down in an armchair in the foyer of the hotel. He was almost twenty-five years younger than his opponent. He had been a serving soldier until a few months before. He was not fat. He exercised regularly. All he had to fear was a freak accident of some sort— which he had been in the army long enough to know was always a possibility when men and weapons were brought together. But in this particular case, he thought, he would never be tempted to take a bet against himself—a sardonic silent calculation of the odds that gave him pleasure. He also spent some minutes preening himself on the sangfroid he had displayed during the meeting with Philipp's emissaries and on the admiration Louise would lavish on him when he returned triumphant from Vienna once it was all over. As for what Philipp must be feeling and how the differences between them would be preying on *his* mind—well, that was a source of satisfaction too.

Yet the longer he sat there the more uneasy he began to feel. First, he had had no idea that anything of the sort was afoot in Vienna, and for some absurd reason this seemed to him unfair; he should have been told about it beforehand, though he could not think of anyone who might have done so. Second, and more important, he realized that he was in no position to inflict any further hurt on Philipp. He could not deny that he felt a certain compunction toward the man. Yet that was not the issue.

There were other, more hard-edged reasons for him to do as little damage to Fatso as possible. The gulf in social and political standing between them was one such reason. Who could tell what retribution he and Louise might be made to suffer if he were to kill or seriously maim a senior member of the Saxe-Coburg family? (Especially after having stolen his wife!) Much more significant still was the state of Louise's finances, about which he knew far more than she did. Notwithstanding the "allowances" she received from Philipp and her father, and the innumerable invoices she had continued to pass on to Philipp for settlement, she was atrociously in debt. Worse still: back in Vienna there were promissory notes lodged with the moneylenders that, for reasons he alone was aware of, carried endorsements best left unquestioned for as long possible. But if Philipp were to be killed or seriously injured, what then? Where would they go? What would their enemies do? It did not bear thinking about.

No, he had no choice in the matter. Either he should go back on his word and refuse to meet Philipp's challenge—which was a moral impossibility—or he had to do his best to avoid seriously injuring him. If that meant exposing himself to greater dangers than he would have done otherwise, so be it.

At this point he got up abruptly from the armchair and went straight to the Villa Paradiso, the grandest of the villas they had so far hired. But it was not Louise he was looking for. Instead, he skirted the house and there, in the stable yard behind it, he found Ozegovich: cap on the back of his head, hands in the pockets of his gabardine breeches, lips pursed, plump freckled cheeks pushed out as if he were forever whistling—which he wasn't. Anyone seeing him there would have thought him to be an honest, simple fellow—which again he was not.* Several years older than Mattachich, his career in the army had come to a dead stop after a series of financial and sexual scandals; he would never be anything more than a middle-aged second lieutenant, one rank junior to Mattachich. In effect, he was now Mattachich's employee rather than friend and fellow soldier;

---

* On Ozegovich's past see Holler, *Ihr Kampf,* p. 107.

but in the absence of the casual quasi-institutional relationships of bar-racks life that had sustained them both for so long, they were closer than ever before. Mattachich was grateful for Ozegovich's matter-of-fact incuri-ous acceptance of his improbable relationship with a royal princess; also, for his unashamed readiness to get whatever benefits he could from the arrangement. So he took pleasure in the sight of Ozegovich's snub nose, cinnamon-colored freckles, unlined brow, comfortable belly and bottom, neat, pigeon-toed feet, and elbows poking out sideways above his pockets.

"Coffee?" Mattachich suggested, in a tone quite unlike an employer's, and Ozegovich did not hesitate. He went off to wash his hands and came back buttoning his tunic.

They walked down toward the main road but, before reaching it, turned into the first estaminet—Les Trois Singes—they came across. It was not much of a place, looking across at a view of pale rocks and sallow growth in the steeply sloping gardens of the villas opposite. They sat more or less in the doorway, their backs to the interior of the bar, with its speckled mirror and bottles in pharmaceutical colors and the three brass monkeys, who saw, heard, and spoke no evil, on a shelf above the counter. It was sunny but cold outside, and they were glad to be protected from the wind. And for the tot of brandy each had ordered with his coffee.

On hearing what his boss had come to tell him, Ozegovich naturally assumed that he would be asked to stand as one of his seconds and was disappointed to be told that this wasn't the case. Mattachich did his best to assuage his injured feelings; there was no one else, he explained, whom he could rely on to remain with the princess should something go wrong in Vienna. ("Not that it will.") What he asked of Ozegovich instead was his advice on other possible candidates for the job—from the Thirteenth regiment, obviously. It did not take long for them to settle on their first two choices (Lieutenants von Saba and von Veith) and a couple of reserves.

"Anything else?" Ozegovich asked acutely, in the silence that fol-lowed, and Mattachich had to admit that actually, yes, there was. He'd decided, he said, to do his best to avoid injuring Philipp severely, what-ever the consequence might be. He wanted Ozegovich to know that. His motive, he claimed, was solely his reluctance to hurt somebody whom the whole world believed him to have wronged. ("Though my blood boils when I think of how he treated her highness. Just boils!") Of the difference in status between himself and Philipp he said nothing. Of money, nothing again.

Ozegovich, who had not yet got over his disappointment at being excluded from the big event, stared skeptically at him and finally, having come to a conclusion, gave both a small nod and a cynical shrug. "Listen," he said, "if he comes out all right and *you* get smashed up, I'll tell everyone what you've just said to me. You won't be shamed after your death. That's a promise. You can write it down on a piece of paper if you like. I'll keep it for you and tear it up when you get back."

"You bastard!" Mattachich exclaimed gratefully. Then he said, "As long as we understand each other." Then: "Now, for the most important point of all. I'm not going to say a word about this business to the princess until it's over. Not a word. And I want a promise that you'll do the same."

❖

Von Saba and von Veith instantly telegraphed back to Mattachich their agreement to act as his seconds. Prince Philipp of Saxe-Coburg? A minister in the War Office? A *Feldmarschalleutnant*? This was not an opportunity that two undistinguished subalterns could afford to pass up. Three days later they sent Mattachich a further telegram, giving him the date and time arranged between themselves and Philipp's seconds. They added that "everyone" knew that Philipp had issued his challenge only after being goaded to do so by various people in the Hofburg, the "highest authority" among them. That last phrase being a coded term for the emperor himself.

By then Mattachich had told Louise that he had to go to Vienna early the following week; he would stay there just the one night and return the following day. His story was that he had agreed to appear as a witness before a court of honor for a friend in the regiment who was accused by some other officers of having stolen money from them. No, he was not personally involved, but he had sworn to keep the whole thing secret until it had been dealt with. No, he could say no more than that about it, not even to her. No, Ozegovich knew nothing about it. No, there was nothing for her to be anxious about; there was no chance the authorities would hear of his presence in the city and seize the opportunity to make trouble for him.

He spoke quietly, putting no particular weight on any of his words. Louise believed him and doubted him at the same time, a state of mind that was not new to her. Sometimes she even had difficulty believing that she was involved with "this fellow," while dreading that he might leave her.

"When are you going?"

"Thursday."

"Thursday! Thursday! How can you say that? You'll never be back in time!"

"For what?" he asked innocently.

"Think! Think!" she cried out, in her iterative fashion. He did as he was told but failed to come up with the answer she wanted, so she then had to suffer the additional injury of being obliged to tell him. Friday was her birthday; he knew it; he must have heard her say it; she'd made special arrangements for them; didn't he remember? How could he do such a thing? Was this all she meant to him?

He apologized but remained firm. He couldn't change the arrangement. It was too late. Too many other people were involved. He'd made a promise and he had to keep it. He would leave Vienna the moment his business was finished, on the earliest train he could get, and they would celebrate the day after.

She had her back to him and a handkerchief to her eyes, and he could see from the stubborn set of her wide shoulders that his words were making no impression on her. She was wearing a frivolous, frothy white blouse, much too young for her, which made her unhappiness seem more painful to him. At last his stumbling tongue found a way to reach her. "My darling, I'll bring you a *surprise* when I come back. No one has ever given you a birthday present like the one I'm going to bring you from Vienna. It's something that can't be bought with money, and I could never give it to anybody else in the world. You wait—when I tell you what it is you'll hug me and kiss me and know forever how much I love you."

There, it worked. He saw it. She was surrendering to the childishness of the curiosity he had provoked. He had turned his absence into a kind of game. Kissing her, seeing her smile, it became easy for him to evade her questions. How could a man help feeling sorry for women, all women, when they were made as they were?

He was especially tender to her that night, and during the days and nights that passed before he packed his bags (one of them containing his dress uniform) and left for Vienna. There he put up at the Hotel Sacher. Only the most fashionable hotel in the city would do for him. It pleased him to think that he and Louise had been there together once before, though for a few hours only; also, that it was where the emperor and his Katti Schratt entertained each other. For all he knew, he and they might be under the same roof.

❖

Imagine yourself in Philipp's position. Everyone knows that your wife has left you; that she has no intention of returning and you have no intention of taking her back. Everyone knows too that you are believed to be no less responsible for the failure of your marriage than the man who has taken her from you; more so, if anything, since she has sacrificed her grand position in society for his sake. Yet here you are compelled to fight a duel, ostensibly to take revenge on him, if you can, and thus reclaim your honor. This is not a case of some big talker going among your friends and enemies with the claim—or suggestion, at least—that he has slept with your wife and of your being determined to punish him for doing so (*à la* the unfortunate Pushkin). Nor of a third-person busybody whispering the same thing about her relationship with another man. So what will belatedly fighting your supplanter do for you? De-cuckold you? Stop the sniggers? Restore the dignity you have lost? You might as well try to restore her virginity, or your faith in her fidelity to you.

All this was painfully clear to Philipp. So were the differences in age and in fitness for combat between himself and his opponent. But once Franz Josef had been provoked by the people around him (the Archdukes Friedrich and Franz Ferdinand particularly) to interest himself again in the matter, Philipp was done for. In a letter on the subject, the emperor (ever a stickler for protocol) had carefully noted that what Philipp did in his private capacity "as a prince" was his business; what he did, however, "as a general in the Austrian army" whose "honor had been stained (*befleckt*) by the behavior of his wife" was "a matter of public concern."[*]

The implicit threat in this letter was plain. If Philipp did not issue a challenge to Mattachich, he would not only have suffered the ignominy of his wife's having bolted with an unknown subaltern but the further ignominy of losing his rank in the imperial army. That the rank was purely nominal made no difference to the emperor—nor indeed, once the emperor's view had been conveyed to him, to Philipp. The only person who urged Philipp to defy the emperor was his mother. She had always detested Louise and was concerned, as any mother would be, for her son's well-being. But had he listened to her he would merely have heaped more ignominy on his balding head.

❖

So at 9 A.M. on Friday morning, February 18, 1898, there assembled at the Military Riding Instructors' School in Vienna (not, as one historian

* Quoted in Holler, *Ihr Kampf*, p. 69.

has suggested, at the more famous Spanish Riding School, where the horses are trained to walk about on their hind legs) a party consisting of the following persons: Prince Philipp, the challenger, and his two seconds, Fejérváry and Wurmbrand-Stuppach; Mattachich with his two seconds, von Saba and von Veith; two doctors, one for each of the duelists; and a long-legged, long-toothed master of ceremonies (*Kampfleiter*) who was the only person in the party plainly enjoying himself. Like the two overcoated and top-hatted doctors, he was in civilian dress, as were the gunsmith and two servants carrying leather-bound cases of weapons whom he had brought with him. The duelists and their seconds were dressed in the full regalia of their respective regiments, Philipp included. He looked depressed but more composed than Mattachich had expected. Mattachich himself had the air of an actor miming respect for the gravity of the occasion, yet as he stepped down from the cab that had brought him he could not prevent what was intended to be a shrug of his shoulders from turning into a small stagger.

You can visit the site of the duel today, if you wish. It is now the Renaissance Penta Hotel, Ungarstrasse, Vienna, one of the international chain of Penta Hotels, a four-star affair complete with a few hundred rooms and suites, a business center, health club, indoor swimming pool, gift shop, coffee shop, bar, and "beer pub." The usual sort of thing, in other words, if four stars are what you are after and can afford. Fronted in an ochreous-pink stucco, with elaborate arched window frames and cornices in white plaster, the central building is adorned at its corners by wedding-cake columns with crowns on their heads; these rise higher than the roofline and give the whole structure an oddly playful, theatrical appearance. The two circular riding halls, with their sanded floors and wooden chest-high perimeter barriers, have long since given way to the amenities just described. In none of the public or private spaces of the Penta Hotel will you hear trumpet calls, shouts of command, the thud of shod hooves, or the reverberating loose-lipped exhalations, head-shakings, and bit-and-bridle janglings that highbred horses use to relieve their feelings. No smell of dung will trouble your nostrils. Nor for that matter will you hear pistol shots or (outside the health center) the groans of men violently exerting themselves. Whatever clashing noises come to your ears will be made by hi-tech gymnasium equipment, not the blades of sabers.

On this particular morning the smaller of the two halls was deserted. Only the dueling-party, preceded by a grubby-looking sergeant with a bunch of keys in his fist, was permitted to enter it. It smelled faintly of horse and of swept, newly dampened sand. Light came through clerestory windows immediately beneath the vaulted ceiling. It was a raw morning, and the men's breath rose in the air and lingered above them. The participants had met outside, where the two principals had been introduced to all the members of the party—except each other. No greeting had passed between Philipp and Mattachich; just stares as expressionless as they could make them. The servants, who were as solemn and as soberly dressed as their superiors, were of course also excluded from the introductions. Since it was so cold, everyone kept on his gloves, hat, and overcoat, like mourners at a graveside.

The servants placed the boxes on a table to one side and withdrew to a discreet distance. The doctors put their bags on the same table. The *Kampfleiter* doffed his top hat, revealing a bald narrow head, on one side of which ran a scar several inches long. Like a damaged worm in shape and an all-but transparent mauve in color, it served presumably as a warranty of his fitness to preside over the occasion. And preside he did, with a mixture of gusto and unction, his words slathering about in his mouth as he read out the conditions of combat agreed by the seconds. To each condition he punctiliously attached the article from the Code of Honor that covered it. The antagonists were to stand facing each other at a distance of twenty-five paces, and each was to fire a single shot in turn. Philipp, as the Insulted Party (*Beleidigter*), was to have the privilege of the first shot. If the first exchange of shots failed to disable either man, the procedure would be repeated. If a second exchange also had no effect, the pistols were to be put aside and combat with sabers would commence. It would continue until one of the combatants suffered a wound that the doctors in attendance declared to have rendered him incapable of continuing.

Dueling—the grievances that led to it, the weapons employed in it, the punctilio elaborated around it, the serious or fatal outcomes to which it occasionally led—was this man's obsession; he couldn't get enough of it. It was also his part-time profession; like the doctors, he was being paid by the participants for his services and for the use of the weapons that lay in their boxes behind him. His audience shifted from foot to foot while his phrases came out, crashing and hissing at the same time, like waves on a beach, each remorselessly succeeding the one before. The longer he went on, the more brightly his eyes gleamed in the dismal, brownish air. Or perhaps that was just the effect of the light silently coming and going in the clerestory windows high above.

At last he desisted and motioned the gunsmith forward.

Everyone's gaze followed the man to the table. This was his moment, and he made the most of it. He unbuttoned his black overcoat all the way down, as if to show he had no weapons concealed within it, and only then opened one of the boxes. The pair of pistols in it—black metal barrels, ebony stocks and butts—lay mouth to mouth in silk-lined hollows, royal blue in color. As if from a life that someone else had lived, there flashed through Mattachich's mind a memory of a jeweler opening a display case in front of Louise; then the image was gone. The gunsmith primed the pans of each of the two pistols with coarse black gunpowder—which he weighed out exactly on a small spring scale that emerged from his overcoat—loaded each gun through the muzzle with a single round ball, and finally presented them in quasi-sacramental fashion to the *Kampfleiter*. In equally ceremonious manner the latter took them and displayed them to both sets of seconds. Then he hid them behind his back and passed them out of sight, from one hand to the other. When satisfied that no one would now be able to tell which gun was in what hand, he invited one of Philipp's seconds to choose a weapon by pointing to his left or right arm.*

❖

With trembling hands the Insulted One stripped to his shirt. Mattachich did the same. They faced each other at the set distance. Even in that light, the onlookers could see that the color had gone from their cheeks. Philipp raised his pistol. It had no front or back sight; he could take aim only by peering along the top of the barrel, which he had difficulty keeping level. Almost at once he pulled the trigger. The gun reared in his hand. Its report sounded less impressive than the echoes that went chasing each other around and around the circular hall. The acrid stench of gunpowder was suddenly everywhere. Mattachich stood where he was, untouched. Now it was his turn to raise his arm. Philipp took off his pince-nez. His face looked naked without them. Mattachich fired. His ball too went wide.

After the drawn-out preliminaries they had been through, the exchange of shots was over in an instant, almost an anticlimax. The two pistols were put away and a similar pair extracted from the second box. The same procedure—priming, loading, concealing—was gone through as before, though this time it was one of Mattachich's seconds who made the blind choice of weapon. The chill in the hall and the tension of the occasion had got to both men, who had nothing but their shirts to shield them above the waist. Philipp was plainly shivering; Mattachich's lips quivered and were still, in little spasms.

Philipp lifted the gun he was given and fired at once, barely looking

---

* In *Ihr Kampf*, Holler (pp. 69–85) goes to town in describing the procedures governing the duel. (This is not a complaint; far from it.) He also reprints various protocols and exchanges of letters both before and after the event, and considers at length how the articles of the Codes of Honor in Austria-Hungary differed from those prescribed in France (as outlined in *Conseil pour les Duels* by Prince Georg Bibesco and a certain Féry D'Eslands).

ahead, determined to get it over with. Another miss. He passed a vague hand over his face, realizing that in his haste he had forgotten to put on his pince-nez. Mattachich's grasp on his pistol was a little less steady than before, and his ball flew wide also. So that was done. The men waited, clasping and rubbing their upper arms, trying to keep warm. The guns were put away and the oblong box containing the sabers was opened. They lay side by side, shining brightly in their double bed of velvet. Like man and wife asleep, they lay, with their heads turned in the same direction.

With the cumbersome weapon in his hand, Philipp was so plainly at a disadvantage that even the *Kampfleiter* looked discomfited as he watched him gauging its weight and flexibility and making passes with it in the air. Mattachich, at a distance from him and with his back to everyone, was also warming up. After some minutes the men were brought together. They had not saluted each other before the exchange of pistol shots (as stipulated, according to the *Kampfleiter,* in article 145 dealing with cases of Aggravated Insult) and did not do so now. The tips of their weapons, each with its single sharpened edge facing down, were lowered to an inch or two above the ground. The one-word signal followed.

"Go!"

The heavy blades clashed, the men lunged and parried several times before Mattachich, backhanded, like a tennis player, struck his opponent across the chest with the flat of his blade. Philipp staggered back and went down, the breath knocked out of him. There he sat, on his bottom, on the sand. The two doctors came forward immediately, calling for a halt to the whole business. But the old *Kampfleiter* showed his teeth, literally, in an angry grimace. Blood had to be drawn. The doctors had to declare one of the contestants physically incapable of carrying on. The Code was clear on this point. Were they ready to make such a declaration? No? Well then! He gestured and waited until Philipp had gathered his breath and was dusted down by his seconds. Again he gave the word.

"Go!"

Mattachich closed at once on his opponent. Aiming directly at Philipp's right hand he slashed down at it, and in the same movement whipped his own blade away. There was a curved steel guard over the grip to protect the swordsman's hand and wrist, but the blow got home. Philipp gave a cry, his saber fell, his left hand made an instinctive grab just below the wrist of the other and held it above his head. Blood began to run between his clutching fingers and down his forearm. Both doctors were already with him. This time, no nonsense; the blow had been damaging enough. One of the sinews connecting his thumb to the side of his wrist had been severed. It was plainly impossible for him to continue the fight. The duel was over.

❖

Mattachich left the building almost immediately, on his own. His seconds, whom he had arranged to meet later for a celebratory lunch, remained behind with the other two to put their signatures to the document which the *Kampfleiter* was drawing up and which duly declared that the combat had taken place "in strict accordance with the rules of chivalry."

In the meantime the doctors tended Philipp's wound. The table on which the boxes of weapons had been placed was immediately cleared by the gunsmith and Philipp was laid upon it. The odor of gunpowder in the hall was now overwhelmed by other smells: that of brandy first, then iodine. Two or three tots of brandy were the only anesthetic administered to the wounded man. Everyone else, servants included, drank from small silver cups produced by Fejérváry. The severed sinew was stitched together; then the broken skin was stitched over the deeper stitches. It was a horribly painful business, but Philipp suffered it in silence, aside from an occasional irrepressible groan or gasp. When it was done and his wrist had been bandaged, he lay with his left hand over his eyes. He did not dare move until he was sure he would not fall to the floor when he stood up. He did not want that to happen again; not with everybody still looking on.

They all knew he had been pushed into the duel; they had all seen what an unconvincing marksman he had made and how little of a swordsman he was. So his stoicism before the duel, during it, and afterward made a strong impression on everyone. They talked about it among themselves and to others subsequently. Within a few days those people who had been most scornful of Philipp beforehand were loudest in their praise of him. There it was, he had done it; he had got through the ordeal itself without disgracing himself.

This was more than could be said about Mattachich. It took no time for rumors to begin circulating in Vienna that there had been something demeaning, something fishy, about the whole encounter. For this Mattachich bore much of the blame. He was the one who boasted during the celebratory luncheon with his seconds that he had deliberately shot wide both times and had contemptuously knocked Philipp over with the flat of his sword because he had wanted to save him from something worse. Such a claim or confession, which in the eyes of all right-thinking people had the effect of turning the whole event into an elaborate charade (not to speak of breaching the sacred Articles of the Code of Honor), was too appetizing for von Saba and von Veith to keep to themselves. The story soon reached the ears of the "highest authority," whereupon the Archdukes Friedrich and Franz Ferdinand, the prime instigators of the whole affair, were obliged by the emperor to consult all who had been involved in it (Mattachich aside, naturally). After various interviews and exchanges of letters, they reported to their ruler that there was nothing to be concerned about—everything had gone off with the strictest regard to the rules—and he was happy to take their word for it.

As for Mattachich's version, what else was to be expected from a man whose scoundrelism, always self-evident to everyone of rank in Vienna, was becoming more and more apparent with every day that passed? Lies and dishonor were his métier.*

---

* In his *Memoiren*, p. 27, Mattachich writes that "the ostentatious concern" for Philipp's welfare he had displayed throughout the encounter received "special acknowledgment" from the prince's seconds. In view of the pains taken by all involved to affirm in writing that everything had been conducted with scrupulous attention to the Code of Honor, this seems unlikely. It is more plausible to assume that Mattachich wrote as he did in order to inflict a further belated humiliation on Philipp.

❖

Mattachich stormed back triumphantly to Nice and the Villa Paradiso and delivered into Louise's wonderfully receptive ear his account of where he had been and what he had done during his mysterious visit to Vienna. This was the belated birthday present he had promised to bring her; and she listened like a glutton to every word of it and told him he was right, he was right; it was the best birthday present she had ever received. Later that evening, in bed, she repaid him for it as fully as possible. Later still she got him to tell her again about what she called "the funny parts"—shortsighted naked-faced Philipp peering down the barrel of a pistol, Philipp trying to wield a saber, Philipp sitting on his backside in the sand.

The next morning, as usual, a copy of *La Gazette du Midi* was brought into the princess's bedroom. Mattachich lay at her side, half asleep after a night that had been a restless one, full of dream—confusions from his journeys of the past few days and the tensions of the duel. Now he was on the train, halted at some little station; now two ragged men labored to push a barrow heaped with earth-clotted potatoes; now a tower in the distance turned into a toy as he looked at it; now his father, whom he had not been near for many years, came forward, head tilted reproachfully to one side, as in life. After such a night it was more restful than sleep to lie with his eyes closed yet conscious of light, the warmth of Louise's body mingling with his own, a smell of coffee, the rustle of the newspaper as she turned its pages.

Until her body heaved violently and a scream of "My God!" burst into his ears. Suddenly he was fully awake and wholly uncomprehending, both in the same instant. She was pushing a page of the paper at him. Her mouth was open, her hands trembling. "Look what he's done to us!" she shrieked. "Why didn't you kill him? You had a chance! You should have done it!"

It took him some moments to get hold of himself and find what she was pointing at. It was a small paid announcement among a host of other items:

> *His Royal Highness Prince Philipp of Saxe-Coburg and Gotha wishes to make it known to all interested parties that he accepts no responsibility whatever for any debts incurred by his wife, Her Royal Highness the Princess Louise of Saxe-Coburg and Gotha.*[*]

[*] Quoted in Holler, *Ihr Kampf*, p. 93.

II

CHAPTER FIVE

A WEEK LATER, LOUISE GAVE AN IMPROMPTU BALL in the Villa. Ostensibly held to celebrate Mattachich's safe return from Vienna, it was also intended to demonstrate her contempt for the notice Philipp had put in the newspapers. Her servants were sent scurrying around town with handwritten invitations addressed to people she had met during her stay in Nice or whom she knew to be visiting the resort. The glassed-in double doors between the terrace and the saloon to the side of the Villa were folded back, concertina fashion, to take advantage of the suddenly mild weather, and in this bald, brightly lit space, and among the theatrically shadowy trees and shrubs in the garden below, her guests gathered with glasses of champagne in their hands and expressions of foxlike curiosity on their faces.

Gleeful, prurient, eager to attack, ready to flee, they knew why they had found Louise's invitation impossible to resist. Scandal! Bankruptcy! Excitement! The servants who attended them were affected too: some were subdued, even weepy; some just perfunctory in performing their duties, preferring to stand about in groups discussing their fate. Two or three were obviously drunk, while those posted at the gates and along the stone wall that encircled the property allowed various undesirables to enter—journalists, shopkeepers, holiday-making idlers—and turned away much grander guests whom Louise had especially hoped to impress with her sangfroid. Inside the house the guests took liberties they would not have ordinarily allowed themselves—they asked the servants when her highness and the count planned to leave, fingered the curtains and cutlery, scuffed up the pile of the carpets to test their quality, wondered aloud whether the pictures on the walls had been rented with the house, crept upstairs to peer into the private rooms and to construe the sleeping arrangements there.

Their hostess and her lover they avoided, preferring to study them from a distance, while drinking as much as they could of their champagne and eating the haphazardly arranged comestibles. The dancing had barely started before the band—which had unsuccessfully demanded to be paid in advance—went on strike, forcing Mattachich and Ozegovich to take its leader into the darkest corner of the garden and give him a few slaps around the head to remind him of his obligations. A public row began when one of the shopkeepers (uninvited and drunk too) broke loose and demanded of Louise that she settle the bill she had run up with him. There and then too. A small plump red-faced man with a bald but deeply wrinkled scalp, as if the wrinkles that should have appeared on his forehead had migrated northward, he stuck his hand into an inside pocket of his coat, pulled out a businesslike piece of paper, and brandished it in her face. "When? When? When?" he shouted, and several of the uninvited guests who had been shamefacedly avoiding Louise, as if she were the creditor and they the debtors, also surged toward her, shouting things like "He's not the only one!" and "What about me?" and "You take us for fools?"

The man who led the charge was later said to be a butcher; others claimed he was a wine dealer, enraged at seeing his expensive and unpaid-for champagnes disappearing down the throats of beautifully dressed women who snubbed him when he tried to make conversation with them. In any case, whoever he was, he brought the princess's ball to an early end. A loyal servant moved to throw him out, two or three of his new allies fought back, women shrieked, men swore, glass was broken and collars torn, the bandsmen packed their instruments and fled, and most of the guests were left to make their getaway as best they could. This was not easy, for the servants supposedly on duty at the gate barely tried to control the vehicles waiting outside. The result was more shouting, shoving, the occasional blow, horses' hooves slithering on the roadway, wheels and shafts grinding together, the sullen buffeting of one coach against another. It was a wonder nobody went home that night with anything worse than bruises and grazes.

However, even those guests who most relished the whole fiasco (retrospectively) had to agree that Louise had been magnificent throughout. Got up in long gloves that came almost to her armpits, a trailing ivory-colored skirt patterned with leaves, a golden bodice carrying bunches of gauze at each shoulder like truncated wings, with double rows of tiny bell-shaped silver objects suspended from waist and bust, a many-stranded pearl choker and wristlet, and, in her left hand, an ostrich-feather fan—got up in this fashion, as if for a coronation ball at one of Europe's courts rather than for public humiliation in a hired house, she shed no tears, made no grimaces, did not raise her voice. At the end she inclined her head to those guests who took the trouble to say goodbye to her, stared expressionlessly at others who were being hustled out by Mattachich and Ozegovich, gave instructions to those servants who seemed ready to listen to them, and went upstairs only after the last of the visitors had left the house.

She was accompanied by a maid and the Baroness Fugger, her lady-in-waiting, but did not allow either woman to undress her. Instead, she sent them away as soon as she reached her bedroom. Alone at last, she took off her gloves and her satin shoes, which no one had seen all evening because of the length of her skirt, removed the belts of pearls from her neck and wrist and placed them flat on the dressing table, and stretched herself out on the bed, still in her heavy skirt and stiff bodice, stockings, and underclothes. Every time she moved the little silver ornaments on her outfit gave a soft tinkle. She heard some of the uproar from outside the house, where the disentangling of the coaches was still going on, but saw none of it.

Eventually, when everything was silent, when the last footsteps of those who lived in the Villa had died away and the last of the empty bottles and scraps of uneaten food had been thrown into wooden barrels behind the house, Mattachich came into the room. He found her lying flat on her back, with her hand over her eyes. He leaned over and took her other hand into his own.

She let him do so. Then, in a tone more somber than any he had heard from her before, she said something that sounded so strange, so implausible, he had to ask her to say it again.

Which she did.

"Je m'appelle Louise, et toutes les Louises sont malheureuses."*

He was to hear this sentence many times again in the agitated weeks that followed, and to hear it once more, years later, when they were reunited after their protracted enforced separation. Now, speaking solemnly, childishly, tearlessly, she told him that the meaning of her name had been explained to her during her childhood by one of the servants in the palace of Laeken, an evil woman with staring eyes who hated her and whom she feared, and whose Gypsy blood gave her the power to see into the future. It was a curse or spell this woman had cast on her, she told Mattachich: something she had never dared to repeat before, not even to her mother, for she feared that the woman would be sent away and in revenge would call down an even worse punishment on her. Nor had she spoken of it subsequently, though the evil female had left the palace of her own accord just a year or two later. The witch left knowing what she had done, however. She knew her victim would carry the curse in her heart forever.

The back of her hand still over her eyes, only her lips moving, with the palm of her hand and the underside of the rings she was wearing exposed, she ended the tale by ordering Mattachich to go. To leave her. At once. Tonight. Her name was Louise and misery was her fate. For her there was no escape. But he was free. He could separate his destiny from hers and go now, choosing to live elsewhere on his own terms, like any

---

* "My name is Louise, and all Louises are unhappy." Quoted in *The King Incorporated* by Neal Ascherson (London, 1963), p. 209.

other human being. She had thought that he of all people might save her from the curse; but not even he could help her. No matter how much she loved him.

"Go!" she said, suddenly turning over to grasp his hand in both of hers. She brought it to her cheek. "Go!" He saw her pale cheek, the white flash of her eye, her disordered hair, and sank on his knees beside the bed. "Princess," he said. "Never."

❖

That was the beginning of the collapse of the fantasy structure Louise and Mattachich had built around themselves. It took longer to disintegrate, however, than you might expect. Its momentum was not that of a frenzied *danse macabre;* rather, it resembled a lesson in old-fashioned ballroom dancing—slow-slow, fast-fast, slow-slow again. With occasional intervals when nothing happened. Then it would start up again, sometimes in several locations simultaneously. The people witnessing or taking part ranged from monarchs like Franz Josef and Queen Victoria to three former servants of the couple (an under butler, supported by two of Louise's dressers), who tried to sue her for unpaid wages and found themselves accused in turn of fraud and perjury. They claimed they had been taken on to work in the princess's household by her chamberlain, a certain Count Keglevich—but a lawyer hired by Mattachich pointed out in court that there was no such person in her entourage and indeed no such "Count" in existence anywhere!*

Over the following weeks many other servants found themselves jobless, out of pocket, and far from wherever they had originally been hired. Some made a nuisance of themselves by pleading, writing letters, weeping.

---

* *"Ein Graf Géza Keglevich existiert überhaupt nicht"* (statement by Mattachich's lawyer quoted by Holler, *Ihr Kampf,* p. 56). In other words, when it suited him to declare that the title he had given himself was fake, Mattachich had no compunction about doing so. When the case was over, he immediately took up the title again and continued to use it until the day of his death.

In lieu of wages others simply took whatever they could smuggle away from the household—shoes, dresses, fans, cutlery, bits of jewelry, the brass- or silver-buttoned livery issued to them, even tackle from the stable—and disappeared. Several local businessmen who had been supplying the household with necessities would have done the same if they could have. Inevitably it was the humblest providers who came off worst, for the staples they had delivered to the Villa (firewood, milk, fish, bread etc.) had long since been consumed, turned into dung and ash, while the wealthier merchants could send in local toughs to try and pick up movables (plate, furniture, even horses) that had not been paid for. Richer or poorer, all were angry and ashamed of themselves for having allowed the social and financial luster of these customers to dazzle them into extending credit too generously. So they felt all the more vindictive toward them as a result.

The task of dealing with such people—and with bigger creditors yet, from more distant places—was left to Mattachich. He was the one who had to wheedle, placate, promise, find new suppliers wherever he could, fork out money ("on account") when he could not. Louise was docile and depressed, except when she thought of Philipp; then she became incoherent. Searching for some possible source of funding that hadn't been tapped, Mattachich made her go through lists of more and more remote members of her mother's and her father's family, and even of Philipp's, before he finally gave up on the idea that hidden in some remote Schloss there was bound to be a forgotten great-uncle or second cousin who would come to their aid. Another recurring fantasy with which he struggled—in silence—was that of following the advice Louise had given him on the night of the party and simply clearing off. Leaving the house with his passport in his pocket and a briefcase in his hand, as if he were going to Nice or Monte Carlo on business, taking the train from there to Marseilles or Hamburg or Brest, and then boarding the first available steamer to America, north or south, who cared where?

He cared. That was the trouble.

He cared for Louise. He cared for himself as her consort. He cared for the life they had lived together. It was by far the most important series of events that had happened to him. He could not imagine anything so remarkable occurring again. The only remotely comparable transformation he could recall—and how transient and childish it now seemed— was the experience of ceasing to be a cadet and finally receiving his commission, and expecting everyone in the garrison town who saw him, on that day and for weeks afterward, to envy him for the star on his shoulder, his youth, his uniform, his shiny boots, the future that lay before him.

Now here he was, living through that young man's future, which had turned out to be richer and more dreamlike than he would then have dared to envisage. Only, in dreamlike fashion, it had suddenly revealed its evil underside; it was charged with a menace he himself had provoked. Long before his duel with Philipp, when he and Louise were still living in Carlsbad, doing as they pleased, confident of their immunity from the rules and obligations governing others, he had committed a criminal act—idly, vaguely, blithely, without consulting Louise beforehand or telling her about it later. He had thought of it then as not much more than a kind of joke, a scornful gesture, a quick fix (as you might say).

But how differently it looked now that Philipp had struck back at them!

❖

What he had done, this hidden deed, sprang directly from an invitation Louise had received to spend a long weekend with the parents of Dora's fiancé, Günther. The invitation, which reached her in Carlsbad, was the first of its kind since her expulsion from Vienna, and it encouraged her to hope that she had not, after all, been irrevocably cast out of the ranks of Europe's highest society. As it happened, the day after receiving the invitation she heard that one of Germany's most famous jewelers, a certain Herr Ludwig Koch of Frankfurt, was visiting Carlsbad to do business with various notable visitors. The coincidence was impossible for her to resist. She sent for Herr Koch, who got into his carriage and came over immediately. From the wares he brought with him she chose something for Dora; then something for Günther, the oversized groom-to-be; then something for his immobile, big-chested, thick-necked, waistless parents. ("They're like sea lions," she told Mattachich, expanding her chest and weaving her head to and fro.) Finally, inevitably, she chose something for herself too: a brooch so thick with rubies it looked from a yard away like a clotted wound—a fatal one, you might think, when worn as intended in the hollow just below her left shoulder.

The cost of these items made even Mattachich blink. The obliging Herr Koch left them with her, pending a promised "release of funds." Then, taking her gifts, she went off to visit her in-laws to be, the Duke and Duchess of Schleswig-Holstein. Mattachich was left in Carlsbad to sort matters out. Which he did by instructing Louise's lawyer in Vienna, Barber by name, to borrow from Messrs. Spitzer and Reicher the sum of 475,000 gulden, for a period of one year, with interest to be paid quarterly.* This time, however, Barber found the moneylenders reluctant to advance further large sums to Louise. Too many stories had reached them about the debts she was running up elsewhere. But since they wanted to keep her custom they suggested she should find a suitable additional guarantor for these new loans. Mattachich responded by asking if the Princess Stephanie would do. Oh, certainly, came the reply, of course; indeed, they would consider it a great honor if her royal highness the archduchess would be so kind as to condescend.

On her return, Louise found the promissory notes covering the entire sum waiting for her. She put her signature to them with barely a glance at what she was signing and gave them to Mattachich to send on to Dr.

* The figures given here and in the next paragraph are quoted in Holler, *Ihr Kampf,* p. 67. Two gulden were the equivalent of one krone.

Barber (which, after a short delay, he did). By then Louise was sorry she had spent so much money on the Holsteins. She had not enjoyed her visit with them and had come back convinced they were interested in her daughter chiefly in order to "replenish their coffers."* A month or two later Mattachich sent the lawyer in Vienna back to Spitzer and Reicher to negotiate two further loans totaling a further 125,000 gulden, on the same terms as before and with the same co-guarantor. The moneylenders agreed and the documents were forwarded to Carlsbad; in due course they came back to Dr. Barber in Vienna with the signatures of both royal sisters inscribed on them.

Once the money was received, Ozegovich was dispatched to Nice to finalize the lease of the Villa Paradiso, "one of the most beautiful properties on the French Riviera" (whose owner was inconsiderately asking to be paid in advance for a six-month lease); and Louise, Mattachich, and Dora got ready to follow him.†

So for the time being, all appeared to be in order. The only trouble was that the second signature on both promissory notes returned to Spitzer and Reicher was fraudulent. Louise's signatures were genuine; but Stephanie knew nothing about the guarantees she had ostensibly offered

---

* Louise writes of all the Holsteins with contempt, but Günther gets it in the neck especially. This on account of (a) his treachery in inducing Dora to leave the household in Nice just before the crash; (b) his preoccupation with money; (c) his failure to invite her to the couple's wedding; and (d) his appearance.

In the English translation of her autobiography—but not, strangely, in the original French—the following passage about young Günther appears: "It was imperative for him to make a good marriage. He failed at many attempts at matrimony. Presentable enough as a youngster, he did not improve as he grew older. . . . When he first asked for my daughter's hand in marriage, and [Philipp and I] had consented, he asked me to fix the date. I could not help saying, 'What—do you seriously propose to bring my daughter to the altar before you have had something done to that dreadful nose of yours?'" (Louise, *My Own Affairs*, pp. 146–147.)

A possible reason for Louise's sensitivity on the subject of noses has already been suggested. Of the size of her father's nose, Disraeli wrote, "It is such a nose as a young prince has in a fairy tale, who has been banned by a malignant fairy, or as you see in the first scene of a pantomime" (quoted in *The Coburgs of Belgium* by Theo Aaronson [London 1969], p. 34).

† They left behind them in Carlsbad a trail of unpaid bills (baker's, builder's, laundryman's, etc.). The usual, in short. (See Holler, *Ihr Kampf*, p. 63.)

in order to help her sister. The countersignatures had been added by Mattachich, no one else, inscribing himself in each case as *The Crown Princess Stephanie, Archduchess of Austria.*

❖

It had been done on an impulse, as much for the thrill of transgression as for the money. The first time anyway; the second time more anxiously— but superstition forbade his going back on what he had already done: to show fear now might in itself bring down on him the retribution he feared. Stephanie was Louise's devoted sister and (he believed) his friend: someone who perhaps wished to be more to him than just a friend. There was no likelihood of her being asked to pay up, should the quarterly payments of interest fail or when the period of the loan expired. Philipp had already disgorged bigger sums to keep his wife's name out of the paper and would no doubt do it this time too. It was only *money,* after all. No real harm could come to them in that connection. Or from that direction. For Mattachich, Louise was padded in money, wadded in it, money sprang up from her footsteps like flowers at the feet of Primavera; it showered on her from above in a golden rain, as it did on that other mythical woman whose name Mattachich had forgotten, but the paintings of whom he had seen all over the place. The endlessly put-upon Philipp would manage somehow, or the Midas monster who served her as a father would do the business, or the fools who were ready to advance her goods and services and cash simply because she was who she was. Or indeed Stephanie herself would be indulgent, if the matter ever came to her notice and they begged her pardon humbly enough. In this case especially—Mattachich felt, with some moral unction—Philipp would be in no position to complain, since so much of the borrowed money had been spent on buttering up his only daughter's parents-in-law to be.

Then came the wholly unexpected challenge from Philipp, the duel, and immediately after it Philipp's "betrayal" of them—which was how both Mattachich and Louise instinctively thought of the notice he had put in the papers. To Louise the notice came as a vile shock and a humiliation; to Mattachich it was something worse. His self-confidence, the sense of invulnerability that keeping company with Louise had conferred on him, suddenly guttered away. All Vienna knew that Philipp had abruptly disowned his wife and her debts and suspected that without his resources and those of Louise's family, the runaways were nothing. She was a pauper, effectively—and what was he? How could he possibly go to her now and confess what he had done? Or go to Vienna and make the same confession to Stephanie and, while he was about it, ask her kindly to let the signatures stand until . . . when? Until Philipp announced publicly that he would continue to meet Louise's debts? Until Spitzer and Reicher agreed to overlook the "mistake" he had made? Until Louise went on a penitential pilgrimage to Brussels and talked her father into helping out? Or would she do better to travel instead to Spa, Belgium, where her mother, Henrietta Marie, lived in seclusion—or to the Château de Bocottes where her great-aunt Charlotte, the insane ex-empress of Mexico, was even more rigorously confined—in the hope that one or the other would agree to rescuing her jumped-up Croatian "friend" from the consequences of his own folly?

No, no, no. They were all mad, one way or another, in that family, but not that mad. They were cunning too. Never once, since Louise had left Vienna to travel around Europe with her so-called chamberlain, had any of them (Stephanie included) sent her a line of greeting or inquiry, let alone an invitation to visit. Not the kind of people, then, who would stand by their outcast sister and her lover in a moment of self-inflicted crisis.

❖

Morning after morning he got out of bed early, before dawn, and walked along the seafront, looking at the incoming tide constantly folding and spreading its white linen like a distraught washerwoman, or he gazed farther out, to where great weights of water silently slid and heaved against one another in the dimness—while the same substance in another guise chuckled idiotically among rocks at his feet—and tried to see himself walking straight into it until he could walk no farther. Then swimming out deeper until that too became more than he could manage. And then? What followed was always the same. Days or weeks later he would be dragged out of it: dead, sodden, bloated, barely recognizable.

Ach, that was always the problem. It was not fear or horror that held him back, or so he believed; it was that he was incapable of excluding himself from the scene. He *had* to be a participant still: to know what was going to happen, to be there, looking, listening, responding when it happened. Not out of it! Not yet! He had to struggle on, trying to make the best of the situation they were in. It sickened him to be preoccupied with such stuff; he was a soldier, a lover, a man of action, not a pettifogging businessman, a Jew-boy moneylender, a bankrupt greengrocer with bills and invoices forever on his mind. Yet their debts, all of them so lightly assumed, had been transformed into an inert, congested, horribly uncomfortable mass somewhere inside him, like a packed intestine, with the forged promissory notes as the final bug up his ass. And to think he had spared that Fatso's life when he could have finished him off!

Very well then, something had to be done and he was the one to do it. Jewels were obviously the most valuable of Louise's possessions, as well as the most portable and pawnable. First they had to establish which of the rings, brooches, bracelets, necklaces, earrings, aigrettes, and the like, which she kept in all those fancy cases and little kid-leather bags—some in the bank, some in the Villa—had been fully paid for, and how much was still owed on the others and to whom. To do that they had to relate the individual items in those receptacles to the bundles of letters, invoices, and receipts in their possession. Then they had to find out how much cash they could realize from them. That was the program, anyway, and it depended largely on his capacity to persuade Louise that this act of stocktaking and inventory-making was not a malign game he had invented in order to torment her but an absolute necessity. It would be a struggle, he knew. In particular, she could not understand why he was so insistent about their need to meet the next installment of interest due to Spitzer and Reicher. What was so special about the money they were owed, anyway?

But on that subject he was dumb. Dumb.

By the end of three or four days of argument and tears on her side and restrained rage on his, he had brought her to accept that cash, cash, cash was what they needed above all. By then too they had prepared a rough and ready list of items that it would be best or most convenient or at any rate least anguishing for her to release. But when he swallowed his pride and went out like a traveling salesman to raise the cash, cash, cash he had spoken of, he ran into another difficulty. Their plight was known up and down the Riviera and beyond it, and every purchaser or pawnbroker he approached was determined to secure the maximum advantage he could from the weakness of their position. The buyers knew they had nothing to lose by holding off, keeping him waiting, turning their mouths down, and declaring that this kind of setting or that kind of stone had gone out of favor and would never come back. Suddenly these previously fawning and smiling creepers, forever giving their hands a dry wash while they listened to them with bent heads, as if he were the wisest man and Louise the most beautiful woman on earth, had become experts at pulling long faces and declaring how little time they had to spare for him and how short of cash they were, alas, just at the moment.

In other words, he and Louise were too poor to sell! After several such encounters, Mattachich decided that the most valuable items would have to be sold or pawned incognito and piecemeal and as far from the Riviera as possible. For this he needed third parties he could rely on. So he decided to let Ozegovich go to Vienna and do his best, since he was in himself too insignificant for his friendship with Mattachich to be known there; and to let a new friend, Maximilian Jean Fuchs, a French-German *alsacien,* a hotel manager by trade, go on the same mission to London. Both men readily accepted the proposals, which naturally included payment of their expenses and the promise of a commission on whatever deals they secured.

❖

With Fuchs, Mattachich went further. Depressed, sorry for himself, and longing to find someone else to feel sorry for him—also half hoping to hear of a solution to his problem that he had somehow overlooked—he took Fuchs into his confidence. He told him everything.

No, not Ozegovich, who was too close to him, too dependent, too *heimisch* to be entrusted with his secret. For Mattachich, Fuchs had the perverse advantage of being a newcomer. Nor was that all. There was something else about him that Mattachich found attractive, even irresistible. When the two of them first met he had wondered if this stranger weren't perhaps a Habsburg spy, sent down to Nice to keep an eye on him and Louise. But he soon decided that was nonsense. What most attracted Mattachich to Fuchs was precisely and perversely the fact that the latter did not take him seriously. Not as a knightly defender of a forsaken princess, anyway. Not as a man hounded by the emperor of Austria-Hungary. Not as a soldier who had thrown away his career in the imperial army for the sake of a great passion. He spoke of Mattachich's *grand amour* as if it were the moral equivalent of the big killing that he, Fuchs, had made in the casino in Monte Carlo a few months before—a killing so big it had enabled him not merely to look like a gentleman (of an unconventional kind) but to live like one. On the strength of it he had given up his job as assistant manager in one of the big hotels on the seafront and had not looked for another position since.

The two men had met by chance in a bar, and chance—or "luck," as Fuchs preferred to call it—was one of his big subjects. Luck was one of the qualities they had in common, Fuchs said firmly the second time they met. "The other thing we share is that we're not apologetic about our luck. We grab it. We use it. We *love* it. Lots of people can't bear being lucky. It makes them nervous; they punish themselves for any luck that comes their way, because they think if they don't dish out that kind of punishment to themselves, someone or something worse will come along and do it to them. Or they run away from it because they don't 'deserve' it, they feel they're not good enough for it. As if goodness has anything to with luck! As if only the virtuous are rewarded. And you know what happens to them as a result? They stop being lucky. Then you ask yourself, What did they really want, to be lucky or to feel badly done by? For people like you and me, though, luck is no burden. We're just grateful for it."

"We have to work for it too."

"Of course. Nothing for nothing. We take risks. You had to take risks and you took them. So did I. Risk-taking is our kind of work, you and me both."

Mattachich protested from time to time against this kind of talk but always returned for more. In Fuchs's company he could come to terms with the additional secret cynical self lurking within him, the inseparable twin brother of the one who wished only to be admired. With Fuchs he did not have to make the effort to see himself as an austerely passionate hero, nor did he have to meet the sly envious scorn he so often felt to be just beneath the surface of the friendliness he encountered among others. Even with Louise he had to keep up a sturdy, reassuring front: not because he feared her judgment but because she was so prone to misgiving and self-reproach, he had to be on guard for her sake rather than his own.

With Fuchs none of this was necessary and Mattachich warmed to him, even became enamored of him, as a result. He felt as if he were an understanding stranger met on an overnight journey and never to be seen again, from whom no secrets need be kept. A man of about Mattachich's age and height, Fuchs's background was humble—that was as much as he ever said about it—but his years in the hotel business, he claimed, had made a gentleman of him long before he had actually "come into the money." He had never done military service of any kind and admitted to Mattachich that he felt diminished in consequence. The army doctors had discovered he had "a heart," he said, meaningfully pointing a finger at his left breast. "Since then," he added, with calm self-satisfaction, "I've done my best to manage without one."

He wore pale linen suits, which in a raffish style of his own invention he had married to one of the newly fashionable black homburg hats, complete with broad flat brim and indented crown. He was the first person Mattachich had met who wore such a hat. Something direct and insouciant in his manner, as well as his dark hair and sallow skin, the droop of his eyelids over his wide ocean-green eyes, the set of his never entirely straight lips, which were pale and yet had an almost purplish tint to them, the small assured movements of his wrists and fingers, the smoothness of his voice, and his fluency in each of the several languages he spoke—all this endowed him with a singular glamour in Mattachich's eyes. It also helped to make plausible his claim that the only thing he missed about his former job was the ever-changing supply of women that had gone with it. Chambermaids, kitchen staff, lady guests, their daughters, their companions, whatever came up. Or lay down.

This was the man that Mattachich was unable to restrain himself from confiding in. Who else did he have? Did not this Fuchs already know him better, in some ways, than someone like Ozegovich ever would? But after Philipp's "betrayal" had been made public in the papers, that was exactly why he avoided the places where he and Fuchs used to meet and thanked God that Fuchs had not responded to the invitation to Louise's disordered, humiliating ball. Now that Mattachich's luck had left him, how could they meet as equals?

Yet they were bound to bump into one another sooner or later, and it came almost as a relief to Mattachich when they did finally do so, on the seafront. Each exclaimed each other's name as they shook hands; then both fell silent. It was for moments only that they had nothing to say, but it seemed much longer.

Fuchs was the first to speak. "I hear you've fought a duel."

That was all. Not a word about the notice in the newspaper, none about those disgusting scenes at the Villa, of which he must have heard; nothing about the bullying, buzzing creditors. The man's tact tore something like a sob out of Mattachich's throat. He heard the sound and it astonished him, as if had come from someone else. It also undid him. It revealed his distress so plainly there was now no point in struggling to deny what he was going through. Without a word, with just a gesture of the shoulder by way of invitation, he continued walking eastwards, as if he had some specific destination in mind. Fuchs fell in beside him. To the right, intermittently cut off by buildings, lay a calm blue sea, like a platter warming under the dome of the sky. There were a few boats out there; otherwise no life, only the sheen and shiver of light. Nearer, around them, were palms, hotels, terraces, horse-drawn vehicles, even the occasional ungainly motorcar, stared at by passersby as if it were a creature escaped from a zoo. Looking straight ahead of them as they walked, Mattachich spoke of how heavily Louise was in debt and admitted that he and she had always relied, ultimately, on Philipp's bailing her out, no matter how belatedly and ungraciously he did it.

And now he had let her down! He had deliberately called for that idiotic duel, knowing that Mattachich would treat him kindly, and always intending, the fat bastard, the coward that he was, to kick his wife in the teeth once his "honor" had been restored.

"Honorably, you understand. Honorably. . . . "

So they were in trouble now, up to their eyes in trouble, and everyone in Nice knew it. (Still staring in front of him.) The world knew. Fuchs knew. And that wasn't the worst of it. By no means. Months ago, when they'd still been in Carlsbad, he, Mattachich, had done something "unbelievably stupid." (A phrase he illustrated by a one-handed gesture, as if throwing an object behind him.) Fuchs must swear never to breathe a word of it to anyone. It wasn't just money trouble he was in but something worse, something that had happened because of their money troubles, months before, and now threatened him with utter disgrace and ruin . . . and God alone knew what else.

"It didn't mean anything to me at the time. Truly! I didn't intend to harm anyone. It was just a little thing! A trick to save bother, that's all. . . . " One hand flew upward again, in an abrupt oath-taking gesture.

He spoke with great intensity, as if the casualness of his intention was still far more important, morally speaking, than any consequences his *trick* might now have.

"But who'll believe it?" The words came out despairingly. So did the broken sentences and exclamations that followed. "They have me by the neck. . . . They've been waiting for this. . . . The princess knows nothing. . . . How could I? . . . I must have been mad. . . . But you know, it's difficult. . . ." And, pointing to the sea, "You won't believe how often I've thought of simply. . . . It's there, it's waiting, so why not . . . take advantage?"

Finally he fell silent. They walked on. Still Fuchs said nothing. Not even "Well?" or "What?" or "I'm sorry." Mattachich stared ahead of him. He had not once looked at his companion since they had set out on this walk; his friend had been no more than a silent presence alongside him, footsteps, a body, movements keeping time with his own. Company enough.

Minutes passed in this way. Suddenly Fuchs slowed his pace, trailed briefly behind Mattachich, halted, brought his hand to his mouth in a gesture of recollection. Then he hauled his watch out of his waistcoat pocket, swore calmly, and said he'd forgotten he had an appointment he simply had to keep. They shook hands and Mattachich stood where he was, his eyes following the other as he crossed the roadway, making toward the town center.

"Fuchs!" Mattachich called out. He felt shaky, conscious of a kind of trembling in his breast. Then louder, as Fuchs plainly had not heard the call above the sound of the traffic, "Fuchs!" This time he halted. Mattachich waved to him to return. Which he did, attentive and unsmiling as before.

❖

Fuchs, then, became the specially chosen friend, the sole confidant, the person who knew something about Mattachich known to no one else, the one sent to London with some particularly valuable items of jewelry worth tens of thousands of gulden apiece. And Fuchs was the son-of-a-bitch who returned from London three weeks later with a sum that fell so miserably short of Mattachich's expectations that the two men's friendship—always a showy affair, starting out of nothing, like a cactus flower—was destroyed in minutes. It was replaced by anger, suspicion, accusation, and mutual contempt. Mattachich was convinced that Fuchs had done deals on the side with the people he had sold the goods to; the signed and stamped receipts from London he brought back with him meant nothing, since both sides would benefit by not revealing the true sums involved in the transactions. In other words, Fuchs was a thief. To this accusation Fuchs—his sallow skin gone yellow, his teeth appearing at unfamiliar angles in his lower jaw, the veins in his eyes suddenly showing—replied that of course a forger would be bound to see everyone else as a crook and a confidence man.

"That's it!" Mattachich said, keeping his voice as low as his rage permitted. "I see what you're up to. Because I trusted you, you think you can do what you like with me. You think, Oh, he's finished, he won't dare to complain; he'll take whatever I bring him."

It was the morning after Fuchs's return from London. They had met in one of the rooms downstairs in the Villa. The doors and windows had been closed and the curtains drawn, so that no one could look in or hear what they were saying. On the table between them were a few receipts and piles of banknotes tied in bundles. Their eyes gleamed in the half-light. Only their unsteady breathing could be heard in the room until a chatter of birds suddenly erupted in the garden, some of them twittering, one larger bird angrily rattling the wooden beads it seemed to carry in its throat. Fuchs stood up, took the bundle of notes nearest to him, and put it into a small portmanteau that had been at his feet. He began to move toward the door. In the same moment it opened of its own accord. Louise stood there. She was wearing a long pale garment with a frilled collar and carried a handkerchief in her hand.

"Herr Fuchs," she said.

He responded with the briefest inclination of his neck. He still held the portmanteau in his right hand. "Your highness."

He and Louise barely knew one another; the men's friendship had flourished outside the house, in bars, restaurants, cafés, gaming rooms.

"You're talking business, I see."

"We were, yes."

"When did you get back from London?"

"Last night."

"And did you accomplish what you set out to do?"

"No!" Mattachich said. "He didn't. He's betrayed us. He's come back with nothing."

"Nothing?" Louise asked ironically, with a faint gesture towards the money lying on the table.

"Nothing. Nothing." Mattachich repeated. "Nothing but insults."

Coming forward into the room, she said calmly to Fuchs, "You must forgive the count. We're going through a difficult time."

"Madam," Fuchs said, struggling to speak calmly too, though his voice shook, "let me warn you. This . . . friend of yours is leading you into great trouble. What he's told me—"

He got no further. Mattachich jumped from his chair and made a rush at him. He grabbed at his neck with one hand and at the portmanteau with the other. Fuchs tried to parry him but was sent sprawling to the floor. Mattachich held the portmanteau up in the air, like a trophy. Or a weapon he was about to smash down on his opponent's head.

"Bastard! Blackmailer!" he said. "I know your game." Then he simply flung the bag at the man, who lay panting on the floor. It struck him on the shoulder. "Get out!"

Louise had given a cry when the fight began; now, silent, pale, looking nowhere, she sat down at the table. Mattachich stood back. Breathing heavily, he covered his face with weary hands. Fuchs remained on the floor, his shoulders moving with every breath. Eventually, in silence, he scrambled to his feet and looked down at the portmanteau, as if not knowing what to do with it. Before stooping to pick it up he glanced apprehensively at Mattachich, afraid he might attack him again, even kick him on the backside. But Mattachich stood where he was, his hands now fallen to his sides. Fuchs put the portmanteau under his arm and left the room without another word. His homburg, which Mattachich had envied and despised, remained on one of the chairs.

❖

The fortnight before Fuchs's return from London had been a bad period for the couple, even within the general rout. Ozegovich had returned from Vienna with less cash than they had expected (though he had done better with the goods entrusted to him than had Fuchs). Creditors they barely remembered continued to appear from unexpected quarters. They had failed in their attempt to raise money by means of the simple ruse of pawning locally the heavyweight agglomeration of silverware hired from the owner of the Villa. Throughout, gnawing privately at Mattachich as a painful part of his larger secret, was the conviction that he had made a stupid error in sharing his secret with Fuchs. Just minutes after he had spoken, minutes after they had parted on the seafront, it had been plain to him. Why had he done it, for God's sake? What good could come of it? How much harm?

Hence the contraction of hope, the sense of utter desertion, he felt when Fuchs told him what his trip to London had netted. His own fault again! How familiar the sense of failure and folly, the self-sickness that seized him then. There it was again: just as it had been in childhood, always waiting within for its opportunity to strike him down. At such moments everything essential to his well-being died instantly. He was done for, judged, charred.

This particular "moment" lasted longer than usual. Depleted, useless, he left it to Louise to do the best she could over the next few weeks. She dealt with the remaining servants, read the letters that came in from angry creditors or their lawyers and responded to them with promises, evasions, and lies, denied entrance to those who turned up at the gates of the Villa (now kept permanently locked), and speculated about possible sources of help she might yet turn to. All Mattachich could suggest was that she go to London and seek assistance from Queen Victoria, her distant cousin by both blood and marriage, but this sounded so implausible to Louise she dismissed it out of hand. Instead, hoping to gain time and to spread confusion among her creditors, she went in for a little creative forgery of her own by sending a cable—ostensibly from a Count Bechtolsheim in the Austrian-Hungarian embassy in Paris—to the press agency Agence Havas, declaring that Philipp's formal repudiation of his wife's debts had been issued in error and that the agency's outlets should print a withdrawal of it.* She had no idea how tempted her lover was, when he heard of this relatively trivial forgery, to tell her about his own. But he simply could not do it.

Slowly Mattachich began to recover his will and energy. The example she had just set encouraged him to compose two further communications that used no pseudonyms or forged signatures but were fraudulent nevertheless. The first was a letter, signed by Louise, which was addressed to King Leopold but never posted to him, since it was drafted solely for Dr. Barber to show to the dreaded Spitzer and Reicher, in the hope of calming them down.† The second was a telegram sent by Louise to Stephanie which read, mystifyingly, IF YOU LOVE ME, SAY NOTHING BEFORE YOU RECEIVE MY LETTER. EVERYTHING WILL BE MADE CLEAR IN IT. HOWEVER THINGS MAY APPEAR, I AM INNOCENT. THE FAULT IS PHILIPP'S. IT WILL BE GREATLY TO MY ADVANTAGE IF YOU SAY YES. WAIT FOR MY LETTER. LOUISE.‡

Not surprisingly, both these miserable initiatives misfired. The imme-

---

* Quoted in Holler, *Ihr Kampf,* p. 94.

† "Dear Father! The situation to which my family has brought me has compelled me to raise money . . . on generous terms. . . . I have asked Stephanie to stand by me, which she has agreed to do, but I have no alternative now but to ask you to help us put things in order. . . . Please do this in the interest of both Stephanie and your loving and grateful daughter" (quoted in Holler, *Ihr Kampf,* p. 96).

‡ Quoted in Holler, *Ihr Kampf,* p. 96.

diate effect of Louise's letter supposedly addressed to her father was to frighten Barber into laying down his mandate as Louise's legal representative in Vienna. Feeling himself being drawn more and more dangerously into a web of deceits, he decided to disentangle himself from the whole affair—and to let "the other side"—Philipp—know he had done so and why. As for the telegram sent to Stephanie, it simply never reached her, for a few days before its dispatch she had been admitted to hospital with a life-threatening case of pneumonia. So the incomprehensible message from Louise went to her chamberlain, Graf Choloniewski, a man as ponderous as his name, who took it straight to Philipp.

All this was bad enough; worse still were the two letters Philipp received from the infuriated Fuchs. If Mattachich were to come to Vienna, Fuchs wrote, Philipp should take steps to have him arrested immediately. "This starveling who tries to pass himself off as a grand lord," Fuchs wrote, "is nothing more than a fraudster and a scoundrel." Fuchs's next letter, which arrived on the following day, was even more dramatic in tone: "Things are looking darker than ever! The princess has bought on credit jewelry from a Monte Carlo firm . . . and sent a certain Ozegovich to Vienna to pawn them so she'll have cash in hand for her flight. . . . The moneylenders want to take her to court for perjury and theft. . . . The whole business has been cooked up by Mattachich."*

❖

Ten days later a meeting took place in the "portrait room" of the Coburg palace. It was attended by Prince Philipp, Spitzer, Reicher, Philipp's aide Gablenz, Graf Choloniewski, and the indispensable Dr. Bachrach. Under the cracked dusty eyeballs of a score of bearded, high-booted, gold-braided, bemedaled, besashed, and bestarred eighteenth-century Coburg males, most of them intermittently lit up by sunshine coming in through tall windows, the promissory notes purportedly signed by both Louise

* Quoted in Holler, *Ihr Kampf,* p. 92.

and Stephanie were produced for inspection. Choloniewski took one look at them and declared Stephanie's signatures to be fakes. He explained that she would never have signed any formal document of any kind as Crown Princess Stephanie, Archduchess of Austria. Her official title was Crown Princess-Widow (*Kronprinzessin-Witwe*) Stephanie, and except in letters to the closest members of her family that was how she invariably wrote her name.*

* See Holler, *Ihr Kampf,* p. 97.

CHAPTER SIX

SOME YEARS LATER A GREAT FUSS WAS MADE about the role of the moneylenders in the whole affair. Two questions in particular were asked about them. Why did they demand a second guarantor of the promissory notes covering their most recent loans to Louise (something they had not asked for previously) and why did they belatedly insist on verifying this guarantor's signature so long after they had apparently accepted it as genuine? Up to that point Louise had met the payments of interest due on the various loans made to her, so why their sudden misgivings about the underwriting of these documents?

Some of Mattachich's supporters gave a simple answer to both questions. Or rather, they answered them with another question. What else could you expect from a pair of Jews? Archetypal Jews, indeed, moneylending Jews, who as always had just two aims in mind: to make money and to exercise power in malign subterranean fashion. Their belated queries about the authenticity of Stephanie's signature were bogus from beginning to end. They had always known her supposed signature on the documents to be faked *because they themselves had put it there.* They were the forgers. With the incriminating notes in hand, they had waited patiently for the appropriate moment to strike. Now that moment had come.

Strike at whom, exactly? Well, listen to the testimony delivered to the imperial parliament—the *Reichsrat*—by Ignaz Daszynski, a member of the Social-Democratic Party. From the moneylenders' point of view, Daszynski explained, "it was entirely convenient" to add a false signature to a genuine one "since it is a universally acknowledged fact that a false signature is worth more than a genuine one, above all in usurious transactions of this sort. Then the usurers can say, 'With a forged signature there is scandal, threats, we hold a pistol not only against the forehead of the Prince of Coburg but against all the leading elements of the imperial court.' . . . For we are dealing here," Daszynski went on, "with the fiercest, most fanatical moneymen, who advance their money at exorbitant rates of interest to countless numbers of people in the court"*

And more in the same vein. Useless to ask why it should be entirely convenient for Messrs. Spitzer and Reicher to add a false signature to a genuine one, thus rendering the documents worthless in any court of law. Or since when exactly has it been "universally acknowledged" that a forged promissory note is more valuable for blackmailing purposes than a genuine one. Especially when the proffered forgery is instantly detectable to all who know the hand of the supposed signatory. Or why the moneylenders should conspire to issue documents that would not only put at risk such large sums of their own money but would also lay themselves open to prosecution as forgers, perjurers, and abusers of the name of the king-emperor's daughter-in-law. No less. Or whether Spitzer and Reicher were alone in the alarm they felt about the state of Louise's finances after Philipp's public disavowal of her debts and the fusillade of messages that had been reaching Vienna from Nice and elsewhere about the state of her household.

Doubtless you can think of further posers that might have been put to the now long-dead Daszynski, but since such questions were useless even when he was alive, why bother? It is more to the point to note that, the anti-Semitic tenor of his speech notwithstanding, Daszynski also chose to compare Mattachich to the innocent Captain Dreyfus, the French-Jewish army officer who was sentenced to imprisonment on Devil's Island, ostensibly for treason but in fact on grounds of his race alone. At

---

* Daszynski was the man who referred to Philipp's lawyer, Adolf Bachrach, as "a little Jew with feudal pretensions" (see Chapter One). The phrase was reported to have roused "lively mirth" (*lebendise Heiterkeit*) in the legislature.

these moments Daszynski suddenly seems to remember his socialist credentials, which are displayed elsewhere in his speech by references to "the fatal hand of the Habsburgs," "Coburg greed," and the empire's "high society . . . stuck in its own filth." Occasionally, too, he manages to weld indissolubly both prongs of his argument, as in his characterization of "the Jew Bachrach" as "one of those figures who are always to be found creeping behind the shelter that despotism is only too eager to give them."*

❖

All that said, Daszynski was absolutely right in one respect. The members of the group meeting this morning in the portrait room in the Coburg palace, to examine the forged promissory notes and decide what was to be done about them, are agreed that the matter should be handled as discreetly as possible, and at the lowest cost (in every sense) to those around the table. Spitzer and Reicher want their money back from whatever source might provide it. Philipp, whose plight is the unhappiest of them all, wants to be permanently shut of Louise and the debts and humiliations she is forever dragging him into. Choloniewski, on behalf of the ailing Stephanie, is simply anxious to keep Louise's connections out of the whole unsavory business.

But how? *How?* When the promissory notes have been handed back

---

* Extended extracts from Daszynski's speech appear in both Louise's *Autour,* pp. 232–236 and in Holler, *Ihr Kampf,* pp.193–198. Just two decades later a far more deadly combination of radicalism and virulent anti-Semitism—as first tried out in Vienna by Daszynski, Schönerer, Lueger, and others—was to be peddled in the streets of the German-speaking world by an incomparably more effective demagogue.

A recycling of Daszynski's arguments about the Mattachich-Louise affair can be found in a pamphlet entitled *La Princesse Louise en fuite* ("Princess Louise in Flight"), published in Brussels in 1905. Subtitled *Le Roman d'une Vie* ("The Story of a Life"), its authorship is left unclaimed. Complete with a pen-and-ink-sketch of Louise, the pamphlet dishes out dirt in various directions—it claims, for example, that Louise's "lout of a husband" (*son butor de mari*) used to "slap her about like plaster" (*la battait comme plâtre*)—but its treatment of the forged documents relies wholly on Daszynski's version of events.

and forth around the table and finally returned to the folder from which they were produced, and the complaining, the sighing, the head-shaking, the disgusted or despairing *Achs!* are all done with, everyone turns to Bachrach. There he sits: erect, portly, pale, self-confident, his round head shaven, his sharp waxed mustache points directed pacifically downward, not sideways or forward, his mouth firm, his brown eyes equipped with bags beneath them, and a set of wise-looking wrinkles fanning out from their corners. The whole ensemble, in short, carefully composed— composed literally, you might think, as if he'd been offered a choice of habitual expressions to wear and had finally settled on a mixture of "wry" and "cautious," with more than a hint of "stern" thrown in. Having kept them waiting in silence for what he judges to be the right length of time, he coughs, looks at the paper that lies on top of a little pile in front of him, and begins talking in a light, manly tenor voice into which something almost purringly basslike comes and goes.

"Your Highness, gentlemen," he begins, "I speak candidly about the problem facing us since I know everything that passes between us will remain confidential. We have been given direct evidence this afternoon that a crime, the insidious and vulgar crime of forgery, has been perpetrated not only against her royal highness the Crown Princess-Widow Stephanie but also against the two . . . um . . . financial gentlemen present with us who were inveigled by falsified signatures into making large sums of money available to the Princess Louise. It is some comfort to know that the forgeries have been revealed when only a portion of the money loaned has been drawn on. We have also had direct evidence from at least two sources, from a certain Jean Fuchs of Nice, of whom I know nothing, and from my Viennese colleague Dr. Barber, that the forgeries were inscribed on the documents by Lieutenant Géza Mattachich, who describes himself as chamberlain to the Princess Louise."

A long pause follows. Then, as if rebuking not himself but someone else: "Correction: what has just been said is not quite accurate. The allegations made by Fuchs and Barber are not evidence. Rather, they have made accusations against Mattachich that would have to be tested in a court of law, if—*if*—the case were to be directly turned over to the police. Which might seem the simplest way to proceed."

Another long pause. Bachrach's eyes turn to Philipp, who acknowledges the glance with a half-hypnotized nod. A spark of light from the sun, reflected off his pince-nez, strikes one of his ancestors on the wall opposite him and dies there instantly. Bachrach lowers his head.

"As the aggrieved parties, Messrs. Spitzer and Reicher are perfectly entitled to go to the police, to report the crime, and, if they so wish, to lay criminal charges against the alleged culprit. . . . Or culprits." The longest pause yet, while he allows the implications of this plural noun to sink in. "The point I am making is this. We know that a forged signature purporting to be that of her royal highness was inscribed on the promissory notes issued by our financial friends. We have strong reason to believe that the person who committed this crime was Lieutenant Mattachich. But do we *know* he was the one who did it? Can we *prove* that he was responsible for it? Do the people who accuse him of the crime claim to have *seen* him committing it? In my view the one thing that is indisputable about these documents is that Princess Louise, as their ostensible beneficiary, had privileged access to them and that her signature appears on them, alongside the supposed signature of her sister."

Someone's chair creaks. Someone else clears his throat. No one dares to speak.

"I leave it to Count Choloniewski to decide what to tell the Crown Princess-Widow Stephanie—to whom we send our best wishes for a speedy recovery from illness—about our meeting today. It is important that she understand her honor and her interests are no way endangered by this unhappy business. The fraud has been discovered and is acknowledged by everyone here. No demand arising from it can possibly be made against her. There is no need for her to feel personally involved—except through her sisterly feelings, of course—in this sordid affair."

While speaking, Bachrach directs his gaze to the table in front of him; only during his silences does it go from face to face around him. At this point he looks straight at Choloniewski, who solemnly reflects for a few moments, or makes an effort to look as if that is what he is doing, before announcing, "It is my duty to inform her royal highness of all that concerns her. I will repeat to her the assurances you have just given."

Now comes the crunch. Everyone knows it. Bachrach's neck and shoulders stiffen; his voice rises a little, not in volume but in pitch. This time his gaze finds Spitzer and Reicher. They know and he knows, and so do the three others in the room, that what lies between the speaker and the spoken-to at this moment is not just a legal or financial problem but a racial one too.

❖

In their Hasidic beards and Hasidic garb, Spitzer and Reicher, the aggrieved parties, as Bachrach has just described them, are seated side by side, gazing intently at this smooth-talking, smooth-shaven, semi-apostate lawyer, this probably-pork-eating Jew, of whom they are plainly suspicious. On his side Bachrach—child of the Enlightenment, a third generation beneficiary of the Edict of Tolerance and of Franz Josef's opening of Austria's universities to Jews—regards them quite differently. Described in every social and professional directory published in Vienna as "advocate to royalty and the high aristocracy (*des höheren Adels*)," he is determined not to be abashed or irritated by the manner in which these two men display the "medieval" Jewishness that he and his family have long since left behind; determined also to rebuff any hint of an intimacy with him that they or anyone else might dare to assume or suggest. He does not take them for fools and primitives; nevertheless, he feels himself to be an emissary from the real world, the world he knows so well, to the sequestered milieu they presumably inhabit. He feels the need, too, to preempt the suspicion that he might be swayed from his duty toward Philipp by any improper sympathy for them.

Yes, he tells them, it is they who stand to incur losses that can be calculated in hard cash rather than hurt pride. For that reason they are entitled, as he has said, to turn to the courts for protection. But what good will come to them if they do? Punishment of the man "who has led the princess so sadly astray" will not bring back their money. And as for restitution . . . well, their only hope of recouping any of the money they have lost lies with Prince Philipp, and it is the prince's wish that the police are not to be called in. Not at this stage, anyway. The newspapers are not to be informed of the crime. No approach is to be made to Princess Stephanie. No steps are to be taken through the civil courts to distrain any property Princess Louise might still possess.

"So what are you suggesting?" Reicher asks eventually. He is the shorter, stockier, more stubborn-looking of the two. "That we do nothing? Just let ourselves be robbed? Like fools? Like helpless things?"

Philipp draws in a breath. But Bachrach smiles for the first time since the beginning of the meeting. It is a concise affair, just a twitch of his lips.

"Yes."

"And in return?'

"His highness will consider your position sympathetically, once the matter has been resolved."

The two men put their heads together, so far as their broad-brimmed hats permit, and whisper a few sentences to each other.

"What does 'resolved' mean in a case like this?"

Again Bachrach's mouth twitches. "I have no idea. Not at present."

Now it is Spitzer's turn to show a stubborn streak. "Forgive me. Perhaps you are forgetting that the prince repudiated the princess's debts well after these promissory notes were issued? He is her husband. If she fails us, surely he is still obliged therefore to—?"

Bachrach interrupts him. "My legal opinion is no, he is not. The notice in the newspapers was nothing more than a warning to the public. It carried no implication that his highness accepted responsibility for all the debts his unfortunate spouse had incurred until that moment. You did not consult the prince before you made the loans to the princess. If you had, he would have advised strongly against your going ahead with the transactions. Of course you're still free to take a criminal case to the police regardless of the consequences. Or you can sue the prince in the civil courts. But there are other considerations. Leave aside all the problems of extradition and jurisdiction that will arise—given that the princess and Mattachich are abroad—and consider the following points. If you do go to the police, and they manage to secure the cooperation of the French authorities, you may find yourself in a court, here in Vienna, where the person in the dock will turn out to be not this Mattachich creature, whom we all know to be the fraudster, but the princess herself. I have already implied as much, now I say it to you explicitly. How would you feel on seeing so highborn a woman, the daughter of a king, a princess of the house of Saxe-Coburg, a sister to the widowed Crown Princess of Austria and Hungary, standing in the dock as a result of your actions? How do you imagine a scene like that will affect her husband, who in all the frankness and humility of his generous heart sits here with us today? And if you choose to sue him for your losses in the civil courts, remember that this would mean dragging his highness's most intimate family affairs through the newspapers. What will that do for you? What reconciliation with him can you hope for subsequently?

"I've already said that I don't believe the courts will uphold your claim against him. But there is a further element in the case you must take into account. I mean the climate of opinion that exists in the streets of Vienna today. And not only in the streets, but in the salons and palaces too. And the parliament. Gentlemen, you know well what I'm referring to. You've witnessed—suffered—the excesses that certain extreme elements in our city are ready to indulge in, given the slightest encouragement. Frankly, if you do go to court, then whatever happens to you, win or lose (and I'm confident which of the two it's likely to be), you will have it on your shoulders that you have done a great disfavor not only to yourselves but also—I have to say it—to your people. To your entire community."

❖

He could blackmail them in this fashion with a clear conscience because he was Jewish himself. He knew it; they knew it; the others in the room knew it.

Silence. More whisperings. Spitzer and Reicher had gone through the shock of learning that a signature they had relied on was a fiction. Now they found themselves instructed to do nothing, to wait, to rely on Philipp's good nature. Had a few dozen sentences from his lawyer finished them off? And perhaps their cash too?

Finally their confabulation produced a heavy-hearted inquiry. If they gave the undertakings that had been asked of them, might they expect to receive something, you know, in the meantime, on account, in a manner of speaking?

No, Bachrach answered, as quietly and obdurately as before. Nothing could be done now that might prejudice an eventual settlement. But they would be kept informed of the steps that would be taken. Their cooperation was highly valued. It would not be forgotten by his honored client. Their losses were not taken lightly. Far, far from it.

The prince, who had listened with intent wonder to everything his lawyer had said, spoke at last, his gaze and voice pitched toward the ornately molded ceiling above.

"This is a nightmare," he said. "Everything to do with it is just . . . awful."

A respectful silence followed this announcement. Then Reicher began argumentatively, "For you"—with a motion of his forefinger that managed to point neither at the prince nor anywhere else—"this is a family matter, but for us—"

"I will do my best for you, be assured," Philipp said. "That is my undertaking."

Spitzer spoke up hastily, as if to keep his fractious colleague at bay. "Yes, yes, for us too it is a nightmare. We are honest people. Our business is money. We buy it and sell it. We borrow it as well as lend it. We do the one in order to do the other. That is how we live. Your highness must not forget that we have creditors too, to whom we owe money. So this is a double blow for us."

The two men exchanged glances; then Reicher spoke up. "If your highness will permit, we will leave you now. We have much to consider. We have our own lawyers to consult."

He put his papers into the black leather bag, rather like a music folder, that accompanied him everywhere. His colleague, equipped with a similar but smaller bag, did the same. They stood up and bowed to the prince, who acknowledged their obeisance with a nod. They exchanged the briefest farewells with the others—a nod here, a "good day" there. Reicher gave a last look, heavy with animosity, at Bachrach, who met it with a straight face and a bland undertaking: "You will be kept informed of how we proceed."

No sooner were the two men out of the room than everyone in it relaxed. Sounding almost cheerful for the first time that morning, Philipp called out, "Bachrach, you handled your friends beautifully."

"My friends?"

"Yes, well, you know what I mean," Philipp replied imperturbably, and indeed Bachrach did know what he meant. So did the others. Even Choloniewski managed a prim smile. Philipp went straight on. "Now you must tell us what is to be done next. It's a desperate business, this."

"It is, your highness. For all we know, the princess may be in danger—not just from the law or from her creditors but possibly in physical danger too. Think of the company she's keeping! Who knows what such people are capable of? If we want to save her and to keep your highness's house from further scandal, we must move forward very carefully. We've secured the silence of those two, which is a mercy, but I don't know how long their patience will hold out. First, we must get someone down to Nice to tell us exactly what's happening in the Villa Paradiso and around it. And then—"

"And then?"

"Your highness, as I said to those you call my friends, I don't know. Something is going to give way in that ménage, that's all I'm certain of.

Our chance will come. We must take advantage of it when it does. Who knows, maybe this Mattachich has got up to some other crimes with which the princess cannot possibly be connected. Then we can act. Until then, we wait and watch."

When the meeting was over, Philipp complained to Gablenz that it was all very well for Bachrach to advise those two moneylenders to sit tight and do nothing, but it was another matter for the devilish lawyer to "tie him up" in the same way. But as he had great respect for Bachrach's judgment and couldn't think how else to go about the business, he consoled himself for the next week or two with whatever fantasy outcomes to the situation his imagination could contrive. Such as: Mattachich jumping off a high building and lying crushed on a pavement below. Mattachich stricken by a swiftly developing cancer. Mattachich caught red-handed committing a heinous crime—raping one of the maids at the Villa, trying to burgle one of the other villas nearby, passing on a forged banker's draft. The French police arresting Mattachich, throwing him into jail, banishing him to Devil's Island, returning him in chains to Austria. Better still, guillotining him. Louise shipped back to Belgium and given a modest pension and a house in the country, Philipp never to see or hear from her again.

None of these desirable events occurred. Instead, the retired police officer whom Bachrach had sent down to Nice with instructions to find out everything he could about the couple's doings telegraphed Vienna with some unexpected news. It appeared that Mattachich and Louise, accompanied by her lady companion, the Baroness Fugger, had suddenly left Nice and that nobody knew where they had gone.

What should he do now? the man asked. Remain where you are, Bachrach telegraphed back, and keep your eyes and ears open. Which he did for the next couple of weeks, to no purpose whatever.

❖

In the end, the flight of Mattachich and Louise from Nice turned out to be as pointless as the arrival there of Bachrach's hireling. And more pitiful in its sheer inefficiency. They and Marie Fugger had gone to Paris where under assumed names they holed up in a hotel for a few days. From there they set out for London. Louise had finally succumbed to Mattachich's urging that she should pay a visit to Queen Victoria and ask her for a handout. After all, she was empress of India, monarch of the greatest empire the world had ever seen, Louise's cousin of sorts, and if she did not turn to her now when would she ever be able to do so? They had nothing to lose. So why not aim as high as she could? Why not go to the very top of the tree? Victoria had celebrated the silver jubilee of her coronation just a year before. She could not have long to live.* She was as rich as Croesus in her own right, probably as rich as Leopold—though her money, being "older," drew less attention to itself. What better use could she make of a tiny part of her fortune than to bail out her not-so-distant kinswoman?

That was as far as his reasoning went. Louise's understanding of the queen went further, which explained her skepticism about the project. The two women had met perhaps a few times before, and the impression Victoria had left with Louise was not that of a softhearted, impulsive creature who would open her purse for a pair of runaway adulterers, rule breakers, and social outcasts. Far from it. "How shall I describe the witheringly cold gaze with which Victoria scrutinized her family?" Louise wrote later. "Any lapse of taste in appearance, the slightest lapse in manners, was immediately noticed. . . . Then she wrinkled her nose and pressed her lips together, while her face turned even redder in hue than it ordinarily was."†

---

* Victoria died less than three years later, in her eighty-second year.

† Louise makes some respectful references to Victoria's "air of great distinction" and her "imposing presence"; yet her description of the great queen is filled with malice. "[She] was very short, and had a very red face, and was corpulent to a degree that made her look almost deformed." She slyly describes the queen's famous manservant, John Brown, as "that devoted Scot whose doings occupied such a prominent position in the *Court Circular,* and who like others of his kind . . . belongs to an unpublished page in the history of royal courts." With her tongue in her cheek, she goes on to wonder whether his eagerness to curtail the evening drives which he took with Victoria "sprang from a fear of catching rheumatism or a cold that might have affected his health and limited his capacity to fulfill his duties to the queen . . . I simply cannot say" (Louise, *Autour,* pp. 207–208).

Still, what did they have to lose by trying? Mattachich had asked. Once they got to London, however, they discovered that they had their self-esteem to lose. Or their esteem in each other's eyes, which amounted to much the same thing. In London, in their hotel suite, they had one of their rare shrieking, blaming, mutually insulting rows. Why? Because they hadn't done their homework. On the day of their arrival, they learned, Queen Victoria had left London for Nice—of all places. Her ferry and theirs had actually passed in the English Channel. How shaming this was! How farcical! What a revelation of their unfitness for the life they had tried to live! And when their anger had died down, and her tears had dried and the angry tremor of his hands had abated, they were left to stare at the ashes of their own expectations and accomplishment. What next? Where now?

For the moment, nowhere. They stayed on in London. They tried their luck with the notoriously high-living Prince of Wales, the future King Edward VII. But he, being permanently in hock to his bankers and having heard of their troubles, took care to avoid meeting them. Under assumed names they booked for a passage to the United States but never got as far as paying out the money, let alone traveling to Liverpool and setting foot on the boat. For Louise in particular it was a journey too far— a turn toward a country and a future too difficult for her to imagine. Yet she halfheartedly urged Mattachich to leave: to escape from "this mess" and start a new life. Her suspicion that he knew something dire about their position which she did not know had deepened since she had witnessed his falling-out with Fuchs; but even now she did not dare to ask him what it was. It was enough for her to label their situation as "this mess," to tell him that it was *her* mess ultimately, not his, since all their debts were in her name, and to assure him that nothing too terrible would happen to her because of them. When everything had settled down he could come back to Europe. Or she would join him on the other side.

His answer was unwavering.

"I said *never.* It's a word with only one meaning. Only death can change it. And I don't want to shoot myself, yet."

So they turned and went back to Paris with a strange sense of relief, almost of elation. Nothing had gone right for them; but at least they had escaped America.

❖

That mood did not last long. When they got back to Baroness Fugger, whom they had left behind in Paris, they found her holding a letter from Ozegovich. It warned them on no account to return to Nice. Though they had tried to leave the resort as unobtrusively as possible, word of their departure had got around instantly. As a result yet more creditors were besieging the Villa, many of them armed with distraining orders that magistrates up and down the Riviera and farther afield were distributing to all comers. One of the claimants was also insisting that he carried a warrant for the arrest of Mattachich, on the grounds that he had taken with him items of jewelry that had been in Louise's possession "on approval" merely. Journalists from French, German, Austrian, and Hungarian newspapers were infesting the place: badgering neighbors, creditors, servants, even street sweepers for whatever bits of gossip could be sucked out of them. They would "run amok," Ozegovich wrote, if the couple reappeared.

Mattachich telegraphed his friend to close the house down completely, discharge any servants who still remained, and set out as soon as he could for the Ozegovich home in Breznica, Croatia.* Not forgetting to take with him whatever valuables, clothes, and items of furniture he could save from the wreck. The princess would join him there. Of his own movements Mattachich said nothing. Yet when the train carrying the princess arrived at Breznica, he was with her. So was Marie Fugger.

In his *Memoiren* written six years later, Mattachich offers a lofty reason for his decision, which he took at the last moment, to accompany Louise on her journey to his native country. "Now I had just one aim in mind: to

* See Holler, *Ihr Kampf,* p. 101.

get back to Austria in order to give not the slightest hint of plausibility to the idea that I or the princess wished to evade our responsibilities."[*] Even in retrospect it was impossible for him to confess to the banal truth—they had no money and hadn't been able to find anyone to shelter them in any other European country. (The last beseeching letters sent by Louise before their flight from Nice had been addressed to Kaiser Wilhelm of Germany and to the much-hated Schleswig-Holsteins. Both parties had failed to reply.) Still less could Mattachich confess that something more compelling—perhaps more shaming—than the lack of an alternative was drawing him back to Croatia. Initially he had intended Louise to be "stored" anonymously in backwoods Breznica, until he found a place of refuge for them both somewhere in western Europe. But when the time came for Louise to leave, the thought of being left behind, on his own, was more than he could face. Equally, the thought of her alone in Croatia had no appeal. Croatia was his place, not hers. It was his home. At this moment of crisis it was where he wanted to be. In almost childlike fashion he found himself thinking he would be safer there. Home. Home. Look how he had loved his homeland during his last visit, longed for it even while there, when he had stood at the window of his room, those wintry nights in the Schloss, and gazed out at the white snow and brilliant stars and the embedding darkness around them.

Louise was agreeable to traveling to Breznica and was delighted that he would be accompanying her. She was in a docile mood. She knew their situation to be bad however it was viewed, and in more ways than she could understand. But since everything around her was so plainly beyond her control, it seemed reasonable to her that she should not be blamed for any of it, and that sooner or later it would become obvious to other people that she and Mattachich needed help in sorting matters out. Therefore help was bound to arrive eventually. This irrational conviction endowed

---

[*] Mattachich, *Memoiren* (p. 33). The fact is, they did not go "back to Austria" as Mattachich writes; they went to Croatia, admittedly then a *Bannat* (governorate) of the Habsburg empire. But it is odd to see Croatia being referred to simply as "Austria" by someone who is himself a Croatian.

her with a kind of calm that was to be useful to her during the weeks, months, and years that followed.

❖

Let a fortnight pass. Imagine Bachrach at the center of things once again. Bachrach receiving messages from various sources about the arrival of the runaways in Croatia. Bachrach convinced that, with the couple inside the borders of the empire, an opportunity "to resolve the problem" will soon arise. Bachrach traveling to Croatia to spy out the land and establish the truth of the reports reaching Vienna about what is happening there. Bachrach finding things to be even worse than he had expected.

Now imagine Bachrach on his way back to Vienna, turning over different plans but postponing a decision on any of them. His first duty is to inform Philipp of what he has seen and heard in Croatia. Imagine Philipp listening attentively to his report and suggesting that it be presented also to various officials from the Hofburg. This time it is essential, though, that the Lord Marshal be among them.

Fine. Here is the Lord Marshal, a more detached, diminished-looking creature than his title might suggest, though his pale blue gaze is confident enough in dealing with all comers (the emperor aside). The group from the Hofburg meets Philipp, Choloniewski, and Bachrach in the same room in the Saxe-Coburg palace as on the previous occasion. Bachrach begins. Point One: He has found Mattachich and Louise living not in Breznica, as he had heard before his departure, but in the Schloss Lobor, where they have taken refuge after falling out with members of the Ozegovich clan and offending other people in the neighborhood, mostly because of Mattachich's aggressively erratic behavior. Two: Count Keglevich, Mattachich's stepfather, is no longer residing in the Schloss, having left as soon as he heard that Mattachich and the princess intended to move in there. Three: Whether legally or not, the house is now in the hands of Countess Keglevich and her estate manager, Fiedler by name, with whom she appears to have close relations. Four: The countess is silent and unapproachable but apparently unabashed by the change in her domestic arrangements. She shows no particular warmth toward her son or his companion but is evidently loyal to them. So she will be of no use to what Bachrach calls *our cause*. However, Bachrach has already reached an understanding with Fiedler. Five: The Schloss is kept constantly under guard, and the servants are under strict orders to admit no one without getting Mattachich's permission beforehand. Six: The position of Baroness Fugger—a widowed, childless, presentable lady of a certain age—is hard to assess. Outwardly she is loyal to the princess, but the tone of her voice and the look in her eye have suggested to Bachrach that she has a *tendresse* for Mattachich. Seven: Before his meeting with Mattachich, Bachrach is warned by Fugger that the man carries a revolver at all times and swears he will shoot the princess and himself if any attempt is made to take her away from him by force. Eight: The baroness also tells him that the princess appears to have no will of her own; she agrees with whatever Mattachich says and complies with what he tells her to do.

An unhappy picture, yes. But worse follows. When Bachrach and Mattachich finally meet, the latter greets him at the door of the Schloss with a gun in his hand. He brandishes it about and warns the lawyer he will kill the princess and himself before allowing her "to fall into the hands of her enemies." During this conversation, Bachrach takes it on himself to suggest that if Mattachich were to swear to leave the imperial territories instantly and on his own, never to return, unhindered passage abroad might be granted to him. (This offer is rejected, Bachrach primly reports to the group in the Coburg palace, with "barrack-room insults.") However, Mattachich eventually does give him permission to meet the princess privately. When he does so he is shocked by what he sees—her expression, her pallor, the clothes she is wearing, the state of her hair—despite the fact that Fugger and a maid are still in attendance on her.

Nevertheless, he puts to her the proposals he has been formally authorized to offer on Prince Philipp's behalf. She and he should jointly make application to the Viennese court for an uncontested divorce; they should approach her father for help in paying off her debts; she should hand over to her creditors whatever items of jewelry are still in her possession and return to the family those belonging to the Coburg collection. To all this the princess agrees, without appearing to pay attention to what is being said. Then she suddenly rouses herself to declare, "I have heard from my sister about those moneylenders' notes. I don't know who put her name on them. It is a mystery to me. That is all I have to say on the subject."*

❖

In neutral lawyerly tones, Bachrach delivers his report to the officials from the Hofburg. It is what he was born to do; or so he feels while doing it. And he is not quite finished yet. With a perceptible change of tone, he goes on to say something about himself that everyone there already knows. He is not a medical man. But as a layman he must confess that he came away from his meeting with the princess much alarmed about her mental condition.

"Let me put it starkly, gentlemen. You may think that Mattachich, with a pistol in his pocket and his threats of murder and suicide, is the more unstable of the two people we are dealing with. In my opinion he is not. I believe the princess's state of mind is more worrying than his. He is the planner, the actor, the striker of attitudes, the maker of demands; she is the follower. It is her apathy, her suggestibility, her subjection to his wishes that make her vulnerable to a degree I can hardly exaggerate. I'm afraid he has so strong a hold over her that she will do whatever he might command her to do. No matter how outlandish it might be. Or self-destructive."

---

* For Bachrach's visit to Schloss Lobor, see Holler, *Ihr Kampf*, pp. 107–114. About that visit—and about Bachrach himself and those employing him—Mattachich writes in his *Memoiren* (p. 37): "I could not suspect that so much wickedness could be found within such a harmless-looking little man. Later I would see how this person, in the service of his "higher clientele," would cold-bloodedly destroy all lesser mortals who stood in his path. All doors were open to him . . . and it was grotesque to observe how sycophantically everyone from the loftiest general to the most recently discharged soldier played his part according to the signals given them from 'above.'"

At this point Bachrach produces his trump card. It is a phrase that had occurred to him on his lengthy train journey across the flat, green, unfenced plains of Hungary. (A route, as he knew, laid out for political and strategic reasons, not to oblige an impatient lawyer.) Lulled by the rhythmic rattle and sway of the train and the slow circular motion of the view outside his window, where newly emerged ribbons of wheat turned now glossy, now matte, as wind and sun determined, and villages of moss-smudged tiled roofs half hid themselves among clusters of trees, while apparently immobile streams shone in the distance—lulled by all this into a state of abstraction, even trance, there slid into his mind a few words that suddenly gave him the key to the situation in the Schloss. They would also settle the outcome of the discussions that lay immediately ahead.

"We can't have another Mayerling."

❖

Now, saying the words out loud for the first time in that somber overblown room in the Coburg palace, he heard an intake of breath from the others and saw the expression on their faces change. Even Philipp, to whom he had said the phrase the day before, looked down, unable to meet their eyes. He, Philipp, knew far better than anyone else there what the words meant. He had been among the very first to come upon the grisly scene at the original "Mayerling."

Not that the people around the table needed any further prompting. They understood Bachrach at once.

And you? How much do you know about Mayerling? How much do you need to know?

Not all that much, actually. Once it had been merely the name of a building used by the Crown Prince Rudolf as his hunting lodge. Then it was transformed into the name of an event that "shook the empire," as people said. During the lifetime of Rudolf's parents it would evoke a self-renewing catastrophe every time they thought of it. To the public at large (and later to novelists, playwrights, and movie producers) it would remain a topic of ghoulish fascination for a century and more. For it was at Mayerling that Rudolf—the only son of Franz Josef and Elizabeth, husband of Princess Stephanie, brother-in-law of Louise, heir to the thrones of Austria, Hungary, and the Habsburg lands—there Rudolf had killed his latest mistress, the infatuated eighteen-year-old Mary Vetsera, before killing himself.

He was handsome, unstable, liberal-minded, gonorrheal; she, eagerly complicit in her own immolation. With a bullet through her skull she lay in the bed the couple had shared earlier; he sat in an armchair nearby, his pistol still in his hand. That was how they were discovered in the morning by the manservant and the two companions Rudolf had invited to join him for a weekend hunting party. One of these was a Count Hoyos, who is of no interest here; the other, Prince Philipp.

The grief that gripped Rudolf's parents at the news is probably best left unimagined. For the officials of the Hofburg it was a cue for sorrow too, but also for lies and panic. Initially they claimed that Rudolf had died of a stroke, then of a heart attack; finally they admitted that he had died by his own hand "during an attack of insanity." (Which enabled the church to give him a full funeral mass.) They also made hysterical attempts to suppress the fact that two bodies, not one, had been found in the hunting lodge, and thus to erase entirely Mary's part in the drama. Dispatched by the authorities to the murder scene—a gaunt rambling structure, more like a monastery than a place of recreation—two of her uncles dressed her corpse in coat and hat, "marched" it out of the building into a hired cab, and kept it seated upright between them until it was delivered for speedy and secret burial in Heiligenkreuz near Vienna.*

The attempts at a cover-up—the macabre charade with Mary's body not least—inevitably had the opposite effect from what had been intended. Nothing remained hidden; everything was distorted by rumor.

---

* Since then Mary's grave has been dug up several times: by Russian troops in 1945, among others, and some years later by an obsessed furniture merchant named Helmut Flatzelsteiner (see *Last Ride to Heiligenkreuz*, www.xs4all.nl).

It was said that Mary had tried to poison him and that he had shot her in revenge for her treachery before doing away with himself; that the couple had succumbed to the *fin-de-siècle* decadence and neurasthenia that godless people of the middle and upper classes were supposedly falling victim to on all sides; that the double suicide was a cover for a diabolically cunning political assassination (with the death of Mary serving as nothing more than camouflage for the conspirators); that the Jesuits were behind it all, or the Freemasons, or right-wing elements of the Austrian army who detested Rudolf's social and political views. (If the Jews were excluded from the list of suspects it was only because he was known to be strongly philo-Semitic in sentiment—a fact that was held against him by his ene-mies.) Others blamed his state of mind on an unsympathetic father, who had just sacked him from his job as Inspector General of the empire's armed forces; some blamed his wife, the coldhearted Stephanie, who loathed him for having infected her with the disease that was rotting his mind and body; some his mother, for passing on to him an obsessional self-destructive streak that she had never made any attempt to hide.

And so on. A few years after the event, the Mayerling buildings were converted into a Carmelite convent at the wish of, and with an endow-ment provided by, Franz Josef. In the mind of the public, however, noth-ing could lift from the place and its name the taint of scandal, melodrama, political intrigue, and the allure of an orgasmic suicide.

❖

Another Mayerling? With yet another daughter of King Leopold caught up in it too?

Once said, the phrase could not be retracted. Once perceived, the dan-ger appeared imminent. Of course this jumped-up Mattachich creature, this self-appointed Croatian "count," would be thinking of it! How could such a self-dramatizing scoundrel *not* relish seeing himself as a compan-ion and competitor to the crown prince; not welcome the idea of inflict-ing another blow on the house of Habsburg; not dream of winning a degree of posthumous fame for himself and his royal whore comparable to that of Rudolf and his besotted victim and collaborator, Mary Vetsera?

In the emperor's eyes the vileness and vulgarity of the threat were equaled only by its cruelty. On hearing from his Lord Marshal what had been said at that meeting at the Coburg palace, Franz Josef reacted by immediately sending him back to Philipp with the message that "the highest authority" agreed to the use of "any means" that would bring about the physical separation of Mattachich and Louise and thus prevent so horrific and degrading an end to the affair between them. All organs of state were to cooperate fully with those engaged in carrying out this task; the requests they made, whatever these might be, were to be unhesitatingly fulfilled.

Franz Josef had no compunction in issuing these orders. However, he did attach two conditions to them. The first was that the separation between the parties be carried out as discreetly as possible. The second was, simply, "No bloodshed!" What the emperor wanted was to avert another Mayerling, not to produce one. How could that be done if lives were lost once again? How much more disgrace and humiliation could the family bear? So he repeated the two key words several times, lifting an aged forefinger at each repetition, before dismissing his high-ranking official with nothing more than a brief sideways movement of the head.

CHAPTER SEVEN

ALMOST FROM THE MOMENT LOUISE AND MATTACHICH crossed the border into Croatia, he realized that their return to his native country was a mistake. The fantasy that once there they would somehow find a solution to their problems disappeared as soon as the country itself became a reality. In backwoods Croatia they were as deep in debt as ever, in greater danger of arrest than they had been before, and dependent on others for their accommodation. Everyone from the *Banus*—governor—of Croatia downward knew where they were, the newspapers in Agram included. They both had to submit to the humiliation of being transformed from Ozegovich's patrons to his beggarly lodgers; and Ozegovich's wife (his platonic wife, since she and her husband were barely on speaking terms) made no secret of her resentment of their presence.

Nevertheless, she asked neighbors from miles around to come and goggle at this notorious couple, and encouraged them night after night to drink too much and to pester the newcomers with unwanted questions. Formerly an actress, Eleana Ozegovich was a tall, slender woman with long arms that hung from her shoulders in a curiously inert, sexually provocative manner. She also had a round chin and baby-blue eyes and gave herself airs when merely walking across a room—arms dangling, hands dangling, pointed shoes turning out at every stride. When no neighbors were present she herself took up the role of inquisitor and hint dropper and did it crudely too. "Why don't you tell us what *really* happened? . . . You know *so much more* about that money business than all those stupid people in Vienna. . . . Last time I was there people were talking about *nothing* else," and so forth. Eventually, this nagging produced the effect she was perhaps seeking. One evening Mattachich snarled at her that he'd had enough, she had better fucking leave him alone. At that point, both husband and wife turned on him. Who did he think he was? They owed him nothing; he was a guest in their house, he was nobody's boss here; everybody knew what he'd got up to with those moneylenders; and so on. It ended with the two men challenging each other to a duel with swords, pistols, stones, bottles, who cared; yes, now, outside the house, yes, in the bloody dark, why not? He, Mattachich, couldn't miss anything so big and fat while Ozegovich swore to God that he'd just aim at the smell. . . .

By that time the women were in tears. Louise was clinging to Ozegovich and Eleana to Mattachich, with Marie Fugger going from one pair to the other, pleading with the men to shake hands. Which they refused to do—before staggering upstairs to bed.

So they had to leave. After an exchange of telegrams, the Mattachich party went to Schloss Lobor. This was something Mattachich had hoped to avoid. Keglevich had made it plain that he wanted to have nothing to do with the runaways, and in any case Mattachich's pride made it difficult for him to run home to his mother. But he had nowhere else to go. When they arrived at the Schloss they learned that Keglevich had left as soon as he heard they were coming. Mattachich also found his mother and Fiedler, the estate manager, on such close terms he had to wonder if Keglevich's departure hadn't been imminent anyway.

❖

All this took place before Bachrach's visit to the Schloss; by the time the lawyer arrived, Mattachich's attitude to his situation and Louise's was both more settled and more desperate. He now had a trick up his sleeve—or in his pocket—that freed him from fear of the actions and judgments of others. If he and Louise were attacked, as he put it, he would shoot her and then kill himself; it was as simple as that. To show how serious he was, he carried his revolver with him at all times by day and kept it at night on the cabinet beside the bed.

These threats succeeded in alarming everyone around him, his mother and Louise aside. His mother did not believe he would go through with it—and said so—which made him watch his tongue in her presence. Louise on the other hand did believe him and was unperturbed. Even before leaving Nice she had told him that she was as ready to die with him as Mary Vetsera had been with Rudolf. ("Do you think that little tart loved Rudolf more than I love you?") The two of them had even taken to playing murder-and-suicide games together in the privacy of their bedroom. He would empty the chamber of the gun in front of her, put its muzzle to her temple, and pull the trigger. To his delight, Louise sometimes collapsed theatrically in her chair after the resounding metallic smack of the hammer; sometimes she just waved her pseudo-murderer away like an importunate waiter. Then he would hold the gun to his own head and repeat the performance. Each time he carefully reloaded the pistol and put it back in his pocket or on the cabinet. Since they were going to die anyway, sooner or later, why should they not rehearse doing so on their own terms? Take comfort in the thought of the disappointment they would inflict on their enemies?

And if they were to die soon, what then? He was a materialist, a nihilist. He believed that all the meanings people gave to their existence were nothing more than illusions that were necessary to them. "Necessary" because humans simply couldn't live without trying to find meaning in the world around them—which wouldn't exist *as a world* if they were not there to think of it as such. "Illusions" because not one of the meanings they proclaimed could be justified by anything outside the words used to express it. Louise, by contrast, insisted that she still thought of herself as a Catholic, though a very bad one. A world so complicated, she argued, could not have just happened; it had to have been made by a Creator with a purpose in mind. And what was that purpose? He had to make himself known to mortals almost as intelligent as himself, who would be capable of recognizing and responding to him. Then, if they deserved it, he would take their souls back into his own. If not, goodbye.

"Poor, lonely God," Mattachich teased her. "He needs us to talk to. Us, of all people!"

Conversations of this sort made them feel refreshed, even virtuous; they helped to renew their attachment to each other; it wasn't all money and defiance and passion between them; they were soul mates too. (Especially now that physical passion was failing them, and the time Mattachich spent alone with the faded yet fine-featured Marie Fugger, with her pale lips, watchful hazel eyes, and heavy head of hair, was a topic he and Louise never discussed.) In the mornings Mattachich got up early and in a bizarre parody of his habits as an army officer inspected his guards—pairs of household servants or men from the estate farms equipped with shotguns—whom he had conscripted and kept posted in shifts for a full twenty-four hours a day around the Schloss. He genuinely feared that *they,* the authorities in Vienna or their minions in Agram, would mount a raid on the house and try to snatch Louise from him. The purpose his guards would then serve was clear in his mind. He wanted them outside the house not because he dreamed of fighting off the armed forces of the empire but to give himself and Louise time to cheat their enemies of victory.

After exchanging words with the men, he would walk across the fields, if it was a fine day, enjoying sole possession of the gleaming world around him: grass dew-heavy; soil breathing out the last of its wintry odors; meek, inexorable sunlight creeping into furrows and ditches; green leaves unfurling day by day; the occasional copper beech and early sycamore mimicking for reasons of their own the ruddy colors of autumn. How remote and veiled, unimaginable really, that autumn seemed, waiting for him on the far side of yet another summer he might never live to see. Birds wheezed, whistled like urchins, snipped at the air with their scissorlike beaks, while down below crows did their ungainly double-legged hop about the fields. Then he would turn back to the house for breakfast, which he had alone with his mother. Louise, always a late riser, usually ate hers with Marie Fugger from trays sent upstairs. After what had gone on in their previous resting place—the drinking, shouting, gambling, shooting for fun into the night, punctuated with tantrums from Eleana—Mattachich was grateful to his mother for the restraint she had shown in greeting her unexpected guests and taking care of them subsequently. Not flustered, not reproachful, not overawed, not indecently curious: just businesslike. She knew they were in trouble, deep trouble—everyone knew it—but she was too proud and too considerate to press him to speak of it. So he did not.*

And to think of a woman like his mother chucking herself away on this Fiedler! (If that was what she was doing.) It was a mystery to him, but he was careful not to let her know how he felt about the man. There was a kind of truce between mother and son: if she did not ask him about money or forged documents, he asked no questions about the departure of Keglevich and his replacement by Fiedler. However, when he was alone with Fiedler, a stout, shifty, self-important fingerer of his graying beard, the two men wrangled about any idiotic subject that came up between them—the correct names and social ranking of regiments, the derivation of words, varieties of apples and cherries, the training of dogs. Fiedler made no attempt when alone with Mattachich to hide how much it irked him to have his unlikely triumph with the countess trampled over by these fugitives; nor his distaste at the intruders' carrying on as if the

---

* In fact, both Louise and Mattachich remained remarkably reticent on the subject of the forgeries to the end of their lives. In her autobiography, Louise devotes a dozen enigmatic lines of a 250-page book to the subject that had occasioned so much suffering to herself and Mattachich. "My signature was well and truly my own," she writes *(Autour,* p. 230). "That was why I had to be silenced. My sister's signature, added later, was a forgery—but perpetrated by whom? And why? I was not permitted to ask such questions. . . . Count Mattachich knew nothing about these bills and of the use made of them." For his part, Mattachich insists in his *Memoiren* that the forged signatures were added to the promissory notes after they had passed out of the princess's household, and makes a general nod at the Daszynski thesis about them. His only other suggestion appears in a formal statement (quoted in Holler, *Ihr Kampf,* p. 178), in which he claims the forged signatures to have been the work of Dr. Barber, Louise's lawyer. He offers no reason, however, why the lawyer should have done something from which he could draw no benefit and which would be professionally so damaging to himself.

entire household was at war with the *Banus* and everyone else in the empire. Sentries, if you please! Shotguns!

What Mattachich did not know was that at the end of Bachrach's visit to the Schloss, Fiedler had waylaid the visitor at a point out of sight from the house. Standing under a clump of trees by the side of the chalky road, the two men came to an understanding. Fiedler assured the visitor of his unshakable loyalty to the crown and offered to keep the *Herr Regierungsrat* informed of everything that went on in the Schloss. In return, Bachrach gave him the address of a colleague, a lawyer in Zlatár, Tonkovich by name, with whom he should get in touch when he had something to report. His services would not be forgotten, Bachrach assured him, when this "unfortunate business" was finally cleared up.

❖

Now imagine yourself on your way to Agram, several weeks later, immured in a carriage with Mattachich and Louise. A cheerless afternoon. Rain falling heavily at intervals. Wind moving the clouds about and draping them at random over hilltops. Trees going spectral in the mist and emerging in fragments from it. Patient cattle, their hindquarters turned to the wind, tolerating what they cannot change. All this accompanied by the elaborate music of a horse-drawn carriage traveling on a wet highway—grindings, squeakings, slappings, rumblings, with an occasional splash or squelch in addition. Look at the coachman on his perch outside, his green overcoat almost blackened by the rain, falling directly on him or shaken in spatters from the brim of his tall hat, while Louise, Mattachich, and Marie Fugger are seated within, behind blurred glass and padded carriagework. Marie sits with her back to the driver, facing the other two; all three have traveling rugs over their knees and are trying to sleep. They have spent the night in Breznica, chez Ozegovich, which is why they are now catching up on sleep lost the previous night.

The visit had been something of a kiss-and-make-up affair, by intention anyway, after their ruinous previous stay in the household. Subsequently, neither side had communicated with the other until, to his surprise, Ozegovich received a note from Mattachich in which he wrote that he, Louise, and Marie Fugger were leaving shortly for Agram and were wondering if they could spend a night in Breznica on the way. He had some questions to ask of his "old friend and comrade-in-arms." Ozegovich responded in equally friendly fashion, though on one subject his mind was made up. Should he be asked to perjure himself when Mattachich was put on trial—which he had no doubt was going to happen sooner or later—he would not do it.

But that, he learned, wasn't the reason for the visit. Mattachich had received a summons from the headquarters of the Thirteenth Uhlans in Agram, addressed with the utmost punctilio to "the on-extended-absence-from-duty lieutenant." The letter commanded him to appear in the city for medical examination and reregistration, as the period of leave granted to him had expired. Had Ozegovich received such a document? That was what Mattachich wanted to know. The answer was no, nothing of the kind had come Ozegovich's way. After a silence, he added that if he were Mattachich he wouldn't answer the summons. It smelled fishy to him. Why after all this time was the regiment so curious about his fitness to serve? Even if he hadn't had—you know—question marks hanging over him.

Mattachich was disappointed, and it showed. "Christ! I've had two letters from the *Banus*—if you please!—telling me to report to the prefect in Zlatár and I've done bugger all about it. But this is different. It's my regiment. And yours. If I can't trust them to be straight with me, who in God's name can I trust?'

"Nobody," Ozegovich answered.

Another stare, another silence.

Mattachich groped in the inside pocket of his jacket and took out a folded letter, which he did not open but just shook in the air. "That's not the only letter I got from Agram this week. This is from some lawyer there. He tells me my stepfather's given him instructions. First of all, his lordship says I must get out of the Schloss or he'll call the police to chuck me out. It's his property, not mine. Or my mother's. Second, he's already written to some office in the capital telling them he's determined to cancel the order he made to adopt me. . . . Can he do such a thing? Who knows? I must find out while I'm there." Mattachich put the letter back in his pocket and went on as if he had not changed the subject at all. "Now you say the regiment's also plotting against me. I just don't believe it. I can't. We took an oath at the passing-out parade; we'd be faithful to one another to the end. Remember? *Bis in den Tod.* One by one we said it, and then we shouted it together. Now you tell me it means nothing? That they're double-crossing me, just like everyone else?"

Ozegovich did not notice the implied slur in what Mattachich had just said. He saw in the man's eye the hunger to believe and heard the obstinacy in his voice. So he kept silent.

"Anyway," Mattachich said, conceding defeat, or at least the possibility of it, his hope now indistinguishable from despair, "the princess will be with me. They won't dare do anything to me as long as we're together."

The rest of the evening they spent drinking. The women in the house joined in. All went peacefully, and all went on for too long.

❖

The carriage slowly making its way toward Agram now comes to a halt at a roadside inn. The passengers get out to relieve themselves and drink coffee. Soon they return to the vehicle and try once more to sleep—or to doze at least, feeling their bodies shake to the rhythms of the carriage, constantly hearing the noises from below and around them for what they really are and also as what they are not: cries, musical notes, floorboards creaking under footsteps, human voices saying the same word over and over again. Then a real human voice intrudes; it is that of Mattachich. To his shame he has suddenly been seized by stomach cramps. Marie Fugger bangs on the partition between herself and the driver, and the carriage comes to a halt. Mattachich clambers out and hurries behind some bushes. Through the still-open door they hear retching noises. The two women exchange concerned glances. A silence follows. When Mattachich reemerges, the look of his rumpled clothes shows that retching is not all he has had to cope with. He is pale; his breathing is irregular.

"I don't know what it is," he says shakily, as people do at such moments. "I haven't been feeling right all morning. And all of a sudden . . . It must be something I ate last night."

He pulls his blanket over his head this time and huddles in his corner of the carriage. Pulling up the blanket has left his knees and ankles exposed, so Fugger puts her blanket over his lower limbs and Louise helps her to tuck it around him. He remains swathed in this fashion until the next emergency stop is made.

Their plan had been to be in Agram by nightfall, but the journey is slowed by the repeated stops they have to make. Only toward sunset does the sky perversely break and brighten spectacularly. Crucibles of fiery stuff are spilt in all directions, as if a new world is being smelted and fused up there. But within minutes the gushes of gold, bronze, and silver begin to curdle and go dark; the clouds thicken; the mist returns; the rain falls; night has begun. At last there is a change in the sound of the turning wheels beneath them. They have struck a fully paved road and entered the outskirts of the city. Revived by the imminent end of the journey, Mattachich pushes aside his cocoon of blankets and looks out the window. In a thin voice he assures Louise that he is feeling much better; it was just . . . something. Nothing.

Soon they will be approaching the Hotel Pruker on the city's main street, where the obliging Fiedler, on his last trip from the Schloss to the telegraph station, had booked rooms for them.

❖

In the end, Mattachich made things easier for his enemies than they could ever have hoped. That a man who had ignored a pair of summonses from the *Banus* should quixotically obey a call from his regiment was something Bachrach, who had been behind both initiatives, had hardly dared to believe. It had always been the call from the regiment, rather than that of the *Banus,* that he thought the better of the two options from his point of view; and that was the one Mattachich had chosen to obey. That he would also have had a helpful stomach upset beforehand was just pure luck; nothing else. By the time the couple had wearily gone to bed in their room and Marie Fugger in hers, plainclothes detectives were already on the watch in the hotel foyer downstairs; before dawn the next morning additional policemen had been posted in a coffeehouse across the road. Observing from a slightly greater distance were Bachrach, the local chief of police, the lawyer Tonkovich from Zlatár, and yet another lawyer. The particular rooms booked for the visitors had actually been chosen by the chief of police himself, who had been in touch throughout with Fiedler and Tonkovich and had called at the hotel and studied a plan of its layout well before the party from the Schloss was due to arrive.

Being on the spot, hearing all this, Bachrach began to believe for the first time that he had truly outgeneraled Mattachich. All the preparations he had been making in the name of the "highest authority" over the last few weeks—the telegrams and handwritten messages he had sent to the *Banus* and to handfuls of key officials in the army, the police, the civil service, and the railway system, as well as the time he had spent coordinating their replies—had not been wasted. But he could not afford to relax. Then one additional item of information was delivered to him from the helpful clerk at the hotel desk. As he was still feeling poorly, Mattachich had asked the regimental doctor to come to the hotel to carry out his examination, and an extra room upstairs had been hired for this purpose.

Perfect.

The ambush itself was carried out with more-than-military efficiency. The regimental doctor arrived and was directed to the room reserved for the examination. A few minutes after Mattachich joined him, the watching policemen and an army major rushed in through the unlocked door, seized the half-naked man, handcuffed him, and hurried him downstairs into a waiting landau. It was done in a moment. "So Mattachich was taken into custody without mishap," Bachrach telegraphed to Philipp that same day.*

Once the landau had gone around the corner, his party made for Louise's room. She was a woman and a princess, so there was no question here of handcuffs or of hustling her in a disheveled state across the hotel foyer and onto the pavement outside. But they were as determined as they had been with Mattachich to see the job through. First the lawyer Tonkovich was sent to knock on her door and call out his name, as it was known that Louise would recognize his voice and open the door to him— which she did. The others immediately followed him through the door. Confronted by this irruption into her bedroom of a handful of men, most of whom she had never seen before, the mixture of hauteur and apathy that was one of her specialties came to her aid. She refused to answer Bachrach's questions about who had slept in the rumpled second bed in the room, or whose night clothes lay on top of it. When asked if there were any weapons in the room, she pointed silently at the drawer of a bedside table and made no comment as Bachrach drew out the loaded revolver. She became agitated only after he told her that she was going to be taken back to the Coburg palace in Vienna. Nothing, nobody, she said fiercely, could force her to go back there or see her husband again. Bachrach then assured her that her wishes would be respected and she would not be compelled to do either. A maid was sent next door to tell Marie Fugger that she was needed. She came into the room, saw at once what was going on, and asked Bachrach if he had "approval of the highest authority" for what he was doing. Yes, he answered, the emperor

---

* Quoted in Holler, *Ihr Kampf,* p. 125. In pp. 123–126, Holler gives a detailed description of the arrest. Not surprisingly, Mattachich's account of the event (*Memoiren,* p. 41) is full of uncontrollable bitterness. Of Fiedler and Tonkovich's contribution, he writes: "They tried to consolidate my trust in them with their so-called good advice and their false concern for my welfare, with the diabolical intention of luring me into the net they had prepared beforehand. Should anybody ask me today for an example of complete turpitude (*Niederträchtlichkeit*), I would answer: the role that Fiedler and Tonkovich played then. And both today enjoy the privileges of respectable gentlemen!"

himself wished it. From then on she cooperated with the princess's captors, though she too refused to answer when Bachrach asked who had spent the night in the other bed in Louise's room.

Conscientious as ever in his master's service, Bachrach was busy looking for evidence that would be useful later, if Philipp were to sue for divorce. With this in mind, Mattachich claimed later, the lawyer snooped through the bedroom—"not omitting to bring the bedsheets into view, hoping to find on them telltale signs of acts of adultery. . . . That was the lowest of all the deeds that took place in the course of the morning. A common prostitute would not have been treated so! That the princess was not driven insane by this shameful event . . . but managed to stay remarkably calm is itself testimony to her psychological stability."*

❖

Within an hour or two, confident that she would not be compelled to meet Philipp or to return to his palace, Louise was in a two-coach special train that had been kept waiting at a siding outside Agram to carry her back to Vienna. Even before leaving the hotel she had been told that Mattachich was under arrest, an item of news that she received with much the same calm she had shown when the men had burst into her room. But she did insist on writing him a letter which she gave to Bachrach—and which its intended recipient never received. As the train drew nearer to

---

* See Louise, *Autour,* pp. 227–228; Mattachich, *Memoiren,* p. 49; and Holler, *Ihr Kampf,* pp. 126–127. Inevitably, Mattachich and Louise hated Bachrach for the rest of their lives, though Louise managed to strike a loftier note than her partner in taking a long-distance revenge on him. "In Vienna recently," she wrote, two decades after that morning in Agram, "I saw a miserable being, near-blind and on the edge of the grave, and the name of a Jewish lawyer—disowned by all respectable Austrian Jews—was murmured in my ear. He had been the agent, prompter, and close adviser of the vicious hatred that had tried so hard to destroy me. . . . Astonished, I asked myself, 'Do they understand. . . . Can they, without dreading what is to come, remember their past without remorse?'" (p. 222). In fact, the Viennese directories show that Bachrach survived for a good ten years after her sighting of this supposedly dying man (see, e.g., *Östereichisches Biographisches Lexikon, Band 1,* p. 42).

Vienna, Bachrach broke the news to Louise that since she had refused to return to the Coburg palace, her destination would be a sanatorium in Döbling, on the outskirts of the city. Shortly afterward he let her know that this sanatorium was actually a private lunatic asylum. A declaration that she was voluntarily committing herself for treatment in the institution was then given to her to sign, which she did. Apparently it occurred to no one there that since she had not "volunteered" to be brought to Vienna in the first place, her signature on the document was in itself something of a forgery.

Louise, Marie Fugger, and a specially hired nurse who had accompanied them on the train were housed in a small villa in the grounds of the institution. Four days later, Louise was put through a lengthy examination by an entire team of physicians and psychiatrists, the "keeper" of the asylum, Dr. Obersteiner, among them. Representatives of the Hofburg and of King Leopold were present in the next room, as well as the indispensable Bachrach. The only physical ailment the doctors reported was an outbreak of psoriasis vulgaris on various parts of her body.* They were agreed, however, that her psychological condition betrayed serious symptoms of "intellectual insufficiency" and "moral weakness." On these grounds they declared it necessary for her to be kept in strict seclusion and under constant observation in the asylum for the next six months. The task of supervising her during this period was assigned to Dr. Obersteiner.

❖

Philipp would have been better pleased with an outright declaration from the doctors, there and then, that she was insane; so would their imperial

---

* In writing of this medical examination (*Ihr Kampf*, pp. 128–129 and pp. 134–135), Holler, a medical doctor as well as a biographer, points out that one of the contemporary treatments for psoriasis was the administration of arsenic in the form of drops or pills. In high doses this treatment could in itself a produce a variety of psychiatric symptoms, "apathy" and "somnolence" among them.

majesties, Franz Josef of Austria-Hungary and Leopold of Belgium. That disappointment aside, however, everyone involved (apart from Louise) was satisfied with what had been accomplished. The danger of her having to appear in any court of law—in what Philipp feared would be "the most scandalous public proceedings imaginable"—had been averted. "In confining her," he wrote, "I have succeeded in preventing future disorders . . . though it has been difficult indeed to bring this about." He admitted that neither the public at large nor the lawyers representing Louise's creditors believed in the story of her mental illness; but, he went on, "I cannot permit Louise to appear before any trial by jury. . . . I cannot do it to my family." With his trademark mixture of helplessness and indignation he went on to grumble that "nothing will move Leopold; he will not lift a finger to help in the settlement of his daughter's debts."*

So much for the sentiments of Louise's enemies. As for Louise herself, twenty years later she described these events as follows

> *Thus I was suddenly kidnapped and found myself in a cell at the Döbling Asylum in the suburbs of Vienna. I was kept under constant scrutiny through a judas hole in the door. The window was barred. I heard screams and yells from outside. . . . I had been put in that part of the asylum in which those most severely ill were segregated. I saw a patient running around a little courtyard during an exercise period, throwing himself with terrible cries against a wall lined with mattresses. . . . I turned away, shocked and horrified, and flung myself down on the narrow bed. All I could do was put my head under the pillow, hoping to see and hear no more. But I could not quench my tears.*†

---

* Quoted in Holler, *Ihr Kampf*, p. 129. Leopold did eventually offer to send him the sum of 100,000 gulden, which Philipp dismissed as "alms I felt obliged to decline."

† Louise, *Autour*, pp. 228–229.

The next day, however, she asked for a piano to be brought to her "pavilion" in the grounds; soon afterward, one of the rooms in the house was turned, at her request, into a studio, complete with an ample provision of paint, canvases, pencils, and paper. The nurse who had traveled with her from Agram was replaced by a lady's maid, Olga Börner, who was to remain with her to the end of her life. And Marie Fugger continued to live in the villa until it was discovered that she was helping to sustain a secret correspondence between Louise in her asylum and Mattachich in his cell.*

How can the latter facts be reconciled with her account of the horrors accompanying her admission to the Döbling asylum?

Readily enough, if you are prepared to try. Imagine that both accounts of her reactions to what had happened to her are essentially true. Imagine that she was outraged *and* relieved to be confined. Humiliated *and* comforted, after the alarms and escapades of the previous months, to know that she would be living in the same place for the next half year. Degraded *and* gratified to know that she would not be asked to make any decisions about her future during that period. There is no need therefore to jump to the conclusion that what she wrote twenty years later was merely retrospective playacting. Without warning she had been snatched away from her lover, rushed across hundreds of miles, thrust behind high walls and locked gates, stripped of her rights in law (including the right to be prosecuted as well as to defend herself in a courtroom), and declared fit to reside only in a closed institution filled with demented strangers.

The stark truth is that any enforced confinement among sick, desperate, and self-torturing people is bound to be regarded—even by those who may be most in need of it—as in itself a form of torture.

So who can blame her if she later chose to remember just one side of the "bargain" that others had struck on her behalf?

---

* See Holler, *Ihr Kampf,* pp. 137, 146. Since the baroness was a German with a German passport, it was easy for the authorities to expel her from Austria.

❖

From the Pruker Hotel, Mattachich had been taken immediately to the detention barracks of the garrison in Agram. "Though I had offered no resistance," he wrote later, "the upstanding major who had carried out the arrest kept on telling me to keep my temper. I saw from his demeanor that he had been expecting to carry out a heroic deed and was disappointed that I kept so calm throughout."[*]

Since he had been arrested under military law, not the civil law of the empire, the authorities were not obliged to bring him to trial within a set period or even to tell him what charges he would eventually have to face. In other words, with both lovers consigned into limbo, Philipp and Bachrach could now gather at leisure whatever evidence they could find against Mattachich and await without misgiving the next psychiatric examination Louise would be put through. No wonder that Daszynski, the deputy who was eventually to bring the whole business to the attention of parliament, spoke of what was done to the lovers as an example of "court justice" or "royal justice"—arbitrary justice, that is—the justice of a despotism, not that of a state bound by its own laws.

For something like seven months, Mattachich was left in the garrison prison in Agram. Through its walls he heard the familiar sounds of military life going on without him, as if to remind him day and night of what he had lost. Lost in every sense, since he was not merely shut out of it, as of everything else that had made up his life, but because he was convinced that the army itself had betrayed him.

> *Five weeks passed {Mattachich would eventually write} before proceedings were put in hand relating to the offense—the forging of documents—for which I had ostensibly been arrested. . . . For the following six months, until December of that year, I was forced to travel through a world that was new to me: that of the Austrian system*

---

[*] Mattachich, *Memoiren*, p. 43.

of military justice, an atrocious institution about which the Austrian
public cares little or nothing and which is therefore left free to carry on
in its own way. I have felt the workings of this institution on my own
body. . . . And you, Austrian fathers and mothers, who have a caring
heart for your children {who will have to do their military service}, do
not believe the ministers when they tell you that reform is on its way,
because I know that it is not. *

By any standards, Mattachich's trial was a travesty. Once he had been informed of the charges against him, a further three months passed before he saw any of the evidence that had been gathered in Vienna. It was made available to him only in written form, so he had no opportunity to question witnesses before or during the trial. No lawyer was permitted to speak on his behalf at any time, for the trial was handled throughout by a military "auditor" who served simultaneously as prosecutor, defense counsel, and judge and who also had total discretion over the rights of the accused at every stage. The proceedings came to an end on New Year's Eve, seven months after his arrest, when he was instructed to put on full parade uniform—brought up specially from the Schloss—for his appearance before the panel that would pronounce judgment and sentence. He was taken into a chamber, a trumpet sounded, and the chairman of the panel (also in full parade uniform, as were his colleagues) pronounced him guilty and imposed on him a sentence of six years' imprisonment for his crimes. Chief among them, of course, was the forging of the signatures on the documents put before the court; lesser offenses included his sojourn abroad without the prior permission of the War Minister, his unauthorized extension of the leave of absence granted him, and his failure to respond to messages dispatched to him while absent from duty. No allowance was made for the seven months he had already served in prison,

---

* "I tell all those who committed this act of violence against me," Mattachich wrote, "that at no time did I weep, wail, curse my fate. All my anxiety and care were devoted to the thought of the unfortunate woman who had been robbed of her protector and given over helplessly to the brutality of her enemies" (*Memoiren.* p. 43).

and the sentence was made much harsher still by additional penalties attached to it; he was condemned to go without food on the fifteenth day of every calendar month; to sleep on a "hard bed" (*hartes lager*) on the twenty-fifth day of each month; and to spend the first and seventh months of each year of his sentence in solitary confinement. He was then stripped of his commission and his "noble status" (such as it was) and sent back to his cell to await immediate transport to the military prison in Möllersdorf, Austria.

Of his response to the sentence and his immediate return to the cell in the garrison prison he wrote later:

> *I could not help it, but the reading of the sentence made a strangely comic impression on me. Quietly and firmly I followed the duty officer to my cell. Once there, however, I fiercely tore off the uniform I had worn for eleven years and would never don again. In doing so I suddenly felt a terrible distress and an overwhelming wish to be alone. . . . These feelings lasted for seconds only. I had no time for sentimentalities; I needed composure and understanding. . . . Only with strength and calm would I be able to overcome the despair into which I was being deliberately driven.*[*]

---

[*] Mattachich, *Memoiren*, p. 54.

CHAPTER EIGHT

IMAGINE THAT A YEAR HAS PASSED since Louise and Mattachich were incarcerated.

How has it passed for them?

Slowly.

How have they been affected by it?

Badly.

Should you speculate about whose misery was the greater during their captivity?

No. You might as well ask whether he or she was the more sensitive to suffering, or which of them had the greater capacity to endure it. Or how to define the relationship between endurance and sensitivity in each case. Such questions merely lead to other questions, none of which can be answered.

What is certain is that the physical conditions Mattachich had to live under in the gloomy, muddy, rundown military prison in Möllersdorf were incomparably harsher than anything Louise had to put up with. But did he suffer more than she did, for that reason or for any other?

Credit them both with one remarkable achievement. In later years neither ever tried to claim a dismal precedence over the other in that regard.

❖

On his arrival in Möllersdorf, Mattachich was put into a dank cell, cold in winter, hot in summer, airless always. Except at mealtimes (twice a day, morning and evening, when he was led into the small eating hall for ex-officers) and during exercise periods (twice a day also, in thirty-minute stretches), and when he was detailed to do secretarial work in the prison offices, he sat in that cell. Coarse brick walls, a small shelf fixed to one of them, an equally small chest beneath the shelf, smooth cement floor, a fixed bunk, bedclothes, a bucket with a wooden lid, a barred window too high and too small to see out of. During the day the cell was half dark; during the night an oil lamp hanging out of his reach was kept constantly alight. Once a week he was permitted to go to the prison canteen to buy additional food, ink, paper, soap, and other such luxuries. On Sundays there were church services in the chapel, which he attended without believing a word of what was said or sung. On Sundays too, when they were ostensibly on their way to and from the chapel and most of the guards were off duty, the prisoners were allowed to dawdle about the courtyards into which the prison was divided. The yard that surrounded the chapel, prison offices, eating halls, and kitchens was a spacious paved affair, decorated with a few trees; the others, the one outside Mattachich's cell included, were rutted, potholed, and flanked by wretched buildings that could have been stables or cow barns rather than dwellings for humans. Except that the smell that came from the latrines was darker and more noxious than that of any stable. Only meat eaters could produce such a stink. Because Mattachich was an ex-officer he was permitted to employ another inmate, a former private soldier, to do his laundry and to scrub out his cell and bucket; this man also made deals on his behalf (cigarettes, illicit drink) among the captive rank and file in their cells in another yard on the far side of the complex.

Visitors were a rarity. His mother came once every three or four months, bringing with her the money he spent in the canteen; Ozegovich came somewhat less often. The latter's visit he brazened out; his mother's reduced him to tears, though he shed them only after she had left. He had no idea—he was never to know, since he never saw any record of how the investigation of his appeals had proceeded—that Ozegovich had given evidence against him during one such appeal. The other variations in his routine were the periodic extra punishments inflicted on him by the Auditor in passing sentence—deprivation of food on the fifteenth day of every month; sleeping on the cell floor with just his straw pallet beneath him on the twenty-fifth of each month; and, worst of all, the full month of solitary confinement he had to endure twice a year. He had been lucky to escape this on the day of his arrival (New Year's Day), but was compelled to go through it the following July, when he was isolated during meals and took his exercise under a silent guard. During that month the Sunday chapel services were forbidden to him too.

And that was it. In theory anyway. In practice things were looser, or soon became so. His position in the prison was ambiguous from the moment he entered it. His trial may have been held behind closed doors, but it had not been possible for his conviction and sentence, together with the simultaneous dispatch of Louise to a madhouse, to be kept hidden from the press; and the radical and socialist newspapers had made headline news of it. Bachrach's double coup in separating a pair of lovers who had overcome everything that should have kept them apart (social class, national origin, marital status) had been turned by these papers into a political issue: they treated it as a romantic escapade that happened also to illustrate the callousness, cruelty, and essential lawlessness of the Habsburg household, the "Coburg clique" in Vienna, and Louise's infamous father, Leopold. About the forgeries the left-wing press cared little. Compared with Leopold's systematic pillage of the Congo, Louise's so-called *Verschwendungslust* (spending mania) was a trifle.

Then the papers forgot about them. But the immediate result of the publicity given them was that on his arrival Mattachich had been greeted outside the prison by a crowd of curious and sympathetic onlookers. In Möllersdorf of all places! From then on, hagridden by a fear of further scandal, the authorities felt compelled to take special measures to make sure that this prisoner did not embarrass them further by trying to commit suicide. Hence the lamp kept burning all night in his cell; the irregular inspections made of him by day and night through the grating in his cell door; the strip searches he was put through before and after seeing visitors. Hence also the rough treatment he received from some of the guards, who were determined to let him know that they were not impressed by his "fame." But there were others who were gratified to be in charge of such a distinguished prisoner and liked to believe that somehow, somewhere, he or his lady friend had plenty of hidden money at their disposal. So who could tell what benefits might one day come to those who were obliging and helpful to him now?

Thus for Mattachich his consignment to such a rundown, rarely inspected institution turned out to be both a blessing and a curse. The filth and the forms of ill-discipline manifest everywhere—in a place that purported to be a military establishment—disgusted what he liked to think of as his soldierly soul. But could anything else be expected when prisoners, guards, and the epauletted slovens who supposedly commanded them were all rejects, idlers, no-hopers, drunkards, human rubbish and knew themselves to be so? The one exception was the deputy head of the prison, a tall, handsome, large-headed Czech captain named Navratil, whose bearing was not like the others' and who responded to Mattachich's air of self-regard and his efforts to keep himself trim even in such surroundings. Navratil was always correct in his dealings with this prisoner; he showed none of the curiosity or prurience that Mattachich encountered elsewhere; yet the two men knew they had an understanding with one another. In some of his more vulnerable moments (and there were many), it made Mattachich feel breathless, even shaky, to hear the captain address him not by his surname but by the rank he had previously held: *Herr Oberleutnant.* That they should have been trapped in such a dead-end place, though for different reasons, was a source of bitterness to them both; they never spoke of it, but each showed it to the other through his eyes and the movements of his lips; they heard it in the tone of their exchanges. So Mattachich was grateful but not surprised to find himself, before many months were out, working more or less full-time directly under Navratil in the prison office, an act of favoritism that was to have fateful consequences for Mattachich—and unfortunate ones for his benefactor.*

Finally, among everything else that tormented yet perversely helped to keep him going was his obsession with the unfairness of the trial that had condemned him. In his memoirs he presents himself as someone who had made up his mind to endure his imprisonment with a haughty stoicism, tempered only by concern for the welfare of his princess—and who then proceeded to do just that. In fact, from the start he showed up before the prison doctor with such a variety of ailments—head, stomach, heart, joints, eyes, lungs—that the doctor put him down in his notes as a hypochondriac and malingerer, while also remarking that what really ailed him was his "continual sleep-destroying (*schlafraubende*) preoccupation with his trial and his attempts to overturn its verdict."† Nor did Mattachich keep his complaints about the trial within the prison walls. Just days after arriving in Möllersdorf, he was busy with a preposterous long-winded statement for the War Minister in Vienna in which he demanded that Prince Philipp be stripped of his sword and army rank by a "military court of honor." The grounds put forward for this demand was that Philipp had behaved "like a blackguard" (*Schuft*) toward the Princess Louise. "His [Philipp's] feeling for his wife is that of a filthy animal. . . . He would have done better to have married a cook rather than a king's daughter. . . . I insist that her royal highness's companion, the Baroness Fugger, be summoned to give evidence on his scoundrelly behavior."‡

That was his opening shot. Subsequently, one elaborate appeal after another, addressed to a variety of destinations, emerged from the demi-

---

* In his *Memoiren* (p. 27), Mattachich acknowledges Navratil's "straight, honest gaze, his trustworthy speech and nature . . . which enabled me to recognize at once that he was the only official there who tried to fulfill his difficult duties by seeking to better the condition of the prisoners in his charge, rather than to demoralize them." However, he does not mention the trouble he got Navratil into later.

† Quoted in Holler, *Ihr Kampf*, pp. 173–174.

‡ The War Minister, a man with the amazingly appropriate name of General von Krieghammer ("war hammer"), put this overwrought item in his safe and did not look at it again (see Holler, *Ihr Kampf*, p. 175).

darkness of Mattachich's cell and was duly sent on its way. He wrote to the military court that had originally tried him in Agram; to a superior division of that court, which also sat in Agram; to the civil judiciary in Vienna responsible for gathering the evidence that had been used against him in the trial; to the central appeals court of the imperial army; and to the Lord Marshal in the Hofburg—of whose part in the plotting of his arrest and trial he had no inkling. With the exception of the statement addressed to the War Minister, his appeals were not dismissed out of hand. Mindful of the prisoner's special circumstances, the officials on whose desks they appeared gave them special attention. Evidence collected during the trial and subsequently was reexamined several times, and further witnesses were called on different occasions to give their testimony. However, no lawyer was allowed to plead on the prisoner's behalf (though one of Mattachich's appeals had been devoted to that point alone), nor was he ever invited to put questions in any form to new or old witnesses. Ultimately all his labors led to nothing more than the discovery of yet more material unfavorable to his cause. Some of it was on paper (for example, various manifestly untruthful letters and telegrams he had sent at the height of the crisis to Stephanie, Leopold, and Dora); some of it was given orally by people who took the opportunity to speak ill of him behind his back.*

After a year and more of this "sleep-robbing" activity—which went on, in silent or whispered fashion, not just when he should have been asleep but while he was exercising, eating, excreting, sitting on his bunk, lying during punishment periods on his pallet on the floor, and was translated into the penciled scribblings made in the darkness of his cell or

---

* Ozegovich stated on oath before one of these courts of appeal that he had never doubted Mattachich's guilt. Keglevich, Mattachich's ex-adoptive father, did his bit by telling the investigators that more than once he had had to settle debts his stepson had incurred without having the means or the intention of repaying them. A hitherto unknown couple, Bog by name, came forward to reveal that they were still waiting for Mattachich to repay a substantial loan they had made to him five years before. His wretched attempts to swindle out of their wages some of the servants he had hired in Paris and Merano were also put before the courts (see Chapter Five of this volume; also documents quoted in Holler, *Ihr Kampf,* pp. 55–56, 118, 180).

unobserved at his desk in the prison office—Mattachich had exhausted all possible avenues of appeal. He had also exhausted himself. He had no notion that the harder he worked on his documents the more hopeless the judges found them to be. To a lawyer's eye nothing is less persuasive than frenzy mixed with an amateur's notions of legal exactitude—and that was exactly the effect Mattachich achieved. In his case there was the additional element of the writer's (apparently) paranoid conviction that he was the victim of a conspiracy that had involved the organs and office-holders of the state, from the lowest to the very highest, the king-emperor himself not excluded. Plainly, the man must be mad. So the officials did what they believed to be their duty by the case and turned with relief to other matters.

Rebuff, contempt, failure, frustration, exhaustion, a renewed sense of his helplessness before an unassailable bureaucracy deaf and blind by nature to the pleas of a man trapped inside the battered walls of Möllers-dorf prison—that was all the return Mattachich appeared to get from his efforts. Yet those same efforts also helped to make his captivity in some sense more tolerable for him than it might otherwise have been. How could this be? Well, try to imagine how he would have survived *without* his obsession! Yes, it robbed him of his sleep, cleaved his aching head into two halves with a space for vertigo between them; made his heart thrash in his breast and his stomach vomit back the food he ate. But it also gave him an occupation. It was his cause, something to live for. It was a shield between himself and the people who surrounded him, in all their misery, imbecility, and sudden outbursts of violence or hysteria. Compared to the intensity of what was going on in his mind, his fellow prisoners and their guards often seemed wraithlike to him, inconsequential, existing for no better reason than to babble and gesticulate and distract him from his task.

(In later years, though, he would be surprised by how vividly he remembered some of them: the clothes they wore, the things they said, the inane grin of that one, the hobble-shuffle of this one in boots too big for him, the extraordinary habit another had of spitting not in gobs, as everyone else did, but in long jets like a cobra shooting out its venom, so that the front of each expectoration hit the ground before the last of it had left his lips. A thin man he was, with a thin mustache and something both pale and swarthy about his complexion, like a Sicilian or Maltese, thought Mattachich, who had never been to either island. And his fellow ex-officers: Kotze, who had embezzled mess funds; Helfrich, who had hauled shivering boy recruits into his bed; Wahl, who had sold army equipment on the side; the silent von Baalen, who had discovered God in his second year of service and thereafter neither gave orders to anyone nor obeyed those given to him.)

No, better any distraction than allowing people like these to take over his consciousness. Nor was that all his persistence in fighting this hopeless campaign did for him. It produced changes deeper yet. The more elaborately he developed his arguments, the more anxiously he drafted and redrafted them, the further he looked about for authorities to appeal to and studied the law books that, as a great favor, were passed on to him at rare intervals, so the more blurred and uncertain became his memory of what had actually happened, of what he had done, of the crime—if it was a crime—he had committed so long ago. As days, weeks, months, and years went by, his idées fixes erased whatever guilt or remorse he might have felt for the rashness that had actually landed him in this place and Louise in that place, for his memory of things as they had been was overtaken and eventually effaced by a fanatical logic that he could not have worked out beforehand and would never be able to undo subsequently.

It went like this. The trial that had found him guilty had been a mockery of how justice should be dispensed. That was indisputable. *Therefore he was innocent.*

It was as simple as that. It had to be so.

Convinced of his own innocence, he was now free to idolize Louise in an asexual, quasi-religious, Marylike manner. Mother, virgin, princess, blameless woman, she had given up everything for him. She was suffering for him just as he suffered for her. But it tantalized him that he could not summon up her full presence before him; he could remember her in nothing more than snatches, glances, turns of the body, single features. Only in occasional dreams, and even then for instants only, did she become immediate to him, the weight and warmth of her, the sound of her voice uttering a single word, her stockinged instep in the palm of his hand.

When he was driven out of need and despair to coax pleasure out of himself, he made it a matter of honor to try to banish from his mind all images of Louise. For that abject necessity, other women would do; he could call on other half-remembered shadows. If only they were here, any of them!

❖

Imagine lying awake in pain and discomfort, in the darkness, wondering how it is possible for a single night, a single hour, a single minute, to stretch itself out more and more even as you are trying to live through it, as if it exists for one purpose only: to drain from you your understanding of what past, present, and future mean. Imagine longing for day to break while knowing it will bring nothing that is not already as familiar and exhausting to you as your own action in pulling up your blankets and throwing them off, again and again, in search of an unconsciousness that departs the moment it arrives. Or so it seems. Imagine dawn coming at last to reveal to you that the night filled with motionless time has already fallen into a black void, leaving nothing behind it, nothing to mark it off from all the other nights exactly like those that preceded it and those still to come.

Nothing has changed. Time does not pass in this place. It cannot do so for it has nowhere to go. It exists only to prolong itself. It makes itself known on these terms only to prisoners—mad or sane, guilty or innocent—and the very ill.

❖

In one asylum after another, Louise found herself living in small holiday-like villas ("stationmasters' houses," she called them) with steep slate-tiled roofs, little gables, wooden eaves and shutters, a kitchen at the back and a garden of some kind in front. Set among trees and overlooking an unpaved roadway, each offered glimpses of the institution's main building, the smaller structures surrounding it, and of high encircling walls of stone or brick, usually with a triangular coping running along their top.

Louise's household consisted of herself, a lady companion, Maria von Gebauer, and the live-in maidservant, Olga Börner. A female cook came in daily, and a male servant worked on alternate days about the house and garden. Philipp never visited her at any of these places, but he met all the costs of her residence and paid for whatever special treatments were administered to the patient. These varied according to the beliefs of those appointed to look after her: hydrotherapy in one; electric shocks (milder than those administered to patients twenty years later) in another; cranial massage here; a diet consisting mostly of milk and finely milled raw root vegetables there. To people tactless enough to ask Philipp about Louise's welfare he invariably pointed out—his voice rising in pitch, his eyes shining with injury behind his glasses—that he was doing far more for her than that miserable, miserly father of hers, who took care never to go near her and did not contribute a penny toward her upkeep. Her mother, Marie Henriette, kept away too, but whether by her own choice or because she was compelled to do so by her husband, Philipp did not know. Princess Stephanie was another who had made no move in her direction. And Dora? Ditto.

In short, doctors and officials aside, no one ever called on Louise. No one wrote to her; or if they did she never received their letters. So what did she do with herself? Daydreams. Indolence. Bouts of frenzy. She returned to the habit that had partly slipped away from her, while she had wandered about Europe with Mattachich, of holding long conversations with herself: extensive reenactments and revisions of scenes that had taken place with others, or that she wished had taken place, or wished to believe would yet take place. New scenes from a week ago, old scenes from her childhood, scenes that magically opened with someone familiar walking through the trees to meet her: in all of them she took the leading part and emerged triumphant, sometimes pityingly or forgivingly so, more often scornful and vindicated, her rights as daughter or wife, princess or lover, fully acknowledged at last. Her rights as a patient too, often enough.

These reconstructions of her own history as she wished it to have been, or of a future she hoped to see, alternated with spells of vacancy and inertia or sudden enthusiasms. She took up learning languages, painting and drawing, botanizing among the plants and trees that grew on the grounds around her, singing lessons, cutting pictures from those newspapers she was allowed to see and pasting them into albums. Each fad was abandoned as abruptly as it was begun, though some would return later. She wrote long letters to members of her family, friends, and servants from the old days, as well to the editors of newspapers. In these she invariably demanded justice for herself and the imprisoned count. She gave them to her companions to post when they left the asylum grounds; they turned them over instead to the management, which made sure that not one of them ever reached its destination. She read novels and some poetry and tried to write poetry of her own, in both French and German, but was never satisfied with the results.

Fortunately, for her and for them, she had usually managed to get on well with the various women who had attended to her from childhood on, and this knack did not leave her now. They talked together, knitted, did bits of embroidery and tapestry; when the impulse took her, she told them about her childhood and her children and divulged intimate details of her married life and her adventures outside marriage (Mattachich's wonderful qualities of mind and soul being a favorite topic). She came out with memories of her horses and dogs and the underside of life in the Hofburg. She did not care what she revealed at these times and what kind of language she used in doing so.* In return, she expected an equal degree

---

* Some of the doctors who examined her wondered where "so highborn a lady" had learned the language they occasionally heard from her, especially when the subject of her husband came up (see Holler, *Ihr Kampf,* p. 148). Naturally, they chose to presume that she had learned it from Mattachich.

of candor from her interlocutors and believed she got it, which was seldom the case.

Not that either of her confidantes had much to confess. Each was of
different social background from the other, von Gebauer being obviously
of aristocratic descent, which Börner was not, yet they were also alike in
many ways: plain, rawboned, devout, unmarried, almost conventual in
manner. They learned to cope with Louise's outbursts of anger and malice
and her collapses into a surly apathy—though never with the refusal to
bathe that she would periodically announce and then adhere to for days
on end: until, she stank, simply. Then professionals from the medical staff
would come to narcotize her and wash her down limb by limb, crevice by
crevice, from her scurfy scalp to the grubby soles of her feet. Other spells
of noncooperation, some of them taking madder forms than others, gave
them almost as much difficulty. Overeating. Not eating. Cutting the buttons off the many dresses she kept in suitcases (and never wore) and stor-
ing them inside the many shoes she also never wore. Concealing (after
use) the sanitary cloths she needed (now only at irregular intervals). Swallowing sand or coal ash or leaves she plucked at random from whatever
plants she could get her hands on. Sucking paint from her brushes.

She was crazy, you see. Her first admission to the asylum may have
been "voluntary," but her confinement had been made official since then,
and she knew it. Therefore she was licensed to behave as extravagantly as
she pleased whenever she felt like doing so. Overwhelmed by boredom,
claustrophobia, and the need to strike back at her jailers, she would let
them know from time to time just how mad she could be.

❖

The definitive and final declaration that Louise was insane—for which
Bachrach and Philipp had been impatiently waiting—came from Baron
Richard von Krafft-Ebing (1840–1902), head of the department of psy-
chiatry at the University of Vienna. Thickset, with a heavy beard, strong
shoulders, and a firm line in high-buttoned waistcoats, the professor had

the direct unsmiling gaze of a man who had heard everything and whom nothing, therefore, would ever surprise. He had the voice to go with this degree of confidence too: not the booming baritone that a less self-assured and successful medicine man might adopt but its direct opposite— something soft and husky, a voice you had to attend to if you wanted to hear what was being communicated.

He knew, you see, how much you would lose if you didn't attend to him. Was he not the world's greatest authority on the twin subjects of madness and sexuality? The propagator if not the inventor of terms like "sadism," "masochism," "fetishism," "the twilight state," and various others that he had seen pass into common speech? Was not his *Psychopathia Sexualis: A Forensic-Clinical Study*—an immense compilation of case histories that had gone through edition after edition in the twelve years since it had first appeared—consulted and referred to in clinics and courtrooms all over the world? Had he not developed a theory of "moral degeneration" that explained the etiology of many if not all nervous diseases and sexual compulsions? Was it not clear now to all who worked in the field that these were the consequences of a "degeneration" that some victims of hereditary weakness could not resist and others, who were merely "perverse," could have resisted had they chosen to do so?

This was the distinguished person whom the Lord Marshal's office in Vienna called on to draw up the third report it had requested on Louise's mental condition since she had been transferred from the asylum in Döbling to the one in Purkersdorf. The first of the Purkersdorf reports had given examples of her erratic behavior and referred to her "incapacity for self-criticism"; the second had spoken of her "need for the protection of the law . . . in view of her psychological infirmities." Neither of these conclusions was decisive enough to satisfy Philipp or the Lord Marshal himself, acting on behalf of the Hofburg, which wanted this case doubly locked and bolted. The Lord Marshal did not exactly say so, of course, but his wishes were understood.

So the Baron Dr. von Krafft-Ebing obliged. So, in her own way, did Louise. She was used to inspections by visiting doctors and knew the kind of questions they would subject her to. Far from being intimidated by the arrival of yet another of the breed (this one's name meant nothing to her), she was offended by his air of command and the display of excessive respect shown by those around him, the institution's director not least. *She* was the royal princess; she was entitled to whatever show of deference was going; she was the most important person in any room she would ever share with this man. Also, his beard had an unfortunate resemblance to Philipp's, which confused and angered her. The longer the interview went on, the more uncertain she became as to whether or not she was speaking to Philipp, as she so often did in her dramatic monologues. If it was Philipp, why had he taken off his glasses? Was it to fool her? "Speak up, man!" she shouted at him when he asked her one of his particularly husky, intimately self-assured questions, and the others in the room quailed, not because they were afraid of her but because they knew that this was no way to speak to such a distinguished scientist.

Nor was that all. She sulked, she swore, she told Krafft-Ebing several times he would never have dared to ask such questions of her if Count Mattachich had been present. "But then he's an honest man. He would defend me against such infamy. Whereas you—people like you—I know what you're capable of." And she insultingly rubbed her thumb and forefinger together in front of his face, to remind him that he was being paid for his services. If he was really a doctor, that is, and not Philipp in a poor disguise.

Krafft-Ebing refused to allow himself to be disturbed by this behavior. Why should he, after all his experience with mentally afflicted people? Besides, he knew he could—and would—sink her with the report he was going to write.

> *The lady completely lacks insight into the events of the past, has a false apprehension of her present situation, and no grasp of the future. . . .*
> *She sees herself as a pure and aristocratic woman who could resume her place in Viennese society, were she to resign herself to consorting once again with her husband. Her relationship with Mattachich she regards*

> *as noble and beautiful, notwithstanding the efforts of others motivated by envy and spite to drag it into the mud. . . . She dreams of disguising herself in men's clothing and of raiding his prison and freeing him. . . . Of the ruin she has inflicted on her husband and of the decay in her own social and moral position she has no understanding whatever. . . . The princess suffers from psychological weakness and a striking diminution of the higher mental faculties (logic, willpower, ethical standards). . . . Scientifically speaking, her condition may be described generally as an acquired feeble-mindedness. Having fallen under the spell of an unworthy man, she has subjected her will entirely to his suggestions, is indifferent to her high social position and to the values of marriage and motherhood, and wanders around the world with her adventurer seeking—by means of moral degeneracy, financial ruin, and unworthy company—to destroy her marriage.*

Strong stuff. Just what was wanted. It took no time at all for an official declaration to follow the delivery of the great doctor's report:

> *Declaration of Guardianship: The Lord Marshal hereby makes it known that owing to weakness of mind H.R.H. the Princess Louise of Saxe-Coborg, born as Princess of Belgium, has been placed under the guardianship of Dr. Carl Ritter von Feistmantel, advocate and officer of the court.**

And that was it—her permanent "incapacitation," as Philipp described it in a letter to a member of his family, had at last been achieved. Just what he had wanted. No provisional six-months-at-a-time limitation on Louise's freedom was in question here. Thank God.

That was Philipp's first reaction. His second was to try once again to get Leopold to take over responsibility for his daughter. Now that she had officially been declared a halfwit, surely the King of the Belgians and

---

* Medical report and official declaration quoted in Holler, *Ihr Kampf,* pp. 149–150.

King-Emperor of the Congo Free State would feel under an obligation to provide for her upkeep. It wasn't as though she would ever again be able to run around the world spending his money (or her husband's) and generally disgracing herself and the families she was connected with.

Leopold, however, remained unresponsive. He had better things to do with his money than throw away even a tiny part of it on such a creature— especially now that she could no longer do him any harm. So Philipp decided to ship her out of Austria-Hungary to an institution in Coswig, near Dresden, Germany, which would at least put her at a greater distance from himself than before.*

❖

Louise never read that Declaration of Guardianship. The women in her household, who knew their orders, were careful to keep away from her all books and papers that had not been vetted by the management of the asylum. But one of the brown-smocked attendants who worked in another part of the asylum passed on to her news of the declaration. Toughened by the years he had spent in the company of the lost souls around him, this man did not hide the fact that it was in effect a life sentence. An edict issued in this manner by the Lord Marshal could only be rescinded by his own office. There was no authority beyond it, in its dealings with those of royal rank, and it was not in the habit of changing its mind.

For Louise the only immediate consequence of the issuing of the declaration was that doctors from outside ceased coming to see her. However, lawyers continued to do so from time to time; and she knew why. On the one hand she was mad; therefore, her evidence was worthless and could not be used in court. On the other hand, Mattachich's attempts to reopen his case encouraged the authorities to lead her repeatedly through everything she had said during their earlier inquiries. Their hope was

* See Holler, *Ihr Kampf,* p. 151.

that she would let something slip that would implicate Mattachich in previously undiscovered criminal acts. Then they would be able to lay further charges against him and sentence him to another term in prison. And another one after that, if possible. Their master wanted to see him banished from the world as irrevocably as she herself was. But she was not so mad as to be incapable of smelling the intention on them.

Would she really remain behind walls for the rest of her life? In some of her lowest yet most clearsighted moments she saw herself joining the walks taken by all the other unfortunates who were led daily, ward by ward, around the asylum. She saw them out of the windows of her house or when she herself went for a walk with Marie or Olga. She imagined herself as just another old woman among the rest, in clothes just as old as theirs, making gestures as dislocated as theirs, shouting at the sky or at their brown-jacketed guards, or weeping incessantly, just as they did. If she had any hope of escaping this fate, it lay solely with Mattachich, whom she thought of in quasi-magical terms: he was her champion, her savior, her Roland, her Lancelot. And these miserable lawyers expected her to betray him! Sometimes when they came to see her she simply retired to her bedroom and refused to come out; at other times, even more disconcertingly for them, she came into the room where they were waiting for her, seized a chair, turned its back toward them, and sat with her eyes fixed on the ceiling, and remained silent until they surrendered and left.

When she did on rare occasions open up it was only to repeat what she had said many times before. No, she had no idea who had forged her sister's signature. She could not recall the specific content of the documents issued by Reicher and Spitzer but was certain that when they had left her hand they had carried one signature only: hers. That's how it always was: Count Mattachich put papers of all kinds before her, she signed them, he folded them, messengers took them away. She had given him full authority in all matters to do with her business affairs. She had "boundless faith" in his integrity and fidelity. Yes, there could have been someone in her "surroundings" who had been scheming against her and the count and had tried to get them into trouble. Philipp's agents, perhaps. Or thieves in her own employ. Of such people she could not speak. But for the brave true Count Mattachich, her sole defender, the only honest man in her service, the last honest man in the empire, she would speak up on oath before any court in the world. But they would never let her do it. They would never give her the chance. Not as long as Philipp and Bachrach and the almighty emperor, a man with a stone for a heart and a stone for a brain, wanted him kept in jail.

When once or twice it was hinted to her that her circumstances might be reconsidered if she were to cooperate with her visitors, she responded by squaring her shoulders, raising her head and voice, and making a declaration of her own. They could go to hell. She had been betrayed by everyone: her father, her husband, her sister, and her daughter, who never came to see her—even by her mother. But never by the count. And now people came creeping around her like rats—like rats!—expecting her to betray *him*?

So they gave up. The woman was mad. Therefore best left alone, just where she was.

❖

It was from his mother that Mattachich heard about the "guardianship" imposed on Louise. "They want her to die there," he said, dry-eyed, and his mother nodded. She had not been to see him for several months. His voice was listless; his face was lined and without color; he had lost weight.

"The woman doesn't deserve it," his mother said. "I thought she was a weak creature, but *this*?"

They remained silent, her eyes searching his, as if hoping to find something in them she had not seen there before. But they were lifeless. The room they were in was chilly and bare: a wooden table, two chairs, grubby walls, a coarse plaster ceiling and a coarse plank floor, a full-bellied guard seated in a corner, enjoying the eavesdropping that was one of his official duties. If their voices dropped too low for him to hear what they were saying he would emit just one word in peremptory fashion.

"Louder!"

Mother and son sat with their hands flat on the table, his on top of hers. Both felt that the meeting of their hands created the only warm spot in the room. He had told her about the failure of the last of his appeals. There was nowhere for him to go. It was finished.

"You mustn't give up," the countess said.

He answered, after a dead pause: "I have."

He breathed in and out a few times, responding not at all to the protective gesture she made; just readying himself for the effort to say more.

"We're in the same position, me and her. . . . She's there until she dies and so am I—here. I won't last out three more years of this. I know it. I've done everything I could to make them listen." One finger lifted from her hand and came down on it again. "But nothing works. I've failed. Failed. Failed. It's over."

There was no anger in his voice, only apathy. He spoke as if at a distance from his own words. They sat in silence, moisture filming her steady blue eyes. His remained expressionless, extinguished.

"You don't have to come to see me, mother. You see what I am. It's not going to get better. I did what I wanted to do and this is where it's brought me. There's nothing more to say."

She pulled her hands away from his and was suddenly whispering fiercely at him. "Yes, there is! Tell them she's the one who's guilty! Tell them she did it! She's finished. They've got her. There's nothing to lose. Tell them you knew all about it and couldn't speak before, to protect her. But now—"

Belly and all, the guard bestirred himself in his corner.

"Louder!"

"Do it!" she said. "You can't make things worse for her than they are already."

The guard was on his feet.

"Louder! Louder!"

She turned to look at him, giving him the benefit of her flat contemptuous gaze. In a voice just a tone louder, and looking directly at the guard, as though he were the one she was talking to, even the one she had come to visit, she went on, "I've always thought she was to blame and you were protecting her, like a brave stupid man of honor. Well, I'm your mother, and I tell you I'm not interested in my honor or in yours. If you would only blame her and be done with it, you might—you might—free yourself from all this."

Directing her words at him, she had silenced the bewildered, hovering guard. Now she turned her head to look at her son. "There's no point in it for them either. Why should they keep you here? She's safe from you and you're safe from her. So do it, Géza! Do it!"

She bent down to pick up her handbag from the floor, opened it, took out a handkerchief, and blew her nose. Mattachich watched her pale hands return the handkerchief to its place and close the bag.

"No," he said, when she sat still again. "I won't shame her. Never. And it wouldn't work."

She made a move to get up but subsided. Neither spoke. Minutes passed before he broke the silence. It was the first remark he had volunteered since he had been escorted to the room. He told her that he was still doing clerical work in the administrative offices. It got him out of his cell for a few hours every day. But it would never see him through another three years of this. He also told her, even more distantly than before but unable to keep from her this new element in his life, that he had discovered a place in one of the yards where the buildings and walls disappeared completely if he put his head back as far it could go and stared straight upward. That's where he now went during exercise periods. That's what he did. He simply stood there, gazing at the sky. It always looked peaceful, like a dome, even when clouds were chasing one another, or when rain fell from it, or when black flakes of snow wandered about in it until they reached a point where they suddenly turned white. When the sky was all blue there were other squirming, transparent shapes up there to look at.

He would try to focus on them, but they would never keep still, they would never let him do it. He knew they were just flaws in his own vision which he would never catch and which would never go away.

❖

Neither Mattachich nor Louise nor the Countess Keglevich had any idea that help was at hand. In their most wishful dreams they could not have imagined from what quarter it would come. Or the manner in which it would reveal itself. Or what the consequences would be.

III

CHAPTER NINE

HERO WORSHIP CAN SPRING UP ANYWHERE AND SEEK its objects in almost any direction. Lovers hope their love will be reciprocated; religious believers hope to be rewarded in heaven or on earth for their faith; hero worshippers expect to gain nothing from their passion but the pleasure of admiring the beauty, courage, and power of others. Perhaps that is why Thomas Carlyle was moved to write in his *On Heroes and Hero-Worship* that "no nobler or more blessed feeling dwells in man's heart."

He was speaking ideally, of course. The problem is that in certain cases Carlyle's blessed feeling can become a mania and a torment to the person afflicted by it. Look at the fans and groupies who turn into persecutors, stalkers, even murderers of the yearned-after but unattainable figures they are fixated on. Trapped in obsession, they begin to find intolerable their heroes' indifference to—even their ignorance of—the turmoil of emotion unleashed in the breasts of their unknown admirers. Only if the relationship is acknowledged, responded to, evened up, will the worshippers repossess their own lives again. Deny the possibility, and their love will turn into rage.

Maria Stöger's worship of Mattachich, however, was of a kind even rarer than Carlyle's "pure" variety, or that of (say) Mark David Chapman, the murderer of John Lennon. Through the intensity and durability of her passion, she transformed *herself* into a heroine. What is more, she managed to do it without any of the incitements available to today's worshippers—rock concerts, Web sites, movies, the soccer World Cup, and so forth.

❖

Right. Time for Maria to step forward. The first thing you will probably notice about her is a small, flat, perfectly circular birthmark, reddish-brown in color and placed immediately below the lower lid of her left eye. It is no bigger than the nail of her pinkie, too small and too flat to be called a disfigurement. Yet on first seeing it, you or any other stranger will feel that it must be a distraction or irritation to her, a kind of blur in her own vision that she will sooner or later try to blink away. A moment later, the steadiness of her gaze will dispel the notion and her face will emerge as the shapely whole it is—though a sense of something occluded and mischievous about her will remain. She has a clear complexion, regular features, white teeth, an open brow, dark-brown eyes, and soft brown hair cut short just below the ears, leaving her slender neck exposed. Her figure is slight, her tread light, her hands small and deft. Three mornings a week she cleans and does the laundry for a Jewish family in Vienna's Josefstadt; two afternoons a week she serves behind the counter in a hardware shop near the flat. Her employers regard her as an unobtrusive, honest, hardworking young person who deserves a better husband than the unprepossessing one she is stuck with.

Karl Stöger is much older than his wife. Like Maria's father he used to be a regimental soldier, but having retired from the army on a small pension he now works as a civilian clerk for the Viennese police department. His pay is poor and his habit of spending so many of his evenings drinking schnapps and losing at cards in a neighborhood bar means that Maria struggles constantly to make ends meet. He and she have just one child, Viktor by name—a pale anxious boy of seven who frets about his homework and "doesn't run about enough" according to his overweight father, who moves only when he has to. They live in a small apartment near the railway lines leading to the Südbahnhof; it is sparsely furnished but neatly kept by Maria, who also does the cooking and walks the boy to and from school, except when she is away at work. Then a neighbor whose child goes to the same school takes over.

Daughter of a Croatian mother and a German-speaking father, Maria is now twenty-five years old. She has been married to Stöger for eight years. When she met him it was precisely the difference in age that attracted her; he seemed to her so grown-up, so much a man of the world. In his company, she had imagined, she would be able to arrive at adulthood in a single jump. Now she thinks of him as more of a child than she has ever been: more self-indulgent, petulant, begrudging. Much fatter and lazier too. Also dirtier. All this helps to account for their not having had another child. When he tries in perverse fashion to punish and yet get closer to her by bullying the little boy, she responds with a pale face and an expression of silent scorn that he recognizes, hates, and is daunted by. So he goes off grumbling to his drinking den, while she and the boy eat their dinner and do his homework together before she puts him to bed.

Then she returns to the table in the living room, where she reads the daily paper from end to end, advertisements and all. It helps her to keep going, she says. So do the novels she borrows at a few groschen a time from a little circulating-library-cum-tobacconist around the corner. So do the letters she has written occasionally, under an invented name and address, to Lieutenant Mattachich in Möllersdorf prison. (None of which are delivered to him.) She is filled with longings that look not toward any imagined future with Mattachich or anyone else, but to the past she had once been so anxious to get over and done with while living through it. The future had seemed to teem with innumerable possibilities then; all she had to do was make a grab at it and something unimaginable—a shape, a fate for her to wonder at—would be revealed.

This.

Too late now. Time for bed—a bed in the boy's room, behind a locked door, not the bed she used to share with her husband.

❖

So much for your first impressions of Maria. Her first impression of Mattachich was that he was not as tall as she had expected him to be. He was older too. Less upright. Graver in expression. His eyes more sunken. His presence less commanding. His skin was without light; his teeth needed attention. The sketches and the occasional photogravure picture of him she had seen in the Viennese newspapers had always shown him with a full trim mustache but he had evidently done away with it while in prison; his bare upper lip looked long and doleful as a result.

Yet she was not disappointed to see him as he was, not at all. He was *true*, he actually existed, he was not just a half-insane fragment of her own imagining, as she had sometimes felt he must be, when she tried to drive the thought of him and his affairs out of her mind—and found herself failing again and again. Besides, seeing him she felt even sorrier for him than she would have thought possible before. The poor man! Look what they had done to him! That was what her moistened gaze said silently to him—though he did not look to see it. She knew her eyes had gone starry and did not care.

Standing in a room with him, the two of them momentarily alone, she then discovered something else she could never have guessed beforehand. She too was *true*, like him. This mad adventure for which she had abandoned her husband, left her home, parked her son with her parents in Graz, taken the train to Möllersdorf, arrived there with nowhere to stay and no plan in her head other than to tell the prison authorities that she was a relation of Mattachich's and had an urgent need to see him—none of it had been as mad, after all, as it had seemed to her before she had set out. Usually it is in dreams that things sometimes come together with an implausible ease and rapidity, yet in this case her speculations about what might become of her had been full of anxiety, even terror, whereas actuality, the world itself, had yielded to her as if her wish alone mattered. And it had culminated in a success of which Mattachich knew nothing.

But he would learn of it soon enough. "Oh, is Captain Navratil not here?" she asked out of a dry mouth, having entered this office on the chance that the captain would not be there and she would find in it the real object of her quest.

And here he was, behind a desk, having risen to his feet. The moment she had come through the door she knew it to be him; her strongly beating heart told her so even before her eyes and brain. No question about it. He was her own; he had been hers for so long in his absence, how could she not know him when he stood in front of her?

"*Herr Oberleutnant* Mattachich, I have a message for the captain."

She spoke in German and so did he. "No," he said, pointing to the open door behind her, gesturing her back to the empty corridor outside. "The captain is farther down. Two doors down."

She went back to the door, but only to close it. She took a deep breath and spoke again, in Croatian this time. "Please let me say this. I've just started working in the canteen. I do have a message from Mr. Drexler, the manager, for Captain Navratil. But you must understand—you are the person I want to meet."

She spoke earnestly, boldly, quietly, as if they had come upon each other in an office in some provincial city, never inside a provincial military prison. From the moment she had addressed him by his army rank and name she had seen something—an inquiry, a puzzlement—come to life in his expression; it grew stronger when she broke into Croatian. Then it died swiftly. She saw it happen. He was a felon, a prisoner, a convict; she a young woman about whom he knew nothing. The window behind him showed only the branch of a tree and a glimpse of the inevitable high, dirty, plastered wall beyond. Some of the plaster had fallen away in places, revealing rubble and gray earth underneath.

"I don't know who are you are," he said in German, looking down at the papers on his desk and speaking in a subdued voice. He sat down in his chair. "I don't know what you are talking about. If you want to see Captain Navratil, you must go to Office G, as I'm sure you know. I have no wish to see you again." He glanced up—nothing more—before adding, "And you can tell that to the people who sent you here."

She still stood with her back to the door. She was silent and so was he. She looked at the top of his head: his hair was still strong, though it was retreating, and there was a grayness diffused through its tips. His chapped, rough-looking hands rested on the papers. One hand moved to no purpose, as if conscious that it was being looked at. It was just a reflex but it provoked her to speak again, and again in Croatian.

"Lieutenant, I know who are you. I've read about you. That's why I'm here. I wanted to meet you and I want to help you. You've been treated abominably. If you give me the chance I'll show you how strongly I feel about what they've done to you. I am on your side. You must believe it. I have no other reason to be here. I've spoken to no one about this. Nobody sent me. I'm not a spy. Do I look like a spy? Do I sound like one? Do you think a spy would—"

She halted abruptly, before going on more boldly still, unsurprised now by her own boldness, putting at stake everything she had so far gained in her search for him. "If you don't believe me—if you don't want to give me a chance—then go to Captain Navratil and tell him what I've been saying to you. They'll throw me out at once and you'll never see me again. Or they'll put me in jail too."

She blinked and the mark under her eye blinked too, with an improbable effect of humor.

"But they won't put me in *this* jail," she said, "you can be sure of that. We'll never get another chance."

They stared at each other. Mattachich could not remember when last he had looked into another person's eyes for so long, so directly and steadily. These were a woman's eyes, too, soft and steady but unyielding. They reminded him of what he used to be: ordinary, a human being. Not a prisoner—not an outcast—not forever conscious of the ruin his life had become.

He quelled instantly this flicker of rediscovery, this recollection of his personhood.

"I'll wait and see," he said. In Croatian.

She left the room without another word and went on, two doors down, to deliver her boss's written message to Captain Navratil.

❖

For two years previously Maria had been compiling a secret scrapbook of items from the newspapers about the "Mattachich case." The book into which she pasted the clippings, bought specially for this purpose, had plain pages and mottled cardboard covers; it was bound with muslin along the spine. She had covered it in brown paper and used Viktor's crayons to decorate the cover with a pattern of green leaves and red flowers. She had not given it a title.

She collected whatever references she saw to Louise too; but Louise, though indispensable to the tale, was for her a secondary figure. It irked her that the papers devoted so much space to the princess—her failed marriage, her profligacy, her father's wealth, her widowed sister, her madness—in comparison to what was written about the uhlan. His courage in breaching the barriers of caste and protocol between himself and the princess enthralled Maria; the price he had been made to pay for it filled her with outrage. No wonder they hated him for putting them all to shame, by snatching his lover from among them—those Habsburgs and Coburgs and all the other high aristocrats who clustered around the imperial palace, feasting, drinking, hunting, gambling, dancing, sleeping with actresses and dancers and each other's wives, sailing around the Mediterranean on their yachts, buying newfangled motorcars and using newfangled telephones and never giving a thought to the poor and hungry around them. (Not for nothing was the socialist *Arbeiter-Zeitung* the newspaper she read most devotedly.) Yet at the same time she knew that some of the glamour Mattachich had for her lay partly in the fact that he occupied a position in society so far above her own. He had a title, he was an officer, a sword-bearer, the wearer of a frogged and braided uniform, a rider on one of those horses whose clattering, jingling processions through the city she, like thousands of other Viennese, watched and listened to with pleasure. Antiroyalist though she was, these frequent displays made her feel enlarged and exhilarated, along with all the people around her. Merely by looking on, they too became an indispensable part of the spectacle they were enjoying.

Perhaps, she would daydream, she had seen Mattachich on one such occasion, or many times, without knowing it; perhaps she had stood close to him, gazing up—when the procession halted and the shining horses controlled by their shining masters moved restlessly, shod feet striking on the cobbles like steel against flint—and never suspecting that one day this particular horseman would seize her imagination. Now she dreamed of becoming his ideal friend, partner, confidante, inspirer, in whatever way he wanted her to be. And why him among all the others like him? *Because* he had been hauled off his horse, stripped of his uniform and sword, thrown into jail for a "crime" he did not commit, after a trial held behind closed doors because the evidence against him was too feeble to present in an open court of law. To her it was plain that it was Louise—it must have been Louise—who had inscribed her sister's name on those forged notes she had read about. Who else had the opportunity and the motive and knew what Princess Stephanie's signature looked like? Who else would have been so free and bold with the name of the crown princess, if not her?* But never a word of blame or accusation had come from the lips or the pen of her gallant lover. And to do Louise justice, which Maria tried to do, she too had thrown everything aside, her family and royal position included, for his sake. How strange it was for her to think of these sophisticated people, who were socially so far above her, as nothing more than babes in the wood—he because he was too chivalrous to tell the truth about her; she because until meeting Mattachich she would have seen nothing of truth or sincerity in the corrupt world she

---

* Maria never changed her mind on this subject. She went to her grave believing Louise to have been the one who had actually perpetrated the forgeries (see Holler, *Ihr Kampf,* pp. 100, 361). Remarkably enough, Holler bases this assertion on an interview he conducted with Maria in 1952—half a century after her meeting with Mattachich.

lived in. No wonder they had declared her to be mad and thrown him in jail; they had to punish him for snatching her away and punish her for recognizing the values of steadfastness and honor he embodied.

Imagine thoughts like these obsessing the outwardly cool head of a young mother, a refractory wife, a conscientious charwoman and obliging assistant in an ironmonger's shop. Who would believe it? She could hardly do so herself. The scandal had first caught her eye when she had read a report of the duel in the Riding School, followed immediately by the news of Prince Philipp's repudiation of his wife's debts. She spoke about it to her unresponsive husband, in an amazed, outraged, and almost exhilarated outburst—after which she said barely a word on the subject to him or to anybody else. There was simply nobody for her to speak to. Her employers had no interest in such matters, nor did her neighbors or her parents in Graz, who cared about nothing that did not touch them personally. Only she, of all the people she knew, was really affected by the story, and for that reason her discovery of Mattachich became a rediscovery of her own loneliness. Scanning the newspapers for whatever items she could find with a direct bearing on the case and secretly pasting them into her scrapbook made her obsession all the more valuable to her. Sometimes a flurry of items about the affair would appear in various journals, sometimes there would be a drought; often she regretted the time she had lost by not starting the collection earlier.

It was crazy, no doubt, but after some months she suspected she would feel crazier still if she gave it up. There were times when she did try to rid herself of the whole business by simply not buying newspapers; but she was addicted to them; she missed them too much, and not only for Mattachich's sake. They were like a never-ending serial. If it wasn't the Boers and the British in South Africa it would be the Bosnians and Serbs nearer home, or the Americans in the Philippines, or the Russians and Japanese. Anyway, almost any item of domestic news could somehow be related to Mattachich and his misfortunes: court circulars, army promotions, the doings of Saxe-Coburgs who had apparently spent the last few decades taking over half the thrones of Europe. (And one in Mexico.) One way of curing herself of this mania, it occurred to her, might be to set about having another child, but it had taken Karl and herself a year of endeavor before she conceived Viktor, and to go through all that again in order to acquire a responsibility she did not want—where was the sense in that?

❖

Then the unloved and unwanted Stöger settled the matter for her. He discovered the scrapbook. She had been keeping it in the bottom drawer of a chest in the room she shared with Viktor and had chosen that drawer because it was difficult to pull open: it would move only when tugged first left, then right, like a tooth being prized from a jaw. Given her husband's indolence, it had seemed a safe enough place. But he got to it. She could not guess what he had been looking for there, under the folded clothes that she always placed over the book. Perhaps he had been on the prowl for evidence of infidelity. If so, he had found the moral equivalent.

She came home from the hardware store one evening and found the scrapbook lying open in front of him on the kitchen table, revealed in all its naked foolishness, its remoteness from who she was and how she lived.

He had evidently been sitting there for some time, waiting for her to return. He did not greet her, just looked up, scowling. She did not speak. The shock of seeing her secret life exposed paralyzed her. Then, "That's mine," she said and made a grab at it. But the palms of both his hands slapped down on the scrapbook and did not move.

Squatting to one side on the floor, Viktor had been playing a board game against himself. He studied them from there: his mother leaning toward the table, his father seated at it, crouched over the scrapbook like an animal protecting its meal. The boy knew what their rows looked and sounded like. He got up silently and left the room.[*]

---

[*] The game Viktor had been playing was Snakes and Ladders. It had been exported from India to England about ten years before and from there had spread to the continent.

"So?"

"So?" he mocked her. "What nonsense is this? What's all this rubbish? Who are these people? What have you got to do with them? You're supposed to be a grown-up woman, not a schoolgirl. You lie in bed playing with yourself, dreaming you're a princess in the arms of this fine monsieur, is that it? Oooh! Oooh! Oooh!" He groaned and squirmed his wide hips, making the chair he was sitting on squeak too. "Like that, is it? That's what you want? No wonder you don't let me into your bedroom, you bitch. You've got better things to do with yourself."

A flush of anger had been in her cheeks; now it was gone and only pallor remained. She took a step or two back from the table, still bent, as if her hips or knees would give way if she tried to straighten up. Darting a look at her, Stöger snatched up the scrapbook from the table and began trying to tear it in half. The cardboard was too thick for him, so he opened the book and tore at its spine from the top downward. Some of the muslin binding broke and single pages fluttered loose; the whole thing was now in two ragged halves, still suspended from each other. He tried ripping crossways at the pages, but they too were more than he could manage. So he began plucking them in sheaves from what was left of the binding, ten or twenty at a time.

By then she had left the room. They did not speak to one another the next morning, though she gave him and Viktor their breakfast roll and coffee, the father's black, the son's very milky. She herself ate nothing. Of her scrapbook there was no sign; Stöger had gathered up the pages and shoved them into the round black kitchen stove with its detachable lid. It had taken him a long time to burn them. He had not wanted to choke the flames, lest something remain for her to recover.

As usual she walked Viktor to school, Karl having already left the flat. When he came home that evening, she and the boy were gone. So were most of their clothes. No note remained to explain her departure.

❖

Things had gone so easily, after her son had been left with her parents in Graz, that Maria was tempted to wonder why she had not dared to act before. It turned out that Möllersdorf was used to the arrival of single women of all ages coming to visit their menfolk in the prison, so her presence roused no particular curiosity. She moved immediately into a room in one of the town's inns, which she shared with three others. One of them, herself a relatively new arrival, worked in the prison infirmary and encouraged Maria to ask about her chances of employment there. People were always coming and going, she said. Of Mattachich, Maria said nothing; when asked, she claimed she was a young widow who had come to Möllersdorf because she was now engaged to a farmer in the neighborhood.

She repeated this story in the guardroom at the prison gate, when she went there to ask about employment. The guard she spoke to told her she should speak to Mr. Drexler in town; he and his partner, themselves ex-soldiers, ran the kitchens and canteens for the staff and prisoners, as well as the little prison shop. Mr. Drexler revealed himself to be a diminutive man with a great bill of a nose out of proportion to the rest of him. As if to strike a balance he wore a tall felt hat on the back of his head at all times, indoors and out. Despite his habit of nodding encouragingly while he listened to what she had to say, Maria soon discovered that he drove a hard bargain. But her appearance and manner appealed to him and she had her own reason for agreeing to whatever he offered. Barely a week after arriving in Möllersdorf she walked disbelievingly through the prison gatehouse for the first time, a pass from Drexler clutched in her hand.

See! See! a silent voice said to her as she did so. Once through the gates, she found the institution to be much bigger within and more haphazardly laid out than it had looked from the other side.* The prisoners were divided into groups according to a system she could not grasp, and there was a constant coming and going of guards, civilian workers, visi-

---

* One of the oldest of the buildings had originally served as a hunting lodge for the Empress Maria Theresa (see Holler, *Ihr Kampf,* p. 162).

tors, and suppliers of goods. How was she to make sense of it? And find
Mattachich without making her curiosity about him apparent? And to do
so while working at a fierce Drexler-driven pace in a pair of kitchens
much larger and noisier than any she had ever seen before?

Patience. Discretion. Docility. She should have a large supply of them
all. She had practiced them long enough during the silent years of her
married life. Eventually this trio of virtues, if that is what they are, was
rewarded. Her boss sent her to carry a message to Navratil in the administrative block, which she knew by then was where Mattachich worked.
Someone in the front office on the ground floor told her to go to Office G,
second floor. The first flight of stairs was stone; the second was scuffed,
splintering wood. A dozen closed doors looked upon the corridor, each
expressionlessly bearing a single painted capital letter on its forehead. No
name plates on any of them. She seized the opportunity to forget that she
had been told to go straight to Office G. She knocked softly on the first
door she came to. No answer. She tried the handle. Locked. The next
one—C—the same. The next one, Mattachich.

❖

Of course he was unable to resist her. Do you think you would have
done otherwise? If so, think again. Imagine yourself in that prison with
three more years of incarceration still to come, with grueling additional
punishments at prescribed intervals added on. Now try to picture yourself turning down the comfort offered you by a young, handsome, determined, soft-voiced, good-humored female who has appeared from nowhere
and who by her own account has given up everything she possessed in
order to be with you. Well? Yes, you are afraid she is a government agent,
a trap, a liar; sufficiently afraid to have kept her at bay for eight weeks
since you first saw her—during which time she has been just twice more
in your office, but many times in the wretched room where you and a
handful of *Privilegierten,* the other ex-officers, eat their food away from the

hundreds of rank and file prisoners. For it is in that room (so willing a worker has she shown herself to be, and such a good impression has she made on Mr. Drexler) that she has managed to secure a position.

Now imagine this woman—whose expressions and tones of voice, like her walk, the movements of her arms and brows, even the folds that appear in her neck when she lowers her head, have become familiar to you—imagine her coming yet again into this office, which is the one place in the prison, outside your cell, where you are frequently alone. What do you do this time? Send her away? Succumb to her? Attack her? How can you know the difference between succumbing and attacking when you find yourself suddenly making a drowning-man's lunge at her? What is the darkness that has come over you? The force that hurls you toward this unendurably female person with her woman's skin and figure, woman's neck and hair, woman's parts hidden beneath her dress and clumsy apron? She is in front of you, she has sought you out, these are her eyes looking at you, this is her bosom stirring with her breath, her arms now folded around you—all hers, soon to be yours, any moment, this moment, now. Your lips fasten on her neck, your hands fly wherever they can, two hands never enough for what you want them to seize, hold, crush, devour. After so long! Now you are on the floor, pulling, tugging, panting, starving, barely conscious of the help she is giving you; now you are almost there, there, *there*—and her hand comes over your mouth to stop you from crying out loudly the moment she knows you can't help yourself and your saliva runs over her fingers and the life jets out of you below.

❖

There. After they had drawn apart they caught their breath, sat, knelt, struggled to their feet, rearranged their clothing.

He said to her, "Now you're going to tell me how to escape from here, and then tell them where to catch me? Is that the plan?"

He had meant the question to be cutting, scornful, a man going back to the position he had held with her before. But it was impossible. He heard the relief and gratitude in his voice, and so did she. She gave him a look—offhand, smudged, charitable.

"There's nowhere in the world I want to be if you're not there too."

Did her words settle the matter? The flush in her cheek? The hollow between her collarbones, revealed by the undone buttons of her dress? The dark softness of her hair? That birthmark, singular to her?

That was the end of his doubts, anyway. What had been a mad thought for them both was now a fact. They were having an affair. Yes, in the prison itself. Maria alone had brought it about. It seemed no one could resist her, certainly not Mr. Drexler. At her suggestion he had put her to work in the room where the ex-officers ate; then he let her take on an additional job behind the counter in the little prison shop. Behind the shop was a storeroom, which was a less dangerous meeting place for her and Mattachich than the office in the administration building. Maria also befriended one of the guards who looked after the cells in which ex-officers were confined; soon, won over by her pleas and bribes, he agreed to let her know when he would be alone on duty. As a result she was able to visit Mattachich in his cell too. He no longer spoke of dying in prison; instead, he said he would live on in order to disappoint "them." Even if they found new reasons to keep him there, which they were always looking for, he would carry on. Because of her.

❖

None of this would have been possible if the prison had been a less ramshackle establishment run by a less negligent staff; nevertheless, her achievement was extraordinary.* But she was not content with it. Now

---

* Holler, who is not given to overstatement, describes what she accomplished in getting inside the prison walls and what she then did there as *das schier Unmögliche*, the sheer impossible (*Ihr Kampf*, p. 185). The language Mattachich uses about Maria is grateful but much more guarded: opaque in fact (*Memoiren*, p. 135). He pays tribute to her but reveals nothing about the real nature of their relationship. "For some months," he writes, "I had been commanded to work in the administration of the establishment. This gave an opportunity for a large-hearted woman, Maria Stöger, who was employed in the prison canteen, to extend to me a hand of friendship—out of pure compassion for an unfortunate fellow human—and to let the public know how my rights had been violated." Thereafter he refers to her just once, in passing and not by name, as his *Kameradin*.

that her once-distant mythical hero had sobbed real tears of relief and gratitude in her arms, her ambitions had changed. The fantasies she had indulged in back in Vienna of smuggling him out of the prison had withered at the first sight of its guardroom and the high thick walls. So for the first time her thoughts turned to the idea of starting a public campaign for her lover's release. Unfortunately, at this point she discovered she was pregnant.

When she broke the news to Mattachich he suggested, as men are inclined to do even in circumstances less difficult than theirs, that she should do something about it. "I can't be a father to this child," he told her. "Here? In this place? And how will you manage on your own?"

"I'll have to manage. It's *yours*. That's why it's precious to me."

Barely a year after entering the prison for the first time, she produced a little boy. On the child's baptismal certificate she entered *Karl Stöger* as the father—which turned out to be a tactical error.

Stöger had in fact visited her in Möllersdorf a couple of times since she had left him, but they had not resumed marital relations. So when he heard of the birth and the certificate that came with it, he at once set about suing her for divorce. As co-respondent he named Géza Mattachich-Keglevich, whose address he gave as *prisoner, the Military Prison, Möllersdorf.* More mischievously still, he wrote the War Ministry Office to inform them of what he was doing—and why. The office was enraged by this communication, of course, and became even more so when its first inquiries revealed that the relationship between the prisoner and the assistant canteen keeper had been widely known in the institution.[*]

Maria was immediately sacked and forbidden to enter the prison under any pretext. Mattachich was sentenced to fourteen days of solitary confinement in his cell and emerged from it to find the privileges he had previously enjoyed, his clerical job included, taken from him. Over the

---

[*] Holler, *Ihr Kampf,* pp. 187–192 and 199–206, gives an account of the bureaucratic upheavals in Vienna and Möllersdorf and the punishments meted out to Mattachich in consequence.

next months sterner sanctions followed, among them a period of ten days of darkness in the punishment cell—a tiny hole three-and-a-half paces long and barely two paces wide—on a bread-and-water diet, with planks to lie on and a fetid bucket left stewing in a corner for his wastes.

"The darkness," he wrote later, "was more upsetting and tried my powers of resistance more than anything else I had to endure while in prison. . . . Not for the first time I had the feeling that the aim of the authorities was either to kill me or to drive me mad."*

❖

Maria's response to these misfortunes was firm and unrepentant. She took another job in Möllersdorf (as a seamstress) and from this flimsy base returned to the project she had been considering before falling pregnant and producing her baby. Single-handedly, she set about trying to overthrow the verdict passed on her lover by the military court in Agram more than three years before. Over the next months she traveled as often as she could to Vienna—usually going first to her parents, where she left the baby and spent a little time with her older son, and doing the same on her journey back to Möllersdorf.

Young and ardent, handsome and soft-spoken, demure in manner yet trailing a raffish past (look what she'd got up to with this Mattachich, and in a prison cell too!), a working-class girl scandalously involved with people of an incomparably higher social class than her own—what a combination. You can imagine the success she had with the journalists working on the papers and magazines she canvassed for support. Only in one respect did she disappoint her new friends. She did not reciprocate their lingering glances, their special squeezings of her fingers, their accidental brushings of her bosom, their snug placing of a leg against hers under a restaurant table, while a meal came and went and they all talked politics

* Mattachich, *Memoiren,* p. 151.

together. She was not to be distracted from her business. She managed to plant various items in the press about Mattachich's plight, but her breakthrough came when Ignaz Daszynski, a member of parliament, agreed to take up the case.

Daszynski's appeal in the *Reichsrat* was crucial to all that followed.[*] It created a furor, inside and outside parliament, that he and his parliamentary allies did not allow to die down. By this time Mattachich had spent almost four years in jail, his six-month confinement while awaiting trial included, and every aspect of the trial with which Philipp and Bachrach had been especially pleased was now turned against them. The fact that it had taken place behind closed doors in a military court, that Mattachich's appeals had been lodged in secret and rejected without open argument on their merits, that the evidence of Louise had been rendered inadmissible by confining her in a lunatic asylum, and that even her lady-in-waiting, the Baroness Fugger, had been expelled beyond the imperial borders, now looked uglier than before. Antimonarchist feelings had grown stronger over the previous four years, as had nationalist sentiment among the Slavs; so also had the suspicion that the Habsburgs would do anything to oblige the Saxe-Coburgs and vice versa.[†]

Unnerved by the resuscitation of a scandal that they had hoped never to hear of again, the Hofburg and the War Minister did their blundering best to bury it once more. A notoriously brutal commandant by the name of Major Schönett was put in charge of the Möllersdorf prison with special instructions to keep Mattachich under control, and a stream of formal statements denying any wrongdoing by anyone at any time began to emerge from the War Office. Both these measures failed. The coalition of journalists and parliamentary deputies—of which Maria Stöger had been something more than the midwife—leaped on the news of every extra punishment heaped on Mattachich that the prison walls could not con-

---

[*] Referred to at the beginning of Chapter One and quoted at the beginning of Chapter Six.

[†] Even at the time of Louise's admission to the Purkersdorf asylum, Philipp had written to a member of his family, in his customary self-pitying manner, "Everybody regards her as a kind of martyr and me as a crude lecher" (quoted in Holler, *Ihr Kampf,* p. 140).

tain, and the coalition itself grew in size, especially as the Slavs were now seeing him not as a seedy hanger-on to the court but as one of their own. Though he still had three years of his formal sentence to serve, the belief that the whole thing would simply go away, at least until that period had elapsed, suddenly lost all plausibility.

Still, the surrender of the authorities took everyone by surprise. At one meeting it was deemed unthinkable that the current agitation should be rewarded by the man's release; at the next, it was decided that it was more troublesome to keep him where he was than to let him go. To save face it was also decided to get a confession of guilt out of him, along with a petition for pardon, before releasing him. Philipp reluctantly gave his approval to the suggestion; Bachrach, as he had done in a different context four years before, said that Mattachich would not accept the offer.

❖

Without warning, at daybreak, Schönett entered the cell in which Mattachich now moldered in solitude and idleness almost all of every day. "*Aufstehen!*" he yelled, as he always did, and Mattachich rose to his feet from the bunk he had been lying on. As always, again, Schönett let him stand in silence for some time while inspecting him at length and from close quarters—taking maximum advantage of his own lack of inches to make the process as humiliating as he could. An almost dwarfish thick-bodied man with a large flat round face from which there stood out a small, pointed, bridgeless nose, Schönett had had the wit and the audacity to make something frightening and useful out of his repellent appearance. A lesser man, given his shape and face, might have been tempted toward a preemptive amiability, but not this one. Hating, he wanted to be hated. In his left eye he wore a monocle with neither rim nor ribbon; on his close-cropped head he wore a too-small, brief-brimmed cap; when he opened his mouth he displayed blackened teeth, pale gums, and spotted depths below. He could also alter his voice from a whisper to a roar at any moment, and his whole face, even his forehead, was given to swelling, seemingly of its own accord, until the pores on it were as visible as those on an orange.

This was the creature who confronted Mattachich from a distance of a few inches in the half darkness of his cell. In whispering mode, Schönett told him that those fools in Vienna were ready to let him go, he could get out of prison and piss off wherever the hell he wanted to, if he signed a piece of paper that he, Schönett, had right here in his pocket.

He tapped the left-hand pocket on his tunic and waited.

Mattachich suspected a trap, inevitably. So, frowning, he made no answer.

Another long silence and another inspection from inches away followed. Schönett moved to one side; Mattachich stared straight ahead of him, as he had learned to do from his earliest days in the army. "If it was up to me," Schönett growled into the ear somewhat above his own mouth, "I'd keep you here, for the pleasure of watching the shit being kicked out of you. But I've got my orders. Here they are."

He tapped his tunic pocket again but made no move to open it and take out the document he claimed to have there. He came around to stare directly into Mattachich's eyes.

Mattachich began to tremble. It humiliated him that he couldn't prevent it, standing so close to his enemy. Fear and physical weakness made him do it, also the onset of hope. Struggling to control his voice and lower lip, he asked eventually, "What must I do?"

"Sign!"

"Sign what?"

"Whatever piece of shitpaper I give you to sign."

"What does it say?"

"You'll see when you sign it."

"That's impossible!"

"As you wish," Schönett said. He turned and walked out of the cell with a nod to the guard, waiting outside with the keys in his hand. The door slammed shut. The keys turned in the three locks, each revolution producing a different sound: *crunch, croak, grind.*

Three days later Schönett reappeared. As if on cue, Mattachich began to tremble.

"You want to know what I got in my pocket?"

A dry lick of his lips. A nod.

"All right, have a look."

Schönett took the letter from his pocket but did not hand it over. Instead he unfolded it and stuck in front of his face.

"Read."

Mattachich had difficulty focusing on it. The bottom half of the paper, below the fold, sloped away from him.

He looked at the major. "It says that I beg the emperor's pardon for the crimes I've committed."

"Well?"

Mattachich closed his eyes, as if to distance himself from the words he was about to utter. "I committed no crimes."

"Your funeral," Schönett said indifferently. But there was a gleam of satisfaction, even of mirth, in his monocled eye. He folded the paper up and put it back in his pocket, buttoned it down, turned, and walked out. The door performed as it always did, whatever the occasion: *crunch, croak, grind.*

❖

This game went on for about three weeks. At times Schönett was more abusive than at others, but since the only psychology he possessed was that of the bully, it did not occur to him to break Mattachich's will by kindness, by a show of understanding and respect. In his view it was typical of his bosses, anyway, that they should want to release this Mattachich. Just as they were ready to crawl before the cretins and pederasts who filled the benches of the *Reichsrat,* so they wanted to reward this prisoner and his whore for making monkeys out of them right here in Möllersdorf. But it was different with Major Schönett. If the idiot wouldn't sign the plea for pardon, then good, fine, excellent, let him stay where he was, rotting away, suffering the additional torment of knowing it was happening by his own choice.

In Vienna, after the usual delays, the usual gang met to discuss what to do about this stalemate. After much talk they came up with a solution almost as farcical as the dilemma they had got themselves into. It was the boneheaded Choloniewski, Princess Stephanie's chamberlain, who made the suggestion. If Mattachich would not oblige them by admitting his guilt in order to secure a release, they should find a senior representative of his family to make such an admission on his behalf. The War Office could graciously accede to the plea and thereafter the entire Mattachich clan, if there was such a thing, could go to hell. After inquiry it was decided that the obvious person to approach was Count Keglevich, the prisoner's adoptive father. So in due course Keglevich received a cautiously worded communication from the War Office informing him that *if* he were to make such a request on his adopted son's behalf, his imperial majesty *might* be minded to look favorably upon it. The count's reply to this suggestion was courteous, even fawning in tone, but firm too. First of all, he wrote, the order that had proclaimed his adoption of "the former Lieutenant Mattachich" had been annulled at his own request. Second, he had asked for this annulment because the person in question was "to the knowledge of your humble servant and most loyal subject a scoundrel of the lowest order." Therefore the undersigned respectfully begged his excellency's pardon for declining the request made of him.

Not even then did the authorities think of turning to Mattachich's formidable mother. As a woman, her standing was too low and her legal and civic rights too circumscribed (even in relatively enlightened Austria-Hungary) for her to be considered a suitable supplicant in such a case. Clearly, any mother would do anything to get a son out of jail; therefore her signature on a petition wouldn't carry the desired weight. In desperation the ministry then sought the advice of the *Banus* of Croatia, and after consultation he came up with—of all people!—the prisoner's drunken father, old Mattachich, whom Géza had not seen or communicated with since his schooldays. Let him be the one to make the request of his imperial majesty.

Which of course the old man did. He was honored to be asked. His hands shook; his eyes watered; his teeth were gone; his white hair and beard had apparently not been visited by comb or scissors for many weeks. His house had floors that groaned and trembled when walked on, ceilings that dropped flakes of plaster on the heads of those below, carpets that smelled horribly of dog. Nevertheless his hard-faced housekeeper had done something to knock the old man into shape—literally so, to judge from the uneasy glances he kept giving her—by dressing him in a blue uniform with a stand-up collar, tarnished brass buttons, and unraveling gilt braid around the cuffs. His tremor made it difficult for him to sign the document presented by the two officials who had brought it from Agram, but once it was done he asked them to drink a toast to his son's forthcoming release from prison. "Nothing matters more to a gentleman than to see his son set free," he said, with the earnest, unashamed self-centeredness of the aged, and they drank to the sentiment. Then they found other sentiments to drink to (including the health of the king-emperor and the future of their beloved Croatia), until the housekeeper took the bottle and locked it into a wedge-shaped pine cupboard standing in a corner of the room.

CHAPTER TEN

"ONCE AGAIN, IN THE COURSE OF THAT NIGHT, I lived through all
the years I had spent in prison. Nothing of them remained, nothing came
into my mind, nothing but sorrow. . . . As the doors of the prison finally
opened before me I thought of the dreadful people who had rejoiced—
prematurely—when those same doors had closed behind me, never
believing that the day would eventually come when I would emerge from
them."*

So much for the bitterness Mattachich felt on his release. Some days
later, Louise—who had been sent to take the waters in the resort of Bad
Elster, in hope of getting relief from the attacks of psoriasis and gout she
had been suffering from—returned to the asylum of Lindenhof, near
Dresden, which had been her home for the past two years. One of the first
things she heard on her return was that Mattachich was now a free man.
The owner and chief physician of the institution, Nelson Pierson by
name, a neat, small, gray-suited, demi-Englishman with the round chest
and tummy of a sparrow and the highly polished shoes of a mannequin in
a shop window, watched her closely as he broke the news to her. By then
the policy of trying to keep her totally ignorant of information with a
bearing on her own case had long since been abandoned. (Nor had her
stay in Bad Elster been her first licensed period of residence outside

* Mattachich, *Memoiren*, p. 155.

Lindenhof, though there too she had been under close supervision through-out.) That evening Pierson settled down to write in self-satisfied fashion to Louise's Guardian-in-Lunacy, Dr. Feistmantel in Vienna. The patient, he wrote, "seemed fairly pleased at the news of Mattachich's release, but not especially moved by it." He also reported her as having said she hoped Mattachich would not make any effort to get close to her, though she wouldn't mind "seeing him from a distance."*

Apparently it did not occur to Pierson that Louise may have been putting on a show for his benefit. Much later she was to write that during her incarceration in the three asylums, she had always seen in Mattachich her "only hope of liberty." Now, hearing that he had at last been released, her faith in him did not waver: "Once he was set free, the sun of my own free-dom rose above the horizon. . . . I was sure that the hour of my liberation was at hand."† In fact, two more years of imprisonment, during which she went through periods as bleak as any she had already endured, had to go by before her hour of liberation actually arrived.

❖

Now imagine—or try to imagine—the newly freed Mattachich join-ing Maria and settling down with her to lead a commonplace petit-bourgeois life in the shabby Floridsdorf district of Vienna. With no income to speak of.

You can't do it?

No?

Don't be disheartened. They couldn't do it either. Maria had left Möllersdorf ahead of Mattachich and found a small apartment in which she waited while the papers relating to his discharge were processed in various parts of the empire. By the time he got to Vienna, everything was

* Quoted in Holler, *Ihr Kampf,* p. 225.
† Louise, *Autour,* p. 243.

ready: Maria, the flat, the bits of furniture she had bought or rented for it, the baby, and her older son, the anxious Viktor—whose nervousness about how he would fit into this new arrangement immediately got on Mattachich's nerves. He had been a stepson of sorts himself, for most of his childhood, and had not enjoyed the experience; he had always resented the presence of Keglevich in the house and the subordinate position of his pushed-aside father. The fact that he believed his father to be fit for nothing better did not improve matters. Yet here he was, coming out of prison after a grueling four-and-a-half-year stretch and suddenly finding himself not only a stranger to the world at large but a father and a stepfather too, if you please.

After what they had been through, both Maria and Mattachich inevitably felt a reciprocal sense of anticlimax. For Maria there was the anticlimax of living day in and day out with the victim and hero she had created for herself out of newspaper reports and her own imaginings, had then loved in the improbable surroundings of a prison, and for whose sake she had defied the power of the state in order to break twice through the prison walls. (Once to get herself into the jail, once to get him out of it.) Now she had to learn how moody and easily dissatisfied he was, how impatient with the children, how impatient with her, how anxious and self-regarding. Yet what else could be expected of a man who was himself living through the anticlimax of finding how swiftly the initial euphoria of his liberation had evaporated? Yes, it was wonderful to breathe fresh air again, to eat foods he had not tasted for years, to see and hear around him the noise of a city, to go to the theater, to look at shop windows and the multitudes of women passing in the street, to hire a horse and spend days hacking about in the Vienna woods, to marvel at the mechanical changes that had occurred in the years he had been away (more motorcars and electric trams in the streets, more shops and houses illumined by the unyielding worm-shaped filaments of electric bulbs instead of lambent gas flames, more apartment buildings springing up beyond the Gürdel, telephones and motion picture performances available to those who lived in the right districts). But then? What next? There were times when he was so unnerved by his fear of spaces and of unknown crowds of people that he had to sit down or lean against a wall with his eyes closed, fearing he would fall, faint, be trampled on. At other times he was choked by rage at having had so much of his life stolen from him; at such moments he had to restrain himself from grabbing complete strangers and shouting into their faces the story of the injustices he had suffered. Of these moments, and more than moments, he could speak to Maria, but not a word crossed his lips about the bizarre homesickness that overcame him for the stinking cell where he had endured miseries that made him hope many times he would not survive them. The longing to go back there seemed so improbable, repellent, even mad, he had to keep it to himself. Yet he could see its perverse attraction too. In prison the purpose served by each succeeding day was always starkly self-evident. It brought him closer to the moment when this torment of confinement would come to an end—by death if necessary.

But now? What was he supposed to do? How was he to live? Some of Maria's contacts had put his picture in the papers and several of them had published interviews with him, in which he gave vent to his disgust at a society that put a higher value on the word of "the big capitalists and moneylenders of city-wide ill repute" than on the veracity of an officer and gentleman like himself.* That was fine, it pleased his vanity, but for how long could such episodes sustain him? Was he to content himself with being a kind father and stepfather to these children? A good semi-husband to Maria? A conscientious riding instructor to the socially ambitious daughters of shopkeepers and accountants? To live indefinitely in a flat like the one they now occupied?

Facing prospects like these, it never occurred to him that Maria might be learning things about herself that were hardly less shocking to her than his discovery of a nostalgia for the prison cell was for him. He could

* Mattachich, *Memoiren*, p. 57.

not guess at the dismay she felt on discovering that Mattachich the victim hero, the imprisoned martyr, the male creature famished as helplessly as a dog for her body was more appealing to her, more compelling to her mind and her senses, than this sleepless, fretful, commonplace person who no longer wanted to touch her and whom she did not much care to touch either.

Imagine these strange reciprocities constantly at work within them both—and add to them the effect of the differences in social class they had been able to ignore in prison but that now insistently made themselves felt. Here in Vienna he was the aristocrat (he had of course resumed his "title" the moment he had left prison), the officer, the former consort of a king's daughter; she was a shop girl, a seamstress, a canteen worker. Which made it all the more galling that the company they were keeping was inclined to regard him as Maria's dependent, the beneficiary of her courage and single-mindedness. In his glory days with Louise he had learned to recognize a sly patronizing look in the eyes of strangers who saw him as nothing more than the jumped-up fancy man of an aging princess; he had consoled himself then with the thought that most of them would have leaped at the chance to change places with him. But that consolation wasn't open to the companion of a woman who revealed her working-class origins every time she opened her mouth and whose company was nevertheless preferred to his by the only friends they had. Without Maria he would never have encountered such people—Bohemians, journalists, socialists, head-scratchers, wordmongers, detribalized Jews, antimilitarists, sneerers at the idea of empire—whom he simultaneously envied and did his best to despise. Prominent among them was that same Daszynski who had spoken so passionately in the *Reichsrat* about the wrongs done to Mattachich and who now patronized him merely as one of his political trophies.* These people loved Maria for being both working-class and a heroine, whereas he remained (it was in their eyes, again, that

---

* In his *Memoiren*, Mattachich refers (just once) to Daszynski as "my friend . . . to whom I owe my liberty" (p. 98) and quotes from the latter's speech to the *Reichsrat*. However, he gives less of the text of the speech than Louise does in her autobiography.

he saw it) a boring gigolo-esque cavalryman now trying to pass himself off as something he never had been.

More and more, as time went by, Mattachich chose to respond truculently to these new acquaintances, especially after a few drinks. At first he had listened respectfully to them, but no longer. With the authority given him by his army background and his sufferings at the hands of "the Habsburg clique," he began to lay down the law. Gray-faced still, drawn around the lips, lined across the forehead, his hair receding but still brushed straight back in military fashion, he made it plain how different an animal he was from them. Yes, he was just as antimonarchist as they were, just as anticapitalist and anticlerical. But he was also antisocialist, antiegalitarian, antirevolutionary, pessimistic, a believer not in democracy but in the destiny given to a minority to command the gullible, sensual, immitigably stupid mass of men and women. Of all classes. The kind of leadership he had in mind, he insisted, owed nothing to status or blood or breeding. That was all a grand conservative *Schwindelei* and *Betrügerei*. Real leadership, true leadership, was derived from the duty a man owed to himself. And how was that duty to be recognized? Because it demanded of him to act not *because of* but *in spite of*! This was a distinction that had become talismanic for Mattachich, for reasons Maria believed she alone understood.

"You help other people not *because* you think they're worth it, but *in spite of* knowing that they aren't. You risk your life for them *in spite of* knowing they'd never dream of doing the same for you. You help them in their difficulties *in spite of* being sure they won't repay you for it. You work as conscientiously as you can *in spite of* the fact that most people can't tell the difference between a job well done and one not worth spitting at. You do it not for the greater glory of God but *in spite of* knowing that he isn't there, he never was, and there'll be no one up in heaven to give you a pat on the head when you're finished and done with. So why bother? Why make the effort? Out of shame, that's why! Or pride, if you like. Think of the alternative! Think of being one of those people who always do their sums in advance, who always ask, What's in it for me? What's the payout? Priests, shopkeepers, little clerks, hotel managers, Jew moneylenders, lawyers. . . . You know what I call the lot them? *Because-ofs!* They're the lowest form of human life, these *because-ofs,* which means they're the lowest form of all living creatures. The worm that eats you when you're dead and rotten doesn't wear a crown on its head and stars on its chest. The bird that shits on your shoulder means nothing by it. Cockroaches don't write manifestos and stand for election."

That was the figure he now cut: sedentary, scornful, throwing one phrase after another into the cigar smoke and brandy reek of this or that café: his contribution to the tides of vociferation that rose and fell around him. Those sitting near enough to make out what he was saying were part impressed, part amused, part contemptuous of this impassioned forger and ladies' man holding forth on duty and honor. Then they would resume talking about whatever they had been talking of before.

Silent, suddenly exhausted, Mattachich felt a trembling of his ribs, as if fingers were running along them from within. His listeners couldn't believe that he meant what he was saying; but he did, he did. He had worked it all out in his prison cell.

❖

Then there was the matter of Louise. Maria had expected him to try to get in touch with her soon after his arrival in Vienna or at least to talk of doing so. But he did not. So she made allowances for him; he had to get his bearings, find his feet, accustom himself to being a free man again, et cetera. Yet as the weeks went by, his silence and inactivity on this of all subjects made her more and more uneasy. One month passed, a second, a third. Had he forgotten what had been agreed between them a long time before? Surely not. Or had it meant less to him than she had supposed?

In many ways, she felt, that would be even worse. For Maria believed that they had made a compact with each other about Louise. It had been sealed the very first time her name had come up between them, during the summer of her arrival in Möllersdorf. It was then he had sworn to her that if he survived the rest of his sentence he would do everything he could to get Louise out of whatever hellhole her enemies had put her into. He would make it his chief aim in life. Nothing would deter him from it, least of all the risks that might be involved.

She had not prompted this declaration from him. It was his doing. Speaking sullenly, inwardly, as if under compulsion, his eyes resting neither on her nor anywhere else, he stood in front of Maria and told her he would never allow what had happened between them to push Louise out of his mind. Never. He thought of her almost constantly and always with one emotion only—guilt, guilt, guilt. If he had not indulged in his own fantasies, if he had not stood in wait for her on Viennese street corners, if he had not visited her in Abbazia and had not set out with her on their travels, she would never have had to suffer any of the misfortunes and humiliations that followed. This madness business (his phrase) plainly being the worst of them. He had never been her protector, as he had fancied; instead, he been an agent of her destruction. If he ever had the power to reach her again, to help her, to put right what he could, he would do it. He could never abandon her.

That particular afternoon he had supposedly been on his way to the prison hospital, where he was to see the visiting doctor; Maria, having finished her shift in the canteen, should already have left the premises; instead they had met by arrangement in the comfortless little storeroom behind the prison shop. He stood throughout; she sat low down on a wooden box packed with bars of strong-smelling soap, mottled blue and white. There was also a smell of cheese in the room. Late-afternoon sunlight came in at an angle through a small barred window, gilding the wall opposite and imprinting on it a shadow grid of iron bars. They both spoke in whispers, which was how they always talked to each other. Shouts and whistles and raggedly stamping feet could be heard from the yard outside, where the "other-rank" prisoners, returning from their work details, were being counted before going back in batches to their communal cells.

"It's all my doing," he said. "My failure . . . my"—his voice dropped even lower, trailed away, barely emerged from somewhere in his throat— "my . . . confusion."

That was as close as he would ever bring himself to speak of the forged promissory notes that had finally been his undoing and Louise's. "Confusion" was the only word for the blur, the uncertainty, the almost-nausea that opened and closed within him, like the mouth of an octopus, whenever recollection of the episode stirred his mind. What had happened? Had he done it? Who had done it? Hadn't there already been two signatures, not one, on those wretched pieces of papers when he had first seen them? Who could tell the handwriting of the one sister from the other anyway. So when . . . how . . . and what was the point . . . ?

Maria waited. She sat on the soapbox with her arms half folded in front of her, as if protecting her bosom: one hand cupping an elbow, the other her chin. She had always known that a conversation of this kind had to take place, sooner or later, but had never tried to imagine how it would begin, what he would say, what her response would be. All she could think of now was that it was better for the moment to have arrived at last than for her still to be waiting for it. Yet she was afraid of learning something about his past that she did not want to hear and bursting into tears as a result.

As if he had read her thoughts he said, "If you understood how childlike she is," and she herself suddenly wanted to cry. *What about me? What about me?* clamored the child inside her—but not aloud.

Silence again.

She stirred and spoke evenly, like someone asking directions from a stranger. "So you still belong to her? And you always will?"

"No."

"No? You've just said you can't put her out of your mind. That you'll do anything to set her free. So where does that leave me? Allowed to be yours only while you're here, in this vile place?"

She pointed down at the pale, rough, dried-out floorboards of the

room and, a moment later, with a gesture of her arm, the barred window
to her right.

He had not yet met her gaze. "I'm certain she suffers for me," he said.
"I'm certain she blames herself for what's become of me, just as I do for
her." Then: "She'll never begrudge what I feel for you."

"How do you know?"

His hands had been loosely clasped at his waist; now he abandoned
them, letting them hang down empty. His eyes turned toward the sun-
stained wall and its shadow bars. It was to the wall that he made his declaration. "I love you too," he said. "With Louise it's different. I don't think
of her . . . like that. I don't believe I ever will, again. We've been away
from each other for too long. And anyway, even before. . . ." At last he
gazed directly at her. "Lying there in my cell night after night, month
after month, I trained myself not to think of her . . . like that. Eventually
it became easier than you would think. I'm telling you the truth. I have
to look after her. She's my responsibility. She will always be in my life.
But I don't think of her as . . . as I think of you."

"Of me? Or of any other woman—available here—in a place like this?"

"Other woman! Other woman!" Anger made him raise his voice; fear
made her lift a warning hand. "Don't be stupid!" he whispered, as angrily
as before. "What other woman would have come here to find me? Only you."

Her mood changed abruptly. He did not see but rather felt the dazzle
of her dark eyes, come and gone in an instant.

"So you've noticed at last! I *am* stupid. If I wasn't stupid I wouldn't be
here! You should be grateful for my stupidity. Day and night."

Something between a smile and a grimace affected his lips. "I am
grateful," he said. "Day and night."

He leaned toward her and touched her forehead with a single finger,
above her troubling left eye. That was done then, sealed, a compact between
them.

❖

Yet here he was, more than three months after his return to Vienna, hanging around the flat, going into the city on purposeless forays, giving occasional riding lessons (through a small livery stable off the Renneweg), threatening to start writing a book, spending time in cafés, talking too much. He had also paid a visit to his mother in Croatia and returned from it with a surprisingly large bank check by way of a gift. From what source this money had become available to his mother he did not know and had not asked. She was still living with the odious Fiedler, he reported, and was "just the same." She had declined his invitation to come to Vienna and meet Maria and the grandchild. "Apparently she doesn't approve," he said dryly, leaving her to work out, if she wished, what that might mean. With a touch of pride in his mother's obduracy, he said again, "Just the same."

Then he resumed his idler's life. Maria had got herself a part-time job as a proofreader and general helper on a monthly magazine; she also worked two afternoons a week in a baker's shop. He did nothing. Eventually a trivial argument over his refusal to look after the children one afternoon, when she was too busy to do so, flared into uncontrollable anger. She flew at him. "If you can't do that much for me, then for God's sake go and do something for your precious princess!"

She had never spoken to him like that before, and was caught for a moment between shock and relief. But having been the aggressor she was also the first to recover. She went for him again, even more fiercely than before.

"Or do you want me to do it? Is that what you're waiting for? I got you out of that foul Möllersdorf place, so you think you can leave me to do the same for her?"

His face changed color. Without a word he turned and left the flat, slamming the front door behind him. He was away for about ten days. During that time she wondered how he was managing without his overcoat, a change of clothes, his razor. She also wondered if she would ever see him again. But underneath she was confident he would return. More than that: she felt easy in mind, almost serene. The irksomeness of the life they were leading together had at last resolved itself into an expectancy, the prospect of another adventure. Yes! He didn't have the strength or self-confidence to do the task on his own; that was now clear to her, for all his fine words. Nor could she do it alone. But together . . . ?

She was not afraid of Louise. She was not afraid of him. And she felt no fear for herself. As things were going, she had nothing to lose.

❖

Now imagine yourself just outside the Lindenhof asylum. You are sitting with Louise in the modest gig in which she and her maid, Olga Börner, go for their afternoon drives in the countryside around Lindenhof. These outings take place two or three times a week, weather permitting, and are another element of the regime that the avuncular Dr. Pierson has arranged for this special patient. The two ladies are accompanied by a young groom who knows that his job is not just to drive the carriage but also to keep an eye on the princess. Occasionally they go to Coswig, the little town nearest to the asylum; more often they drive at random among the rolling woods interspersed with clearings, cropped fields, farmsteads, and the occasional sawmill, from which terrible shrieks and groans emerge at intervals. Pine trees flourish on the sandy soil, but so do sycamore, ash, hornbeam, oak. It is early in October and the leaves on the deciduous trees have already stiffened and lost their luster, in preparation for the flourish of color and the grand denuding that will take place over the next month or two. Acorns drop solemnly into the undergrowth one by one, while papery seeds are shaken down at intervals from the loose tassels and pagodalike structures festooning other trees. Occasionally the gig has to wait to let a farm cart or wagon carrying timber pass by; or it comes to a halt, the nose bag is brought out to feed the docile mare pulling them along, and the two ladies go for a rustling walk into the wood. Never for too long, though; the coachman shouts out for them when he feels they have been away long enough. He always feels more at ease when they are safely shut behind him in their seats and he has turned the gig toward Lindenhof.

Imagine that that is the direction to which they have now turned, after an hour's sedate jaunting. The weather is mild, the sky is cloudy but calm, and the ladies have asked for the hood of the gig to be folded back. Vehicles are rare on this road; no one is stirring about the farmhouses or fields. So it comes as a diversion when, on a slowly curving stretch of roadway, a solitary cyclist appears at a distance. The incline of the road is against him and he is pedaling hard, his head bent industriously over the handlebars of his cycle. He wears a brown knickerbocker suit and a tweed cap with peaks both front and back.

Hearing the vehicle approach, he looks up sharply. He is clean-shaven, dressed in unfamiliar clothes, and at least fifty or more paces ahead. But Louise recognizes him instantly. How could she not! Seeing the light carriage approach he gets off the bike and moves a little to the side of the road. He too has recognized her; she has no doubt of it. He stares straight ahead as the gig slowly draws closer. It is now almost level with him. He holds the bike upright with one hand, its saddle leaning against his midriff. His eyes are so intently fixed on Louise he does not notice the groom's greeting from above or glance at Olga. He and Louise are alongside each other now; there is nothing between them but air, inches of air only, as the vehicle continues to move ploddingly forward. Only a few immeasurably extended seconds are given to each pair of eyes to devour the other. Too little and long enough: both.

They are no longer level now and time has resumed its usual pace. Hours later each of them will remember not only staring eyes but much they had been unaware of then: hands, hair, even the grass on the side of the road and the attentive pines behind, seeming to hold their breath. The silence too, and the grinding of iron-shod carriage wheels on the gravel that emphasizes rather than breaks the silence. Then a gasp Louise cannot control. It sounds so loud to her she is astonished that Olga seems not to hear it. Both Louise's hands are still clutching the carriage door as she turns to look back at him: his pale oval face, smaller than she had remembered it to be, under a brownish cap with thin thongs tied in a bow on its crown. The cycle has fallen and he stoops to pick it up. He has come for her at last! How faithless she had been over these last desolate months, imagining he had forgotten her, accusing him of abandoning her to her fate while he reveled in his freedom.

Her need to hold someone as strong as her need to speak, she takes Olga's hand between her gloved hands and brings her head close to the maid's. "Olga," she whispers, anxious lest the driver should overhear her, "do you know who that gentleman was?"

"No, madam."

"Olga, do you love me at all?"

"Madam, how can you ask?"

"Then swear to me that you'll never repeat a word of what I tell you."

"Madam—of course—whatever you want!"

"That gentleman we passed—you can't see him now—he's my *friend*!"

"Oh, madam, how wonderful!" was all Olga could say, for which she was rewarded by her mistress with a wholly unprecedented kiss on the cheek. Then they both cried a little.

All next day Louise fretted to go out for another drive, but the weather had turned against her; it rained steadily from a closed-up sky, and this irrational request of hers was turned down by no less an authority than Dr. Pierson himself. The sole resource left her was to try to reconstruct her first sighting of him in the distance and their passing each other, and the more she lingered over the episode the more confused it became with her memory of their first exchange of glances, silent too, in the Prater years before. It had been spring then; she had been sitting in a lacquered, emblazoned, open landau with a liveried footman behind her, a top-hatted coachman up front, and a frothily attired lady-in-waiting beside her; while he, in uniform, had been asserting his mastery over a refractory black stallion.

Not humbly standing aside with a bicycle—a bicycle, for God's sake!—in his hands.

Yet these differences were inconsequential compared with what the meetings had in common. His eyes and hers locked together, not to be torn apart.

❖

The rain stopped late that day and Louise's first thought on waking the next morning was to set out at once for a drive through the woods. But she restrained herself, and it was not until afternoon that the threesome set out again through the gates of Lindenhof. It was not the same threesome as before, however; Olga Börner had been replaced by Frau von Gebauer, whose turn it was to go on the outing.

This time they did not have far to go before Mattachich appeared. Dressed in the same suit and still wearing his "English" cap, he stood in the middle of the road, one hand raised to stop the vehicle. His bicycle lay in the grass to one side. When the gig halted he beckoned to Louise to come down. The groom looked on while she scrambled out. Gebauer followed, determined not to be left behind. Mattachich led them for a short distance into the trees. "Now I could approach the princess," he wrote not long afterward. "She leaned against a tree, extended her hand to me with tears in her eyes, and said, 'So there is a God after all.'"*

Constrained by both their prolonged separation and the presence of Gebauer, they embraced briefly. Louise made no attempt to introduce the newcomer to her companion, who had no doubt about his identity. She stood guiltily aside and let them talk together for a few minutes. The driver, knowing that something illicit was going on, came to her rescue. Hearing his footsteps on the path, she insisted that Louise return immediately to the carriage. Mattachich stood where he was and watched them go. "I parted from her," the passage in his book continues, "knowing that the princess was unaltered in her feelings, in her determination, in her childlike spirit. Her noble features were clouded by years of suffering but were even more beautiful than before."†

That night Gebauer, who had heard nothing from Olga about the pre-

---

* Mattachich, *Memoiren,* pp. 174–175. See also Louise, *Autour,* pp. 243–244.
† Mattachich, *Memoiren,* p. 175.

vious meeting, went straight to Dr. Pierson, as if to a priest, and confessed to him what she had seen in the woods. He immediately wrote to Dr. Feistmantel in Vienna to warn him that Mattachich was up to his mischief again; at the same time he tried to play down Louise's excitement at seeing and talking to her former lover.* As expected, Feistmantel passed the letter on to Prince Philipp, who in turn sent it to Bachrach—who responded in true Bachrachian fashion. Since the Lindenhof asylum lay within Saxony (one of the states of Kaiser Wilhelm's empire), he wrote to the Saxon authorities to remind them that the princess was a certified lunatic currently living within their jurisdiction. They were therefore obliged to frustrate any cross-border attempt from Austria to release her. Failure to carry out this task would gravely affect relations between the two empires, as the princess was so closely connected to the Hofburg and the emperor Franz Josef took a special interest in her case. To help the German police pick out her would-be "kidnapper"—described also as "an ex-prisoner by the name of Mattachich with a mania for 'rescuing' her royal highness and no regard for justice and law"—Bachrach sent them a written description and a blurry photograph of the man.† He also warned the police in Vienna of Mattachich's intentions and asked them to keep a closer watch than before on his movements.

The net result of all this was that Louise was forbidden to leave the grounds of Lindenhof and denied access to all newspapers. Her villa was searched regularly. No communication from outside the institution was allowed to reach her without being thoroughly scrutinized. Relations between herself and Gebauer deteriorated sharply after the latter had admitted her earlier confession to Dr. Pierson. As if to exacerbate Louise's conviction that the whole world was conspiring against her at this juncture, she learned that her mother—who had been banished years before

---

* Pierson (quoted in Holler, *Ihr Kampf,* p. 233) uses the same word about Louise's state of mind as Mattachich: "childlike."

† Mattachich, *Memoiren,* p. 69.

from the presence of the merciless Leopold—was on her deathbed. Pierson indicated that he was ready to allow Louise to pay her mother a last visit, provided she was kept under close supervision throughout, but Leopold would not hear of it. Nor would he allow her to attend the funeral that took place shortly afterward.*

Not a word from Mattachich or about him penetrated the cordon thrown around her. Nor until much later did she learn that soon after their meeting in the woods he had twice returned to the neighborhood in the hope of seeing her again. But the heavy police presence around the asylum forced him to give up the attempt each time.

❖

On his return to Vienna from his first foray to Lindenhof, Mattachich spoke in a calm and unembarrassed fashion of his meetings with Louise. She looked older, he said; she had put on weight; they had exchanged just a few sentences; they had both been much moved at seeing each other again. Then he added, "She doesn't blame me for what's happened to her. Not at all."

"Did you think she would?"

"I was afraid she might."

"Does that mean you have stopped blaming yourself?"

"No."

"Did you tell her about me?"

Again the answer was no. "We had minutes together, that's all, and that other woman was listening. But don't worry. I'll tell her about you when I can."

He and Maria were friends again. But the two brief visits he subsequently made to the neighborhood of Lindenhof left him depressed and angry. The number of policemen swarming around the place had to mean

---

* See Holler, *Ihr Kampf*, pp. 217–218. Leopold also banned Stephanie from the funeral. He could not forgive his second daughter for daring to marry—after many years of widowhood—a Hungarian lawyer by the name of Lonyay who did not have a drop of royal blood in his veins.

just one thing. He was being followed. Spied on. Listened to. It had to be so. "They could never keep so many policemen there permanently. Vienna tips them off when I leave and lets them know when I get back. I can't think what to do."

So Maria gave him something else to think about. Since his release they had often talked of the book he might write about his relationship with Louise, his trial, and the years he had spent in prison. Now she told him that during his first absence she had got in touch with publishing firms in Austria and Germany and had trailed the idea of such a book before them. One of these firms (Ödenburg, in Leipzig) had responded positively but she had done nothing about it, as she was waiting to hear whether he would busy himself directly with helping Louise, or trying to do so. For the moment that seemed impossible . . . so?

Almost at once Mattachich embraced the idea. This would be his way of keeping the case alive in the mind of the public, until he found a better way yet. He became even more enthusiastic about it when she succeeded in finding publishers in France and Spain who also put up some money for the book.*

Once he began the task, he found to his surprise that he enjoyed it. Rewriting his past gave him a sense of power he had not known since Louise's household in the Villa Paradiso had fallen into ruin. With his pen in hand he was the master. It licensed him to be scurrilous and sardonic about his enemies, fulsome in his praise of Louise, and more than just to his own best qualities. Maria was granted only two brief appearances in his pages, and the child who sometimes played about his feet as he wrote at their living room table was not mentioned at all.

Employed in this fashion, he found himself leading a version of the

---

* See *Mémoires inédits: Folle par raison d'État* (Paris, 1904) and *Loca por Razón de Estado* (Madrid, 1904), a title that translates in both cases as "Insane for Reasons of State." The equivalent wording does not appear on the title page of the original German-language version. No English translation of the book appears ever to have been made. The German edition is set in a particularly rebarbative Gothic script and uses typefaces of different sizes in random fashion. The spaces between lines on the page vary at random too.

commonplace bourgeois life that had seemed so implausible to them both when they had first set up house together in Vienna. Even this, however, was predicated on the understanding that the whole arrangement was provisional and that everything around them was soon going to change. Radically.

CHAPTER ELEVEN

ONE OF THE GREAT ADVANTAGES OF BEING a woman, Maria had learned from her experiences in Möllersdorf, was that most people supposed it to be a disadvantage. It rendered her harmless in their eyes, insignificant, virtually anonymous. To the police in Vienna she was merely an adjunct to Mattachich: his mistress, the mother of his little bastard, a flighty, unreliable female who had managed to get herself pregnant by him while employed in Möllersdorf jail and then compounded the offense by letting herself be used by a crowd of seedy left-wing politicians and journalists. Now that Mattachich had been freed the authorities saw no reason to take any special notice of her—which meant she was able to travel alone to Dresden and Coswig without being observed. During these journeys, she befriended a female member of the asylum's staff and through her made contact with Louise's maid, Olga Börner. Maria's story was that she was a journalist interested in Mattachich's case and therefore wanted to learn whatever she could about the circumstances of Louise's confinement. Olga did not dare to take Maria into the asylum to meet her mistress but promised to pass on any letters Maria or Mattachich might write and to report to Maria, via a poste restante address, any changes in the princess's circumstances.

With this shaky line of communication established, Maria set about looking for partners in the project she and Mattachich were committed to: getting Louise out of the asylum. Since she was kept there under a legal guardianship lodged with the Lord Marshal—from which there could be no legal or medical appeal—it was plain that their effort amounted to organizing a criminal conspiracy. They also knew they could neither do it on their own nor hire outsiders to do it for them. Anyone who took part in the scheme would in effect have to pay for the privilege of endangering his own freedom.

Preoccupied with writing the final pages of his memoir, and convinced by now that it would have an explosive effect on public opinion in Austria, Mattachich simply let Maria get on with it. In the end, after a few false starts, she managed to assemble a curious crew of fellow conspirators. There was Joseph Weitzer, a hearty, tough, good-humored, bald-headed simpleton, landlord of a pub around the corner from Maria's flat in Floridsdorf, who was excited by the thought of joining in such a romantic high-society venture and who managed to convince himself that, if they were to succeed, Louise's fabulously wealthy father would reward him with payments far exceeding the sum he offered to put into the enterprise.* Then there was a social democratic deputy in the German parliament and a frequent visitor to Vienna, Albert Südekum, whom Mattachich had met through Daszynski and who joined the conspiracy out of generalized antimonarchist zeal, together with the hope that a stunt of this kind would raise his standing with his comrades in Germany.

Last, and most important, there was a young French journalist by the name of Henri de Nousanne who worked as a freelance in Vienna for the Paris paper *Le Journal* and who ingeniously persuaded his parents and the newspaper itself to pool their resources, in order to provide Maria and Mattachich with the largest of the financial contributions they needed. *Le Journal* did this in terms of an agreement so modern in style and language you may well feel wounded in your twenty-first-century pride to read of it. What was jointly agreed by Maria, Mattachich, and de Nousanne on one side and by *Le Journal* on the other was that in return for putting up

* Needless to say, Leopold did no such thing. Eventually Weitzer was reduced to trying to get his money back from Prince Philipp, of all people. He had no luck there, either. See Holler, *Ihr Kampf,* pp. 228, 317.

the lion's share of the money for the project, the paper would hold exclusive rights to the story of Louise's escape from captivity—to be written, of course, by de Nousanne himself.[*]

❖

The three musketeers they called themselves, the members of the team Maria had brought together. They were all looking for excitement; they admired Maria and were agreed that she deserved someone better than Mattachich; having committed themselves to the project, they stuck with it to the end—until they had indeed succeeded in snatching Louise from her captors and putting her beyond the borders of the Austrian and German empires.[†]

Yet all Maria's helpers were to be disappointed in the end, though for a different reason in each case. Weitzer never saw his money again, let alone the bonus for which he had been hoping; Südekum's career did not take off as a result of the newspaper headlines earned by Louise's escape; and even Henri de Nousanne, the youngest of the three and apparently the clear gainer among them, emerged from the coup a more despondent figure than he had been before. He did write his articles on the escapade; he was paid for them and subsequently promoted to become a staffer on his paper instead of working merely as a freelance. The trouble with de Nousanne, however, was that he had fallen in love with Maria—seriously in love, hopefully, hopelessly, every way he knew how to be in love, including some he would not have thought possible beforehand. Maria

---

[*] Holler, *Ihr Kampf*, p. 228.

[†] Franz Josef of Austria-Hungary and Wilhelm of Germany did not care for each other personally or politically. They were careful to keep on good terms nevertheless, since they and their advisers had begun to cling to the idea that if a war in Europe were to break out, an alliance of the "Central Powers" would save them from being crushed between the armies of France to the west and Russia to the east. (Not to speak of the Serbs threatening them from the south.) What this alliance actually helped bring about was the First World War—which destroyed both monarchies and led to the yet greater catastrophes of the Russian Revolution, the advent of Hitler, and the Second World War.

was not his first love—from boyhood onward he had had a habit of falling in love—but she turned out to be his last love, in the sense that she remained his ideal loss, the one he could not forget, the standard by which he judged all other passions and losses before and after.

Her only shortcoming in his eyes was her attachment to Mattachich—"the jockey," as he venomously thought of him. But even as he asked himself how a woman like Maria could have fallen in love with such a shallow, stupid, self-important creature, he was gnawingly aware that had she not done so he would never have met her, never have managed to get close to her. What a quandary! What a stupid business! She loved Mattachich enough to help his former mistress escape from imprisonment; he, Henri, loved her enough to help her in this enterprise; while for the moment Mattachich himself helped nobody and did nothing aside from getting on with writing his book.

Which left Henri to torture himself with the thought of Mattachich's lips and tongue grazing over Maria's body like a cow's over a pasture, his breath penetrating her mouth and nostrils, his hands going everywhere, to all the places her undeclared lover would never visit. And what was worse, Maria thrilling to every caress! His only consolation was the thought that no one would guess what he felt about her; that no one could see through the light, casual, boyish manner that was both his disguise and his curse, since he could never shed it. Even his prematurely graying hair, with its untrimmed ringlets hanging over his ears and the shafts of his metal-rimmed glasses, was part of that disguise, and so was the one white canine that came to rest on his lower lip when he smiled. Beneath which there lay a melancholy and vulnerability that had long predated his acquaintance with Maria and would remain with him long after his very last visit to her.

He made that visit—to Möllersdorf, of all places—on hearing that after many years she had returned to live there. He set out on the journey in a divided state of mind all too familiar to him: unable to repress the faint hope that she might welcome him now as a suitor and the incurable conviction that she would do no such thing.

Yet he had to go, if only because he knew how he would reproach himself if he did not at least *try*. Years before, Mattachich had felt much the same about his approaches to the Princess Louise. But to what different effect.

❖

The publication of Mattachich's book produced less of an explosion than he had hoped. Philipp and Bachrach were of course disgusted by the insults it heaped on them, and the army high command was enraged by his attacks on its system of military justice. But just as writing the book had distracted him from his failure to reach Louise, so now the thought of reaching her again helped him get over his disappointment at the book's reception. He, Maria, and their co-conspirators discussed various schemes of rescue, some of them more hare-brained than others. An armed daylight raid on the asylum? Kidnapping Louise when she was allowed out for one of her rural drives? Smuggling themselves into the institution in the guise of voluntary patients? Passing themselves off (with forged papers) as members of the staff?

In the end a real opportunity was given to them by Dr. Pierson himself, the master of Lindenhof. Having allowed Louise to resume her drives outside the walls, he proposed to Dr. Feistmantel, her guardian in Vienna, that she should return to Bad Elster for a few weeks in the coming August. He was sure, he wrote, that she would benefit both physically and psychologically from the change. She would stay in the Wettiner Hof hotel, as she had previously, so the surroundings would be familiar to her, and his assistant, Dr. Mauss, and two guards, as well as her maid and lady companion, would accompany her throughout. Feistmantel agreed, provided the local police were advised of her visit and would join in the watch to be kept over her.*

---

* "Dr. Pierson always kept a close watch on me," Louise writes in *Autour* (p. 248), "though his manner always remained courteous. He knew I was not insane, but knew also how much he earned by keeping me in Lindenhof. The prospect of losing me as a 'client' was therefore very disagreeable to him."

Pierson accepted this condition without demur and went bobbing across the grounds of his institution to let the ladies in the villa know of the summer treat he had arranged for them. Louise did not respond to the news, but the Fräuleins von Gebauer and Börner were delighted. For them any break in routine was welcome. Pierson bowed low, as he always did to his apathetic royal prisoner, and left the villa—not knowing that as soon as he had passed through the garden gate that opened on the unpaved roadway, Olga went to her bedroom and wrote a hasty note to Maria. Several months had passed since the two women had met, and in Maria's absence she had developed something like a crush on her, or on the idea of her: this young independent female "journalist" leading a life so different from her own dreary double confinement—no, triple confinement—as a lady's maid in a villa that was itself set in the grounds of a lunatic asylum. And to think of her friend being in contact—daily, perhaps—with the handsome, famously disgraceful gentleman on a bicycle whom she, Olga, had encountered in the woods last autumn! She gave Maria the dates when the princess and her party would be in Bad Elster, where they would stay, and who would accompany them. She could not bear to think of the consequences her letter might have for herself or anyone else, the handsome gentleman included. But she could not bear to keep silent either.

With great daring she added at the end of the letter, *From your trusted and trusting friend, Olga.*

❖

Two days later the letter was read aloud by Maria to Mattachich. It produced an immediate effect.

"Now's our chance!" Mattachich cried to Maria. "I'll show the bastards! I'll teach them a lesson!"

That was his first thought: revenge. Writing his book had discharged a little, though never enough, of the bitterness he felt over his imprisonment, his ruined career and prospectless future; but it had done nothing for the injury he had suffered to his pride as a military man. Big-ass staff officers in Vienna, wretches like Bachrach and Fiedler, traitors in his own regiment conspiring with unknown spies and imbecile policemen in Agram—all of them had laid an elaborate military-style ambush for him, and he, with the trusting Louise behind him, had obligingly stumbled into it. Unable to defend themselves, caught naked (literally so in his case, virtually so in Louise's), they had been torn apart and thrown into their captors' cages. That was all his years of training as a soldier had done for him: the months he had spent on maneuvers, the lectures he had attended, the battle plans he had studied, the military histories he had read and dreamed over in his spare time—all nothing. All wasted.*

But Bad Elster? Where better for him to demonstrate his daring and leadership than a small, peaceful spa town overrun by August visitors? After his travels with Louise how well he knew such places, with their crowds of invalids and hypochondriacs, idlers and quacks, gamblers and servants. Filling the hotels, riding in coaches and bath chairs, following their baggage through the streets, walking in parks, boating on lakes, listening to music, drinking the waters, immersing themselves in the pools of various bathing houses before wrapping themselves in layers of sheets. . . . Who in such a throng would notice him and his co-conspirators? It was perfect. If they couldn't snatch Louise there, they would never be able to do it.

"Give me two days," he said to Maria, "and I'll have a plan worked out. They'll never forget the shock I'm going to give them."

"*We're* going to give them," she said.

He ignored the correction. Rapt, he replied with words uttered by some forgotten officer on some forgotten exercise a long time ago—"Four things I must have"—and began counting them out with the index finger of his right hand on the outspread fingers of the other: "Maintenance of aim, clarity of mind, discipline, courage."

Only his thumb remained untouched. Maria closed her fist around it. "Luck."

---

* "Out of a pure passion to serve, and against the wishes of my parents, I had become a soldier; and I can say with complete conviction that I was a first-class cavalryman" (Mattachich, *Memoiren*, p. 107). Many similar passages can be found in the book.

❖

Rough and ready Weitzer was the first to leave for Bad Elster. He booked himself into the Wettiner Hof for the entire month of August and spent his first few days spying out the general plan of the hotel and learning as much as he could about its routines; he also established which of the rooms Louise, her ladies, and the asylum guards would occupy. The role he assumed in the hotel, the largest and most expensive in the spa, came easily to him: he claimed to be a self-made businessman (which he was) of working-class origins (ditto) who had come to take the waters for the sake of his gout (from which he did in fact suffer). Having worked as a barkeeper all his life, and being sociable and unscrupulous by nature, he did not have much difficulty in picking out which members of the hotel's staff were likely to be the most usefully bribable. His first choice was the head of the room-service waiters, with whom he drank during the man's off-duty hours and to whom he eventually confided his real purpose in being there. His confidant promptly appointed himself as the man who would bring the princess's breakfast tray into her room every morning— in this way providing the conspirators with a means of communicating with her. Weitzer's second recruit was a member of the hotel's security staff, who produced duplicate keys to Louise's room, the hotel's ground-floor back entrance, and the garden gate at its rear. Both men were to show themselves as loyal to the conspiracy as they were disloyal to their employers and were rewarded not only by the money paid out to them by Weitzer but also by an enthusiastic if self-centered reference to them in Louise's autobiography.*

---

* Louise, *Autour* (p. 253): "The headwaiter was a man to be trusted. This is how a correspondence between myself and the count [Mattachich] began. . . . I learned what I had to do and what to be ready for when the time came. A night watchman had also become an ally of ours. This man, like the waiter, was putting more than his position in danger. Such was the degree of loyalty that the persecution I had been made to endure evoked from sympathetic people everywhere."

Next: Maria. Having handed the unfortunate Viktor back to his grandparents, she took little Berthold and departed with him for Bad Elster, together with a recently hired nanny. There she rented two rooms in a modest guesthouse, where she passed herself off as a widow recovering from the sad loss of her spouse. She claimed to be suffering from nerves, as a result of her recent bereavement, and made arrangements with the owner of a fiacre to go occasionally for insomniac moonlight drives—some of which were extended until as late as two or three in the morning. She found these outings very soothing, she explained to the coachman. The first couple of drives she took on her own; later she was accompanied each time by two or three gentleman friends. By day she seldom went out, once the princess's party had turned up, to minimize the risk of her being seen by Olga.

Last, traveling from Vienna in separate trains and to separate boardinghouses, came Südekum, followed almost immediately by the nervous but financially indispensable de Nousanne, and then Mattachich himself, who had been staying indoors in Vienna for a few weeks and letting his beard grow. All three men did as he had done in Coswig when he had been hoping to encounter Louise in the neighborhood of the asylum: they hired bicycles from shops in town on which they went for long rides on little-known roads in the surrounding countryside. They also intermittently accompanied Maria on her nocturnal jaunts. Their intention was to find the best way of crossing the nearby border between Saxony and Bavaria without having to produce passports of any kind.*

Then they waited for Louise and her ladies, her guards, and the medical Mauss to move into the Wettiner Hof. It was Weitzer's job to communicate with her via his friend the headwaiter and to sit on the terrace taking note of the times when police and private guards came and went.

---

* More than thirty years had passed since Bismarck had finally succeeded in uniting Germany under the Kaiser. However each of the various kingdoms, grand duchies, duchies, and principalities (as well as the "free cities") remained jealous of its rights and zealous in upholding what remained of its autonomy.

Weitzer's other friend, the security guard, saw to it that the locks and hinges of the relevant gates and doors were well oiled beforehand. Louise was told to wear her darkest clothes on the chosen night.

❖

Everything went according to plan, more or less, though many tense moments passed before all involved could begin to feel confident their scheme had succeeded. One of these moments, which literally left two of them out of breath, was the lifting of Louise though her open bedroom window, stockinged feet first, and the depositing of her on the veranda outside. The most dangerous moment came when two policemen stood in the road outside the hotel and talked idly together (instead of crossing and continuing their patrol in different directions, as they were supposed to do), while just yards from them the escapee and her friends crouched behind an excruciatingly thin screen of bushes. Almost as tense was the delay at the tree-shrouded crossroads appointed for the rescue party's meeting with the fiacre and its insomniac passenger. It was supposed to have been standing there but was not. De Nousanne went in search of it through the deserted streets and found it waiting in the wrong place.[*]

Such mishaps aside, everyone involved did all that was asked of him or her—from Mattachich, chief planner and overseer of the operation, to the bemused fiacre owner, who could not understand why his last late-night drive with this special client of his, this sympathetic widowed lady, had been interrupted so abruptly and ended so strangely, when three men and a woman he had never seen before jumped in a great hurry into his cab and directed him to drive along minor roads until, just after crossing the Saxon–Bavarian border, they arrived at a small town on the main

---

[*] Louise, *Autour* (p. 259): "A catastrophe occurred. The carriage was not where it should have been. We had a moment of despair. What a night! What suspense! All this agony of mind occurred under trees which seemed peopled with fearful phantoms. At last some of our friends conducted us to the carriage. It started, but how sluggishly the tired horses moved!"

railway line to Berlin. There the party got out and disappeared into a modest hotel next to the train station, after making sure that the driver would be put up for the night and his horses stabled and fed. By then it was past two in the morning. At dawn the driver was paid for the work he had already done and given an additional sum to wait until evening at the station. It was explained to him that the group was now setting out on a further excursion by rail and would be needing his cab later to take them back to Bad Elster. The first northbound train came in, they boarded it, the train departed, he waited all day—and never saw any of them again.*

The three men who had jumped into in the cab were Mattachich, de Nousanne, and Südekum. Weitzer remained in Bad Elster, enjoying the consternation and recriminations that followed—the moment he prized most being a public fainting fit by Fraülein von Gebauer when she discovered that the princess had disappeared. (Leaving almost all her luggage behind, which scandalized Gebauer almost as much as the disappearance itself.) Having waited to see his two friends emerge unscathed from their grilling by the management of the hotel and the local police, Weitzer gave them a wink, quietly paid his bill, and left for Vienna. The nanny and the baby had preceded him there several days before. The three of them would join the others later.

For their part, the travelers stayed on the train until it reached Berlin, then lay low in Südekum's house there, waiting for the excitement in the press to subside. When they judged it safe to do so, they moved (though not as a group, and with various stops between) from Berlin to Paris. This involved passing through Belgium and was thought to be the most risky part of the journey. By then the Lord Marshal in Vienna had issued a stern reminder to all European governments that under the Hague Convention

---

* Extracts from the driver's statement appear in Holler, *Ihr Kampf* (pp. 259, 263, 265). Holler devotes twenty-four pages to the escape; Louise describes it in fourteen. Holler's pages include a discussion of the legal issues arising from the flight, as well as quotations from reports of the episode in German, Austrian, and French newspapers.

of 1896 they were obliged to return the runaway princess to Austria immediately—"and by force if necessary."*

Once in Paris, however, they were safe. The French press and French public opinion were on their side, and the French government had no inclination to kowtow on this issue to Franz Josef and his Lord Marshal. The delighted escapees set themselves up in the Westminster Hotel and gave interviews left and right.

❖

A question remained, though. Exactly who, now, were "they"?

Who indeed? For an answer to that question you have to go back to the spartan little hotel in which Louise and her liberators had waited to catch the train to Berlin. It was a brief night in an inconsequential location; yet an event took place there—if something that passed so quietly can be called an "event"—that was as unexpected as anything else the parties had experienced over the previous seven years.

Imagine once again, then, the crowded fiacre drawing up in front of the hotel. It has been locked up for hours past. Situated in the lower part of the town, it dominates the nondescript little dwellings scattered about simply because it has two stories above ground level. A few trees are the only other tall objects to be seen. No lights burn in any of the neighboring buildings or in the hotel itself. There is no sign of dawn in the sky, but the air smells of late summer and the trees stir expectantly from time to time, only to fall silent until the next small breeze arrives. There is a night bell to the side of the hotel's front door, and one of the men in the

---

* Of the journey through Belgium, Louise writes (*Autour*, p. 261): "At long last I saw my country again but alas I did not dare to get out. The king was working hand in glove with the prince of Coburg. I could not even sit near the window and had difficulty in controlling my trembling hands. How ironic was the standard question directed at me by the customs officials who boarded the train: "Have you anything to declare?" . . . Did I not! If only my declaration could have reached as far as Laeken and resounded through the king's residence there!"

The Lord Marshal's demand that the princess be returned forthwith to Austria is quoted in Holler, *Ihr Kampf* (p. 276).

party pulls it fiercely. The cabdriver remains seated on his bench, high above them, wondering what he has let himself in for and whether this client of his, this young widow who has made such a strong impression on his kindly old breast, is all she has appeared to be. After a long delay a woman with an oil lamp in her hand can be seen squinting through the thick glass panel in the upper half of the door. Reassured by what she sees (the cabdriver, the two women), she turns the lock. She is stout and squat and is dressed in a flimsy gown and a frilly nightcap. Lamp hoisted before her, she tells them yes, she can offer them accommodation for the night. But there is a difficulty: she has only two rooms available, one with twin beds in it, the other with a double bed. A third bed can be brought into the twin-bedded room at a pinch; nothing can be done about the other room.

An awkward moment. An exchange of glances. Mattachich seizes the initiative. The ladies will sleep in the double bed; the three gentlemen in the other room. It is the obvious thing to do. No one demurs. The gentlemen order a bottle of brandy and some glasses to be sent to their room; the ladies ask for tea. Nobody asks for food. Each of the men carries a small valise; the ladies the same, and their handbags. None of this is lost on the landlady, who knows also that none of it is her business. De Nousanne helps a sleepy porter—a strongly built, shirtsleeved, slow-moving young man, with an obscure stammer in his walk—to place the additional bed into the men's room. The porter lights the lamps in the rooms and jerks his way to the back of the building, where he tends to the driver and his horses. The men fall on the brandy the moment the landlady brings it in. Each pours himself a large drink, and even before she has closed the door behind her they embrace, slap one another on the back, laugh, displaying some of the relief and elation they have been careful to hide from the cabdriver.

Things are different in the ladies' room, as the landlady discovers minutes later, when she brings them their tea. The older woman is seated on the only chair in the room, a bentwood affair with a plaited straw bottom; the younger sits awkwardly on the big double bed. There is no relief and elation here, only silence. The room smells of damp and must; the bed leaves virtually no space between it and the walls on both sides; the washstand carries a floral china jug with ancient chips on its rim and a basin in the same state; the net curtain across the single window is yellow with age and tobacco smoke. But the landlady is convinced it is not their surroundings that keeps the ladies so subdued.

The young woman murmurs a word of thanks as the tray is put down on top of a small chest. She gets up to pour the tea, while the other looks timidly around her. The door closes behind the landlady. Her footsteps can be heard retreating down the wooden-floored passage outside.

Sitting with both hands still clutching the handbag on her lap, Louise is the first to speak.

"Who are you?"

"A friend of the count's," Maria answers.

She adds awkwardly, after a pause, "Your highness." After another pause, "Your friend too, madam." Pause again. "If you would like me to be your friend."

❖

They slept little that night. By the end of the first hour Louise knew "everything." She knew about Maria's marriage and her older son; about the scrapbook of newspaper clippings on Mattachich and Louise herself; about her separation from her husband, her journey to Möllersdorf, and the job inside the prison she had managed to get; about her affair with Mattachich and the birth of little Berthold; about the work she had done in Vienna to procure Mattachich's release from prison; even about the visits she had paid to the neighborhood of the asylum and the letter Olga Börner had written giving the dates of Louise's stay in Bad Elster. (To which, for safety reasons, Maria had not responded.) Louise listened to it all with a mixture of amazement, pain, and envy. What an exciting time this humbly born young woman had managed to contrive for herself, while she herself had rotted and grown old in the asylum.

And now this! *She* was the one who had spent so many years thinking of the absent Mattachich, raging against him sometimes, more often trying to remember his arms around her and his body next to hers, trying to picture him in the room with her or simply appearing out of nowhere, from behind a tree or around a bend in a path in one of the asylums in which she had been imprisoned, smiling at her as he drew closer until at last he was close enough to take her by the hand and then simply set her free, release her from imprisonment. Then he had actually done it. Just a few hours before, he had helped her over the sill of an open window and passed her to strangers, all well disposed, who had led her magically through one locked door after another until they gained an empty road and waited for the sound and sight of a cab approaching, with lamps affixed to its body and a single lamp swinging from the front of its shaft. Crouched low in the darkness against a stone fence, she and the others, Mattachich the only one she knew, had not dared to move before the cab came to a halt, its door opened, and a young woman's voice called out softly, "Géza!"

The moment the name came out of Louise's own mouth, she heard it clearly and flung herself full length on the bed. She had no idea how much she had actually said aloud of all that had been surging through her mind moments before. But that name she had distinctly heard herself say. She lay facing the wall, her back turned to Maria.

"Who are you?" she wailed again, as if Maria had not yet said a word about herself. "Why are you doing this to me? Why didn't you leave me where I was?"

"Never! Never!" Maria answered.

She lay down too, behind Louise, and put an arm around her—surprised as she did so by the girth of the woman's body. But she felt no distaste for it. Pity, rather, as she might have if she had been lying next to a child. They lay like that, Maria waiting until the sobs shaking the body beside her ceased. It happened quite suddenly; a sob that sounded exactly like the last was simply not followed by another. After a long silence, and with an unsteady voice, Maria spoke into the head of hair against her lips.

"Now listen to me. I don't hate you and I don't want to hurt you. Géza couldn't live like a free man as long as you were still locked up. It shamed him too much. It was eating him away. I could see it happening, both when he thought of you and when he tried not to. And when he talked of trying to help you. So what was I to do? If you stayed locked up you would destroy us both; I was sure of it. If you were set free . . . perhaps you wouldn't! Is that so bad? Besides, I was curious about you—and proud of what I'd done for him—and I thought I could do something like it again for you. And I have. I have. We've all done it. It's wonderful. . . ."

She went on, murmuring whatever came into her head, growing more and more drowsy the longer she went on. "We're all the same, you and me and Géza. . . . Too stuffed with dreams, too greedy. Too little sense, too little patience. But loyal! Look how loyal you and Géza have been to each other. Look how loyal I'm trying to be to both of you. If I love Géza then I must love you too. . . ."

Eventually she moved to take off Louise's shoes and kicked her own to the floor. There was a folded blanket at the foot of the bed, above the counterpane, and she pulled it over them both. They fell asleep. Later they woke and talked some more.

"You're so *brave*," Louise said into the darkness.

"No, I was just infatuated."

"Are you still?" Louise asked.

"Infatuated?" After a silence: "No."

"But you're still loyal?"

"So are you. It's a curse. To be loyal to your own imaginings! What could be more stupid?"

Another silence, broken eventually by Louise. "But just try to imagine yourself without them! It can't be done."

They did not fall asleep again, nor did they have more to say. When they got up in the morning, they exchanged a kiss. It was settled between them; they were friends. Old friends, in fact. Bizarrely, it was as if the years that each of them had shared separately with Mattachich had become a property common to them both, the source of a stock of shared understandings.

Going into the bleak underfurnished dining room downstairs—its air still heavy with the smell of the meal eaten the previous night—they found the men waiting for them. Mattachich went once more through the introductions that had first taken place in the darkness of the cab during their escape from Bad Elster. The women and de Nousanne and Südekum exchanged stiff, idle words, keeping their voices low in order to prevent anything they said from reaching the ears of the bedraggled handful of guests at the other tables. Once he had made the introductions, Mattachich remained silent. Each time Louise or Maria spoke to each other, or just exchanged glances, his eyes hardened. Knowing him to have been the lover first of one and then of the other, and to be responsible for the presence of them all in this room—a bleak place conjured out of nothing, never to be seen again—his companions thought he might be embarrassed by the situation he had created. But the fierceness of his stare suggested otherwise. Seeing Mattachich's eyes fixed on the two women, and sensitized by his own heartache, de Nousanne suddenly sprang to a conclusion that astonished him and flicked at him with a painful, momentary hope. Something had happened between the two women during the night. They were not jealous of each other. It was Mattachich who was now jealous of them both.

When Mattachich and Maria managed a moment together with no one nearby, he said accusingly to her, "You've told her about us, haven't you?"

"Yes," Maria admitted. "How do you know?"

"I could see it at once. Any fool could see it. We agreed: I was going to be the one to tell her, not you. And the first chance you get, you open your mouth!"

"Yes, yes, yes," Maria answered angrily, standing her ground. "Everything's changed now. Don't spoil it!"

A half hour later the train to Berlin drew up at the one-platform station, virtually across the road from the hotel. By then de Nousanne, who had his own ax to grind, his own hopes to nourish, was sure of his hunch. The princess and Maria accepted Mattachich's leadership, but they were no longer his. If they belonged to anybody, it was to each other.

Hooting, hissing, flourishing a white scarf of steam over its head, the train began to urge itself forward.

CHAPTER TWELVE

IMAGINE THAT A YEAR HAS PASSED SINCE that party of five got on the train to Berlin and subsequently traveled from there to Paris. Of those five people, four are still in Paris; only Südekum has left the city to resume his duties in the German *Reichstag*. Weitzer, without whom success in Bad Elster would have been impossible, has come and gone, having learned that he will never see a pfennig of the 30,000 kronen he put into rescuing Louise, let alone make a profit from his efforts.* De Nousanne is working on his paper, *Le Journal,* but he sees the other three only occasionally.

Mattachich and Louise are living under a single roof in a Parisian hotel, as they had when they were first reunited in the city about eight years before. Yet there are differences between their condition then and now. They no longer share a bedroom. Their health is not what it was. The passage of time and the hardships they have been through have irrevocably marked their faces and bodies. Both move more stiffly than they used to; Louise has put on weight and Mattachich has lost a little. She still carries a great loaf of hair on her head, in color more strident than it used to be. Mattachich dresses trimly, in dark suits and white shirts equipped with unusually tall, stiff collars that compel him to keep his head and gaze tilted well back, like the fine upstanding fellow he would like to be. But he is beginning to bend arthritically at the waist, and his

* See Holler, *Ihr Kampf,* p. 228.

hair has thinned and receded. He tries to make up for the hair he has lost by letting what he has of it grow longer and brushing it back without a parting of any kind. He also dyes it regularly around the temples and above the ears. If you knew nothing about him you might guess him to be a fatigued but successful professional man: an accountant, a doctor, a banker. Or possibly a confidence man, someone with an eye for needy widows.

As before, though in far more modest fashion than in the initial days of their elopement, Louise has an entourage of her own, which is housed with her and Mattachich in the Westminster Hotel. It consists of her faithful maid, Olga Börner, and a lady to whom Louise has officially given the position of "Head of Household." References to this lady in the social columns of the Paris newspapers are often accompanied by metaphorical nudges and winks in the reader's direction. She is described as the princess's "bosom companion," her "inseparable friend," her "ever-helpful associate." Words like *striking, touching,* and *unusual* are used about the warmth of their relationship, and the papers also refer occasionally to the two "orphaned" or "fatherless" sons of this lady, who live in the hotel with the rest of the party.

No need to tell you who she is. The papers do not mention that, had it not been for her, Mattachich might still be in prison and Louise would certainly have remained behind the walls of Lindenhof. Or possibly in the much less expensive institution in Austria that Dr. Feistmantel had inspected at Philipp's urging just before her escape.[*] But that is all history now. The Lord Marshal has given up his attempts to get her extradited to Austria, after having been officially informed by the French government that (a) it is plainly not the case that the princess was brought into France against her will and (b) a panel of leading French psychiatrists has dismissed with contempt the claims made by their German and Austrian colleagues about the lady's "moral idiocy" and "mental

---

[*] Holler, *Ihr Kampf,* p. 254.

incompetence."* One unexpected by-product of this psychiatric report, however, is that Prince Philipp has sued her for divorce, which he could not do while she remained under legal guardianship. In order to get the whole business concluded as rapidly as possible he has offered, and Louise has accepted, a settlement of 400,000 kroner in cash and an annual stipend of 70,000.†

As for the newspapers' hints at some perverse or illicit element in the relations between the two ladies, forget it. The most striking or unusual feature of this threesome's cohabitation is that nobody shares a bed or bedroom with anybody else. A silent agreement has been reached between them to avoid taking unnecessary risks with the situation in which they have placed themselves. It is too fragile and too important for them all to be meddled with—just as it is for Maria to raise questions at this late stage about what *really* happened with those wretched promissory notes. They are living in Paris as free, unpersecuted, unprosecuted people—isn't that amazing enough after what they have been through? Let Mattachich go off in search of other women if he feels like it—which he does from time to time—and let the two ladies say nothing about it to him or to each other, so long as he never brings any of these creatures home. Nor have the ladies looked for gentleman friends of their own, though Maria cannot resist teasing and tormenting de Nousanne whenever she sees him. She is still delighted to be in Paris (her first time abroad) and relishes the novel luxuries Louise heaps on her: jewels, dresses, expensive restaurants, boxes at the opera, a seat beside her princess in one or another of the hired carriages or motorcars they use. Her two boys also benefit from Louise's generosity. They are the regular target of her kisses

---

*"The princess gives every indication of being in sound physical and mental health. . . . She expresses herself fluently and exactly, and always in a manner befitting someone of her rank in society. She is completely in command of herself and her imagination. . . . We wonder how anyone could describe her condition as one of imbecility, mania, or irrational rage" (report quoted in Holler, *Ihr Kampf,* p. 309).

† Figures quoted by Holler, *Ihr Kampf,* p. 314. The annual payment is more than twice the amount put up by the luckless Weitzer to help free Louise from her incarceration.

and caresses, and Viktor goes off every morning in a smart cap and uniform to a private school for which she pays the fees.

To Maria, Louise is always *your highness* now and Mattachich always *the count,* except when she and he are on their own. Yet being of demi-peasant stock and immensely self-willed, Maria keeps to herself the fact that she has taken to trading some of the items Louise gives her and sending the proceeds to her former landlady in Möllersdorf, who is buying a little house for her around the corner from where she used to live. Not until their later unhappy wanderings around Europe will Louise and Mattachich learn of the existence of this house and be grateful to take shelter in it for a while.*

Maria's foresight, you see, never theirs. Her misgivings about what might lie ahead for herself and her two boys. Never theirs.

❖

Imagine it is now your turn to be privileged with a far greater degree of foresight than Maria herself will ever possess. How much longer, then, after his return to Paris will Mattachich live? The answer is seventeen years. And Louise? The same, plus a further six months only. Mattachich will drop dead of a heart attack in a Parisian street at the age of fifty-six. Louise, accompanied still by the faithful Olga, will then leave the city and go to a small private hotel in Wiesbaden, Germany. In her bedroom there, shortly after her sixty-sixth birthday, a thrombosis—followed a few days later by both pneumonia and a lung infarct—will carry her away.

Will she and Mattachich still be living together at the time of his death? Yes. Will the years preceding their death be calm and happy? No. No. No. Not a chance. They are incorrigible. Such an existence will always be beyond them. All they can do with their partnership is try to resurrect the idle yet unflinching way of life that had brought them and others to ruin during their first eighteen months together. Inevitably, the

* See Holler, *Ihr Kampf,* p. 331.

results will be what they were then: bankruptcy, flight, the lot. With yet another spell of imprisonment for Mattachich thrown in. (Not for forging promissory notes this time.) They will suffer ill health too and will be repeatedly overtaken by wars, revolutions, counterrevolutions, and wild bouts of inflation. For those calamities, at least, they cannot be held responsible.

And then? When the First World War has ended and they have managed to find each other and have returned to Paris, what will they do? Pick themselves up and try to do it all over again.

❖

True, their spending will never again be as manic or orgiastic as it was before the crash in Nice. No carriages and equipages, no stables of horses, no hiring of special trains, no renting of mansions, no livery and salaries for tribes of servants, no incessant acquiring of booty from any jewelry shop, couturier, vendor of shoes and silks and antique cabinets they happen to visit, or the owners of which visit them. Only occasionally will Mattachich get carried away at the race track or gaming table. Nor, at first, will things go too badly for them. The alimony payments from Philipp will arrive monthly. Money will continue to come in dribs and drabs from the estate of Louise's mother (with Leopold contesting every payment). Merchants with only a blurred memory of what happened the last time around will be glad to see them. Paris will be as full as it always is of socially ambitious people ready to do almost anything—for a while anyway—to be seen in the company of a genuine if disreputable royal princess. A few optimistic bankers will discount today's loans against the large hoped-for gains that are bound to accrue to Louise once her unspeakably wealthy, demented, childless Aunt Charlotte, the former empress of Mexico, is interred in an appropriately elaborate mausoleum.

Still, the fact is that from the day of their arrival in the city they will live beyond their means, and as time passes the prospect of discharging their earlier debts, let alone the new ones they are constantly accumulating, will become more and more remote. Louise's feud with her father over her mother's estate will swallow more and more of her meager income from that source. She will discover that none of her creditors are more insistent on being paid (in full, and with accumulated interest) than the team of eminent and expensive French psychiatrists who were hired to declare her perfectly capable of handling her own affairs. (She had somehow assumed they were doing it for the glory of dealing with so prominent a patient and the pleasure of delivering a severe snub to their German and Austrian colleagues.) The longevity afflicting her Aunt Charlotte will show no signs of abating.* When Maria's conscience compels her to warn her companions that they are heading for trouble, Mattachich will simply wave her away and Louise will either weep or respond haughtily, as if Maria is impugning her royal blood, or her love for Mattachich, or his love for her, or her love for Maria herself.

In short, it will be the same old story, in a seedier and less sensational version than before, but one that unfolds no less inexorably. If anything, the fact that the sums of money involved are so much smaller than they once were will make the whole process seem even more humiliating than it had been then. The manager of the Westminster Hotel, where their payments on account grow steadily smaller while the account itself swells daily, will be the first to crack. So Louise and her party will disdainfully leave his premises and go to another, lesser establishment foolish enough to let them in. Ahead of them—though neither she nor Mattachich can see it and would probably be incapable of changing their ways if they could—stretches a protracted decline that will lead them from one hotel to another, and then from one boardinghouse to another, in one European country after another. But wherever they go, whether in Germany, Italy, or Austria, creditors and their hired duns will be yapping at their heels. The outbreak of the First World War, which catches them in Austria, will send Maria and her two boys back to Möllersdorf (from where she will

---

* In fact Louise did not live long enough to receive any of her aunt's money. Charlotte was more than thirty years older than her niece, but it was Louise who died first.

continue to extend what help she can). It will also result in a call-up notice, of all things, being served on Mattachich.

Once the army has got him in its clutches, its reason for summoning him will become apparent. No sooner has he responded to the call-up than he will be thrown into an internment camp reserved for those suspected of disloyalty to the empire.* Now you have to picture Louise, accompanied only by Olga Börner, turning up unannounced and in an abject state at the door of the Silesian castle in which her daughter, Dora, and husband, Günther, live. They will offer her shelter and sustenance on condition that she accept immediately the imposition of a new guardianship over her, which is to be administered by themselves and will deprive her of control over her affairs. She will agree, retract, be turned away.

Next, picture her under arrest in Budapest, where, in the chaos of the war's ending, Béla Kun's Communists have seized power. They are busy shooting their "class enemies" left and right, but after repeated inquisitions of Louise in jail and out of it, they will think better of executing her and merely kick her out of the country.†

❖

All of this could have been avoided if Louise and Mattachich had been able to do one of two things. The first would have been to change their habits and live within their means, as Maria advised them to do. The second, as far as Louise herself was concerned, would have been to accept the offer made to her alone by an envoy from her father.

* See Holler, *Ihr Kampf,* p. 334. The charge laid against Mattachich was that he had been in contact with a group of Croatian nationalists plotting to overthrow the Habsburg monarchy. It is impossible not to believe that various high-ranking officers seized the opportunity to settle old scores with him.

† Louise (*Autour,* p. 307) writes of having lived through "a nightmare" of "extraordinary days" in Budapest, where she was put through "visits, interrogations, and seizures of property" by the Bolsheviks. "But suddenly my misfortunes disarmed even the savage representatives of Hungarian communism. . . . At the beginning of this book I reported the words of a soldier in that army who said of me, 'Look at this! Here is a king's daughter who is poorer than I am!'"

The envoy's name was Sam Wiener. He arrived in Paris not long before she was about to leave the city with her three companions (Olga included) and set out on a rerun of the fruitless drawn-out trek across Europe that she and Mattachich had put themselves through many years before. A lawyer, a senator of the Belgian parliament, and a member of the governing council of the Free State of the Congo, Wiener was employed by King Leopold as "his" Jew—much as Bachrach was employed by Philipp and the other Viennese Saxe-Coburgs as "theirs." Believed by their patrons to have special or even arcane gifts as negotiators and makers of deals, such people were regarded also as being peculiarly trustworthy in confidential matters, precisely because of their semi-outcast status. What would these court Jews be if the grandees withdrew their favor from them? Socially speaking, nothing. Hence their trustworthiness.*

However, meeting with Wiener in the unprepossessing sitting room of the hotel she was living in, it was Louise, not her visitor, who felt vulnerable. Ever since her marriage to Philipp, aggression had been her sole resource in dealing with her father. But here? Now? In a room like this? Stuffy, dusty, shiny, its curtains and carpets threadbare, its paintwork finger-marked, its wallpapers yawning from the walls and cornices they were supposed to decorate, the room told her caller more than she wanted him to know about her situation. She felt at a disadvantage too because she had assumed that Wiener would be plump, precise, and fussily self-confident, like Bachrach. But this one, she said to Mattachich later, "looked like an American"—by which she meant that he was a tall broad-chested man with an oversized head and eyes, eyebrows and hands to match. His wiry gray hair was cut short; his voice was deep; he had the haughty nose and cleft chin of a piece of Roman statuary. He also had the

---

* Wiener's intervention in Louise's life is mentioned in both Ludwig Bauer's *Leopold the Unloved* (p. 187)—where he is described as "Leopold's factotum"—and Neal Ascherson's *The King Incorporated* (p. 211). In the mammoth entry on Wiener in *Biographie Nationale de la Belgique,* Supplement vol. XI (pp. 822–837), he is described as a member of a Jewish family from central Europe that rapidly became prominent in various spheres of Belgian life, including engineering, banking, the army, politics, and the arts.

importance of being the first message bearer her father had sent to her for a decade or more. The last such envoy had presented her with a stark choice. Either she would immediately put an end to her "filthy cavortings" with this "Croatian guttersnipe" or she would never see him or her mother again.

Now, after what felt to her like a lifetime later, here was Wiener come to present her with another pair of royal alternatives. But not immediately. First, a preamble. His majesty, Wiener began, was disappointed that she had gone to law in the matter of her mother's estate—

"I didn't go to law! He did!"

Wiener's gaze held steady. But he changed tack slightly. "The king is most unhappy that members of his family are litigating against one another in open court. He believes that family matters should be settled privately, not talked about by lawyers and written about in newspapers."

"If he wants to settle the case, he knows how to do it."

He waited demonstratively before beginning again. "His majesty certainly wants to set that unfortunate business behind him. But that's not the reason for my being here. It's no secret in Brussels that you have once again got yourself into a hopeless financial situation. His majesty has heard that a new scandal is about to burst over your head. The prospect appalls him. He remembers what happened the last time you were in that position. He wants to save you and his family from going through such a . . . process again."

"Then he can let me and my sisters have everything her majesty the queen, God rest her soul, meant us to inherit. He can also use some of his own fortune for my benefit—for once. No kindhearted father would ever think that such an outlandish idea."

"He's ready to do it."

"He is?"

"Yes." He paused, waiting for another sharp response. But she was silent, letting the puzzled, suspicious, scornful look on her face speak for her. Having fully registered the look, Wiener went on. "You must understand. The king's health is not what it was. He is very conscious of how little time is left to him. He wants to be reconciled with the members of his family before it's too late, and to see them reconciled among themselves. He knows that relations between yourself and the Princess Stephanie have been strained ever since those unhappy events . . . of which I shall say no more today. As a king he's accomplished many things—great things—things that have awed the world. But he now feels that for him to make peace with his family and within his family would be a greater thing yet. I've seen the change his recent illness has made to him. So close to his life's ending—as he feels himself to be and as we all hope he is not—he wants to gather his family around him once more."

"What you really mean," Louise answered, leaning back casually to show how little affected she was by these solemn statements, "is that the papers are printing such terrible stories about him he wants the world to see what a loving father he is. Is that it? *Torturer, slave driver, child killer, the real cannibal king of the Congo* . . . what don't they call him? I see it every time I open a newspaper."

Wiener's voice was as steady as before. "Some newspapers. That's just politics. Vile things are said about everyone in public life. Only his political enemies and their hirelings talk like that. It's got nothing to do with the sort of a man he really is. Or with what he feels about you." He added, as if it hardly needed to be said, "Or with what is happening in the Congo."

"None of it is true?"

Sitting in his straight-backed armchair, looking at her across the small table between them, his fingers clasped just below his chin, he looked at her like a man of probity and wisdom.

"None of it."

❖

Then he came out with the king's offer. It turned out to be not so different from the one brought to her by the king's previous messenger. However, this one was larded not with threats but inducements and pleas for understanding. The king wanted no more scandals in his family. He was an old man. His thoughts had turned to matters far more important to him than money.

"More important than money? To him! What can they be?"

With a straight face Wiener answered, "The state of his soul. His debt to God."

"And Caroline Lacroix?" Louise interjected, throwing out the name of the king's latest and deepest infatuation, a former prostitute fifty years younger than himself, whom he had recently ennobled as the Baroness Vaughan.

Wiener ignored the interjection. His majesty's offer, he went on, was this. He would hand over to Louise a château with a fine estate attached to it that he had owned for many years near the city of Cologne; he would also make over to her an annual income of 150,000 francs a year, to be paid without regard to anything she was receiving from her ex-husband or of any benefit she might still inherit from her mother.[*] He would also seek a prompt settlement between his daughters and himself in the matter of their mother's testament. Louise could live in the château in the style appropriate to her status and income. The king would not visit her there and would not expect her to visit him until mutually agreeable relations had been established between them. Then at last, he hoped, he and Louise and her sisters could come together as a family again.

Only one condition, Wiener went on, was attached to this generous offer—

With a cry of vindication, of triumph even, Louise jumped to her feet. "I knew it! I've been waiting for it! The count must go! Am I right?" And again, "Am I right? Am I right?"

He lowered his head in agreement.

Still on her feet, she spoke in a suddenly offhand conversational tone, "Wait here. I'll be back in a moment."

While she was away he wandered over to the window. Like the room he was in, the street below had the hangdog air of one that had seen better

---

* See Bauer, *Leopold the Unloved,* p. 187.

days. Round babyish clouds, gray and purple, clinging together, drifting apart, were suspended at no distance over awnings, steep-roofed buildings, a few plane trees, a few people passing on the pavement.

The door behind him opened. Louise came in, followed by Maria and Mattachich. All three stood near the door. Her manner at once imperious and schoolgirlish, Louise said, "Tell my father that I—" she paused anticlimactically, recalling that the stranger had not been introduced to her companions, and then deciding against doing so—"tell him I'm not interested in his offer. He talks of family. Tell him *this* is my family. If he wants to buy me he must buy my family too. There'll be no sale without them. Tell him that that is *my* condition. He will not get me on any other terms."

From across the room Wiener studied the newcomers carefully, as if committing their features to memory. Then he nodded his head again, more slowly than before.

"I'll give his majesty your message. I'll tell him that I deplore it. Which I do."

He looked around for his hat and coat, took them up, hung his coat over his arm, and balanced his hat on it with his other hand. He took a step toward the door.

The others moved aside to let him through. Another step. A pause.

"The choice you've made is unfortunate. But I think I understand it. That is something I will not say to your father."

Unhurriedly, exchanging a glance with none of them, he left the room.

❖

Not long to go now. You already know that on their second trek through Europe they succeeded only in blundering through a further series of misfortunes—as how could they not, wandering across a continent convulsed by the bloodiest war it had yet seen? "If I were to live for centuries," Louise wrote, "I would not see such torments return. Thrones were overturned and crowns carried away by the storm of events. I asked myself if I was really living in the world I had known or was trapped in some terrible dream. . . . I was convinced, as was everyone around me, that an unimaginable period of history had begun."*

No exaggeration there. Released from internment at the end of the war, Mattachich made his way back to Vienna, where nearly six centuries of Habsburg rule had just been replaced by the newly proclaimed Republic of Austria. From Hungary, Louise traveled in the same direction. Neither knew where the other was; both turned for help to Maria in Möllersdorf. Through her the trio was reunited. Not long afterward, Olga turned up in Vienna too. Maria had left her children at home—though the timid Viktor was a child no longer; rather, a youthful, unscathed ex-soldier. Maria helped to install her companions in a hotel in the city and then tearfully left them. Her parting with Mattachich was particularly prolonged. Together they revisited the house they had lived in after his discharge from prison, but they did not go into it; they just stood outside, looked up at the windows of their flat on the second floor, and acknowledged that they had never been happy there; they had felt closer to each other not only in the Möllersdorf prison but also during their sexless attachment in Paris. Still, this flat had been theirs at a particular period of their lives, no one else's, and nothing done and felt there could be undone or denied. They parted, suspecting that they would not meet again.

Nor did they. At this point Maria disappears from the story—only to reappear some thirty years later, tracked down by the tireless Dr. Holler. A grandmother by then, and a survivor of yet another and more terrible war, she was to relate to him some of her reminiscences.†

Of the three who remained together (Mattachich, Louise, Olga Börner) it was Mattachich who was the most damaged by the experiences he had just been through. Louise was old and tired, but he had come out

---

* Louise, *Autour,* p. 307.
† See Holler, *Ihr Kampf,* p. 348.

of his second spell of imprisonment with chronic bronchitis, recurring bouts of malaria, and—worse still, certainly as far as their finances were concerned—an addiction to the morphine that had been too freely administered to him in the camp's sick bay.* Money, or its absence, remained much more than a problem for them; it was a besetting, degrading preoccupation. Leopold had died not long after Wiener's visit to Louise in Paris, but shortly before doing so he had taken extra measures to ensure that only a fragment of his mighty fortune would ever be divided among his three daughters. Not even his youngest daughter, Clementine, who had never married and had stayed faithfully at his side throughout, was spared his postmortem malevolence. Little enough came in from the estate of Louise's mother. And the alimony payments from Philipp had been rendered virtually worthless by the wild inflation that had gripped the new Austrian Republic.

The three fellow travelers (Louise, Mattachich, and Olga) remained as long as they could in Vienna. Then, not knowing what else to do, they packed the bags they still had and again returned to Paris.

❖

What would you have Louise and Mattachich do now? Grow up? Change character? Redeem themselves? Undergo some kind of Tolstoyan conversion? Cease harming themselves and others?

Or would you expect them to carry on exactly as they had during their years in Paris before the war, only now in circumstances even more abjectly reduced than they had known then? Still harming themselves and others; still deceiving themselves and doing their best to deceive others; still enamored of the drama of their own lives; above all else, still together—thus proving to themselves, with every day that passed, that they had not been mistaken in each other; they had indeed been picked out for one another by God or fate and could no more have avoided their

* See Holler, *Ihr Kampf*, p. 349.

union than have changed the color of their eyes or the length of their limbs.

How could they turn their backs on themselves? Permit their suffering to go to waste? Look what they had been through. Look at the fidelity with which they had clung to each other and the tenacity with which they were still doing so. Look at the changes they had undergone and how much they had remained the same: he forever the young uhlan, climbing high, she the princess captive in her tower, leaning down to help him into her chamber.

❖

During this last period in Paris, Louise's major preoccupation was the writing of her autobiography. It was more than a pastime for her. Like Mattachich, she hoped to make some money out of it, for money—money of any kind—was what she thought about incessantly.

He had written his memoirs more than fifteen years before; now it was her turn. Both their books are full of half-truths, quarter-truths, omissions, and inconsistencies through which they actually reveal more about themselves than they could have known; certainly more than they would have wished. Surprisingly, perhaps, it is the half-educated uhlan who is the better writer of the two; he tells his story with a degree of coherence, a command of detail, and a range of tone that the princess cannot match. Her book, by contrast, is so haphazardly put together that parts of it are almost impossible to follow; it veers erratically from autobiography to moral tract, from apologia to gossip about other royals, from attacks on the author's enemies to religious speculation (Catholicism good, Protestantism bad), generously interspersed with pronouncements about the author's literary tastes, political views, and historical forebodings. And some simpering on the subject of her own beauty.

All that said, the book does contain several vivid passages about people she had known and events she had been through. Yet its most striking feature, the element that dominates it from beginning to end, is the admiration for Mattachich and the depth of the author's attachment to him it constantly expresses. She writes about him as a man of honor and courage, a devoted self-sacrificing truth-bearer, the only man in a corrupt world on whose loyalty she could wholeheartedly rely.

While writing about him in this vein she must have known how ill he was, but it is unlikely she could have guessed how close he was to death. However that may be, and however difficult it may be to match her words to your imagining of them both, can you really be inclined to begrudge her the pleasure she got out of writing of him in this manner? Or begrudge him the pleasure he took in reading what she had written?

He did read it too. The book was finished and published just in time.

A happy ending of sorts, then. If you feel generous enough to grant it to them.

AUTHOR'S NOTE

❖

SEVERAL YEARS AGO, while reading Neal Ascherson's *The King Incorpo-rated,* a biography of King Leopold II of the Belgians, I came across his account of the affair between Princess Louise and Géza Mattachich. The story, which is told by Ascherson in less than ten pages, seemed to me an extraordinary one, and I was immediately attracted to the idea of writing about it. Quite apart from the inherently dramatic nature of the tale, my curiosity was roused by the fact that both leading characters wrote their own accounts of the affair and its consequences. I got hold of their books, and then of others referring to them, and the more I read the more deter-mined I became to write their story in my own terms, not as a historian or biographer but as a novelist, a creator of fictions.

However, since the two leading characters in the tale had spoken up so clearly for themselves, I wanted them to continue doing so. How could this be managed? How could I use their words and yet treat them throughout as fictional characters? Simply to incorporate into the text passages from their recollections, as if I had invented the material I wanted to quote, seemed to me less than fair—and self-defeating too, since a striking feature of both characters was their eagerness to see them-selves, and to compel others to see them, in a heroic, even mythical light. Different modes of self-presentation among the lesser characters appeared too in many of the absorbing documents—letters, reports, and similar items—available from other sources: above all, from Gerd Holler's *Louise von Sachsen-Coburg: Ihr Kampf um Liebe und Glück.* How could I improve on them?

This book is my response to the problems—and opportunities. Some characters in the novel obviously represent historical figures; others do not. The footnotes indicate all quotations taken from the available records. (With the exception of those on pp. 37, 66, and 115, all translations are my own.) Footnotes also provide some items of relevant historical information and show from what sources I derived a general sense of where the runaway lovers went, or were forcibly sent, and how they were regarded by their contemporaries. For the rest, I have invented all conversations and descriptions of scenes and settings in the novel. The same is true of the motives, manners, intentions, and states of mind imputed to the characters. I am wholly responsible for the interpretations given to their actions and to the events in which they were involved, as well as for what is written about their physical appearance—though I have looked at photographs of the chief players. The events drawn on have been condensed, extended, omitted, and reordered in whatever ways seemed to me dramatically appropriate. Names of minor characters, some of them taken from Holler's study, have been bandied about as I pleased.

So let the buyer beware.

In addition to the two biographers mentioned above, and to other writers named in the footnotes, I want to thank the following for their help: Gabrielle Annan, Rosemary Ashton, Janet Hotson Baker, Ivan Danicîc, William Godsey, Bill Hamilton (of A. M. Heath & Co.), Margaret Jacobson, Anthony Julius, Tony Lacey (of Hamish Hamilton and Penguin Books Ltd.), Donna Poppy, Munro Price, Zelda Turner, René Weis, and the staffs of the British Library, the London Library, the library of University College London, the Royal Library of Belgium, the Austrian National Library, and the *Journal de Tramway,* Vienna.

ABOUT THE AUTHOR

❖

DAN JACOBSON is the author of novels, short story collections, and volumes of travel writing and autobiography, including the acclaimed memoir *Heshel's Kingdom.* He is the winner of the John Llewellyn Rhys Award and the Somerset Maugham Award, among several other prizes. He lives and writes in London.